SHIFTER BOUND

PACK BOUND SERIES BOOK 3

LEISL LEIGHTON

PERMIEN PRESS

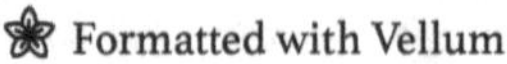 Formatted with Vellum

PRAISE FOR SHIFTER BOUND

Wow! I have found a new author to read! Leisl Leighton has created a world full of intrigue and captivating characters that draw you into the story and hold readers hostage until the very end. I was certainly spellbound throughout.

— EVA MILLIEN - STORMY VIXEN'S BOOK
REVIEWS

Leisl Leighton is an awesome story teller. This whole series so far has me wanting to keep finding out more about other characters and read her other books.

— JESSICA - GOODREADS REVIEWER

I was hooked!

— CYN - GOODREADS REVIEWER

Leisl has out done herself again ... Strong characters and a great story line that will keep you entertained ... I can't wait to read more of her work either too. I have come to love this series.

— KIM - GOODREADS REVIEWER

I found the premise very cool...I recommend to all shifter and witch fans because this is an intriguing story with tons going on and a new spin that you will love! I can't wait for the next book!

— CASSANDRA LOSKOT - CASSANDRA LOST IN
BOOKS BLOG/BOOK REVIEWS

SHIFTER BOUND

To my parents, Kerril and Jim.
Your support means everything.
I love you.

And to Marnie and Anita.
Laughter and friendship truly are the best medicine.
Thank you for yours.

PROLOGUE

Northern Scotland, 1502

Weak, grieving, helpless, Bridgette watched as Morrigan rained fiery retribution down on the village. Like some Celtic Goddess, hair and gown blown back by a Fae wind, wrapped in Darkness, she poured her wrath down on the villagers responsible for the murder of her beloved sister.

Bridgette was the only one left who could stop Morrigan from falling into the abyss, and she'd tried, Goddess, she'd tried. But there was little she could do from the aether. It was like a wisp of fog standing in front of a ravaging storm. However, she had to try one last time. For the dead Morghanna, her baby son, and all the generations of witch and Were who would follow—if she didn't succeed, all would suffer.

Fighting the exhaustion that made every movement through the aether torture, she cried out, 'Morrigan. Please. Do not do this. Morghanna would not wish it.' Morrigan didn't acknowledge she'd heard. But a tendril of the Darkness that surrounded Morrigan, coating her with its unreasoning hatred the way it had done the Were for centuries beyond remembering, broke free and rushed towards where Bridgette's astral self-floated. A whoosh, like the whisper of a thousand voices crying out in the void, followed in its wake.

She turned and fled, the electric cold of the Darkness nipping at her heels. She couldn't let it touch her. Not here. She tried to move faster, but she was too tired; the thread that connected her to her body stretched thin and weak, the aether now almost as thick as mud.

She wasn't going to make it.

An icy tendril caught her heel. Instant despair filled her, pushing aside her raging grief at Morghanna's loss. She almost stopped, almost gave in, but Malcolm's voice came to her out of the distance.

'Mo ghrá. Come back to me.'

'Malcolm!' She tore her foot from the tendril of Darkness and surged forward. It followed, sending a chill as cold as an ice shard through her nerves. 'Malcolm.'

'I am here. Follow my voice. I love ye. Come back to me.'

The Darkness behind her halted, quivered, then continued chasing her. Had it heard him? Goddess no! She couldn't let it get to Malcolm and Morghanna's baby son. There was only one choice to stop that from coming to pass.

Her heart lurched, sorrow almost swallowing her whole at the knowledge of what she must do.

They'd only had ten years—not enough. Not nearly enough—but to save them she'd give up every ounce of happiness she'd ever had. Touching her astral hand to the tether, she said, 'Forgive me, my love. Look after my children and Morghanna's son as if they were your own.' Then she wrapped her hand on the tether and pulled.

It was so thin, it gave with hardly any force. Pain shot through her, bright and sharp. Somehow—she knew not how, it should be impossible given what she'd just done—she could feel her body as if she was still attached to it.

Malcolm's arms were around her, her head pressed to his warm, strong chest. For a brief moment, she wanted to change what she'd done, return to her beloved, but the cold of the Darkness lingered too close.

She must protect the ones who meant the most to her. She would protect them forever.

The heart in her physical form shuddered. It tried to beat on, once, twice and then with a final throb it stopped.

Loss, grief—for Malcolm, for her children, for all she'd miss sharing with them, for the pain this would cause them—made her shriek into the aether as her astral self floated away.

Soon it would break apart, lost in the aether, lost to eternity.

She floated, aimless, sobbing, empty of everything except the pain of everything she'd lost, not even caring that the piece of Darkness that had chased her, was still in the aether with her.

Something touched her. She glanced up from her misery, not even caring if it was the Darkness come to claim her.

But it wasn't the Darkness. A lilac mist had appeared, surrounding her. Tendrils whispered out to her, inviting, caressing, coaxing.

All she was, all she wanted, all she had, was on the other side of that mist.

'For your sacrifice, I will reward you. You will not be lost here. Your essence will go on. Simply come to me. Embrace the possible future.'

The voice shivered through her, filling her with enough energy to dive towards it.

The Darkness screamed; a tearing sound that threatened to shred her mind of happiness and hope. But it was too late. It couldn't stop her from taking this one final leap of faith.

As she fell into the mist, Malcolm's voice rang through the aether. 'Come back to me, mo ghrá. Ye promised me forever.'

She hated the terrifying grief in the sound, hated that she'd made him cling to life to look after their family when she'd taken her own. But he would do it. For her. He'd understand how important his sacrifice—and hers—was.

He would live despite losing his mate.

And then after that ...

'Forever,' she whispered before her conscious thoughts broke apart in the embrace of the lilac mist.

1

'*Forever.*'

The word was a whispered breath of sound, so soft and low that Iain thought he'd misheard it. But then the little shifter's eyelids fluttered and her lips moved over the word again. He sat forward. 'Eloise?'

Her eyes snapped open—those beautiful golden-green peridot eyes—and she looked right at him. 'Mal? Where am I? What happened?'

'I'm not Mal. I'm Iain.'

'Iain?' She frowned.

'It's okay. You're safe.'

She smiled softly, lifted a hand as if to touch him. 'Of course I am safe. You are here.' Her eyes fluttered and then she was gone again.

'Damn it.' Iain thumped the arm of the chair.

'Did I miss something?' Bron asked, entering the room.

Iain gestured at the sleeping girl in the bed. 'She woke up again.'

'How long was she awake this time?' Bron bent over Eloise, putting one hand over her patient's forehead and the other over her chest.

'Not long.'

'Did she say anything?'

'She was whispering something about forever when she woke up, but not much else.' He sat forward, fingertips pressed to his lips. 'She looked right at me this time, and called me Mal.'

'Mal?'

'Must be someone in the rogue coven. I didn't get to ask because her eyes went foggy and she was gone again.'

Bron breathed in deeply and closed her eyes. Iain waited in silence, skin prickling at the use of her magic. Finally, she pulled her hands away from Eloise and straightened. 'She's asleep.' She smiled. 'Her body is healing itself in a natural way now. Finally.' She breathed out a sigh. 'She'll probably wake again soon and be awake longer next time.'

'That's good. You can start working with her then to control it.'

She looked thoughtful. 'Have there been any other episodes?'

He shook his head. 'Not like last time. Her heart's still thrumming like a hummingbird, though, especially when she's dreaming.'

'The dreaming isn't hurting her.'

'The flames don't seem to either.' Flames that resembled the flames of magic that surrounded Skye and Bron and Shelley when their power was building. Flames that usually were only found in witches with ties to the original lines. Flames that were indicators of significant power held within. 'Has Cordy figured out what they are yet?'

'No. She's as lost as we are. But she and Shelley are pouring through the diaries, trying to find out information.' She frowned. 'What they do agree on is that they are an expression of uncontrolled raw magical power, and that is never good.' She touched the leather cuff on Eloise's wrist. 'It seems this is working.'

'I thought Cordy said it was only a stopgap measure.'

'It is. She needs to wake up so we can truly help her.'

He took her hand in his as she stood. 'And we will.'

She touched his face, then brushed his hair off his brow. 'Yes, we will.'

His wolf hummed in pleasure at the caress, but it didn't make the urge inside him go away. He turned back to the bed and the woman in it.

Behind him, Bron sighed. 'If you want to take a break, I'll stay with her.'

'No. It's okay. I'll stay.' He avoided looking at her but could feel her gaze like a hand hovering just above his skin.

'She isn't your responsibility alone, Iain.'

'I know.'

'If I'd known you'd tie yourself to her when I asked you to stay, I wouldn't have asked.'

'I want to stay.'

'I don't want you damaging your wolf.'

'My wolf is fine.'

'I can feel your desire to roam. It's like an itch I can't quite reach.'

'It's my itch, though, and I'm fine with it.'

'Are you?' She touched Eloise's hand. 'And she has nothing to do with the dreams you've been having?'

His jaw twitched. He hated that she could see so much. 'Don't try to see more than is here, Bron. I'm simply here because it's the right thing to do.'

'There are many others who can protect the pack.'

He shrugged irritably. 'It's not just that. This little shifter helped save my life. I owe her. That's it.'

She watched him for a moment longer. He relaxed his shoulders, hoping she wouldn't question him further. He fought the desire to stretch his fingers, release the tension by cracking the knuckles. Bron knew him too well, knew his signs. He had to give nothing away. He didn't want to talk about why he was still here. He didn't fully understand it himself. He'd been so angry when Bron had kept him bedbound for longer than he thought was necessary. He hadn't wanted to wait until his wounds were fully healed. All he'd wanted was to run free. To forget that feeling of helplessness he'd been unable to shrug off since that night before Yule last year when Morrigan had taken him, River and Gareth prisoner and tortured them, almost killing him and Gareth.

He never wanted to feel like that again.

Then he'd found out Eloise was here, had seen her lying in this bed. Many of the pack had taken to referencing to her as 'the little shifter', mostly because of the size of the cat she'd turned into to spy on them, and not for the reasons he thought of her like that. Strangely she wasn't that little. In actual fact, she was on the taller side of average. Even so, she still managed to look small. No, not small. Fragile and delicate, like a little bird. Or like Sleeping Beauty. With her mane of tawny hair and the freckles splashed across her nose like little drops of brown sugar on cream, she did resemble the fairy-tale princess.

Except there was nothing restful about the expressions that crossed her face.

As the days passed, he'd spent more and more time at her side, watching, trying to figure her out, until it had got to the point where he'd been unable to make himself leave, even for more than the time it took to take a run.

It should have been torture to him, to his Lone Wolf soul, and yet his wolf didn't want to leave her either. It didn't make any sense.

His gaze slid back to her face as it so often did. He'd studied her for hours each day, and yet, every time he looked at her, he saw something new. Which was kind of surprising. There wasn't much to her. Fragile bones. Too-pale skin. Lips that held a stubborn pout even in sleep. She wasn't pretty—her eyes too big, mouth too wide, chin too pointed—and yet there was something about her that stayed in his mind even when he wasn't with her. Striking. That's what she was. Ethereal.

Purple smudges marked the skin under her eyes today. Every now and again she tossed her head, lips muttering words he couldn't catch. Her eyes moved constantly under almost translucent eyelids— eyes he'd been unable to forget since seeing them in Morrigan's cave that night. Eyes he'd seen so often in the cat that had watched him warily last year. She'd spied on them, giving Morrigan information that had almost allowed her to destroy them, but then she'd saved them all.

None of it made sense.

She didn't make sense.

He wanted her to wake up, to make her answer his questions, to help him put a stop to this endless fascination.

He realised he was leaning forward, fingers stroking the edges of her hair. Tawny like a lion's mane, it was thick and shiny and silken despite her having been in a coma for over two months.

A noise behind him made him realise the mistake he'd made. How had he forgotten she was there?

He made out like he was just re-settling Eloise's pillow—but when he glanced surreptitiously back at Bron, her raised brows told him she wasn't fooled. Damn.

Thankfully, she didn't say anything about that. 'Did she say anything to let you know who this Mal might have been to her?'

He shrugged. 'No. Although, possibly someone close. She seemed pleased to see me—him.'

'Curious. None of the ones we have are called Mal—although it could be one of the ones who got away with Morrigan.'

His gaze returned to Eloise. He wished he knew who Mal was and why that was the first name to her lips upon waking.

'How about you stop growling at me before River comes in here and shoves that growl down your throat,' Bron said.

He snapped off the growl. 'Sorry, I didn't realise.'

She stroked her hand over his hair. 'I know.'

He thought she was going to say something else, push him further about his need to be here with Eloise, but instead she bent and kissed his cheek. 'I'll bring you some lunch, but after you've eaten, I want you to go for a run. You've been in this room too long.' He opened his mouth to argue, but she held up a hand. 'River will sit with her.'

His mouth snapped closed. If anyone else had a right to look after Eloise, it was River.

'You're evil, you know that, don't you?'

She laughed. 'I try.' She pointed at him. 'Lunch, then run.'

'I promise.'

She flashed him a bright smile. 'Good.'

The door closed behind her. He returned to watching Eloise.

Bron brought him his lunch later and after eating it, he went for the promised run. He usually loved being out in the open spaces, the freedom of running under the clear blue sky, the brush of long grass against his legs, the briny scent of the ocean in his lungs. He could run forever, except ...

He didn't want to. There was a pull inside him, a pull to return to the Packhouse. To not go too far. But he didn't have to go far to let his wolf out to play.

He ran across Packland to the ocean, climbed down the cliff face. His feet pounded on the sand, the spray cold against the warmth of his skin as he ran. It was a private beach, accessible only from the McVale land, and there were sentries around to ensure it stayed that way. Knowing he would be left alone for as long as he wished, he shed his clothes and gave in to the press of his wolf under his skin. With a burst of rainbow glow, he transformed, black and silver fur shimmering in the breeze as he leapt down the beach, paws eating up the sand.

The joy as he ran was almost enough to rid him of the itchy need to return to his sentry duty. With a loud bark, he let his wolf completely off the leash, stretching out muscles that had only recently healed. He romped into the surf, snapped at the waves, chased seagulls off the sand and explored the rockpools at the far end of the bay. A crab snapped at his nose when he upset it sniffing at the seaweed it hid in. He jumped back with a yelp.

Chuckling, he pranced away to go and roll in the sand and enjoy the sun.

Too soon though, the drive to go back and check on Eloise became greater than the drive to keep running. He transformed back into his human skin, threw his clothes on and returned to the Packhouse.

He needed a shower but couldn't help going straight to Eloise's room. River—who was reading aloud to Eloise—looked up as he walked in. 'Hey man. You look better.'

Iain nodded, gaze sliding past the man who'd become his closest friend in the last six months, to the woman lying so quietly in the bed.

'She's fine. Has barely moved,' River said, fingers splayed out on his book. 'I'm happy to stay for longer if you want to take a shower. Or do something else.'

Iain shrugged. 'I might take a shower, but there's nothing else I need to do.'

'Not even making the bench and chair you promised me for the new garden?'

'What's the rush?'

River snapped his book shut and stood. 'No rush. It's just been a while since you did some serious sculpture or carpentry. I know if it was me, my fingers would be itching to get dirty after all this time.' He rubbed his hands on his jeans, as if he could feel the itch. 'Besides, those sketches you did for me were so intriguing, I'd love to see the reality. And there's all that wood Adam and Jason found on the beach just begging to be used. I saw how you were running your hand over the grain the other day. The way your eyes glazed over. I know that look.' His lips hitched into a lopsided smile. 'Have felt it on myself. I'm just a bit floored you can deny it, though.'

'I'm not denying it.' Iain shoved down the annoyance that flared at the other man's pushing. River meant well. And if anyone would understand, it would be River. But for some reason, he still couldn't tell the other Were what was stopping him from resuming his normal life. 'I just haven't felt the push, you know? Not like before. I was kind of waiting for it to come before I started. But you're right, that wood is prime now. I should use it.'

'Great. That's great.' River took a seat again and opened his book, *The Call of The Wild*—he insisted on reading it to Eloise; said it would speak to the animal nature that was at the heart of any shifter. 'I'll come get you if she stirs.'

River's eyes were on him, questions there as Iain hesitated. Seeing them, Iain shot one more look at Eloise and then forced himself to leave. He stood for a moment outside the door, fighting the urge to go back in.

No. He couldn't let the others know about the need, the pull to always seek out the shifter. Not until he understood it himself.

He forced himself to the side door then ran through the garden to his work shed.

The sketches he'd made were on his drafting table, the wood River mentioned piled in the corner. Running his hands over the smooth flotsam, he forced himself to see nothing but the grain, the knots and twists that could be used to form the rough structure of the bench he'd seen so clearly in his mind.

Actually, he'd seen the bench in his dreams. A dream his mind kept returning to, asleep and awake.

In the dream he'd come upon a glade in the middle of a wood. A woman sat there on a bench that looked as if it had grown from the twisted roots and branches of the trees around them. She'd been staring at the clear green pool of water at the centre of the glade, but turned as he entered, a blinding smile of happiness on her face as she'd seen him. That smile had filled him, made him whole in a way he'd never experienced before.

She'd held her hands out as if expecting him. He went to her, took her hand in his.

It felt like home.

A cracking sound snapped him from the dream memory. Blinking, he shook his head and looked down to see he'd gripped a piece of the wood so tightly it had crumbled in his hand. Cursing, he shoved the broken pieces aside. He really wasn't in the mood for this, but he couldn't return to the room. Not yet. Not with River there with that knowing look in his eyes.

How could he explain the inexplicable?

Lone Wolves did not get tied down. It was lore. And their lore had always held true. So, given that this pull he felt towards Eloise couldn't be the mating bond, what was it? And why was he having dreams that were so vivid, they felt real?

Smashing his fist against the bench, he gritted his teeth against the flare of pain and turned from the drawing. He couldn't start on that bench right now—emotion was a savaging rawness in his chest whenever he pictured it—but he could make something else.

A chair. Made out of this wood. He could do that.

Picking up his toolbelt, he strapped it around his waist, clamped a large piece of silky- soft wood onto the sawhorse and began to saw. He didn't need to draw the design out first because he could see it in his mind's eye. See exactly the dimensions it needed to be. Dimensions that would be perfect for a woman who was five foot ten and too thin. Yes, he could see it exactly.

The sun had begun its descent towards sunset and twilight when he finished and headed in to have a shower. He needed to thank River for making him use his hands. The tension locked inside him had been released for the time being. The runs hadn't been enough to smooth out the kinks in his temperament, but creating that chair had.

He couldn't wait to see it being used. He knew exactly where it should be placed. But that would have to wait until River finished what he was doing in that section of the garden—it should only be a few days.

'I know that look,' River said as Iain entered the room after his shower.

Iain laughed and clapped River on the shoulder. 'Thanks man.'

'My pleasure. Bronwyn kept me company for a few hours. She's just gone to check on our other guests but will be back later.'

'Tell her not to bother. I'll call if there's any need.' He took the chair as River stood, pulling it closer to the bed. 'You two deserve some alone-time.'

River halted at the door. 'You shouldn't stay here all night.'

'I'll be fine. I can sleep standing up if need be.'

River chuckled. 'Lone Wolf thing?'

He shared his friend's grin. 'Lone Wolf thing.' He nodded at the door. 'Go kiss your mate. I'll be fine.'

'I'm going to do more than kiss my mate,' River said, his mouth slanting, a glint in his eyes that was such a relief to see after the events of the year before.

But instead of making comments about it, Iain covered his ears. 'Lalalala. Too much information.'

River's laughter warmed him—it was a sound that had almost never come into being—and he waved the other man out the door then settled in for the night.

The room darkened soon after as the sun began to dip below the hills, the curtains a red flare for a brief few minutes. Iain closed his eyes against the glare, the red a blaze behind his eyes. Slumping in the chair, drowsiness took him over and before he could stop them, images —vicious, blood-tinged images—tore through his mind. Desperation clung to the images, the sound of a pleading voice sobbing nearby, the vibrant tang of copper in the air as warm liquid splashed over his face, down his side, thick and viscous. The sounds of wet tearing followed by an ear-piercing scream that brought bile to his throat, choking him.

He coughed, gagging, and sat bolt upright out of the nightmares that had plagued him since that night just before Yule. He shook, skin crawling, as he tried to shove down the terror that left a bitter tang in the back of his throat and constricted his chest. Helpless. He'd never felt so helpless.

A muffled moan caught his attention and he spun, eyes glowing in the dark, piercing the gloom. Eloise was twisting against the sheets, her hands held in front of her as if protecting herself from a blow, her mouth working to hold in a scream.

He was out of his chair in a moment, wanting desperately to touch her, but knowing somewhere deep inside that he shouldn't. Not now. Not yet. But he had to wake her up.

'Eloise.' She moaned again and thrashed against the sheets, hands raised in claws. He ducked, avoiding their swipe, and tried again. 'Eloise. Wake up. You're having a nightmare.' One to rival his nightmares by the look of it. 'Wake up.'

Her eyes fluttered and she stopped clawing at the air, her arms falling to her sides.

'That's it, Eloise. You're safe. It's only a nightmare. Just wake up.'

Her eyes opened, focused on him, flared wide.

She screamed.

'SHE'S AWAKE.'

Jason looked up and smiled at Skye as she stood in the doorway. He lifted his arms and she walked to him, allowing him to gather her onto his lap. He didn't have to ask who was awake—there was only one 'her'. 'I'll call Marcus. He'll want to know.'

'Do you think he'll let Cordy come down and see her? She's going to need help. More help than Bron, Shelley and I can give her.' She smiled that little lopsided smile he so loved. 'We're still learning about our powers.'

He kissed her, loving the way she cupped his face when he did that. 'You're a fast learner, though.'

She smiled into his kiss. 'The best.'

A cough made Jason pull from the kiss. His brother stood in the doorway, a glint in his eye.

'Sorry for interrupting ...'

'No you're not,' Skye said, turning to face Adam.

Adam's smile widened. 'No. I'm not.' He sauntered into the room, leaned against the end of the couch. 'I hear our little prisoner is awake.'

'She's not our prisoner,' Skye said. 'She saved River's life. And Iain's and Gareth's for that matter.'

Jason smoothed his hand down her back. 'He knows that.'

Adam's eyebrow rose. 'Yes, she did, but we don't know why.'

'River says she was sorry for what she'd done. She was trying to do the right thing.'

'After spying on us and giving River up to Morrigan. What she did was almost destroy us.'

'You sound like Shelley,' Skye remarked.

Adam's brows rose. 'You mean Kitten actually agrees with me.' He snorted. 'That's one for the books.'

'If you stopped riding her like you do, she wouldn't be so keen to disagree with everything you say.'

'I enjoy "riding" her.'

Skye's growl was as menacing as a wolf's and Jason smiled. 'Now, now, you two. We're getting off topic.'

'Yes, we are.' Skye glared at Adam as she said to Jason, 'So, we need to go down there.'

'You're not going down there.' Adam snapped upright, his wolf so close to the surface his eyes glowed.

'Yes, I am,' Skye said. 'We've had this discussion before, Adam. I'm your Pack Witch and the leader of our new little coven. I have to do what I feel is best for the pack. And going down to see Eloise is what's best for the pack.'

'Jason?'

'Don't bring Jason into this. He's my mate, not my boss. Besides, I don't know what you're worried about. Eloise is hardly dangerous. Bron says she's frightened more than anything else.'

'But her powers—'

'Are contained for now. We have to go down to see her. And don't look at Jason that way. He agrees with me.'

'Well, that's just brilliant, isn't it?' Adam threw his hands up in the air. 'You're obviously pussy-whipped.' He jabbed his finger at Skye. 'And you're too stubborn to see sense. I'm going to talk to Shelley. I bet she can talk some sense into you.'

'Good luck with that,' Skye called out as he stalked from the room.

Jason chuckled. 'You enjoyed that, didn't you?'

She grinned. 'He's so happy-go-lucky most of the time. It's good for him to experience all of the emotions.'

'He's the pack's Trickster. From what I've been reading,' he tapped the old diary in his hand, 'he feels more than we can possibly understand.'

Her grin faded. 'I know. I don't want to lose him to that like others have been lost.'

'Neither do I.'

'Do you think he's right? That it's a mistake to go down to see Eloise?'

'No. We have to. But maybe we should give her some time to get acclimatised first.'

She nodded. 'Bron said she wanted to spend time bringing her up to date, let her get used to it all. It's going to be a shock for her to discover what happened and how much time has passed. Apparently when she finally woke up, it took Bron half an hour to stop her from screaming.'

Jason shook his head. He couldn't imagine what it must be like for the shifter to wake up and find her entire world had changed. 'Waiting is probably best.'

'Yes. Although Bron doesn't want us to wait too long. The bracelet has helped dampen the power fluctuations, but Bron's afraid it won't last for long now she's awake. She says she's going to need help to dampen the erratic powers while Eloise comes to terms with everything.'

'What about Iain?'

'Bron says he's determined to stay. And while she's worried, she also says that the power fluctuations aren't as bad when he's there. He seems to calm Eloise somehow.'

'Was he there when she woke?'

'Yes.'

'The screaming must have been pleasant for him.'

'Bron said he dealt with it really well. Which is kind of out of character, isn't it?'

Jason rubbed his nose against her neck, breathing in the scent that was nectar to him. 'Not really. He's a stubborn bastard when he gets his teeth into something, and for some reason, he's decided he wants to help Eloise.'

'I'm glad. She needs someone on her side. And he just needs someone.'

'He's a Lone Wolf, Skye.' He brushed his hand over her hair. 'It doesn't work like that for them.'

She smiled, a little secret smile. 'We'll see.'

He shook his head then kissed her neck. She shivered and made the little sound he loved. He smiled against her skin. 'So, when should we go down?'

'Bron says next week.' She sounded a little breathy.

He ran his lips up her neck to her ear. 'Next week it is.'

Skye shifted around to face him. 'Now, where were we before we were so rudely interrupted?'

Her smile warmed through him, the glint in her eye making him laugh out loud. He still couldn't believe this woman was his. 'I think we were here,' he said, as he cupped her face and brought her lips down to his.

2

Eloise's eyes snapped open. She sat up with a gasp, the nightmare still alive and roiling in her mind. Her fingers tingled unpleasantly. Her skin burned. Something had grabbed her in the dream and now the twisted muscles of her deformed foot cramped with a cutting cold.

'Eloise?'

'Iain.'

His large frame was outlined by the lamp in the corner as he rose from his chair. She gasped in a deep breath. His wild earthy scent—pine mixed with something she could only describe as the smell of a storm over the sea—filled her. The tingling in her fingers eased.

He was here. Just as he'd been since she'd woken from her coma two weeks earlier. She'd woken from a nightmare then too, screaming, assuming he was there to kill her.

Of course, he did no such thing. And thankfully, by the time Bron had run in followed by River, she realised how ridiculous she'd been and had calmed down.

These Were wouldn't hurt her. She'd known it last year when spying on them. Had known it when she'd gone to Morrigan to convince her to stop enacting her revenge because two of them were her blood. The scream had simply been a knee-jerk reaction. A lifetime of hearing stories of the Were's savagery was hard to get over even when she saw the opposite was true. Deep in her soul was the knowledge that she was safe with them in a way she'd never been with Morrigan, despite their strength and wild-tinged natures. They'd saved her, healed her, looked after her, kept her body nourished while she drifted in the coma even when they should have left her for dead. Should have hated her for what she'd done. For whom she was.

Just like Morrigan now hated her.

No, she didn't just hate her. She wanted her ex-coven member dead.

She knew this because Morrigan had whispered to Eloise while she'd been in the coma over the last two months. She didn't know exactly how Morrigan had managed it, but she had. The images she'd seen when Morrigan came to her lived too large in her head for them to be a figment of her imagination—quite frankly, her imagination just wasn't that good. In them, Morrigan had worn another face—the body she'd previously worn must have been discarded—and she was wrapped in darkness, eyes filled with madness, screaming that she would kill Eloise for her betrayal.

Her chin wobbled. It wasn't fair. It wasn't right. Morrigan was the one who had betrayed them all. She'd betrayed the coven's most sacred rule. And now Eloise was lost, belonging neither where she once had, nor where she now was. The truth of this rushed in on her every time she woke; a splash of ice water to the face, a stab of ice-cold steel to the heart.

And yet, if Iain was there when she awoke, it wasn't quite so bad.

A fact that made everything somehow so much worse.

She dropped her head into her hands, pressing the heels of them into her prickling eyes. She couldn't cry. Didn't want anyone to see her tears. Besides, tears would do her no good. They'd change nothing. They certainly wouldn't stop her foot from aching. Or her heart.

'Eloise? Are you okay?'

He sat down on the edge of the bed. Close. She jerked away,

pressing against the headboard rather than give in to that strange pull he exerted on her. She might not be afraid of him, but he still made her edgy.

'Eloise?'

She cleared her throat. 'I'm fine, thank you.' Despite the throat-clearing, her voice was rough—full of sleep and stress. She glanced up at him. 'Don't you need sleep?'

He smiled. 'Of course I do.'

'Then shouldn't you go get some?'

'I don't want to leave you right now.'

'Are you worried I'm going to do something bad? To your pack?' That he thought she might hurt them made her stomach curdle.

'No. I know you won't. I just want to make sure you're okay, that's all.'

'Isn't that Bron's job?'

'Bron's gone for two days with River.' He tipped his head to the side. 'Don't you want me to check on you?'

'No, it's not that.' There was something comforting in him checking on her, protective, but it also made her chest hurt, her heart beat hard and fast. Iain was so big and male and ... and ... *there*. So unlike anyone she'd ever met before. She swallowed hard. 'Th-thank you. For looking out for me.'

His lips curled slightly at the corners as he nodded briefly. 'You should get back to sleep. We've got a big session of physical therapy tomorrow.'

'But I thought Bron was away.'

'She is. I'll be taking the session.'

'You?'

He chuckled. 'You don't have to sound so horrified.'

'I'm not. I don't. I didn't mean—'

'It's okay. I get it. You're more comfortable with Bron.' She nodded, thankful he understood. 'But Bron can't be around all the time, so you need to get used to doing your exercises with someone else.'

'You know what to do?'

'I've done some work in that area. Besides, I've watched you and Bron for the last few weeks. And I got her to teach me the program she's set for you. I think I'm more than capable of handling it while she's away.'

'O-okay.' She could see there was no way out of it. She needed to do the exercises if she wanted to get her muscles working properly again and she needed someone to help her with them. 'S-so,' she said, trying to find something else to think about, 'have Bron and River gone back to Melbourne? Oh, I hope nobody's hurt,' she said, eyes widening. Morrigan could have tried to get to them again. She was capable of anything.

He looked at her strangely. 'No. Nobody's hurt. Bron and River are just having a belated two-month anniversary.'

She shook her head. 'Two-month anniversary?' That didn't make sense. 'How could two months be an anniversary?'

'I thought every girl knew about the importance of monthly anniversaries.'

'According to you, I'm not a girl.' She still had trouble coming to terms with what Bron had told her. That she wasn't just a witch. She was also a shifter. Not a Were. A shapeshifter. She was supposed to be able to turn into any animal she wanted, even other humans if she became skilled enough. It seemed impossible, especially given she'd only ever been able to change into a cat.

Apparently she was a failure as a shifter as well as a witch. They had the blood work to prove it though, so it must be true. One more thing Morrigan had lied about and kept from her.

'You're a woman.' His gaze ran over her, appreciation clear in his gaze. 'A beautiful woman.'

She tried to ignore the heated rush that ran through her. Flattery came easy to the Were. River called her darling and sweetheart all the time. It meant nothing. She straightened her back against the head-board and clasped her hands around her knees. 'So, tell me about monthly anniversaries.'

He did, his deep voice winding around her, helping her to forget the nightmare images that had torn her from sleep.

But when he finished and they fell silent, the images came tumbling back. Images of Morrigan and the Darkness.

And Cain.

'What is it?'

She looked up at him through her eyelashes, not able to meet his gaze full on.

Iain's chocolate eyes glowed amber in the low light of the room as his gaze roamed over her face, reading her expression. He seemed to be able to do it so well. Always seemed to know when something was worrying her. Sometimes she refused to answer his questions, but tonight ... She returned her attention to her hands as they clenched her knees. 'I saw Cain in my nightmare. He hates me.' She lifted her head, meeting his gaze this time, daring him to tell the truth. 'He tried to kill me, didn't he?'

His nostrils flared, reluctance clear in his eyes. She was sure he was going to lie, to placate, but then he nodded. 'You remember that?'

'Yes,' she whispered. She'd remembered little when she woke from the coma, but every day, more and more came back to her.

'You believe us now?'

'I don't think I have a choice, do I?'

He sighed. 'You always have a choice, Eloise. You're not our prisoner. You can go whenever you like.'

She lifted her hand, showing the cuff on her wrist. 'This says otherwise.'

'We told you that was just to stop your power from flaring. It's not keeping you here.

It just stops you from hurting yourself or others until you have more control.'

'I don't have any powers beyond a little Healing.'

He frowned at her in obvious consternation. 'That's not what Cordy says.'

'Well, she's wrong. I've never been able to do much of anything with my pathetic powers. Only change into a cat.'

'That has nothing to do with your powers. Not in the way you think.'

'Well, they're even more pathetic.' She stared down at the cuff. 'So this would seem to be useless then.'

'Not useless. It also stopped you from engaging your shifter genes and changing while you were in the coma. It would have been dangerous if you had; we might never have got you back.'

'I'm awake now.'

'You need to get stronger first. Shifting takes up energy you don't have.'

'And when I'm better you'll remove it?'

'Bron said she would. And then it's up to you if you stay or go. We'd prefer you to stay.'

He leaned closer. She could see the grain of his skin, the darkness of stubble across his cheeks and chin, the thickness of lashes that were so long they were almost feminine. But there was nothing feminine about that square-cut jaw and angular slash of cheekbones, nor the determined chin. His lips—full, with a dimple in the corner— were male. Firm. No nonsense. Even his scent was innately masculine, wild and earthy with the tang of the ocean and a winter storm.

It was a scent she liked. In fact, she'd been taking in deep breaths of it; was almost drunk on it. She held her breath.

He watched her, a curious expression on his face, one she couldn't figure out.

'Why do you want me to stay?' she asked on an expulsion of breath.

He leaned forward, elbows on knees, considering her question in that careful way of his before he answered. 'As I said, we want to keep you safe. But more than that, you're like us. The representation of our pack structure in a single being. We are the witch and the Were. So are you. You belong here more than you ever belonged with Morrigan's rogue coven.'

She swallowed hard—that fact still hurt. 'No. I mean, why do you want me to stay? Why do *you* care?'

His frown deepened. 'You saved River. Saved me and Gareth too by your actions, even though doing so almost cost you your life. Of course I care what happens to you.'

'But why are you here every day? Gareth and River are not, and according to your logic, they owe me as much a debt as you do.'

He sat back. 'I'm a lieutenant of this pack, they are not. It's my job to watch over you. In pack terms, I'm your Shadow. It's my job to protect and to see to your care.'

'Shadows are to protect pack.' She'd learned that much last year when spying on them. 'I'm not pack.'

'Neither were Bron or Skye or Shelley before they became bound to us.'

'But they're witches.'

'So are you.'

She sighed in frustration. 'I'm barely a witch. My powers are minimal at best—worse even than I thought they were.'

'I don't know why you've been led to believe you have no power, but Cordy isn't the only one who can feel it inside you. Skye, Shelley and Bron can all sense it too. Cordy and Bron think you've got huge potential. She'd like to help train you.'

'And I suppose you want to teach me how to turn into a wolf too?'

'Not if you don't want to.'

'Why would you treat me so well?'

His frown deepened again. 'Why wouldn't we? Just because we are part animal does not make us uncaring. In fact, I would argue it often makes us care more and in ways humans cannot. But that argument aside, we owe you so much. *I* owe you so much.' He reached out as if to touch her hand, but then pulled away.

'You don't owe me anything. I didn't do it for you.'

He shrugged. 'It doesn't matter. All that matters is that you did. And the fact that it was very brave.'

She shrugged. It hadn't felt brave. It had felt necessary. Because despite the fact Morrigan had turned her back on the first tenet of the beliefs she'd taught the rogue coven—that blood mattered above all —Eloise couldn't. She'd helped River because she'd feared the consequences of not doing so. She'd defied Morrigan, had led her brother away as a distraction, been prepared to sacrifice her life, not because she wanted to help, but because she had to cling to that one belief.

So many of her beliefs had already been shattered by watching the Were, she couldn't have that one shatter too.

No. It hadn't been brave. It had been self-preservation.

She glanced up, cleared her throat. 'I'm not a good person, Iain. I betrayed my coven, my family. Don't make it sound like I did something worthy because my actions suited you.'

He made a strange, wolf-like grunt. 'When you're feeling better, you'll see all this in a different light.'

Eloise's lips trembled. 'I don't see how that will ever be the case when my coven want to kill me. I'll never see any of my family and friends again.'

He tensed and she chanced looking at him. He smiled, a warm, giving smile. 'We'll protect you.'

'That's not the same thing.'

'No. It's not.' His smile faded. Coldness washed over her at its loss.

Silence fell. She didn't want to be the one who broke it. He didn't seem inclined to either. Why didn't he just leave the room? That's what other men would do in an awkward situation. And yet he stayed. Why? Because he was her Shadow?

Her gaze flickered back to him as the question lodged in the back of her mouth, caught there by her desperate need to know and her equally desperate need not to hear the truth from his lips: that she was nothing but an onerous job. One he would be well-rid of if not for the sense of obligation he felt towards her.

'Eloise?' His gaze was too intense. He reached out as if to take her hand.

She snatched it away. 'My head aches and my foot hurts.'

The concern in his eyes stabbed at her. 'I'll get you something.' He left.

The room roared with the silence, with the emptiness he left behind.

She almost sobbed with relief when he came back a few minutes later, a mug in one hand, a heat pack in the other. He gave her the mug—the familiar bitterness of willow bark curled in her nostrils, alongside the floral scent of chamomile, the spice of cinnamon and sweetness of honey. It was one of Bron's tisanes, brewed to help Eloise with the headaches she regularly suffered. She sipped, grimaced.

'Is it too strong?'

She shook her head gingerly. 'It's fine. Just bitter.'

'I put honey in it.'

'I know. But it's still bitter. I've never found anything that fully covers the taste of the willow bark.'

He flipped back the doona and placed the heat pack under her foot where it ached the most. 'Does that feel better?'

'It's fine.'

'Bron said you could have some headache tablets too if you want them.'

She shook her head. 'They've never agreed with me.'

'Not surprising. Sometimes normal medications can have odd effects on shapeshifter bodies.'

'How do you know about shapeshifter bodies?'

He sat on the bedside again facing her, his hip inches from her leg. 'Shapeshifters share some physiology with us. And I've had some dealings with your kind. Enough to know the similarities. I'd like to help you find out for yourself. If you'll let me.'

She wasn't sure what she wanted, so said nothing. Instead, she sipped the drink and tried to ignore the fact that if he shifted slightly, the warmth of him would press up against her thigh.

She shivered.

'Are you cold? Do you need another heat pack?'

'No. I'm fine,' she said, then sipped her drink, keeping her attention fully on the steam rising from the mug and away from the prickling awareness zipping out from her thigh.

After a few minutes, the soothing effect of the tisane made her head feel less like it was going to implode, and the warmth in the heat pack eased the aching cold in her foot.

Nothing much could be done about her awareness of him. She kept telling herself it was because she'd feared them for so long. *Liar!*

She choked on the mouthful of tisane she was swallowing.

'Eloise. You okay?'

She nodded and waved him away. 'Wrong pipe,' she explained after she finished her coughing fit. 'I breathed when I meant to swallow.'

His lips quirked but he said nothing, just continued to watch her quietly as she drank down her tisane.

When she finished her drink, he took the mug and stood. 'I think it's time you try to sleep again. It'll be a big day tomorrow—your first outing since you woke up.'

'And my interrogation.' He'd told her yesterday that Jason and Skye were coming down to see her.

'It won't be like that. They're coming down to see how you are and to answer your questions. I know you have them.'

She did—but she didn't know if she could ask them. Was afraid to find out more than she already had. 'Maybe.' She shrugged. 'But if they think I've got more to tell them, they'll be disappointed.' She didn't know anything. She'd never known anything. She'd barely been useful to her old family. She'd hoped to have a little more time before Iain's pack found out how useless she'd be to them; how little reward they were getting for all their efforts. But worrying about that now was only going to make her unable to keep her wits about her tomorrow.

She lay back down, closed her eyes and, despite Iain's watchful gaze—or maybe because of it—fell into a deep sleep.

3

Iain knocked on Eloise's door not long after she'd woken the next morning.

He waited patiently in the hall while she changed into her workout gear, then escorted her to the kitchen where he'd laid out breakfast for her.

After she'd finished, he took her to the gym where he put her through a round of physical therapy exercises as promised. At the end of it, she wobbled her way to the shower, muscles shaky, but feeling better. For the first time, she didn't have to sit down to shower or get dressed. Humming to herself, she walked out of the ensuite rubbing her hair with a towel.

Iain stood in the doorway of her room, waiting for her. 'Bron and River have just got back.'

'I thought they were away.'

'Bron wanted to be here when Jason and Skye arrived. They shouldn't be long, so we better get you out there. Are you okay to walk or do you want help?'

Her happiness fled. She wanted to say she was too tired, that she wasn't up to seeing anyone yet, but that would be a lie. She was simply afraid. Afraid to see the condemnation in their eyes. Afraid of their accusations. Afraid they would turn on her just like everyone else had turned on her. She'd tried to come to terms in the last few weeks with what she'd done. The betrayal—hers, Morrigan's, Cain's—along with the anger and hurt and sense of shattering loss. She'd almost fooled herself into thinking she'd managed to be okay with it all. But that was a foolish lie. She wasn't anywhere close to being over it. She just wanted to cringe in a corner and never come out. But she couldn't do that. She owed these people more than cowardice.

So instead of curling into a ball, she dropped the towel, raked her fingers through her tangled hair and said, 'Let's go then.' Head held high, she limped out of the room then hesitated, unsure where to go.

'Bron and River are in the kitchen.' He gestured to the left and waited for her to lead the way.

She forced herself to take one step, then another, hoping she looked dignified, despite her limp. Iain's hand under her elbow told her she looked nothing but pathetic. She shrugged away his help, refusing to allow his pity to hurt.

She took two steps into the large room at the end of the hall and came to a sudden stop.

River and Bron stood just inside the patio doors, their bodies outlined by the panoramic vista of sloping gardens, orchards and gentle green hills seen through the floor-to-ceiling, wall-to-wall windows. Bron was laughing, her body turning in to River's. He cupped her face in his hands, body curved in a way that was intimate and protective. Bron's hands slid around him, face lighting with a smile so bright it was almost blinding as she stood on tiptoes to receive his kiss.

A little sigh escaped Eloise. There was something so special about Bron and River together, something that spoke of happiness. No. Happiness was too simple a description. It was joy. Bliss. She'd noticed it the year before when she was spying on them—although back then it had been tinged with grief and confusion as they struggled to come to terms with their feelings. Now it was in full bloom.

She should leave them to their intimate moment but couldn't look away. It was impossible not to smile. Not because of the way they held each other, or the way his body angled towards hers and hers towards his. It was the look in River's eyes as he stared at his mate.

A hot, unbidden shiver chased through Eloise. A shiver that lodged in her chest around her heart. A tear trembled down her cheek. She wanted to reach out and grasp the essence of this moment, to bottle it up and unstop it whenever she was feeling down and unloved—which, quite frankly, was all the time. Especially now given she was an outcast, belonging nowhere and to no-one.

She bit her lip to keep the sigh locked inside her throat, too aware of Iain standing behind her, his silent presence an electric shock zinging along her spine.

Her gaze went back to Bron and River.

Oh! To be looked at like that—as if you were heart and soul incarnate, the centre around which everything rotated—had to be an incredibly heady feeling.

A memory flashed of Skye and Jason standing in the living room of the Packhouse in Templestowe, Skye turning to Jason, her entire body lighting to his presence and his to hers. In that moment, seeing the way they'd looked at each other, Eloise had questioned what she'd been brought up to believe for the first time. She hadn't believed anyone could feel such a depth of love for something that was neither human nor animal, and especially not one of the downtrodden, used and abused witches the Were tied to their packs so they could feed on their power.

But Skye did. And Bron did.

More proof that what she'd been brought up to believe was a massive lie.

That truth had become more and more apparent in the last week as she learned from the Were and their coven what she should have known all her life. That she truly had never belonged. Her parents weren't her parents—how could they be when she was a shifter and a witch and they were barely witches? And her brother, Cain? Was he even her brother? He'd never shifted, but he did have magic. Powerful magic as it turned out. Had he been stolen from some other family too so he could be shaped and moulded to Morrigan's wishes?

Morrigan had said they were twins—two sides of one coin, something special in nature. But had that been a lie too?

They'd been so close until recently; until he'd turned on her at Morrigan's behest. She thought he, like Morrigan, hadn't cared about their blood tie. But maybe the truth was they weren't tied by blood at all.

Goddess! Even though he'd tried to kill her, she didn't want to think that Cain wasn't her brother.

The possibility battered at her, the enormity of all the lies smashing through the numb shell she'd coated herself in. Waves of emotions crashed through her, and at their peak, a sense of betrayal so strong it threatened to swallow her whole. The edges of her vision began to haze and blacken.

No. She wouldn't give into this. Her emotions would not overwhelm her.

Her fingers shook and she clenched them at her sides as she fought the slide back into tears and blubbering or the oblivion of unconsciousness. It wasn't working. So she concentrated on the one thing that had kept her going over the last few weeks: thoughts of paying Morrigan back for every single moment of loneliness, of grief, of pain. She wanted Morrigan to lose everything she ever cared for, everyone she ever loved, to realise she'd been made into what she was with nothing but lies.

'Hey, Little Bird. Are you okay?'

Eloise started, the brush of Iain's breath against her cheek warm and smelling faintly of the sea air.

She realised she was still standing in the doorway, visibly shaking. Damn. Had Bron and River noticed? She glanced at them. No. They were still wrapped up in each other. Whew.

'Eloise? Do you need help?'

She took in a shuddering breath. 'No. I'm fine. I just got woozy for a moment. It's passed now though.'

Before he could offer assistance again, she limped forward. Iain followed close behind her, his hands hovering millimetres from her shoulders as if he was ready to catch her if she should fall. She wished he wouldn't stand so close; it made her want to lean on him, soak up the heat of him that burned through the thin T-shirt Bron had given her to wear. She looked down at herself—the pale pink shorts and green thongs a combination she would never have chosen.

Borrowed. Everything was borrowed.

'*You have nothing,*' a voice whispered in her mind. A voice that sounded a lot like Cain. Although it couldn't be. She'd only ever heard him in her sleep. And besides, she had no idea if he was even still alive. She wished she knew what had happened to him. What had happened that night to her coven. But she was too afraid to ask.

'*Coward.*'

No, she wasn't. That wasn't it at all. Despite the fact that they'd turned on her, she didn't want to find out that everyone she'd ever loved was gone. Then she would truly be alone.

'*You are alone. And the animals are to blame. They took everything from you. Don't let them take more.*'

She shook her head. She couldn't listen to that voice. These people had been nothing but kind. Especially Bron and River. Her gaze flickered back to them just as the Healer cupped her mate's scarred cheek, her other hand curving over the left side of his chest, her finger tracing a pattern of protection over the place where Morrigan had carved her sigil.

Eloise sucked in a sharp breath as a sensation of protective rage and shame surged through her. She was responsible for that pain. She hadn't stopped Morrigan from hurting him. A different voice echoed in her head, '*We will make her pay for what she's done.*'

'*No,*' the Cain-voice screamed. '*You will be the one to pay.*'

Eloise clutched at the side of her head. 'Get out. Get out.'

'Eloise? Hey. It's okay.' Iain was standing in front of her, holding her shoulders. 'Eloise? You're shaking.'

She stared at him. Didn't know how to answer. Couldn't tell him about the voices shouting in her mind or the rage of emotion building inside.

'Eloise,' Iain whispered, leaning closer. 'We don't have to do this now. You can rest first. Skye and Jason can wait.'

She shook her head. No, it was time. She had to answer for her crimes—sooner rather than later. And she needed to find out the extent of the betrayal.

She pulled from his light grasp, trying to get a hold over herself, stop the shaking.

'Hey, Eloise.' Bron appeared at Iain's side. 'What's wrong? Are you feeling okay?'

'Why does everyone keep asking me that?'

'Well, you have been in a coma for almost two months.' Bron's brow rose. 'Besides, you look very pale.'

'That's just the way I look.'

Bron's brow furrowed, her gaze sharp. 'Okay. If you're sure. Come and sit down. Have something to eat.'

'I'm not hungry.'

'You need to eat, Little Bird.'

She turned sharply to face Iain. 'Little Bird? Why do you keep calling me that? I turn into a cat, not a bird.'

He shrugged. 'Your heart often flutters in your chest like the wings of a hummingbird. It did it when you were in the coma. It's doing it now.'

'That's ridiculous.' Her fingers flexed at her side as she tried to ignore the fast beat of her heart.

'Iain.' Bron's tone held a hint of warning as she sidled up to them and took Eloise's arm in hers, her touch a warm balm. 'Come and sit down. Iain's right. You need to eat. Build up your strength. Get you healthy and fit again.'

'I've never been healthy and fit. Or strong. I've never been much of anything.'

'I think you're wrong there.' She took a deep breath, let it out cautiously, and with a nod from River, said, 'Eloise. You need to calm down.'

'I'm fine.'

'No. You're not. Can't you feel that?'

'Feel what?'

'That rising inside you. That hot, heated thing pushing at your skin.'

Eloise stared at her. She could feel it—it had been buzzing inside her ever since she'd woken from the coma, then flared when she'd heard the Cain-voice.

'You don't know what it is, do you? Damn.' Bron rubbed her brow, her eyes shadowed with worry. 'What you feel is your powers. They're trying to get out.'

Eloise sat with a plop on the stool Bron had led her to. 'What do you mean? I keep telling you I don't really have any powers. A little Healing, that's all.'

'That's not true. I think you've got far more power than you know. I think maybe Morrigan dampened your powers somehow.'

'Like what you've done with this bracelet?' She looked down at the cuff around her wrist, the sigils glowing slightly in the dark metal.

'No. Not like the bracelet. Something far more insidious than that.'

Eloise shook her head, her attention jumping from one to the other of them. She'd wanted to know the extent of the betrayal, but this? 'You're wrong. There's no reason she'd do that. She helped Cain with his powers. Why would she suppress mine?'

River leaned across the bench and took her trembling hand in his, meeting her gaze. 'We don't know.' His questioning glance circled to Bron, then Iain. They both nodded. 'All we know is the evidence we feel. What we saw when you were in the coma.'

Something clamped in her throat, making it hard to breathe. 'What are you talking about?'

'Perhaps we should wait for Skye and Jason and the others.' Iain's voice was peculiarly edgy.

'No. I don't want to wait.' She glanced over at him. His worry annoyed her. 'I want you to tell me what's going on.' Her tone shocked her. She'd never been so forthright. But then again, there'd never been such fear and anger rising inside her, pushing her to want answers. To know the extent of the betrayal even if it killed something inside her.

'She's doing it again.' River snatched back his hand with a wince.

'Doing what?' But as she asked, she became aware of a rattling sound coming from the cabinets opposite.

'Eloise, I think you need to calm down.'

Iain moved to her side, glaring at Bron. 'I told you she wasn't ready for this. We needed to do more to shield her. Eloise, why don't you come with me? You can rest and we can try this again later when you're feeling better.' He lifted his hand as if to take her arm.

'No!' She slipped off the stool, backing away. The pans hanging over the stove began to swing back and forth, clanging together violently. 'It's you. You're the ones who want to suppress my powers.'

'No we don't.' Bron and River said together.

'Then take this off me.' She waved her arm in the air, the sigils burning brightly in the metal a blur in her eyes.

'That wouldn't be a good idea. Not while you're this upset.'

'Eloise. Take a deep breath.'

Cabinet doors popped open. Plates fell out to smash on the floor as the rumbling and shaking increased.

'The cuff's not working.'

'She's too strong for it, that's why.'

The voices came to her through the thunder of a swooshing sound building around her. 'Please, just take it off. It's hurting.'

'Bron?'

'I can't, Iain. She'd lose total control without it.'

'And this isn't losing control?'

'She's lying,' the Cain-voice said. *'Lying.'*

The room shook more as she grasped at her head. 'You're lying. You're trying to trick me.' Above the noise, there was the sound of a motor roaring, tires squealing on gravel, the slam of doors.

'No. I wouldn't do that,' Bron insisted. 'You have to calm down. Have to pull the magic back in.'

'She doesn't want you to pull it back in. She wants to capture it. Use it for their purposes. Don't let them. Keep it for yourself. For us.'

'I don't have magic! I can't help them.'

'Help who?'

'I don't think she's talking to you.'

'There's a presence here. It's touching her aura like a dark smudge.'

'Can you get rid of it?'

'I don't know. I'll try.'

Eloise stared at Bron and Iain, the room shaking around her. 'What are you talking about?'

'There's something with you,' Bron said. 'It's talking to you, isn't it?'

Eloise shook harder. 'How ... how do you know?'

'I can see it. It's doing something to your powers. Making them more unstable than before.'

'I don't have powers.'

'*Of course you do. You're my sister after all. Don't let her touch me. Don't let her push me away.*'

She clutched at her head as pain screamed through it. Through her body. 'Stop. Stop.' She just wanted it to stop.

'*Let the power go. Eviscerate them.*'

'Don't listen to it, Eloise. Let me help.'

Gentle warmth pushed at her. The pain in her head sharpened. 'No!' A cabinet burst open above Bron. Glasses rained down towards her. River, a blur of movement, grabbed Bron as she raised her hands to protect herself, and whisked her away from the spray of glass shards.

'What the fuck!'

She spun around. Jason and Adam were running down the hall-way, Skye and Shelley behind them. She skittered away from the new arrivals, over towards the couch, tripping on the rug.

'Eloise!'

'No!' She flung out her hand as she caught herself on the back of the couch. Iain stopped in his tracks. 'Don't touch me!' She didn't want to be touched. Not by any of them. Not when they were lying to her and trying to trick her. People had lied to her all her life and she'd had enough.

'*They haven't lied,*' the other voice, the female voice, whispered.

'*No. They will simply use her until she is nothing but a husk.*'

'Stop it! Stop it!' The light overhead swung wildly.

'Bron?' Jason moved forward cautiously, the intelligent control of him so overwhelming, it was frightening. The room began to shake even harder.

'No, Jason. Stay where you are. We don't want to upset her further.'

Jason stilled, as did Skye and Shelley, who had come to stand beside him. Adam, however, began to inch sideways.

'Eloise.' Her attention snapped to Iain. 'You have to calm down. You have to stop.'

Iain tried to move but couldn't. It was as if the air had thickened around him.

'I'm not doing this.' Eloise's frightened gaze darted around the shaking room. 'I'm not doing it,' she whispered, as if she was trying to convince herself. 'I can't. I don't have the power. You're lying.'

'This is you,' Bron said. 'Whatever was stopping your powers dissolved when you helped us last year. They've bubbled to the surface. We thought the cuff would help until you learned to control them, but something's goading you, tipping you over the edge. You need to keep calm otherwise you'll overload.'

'I don't ... I can't—'

She shook, her eyes wide and frightened. Iain's heart thumped in his chest. Teeth gritted, he managed to move forward a step. 'Please, Eloise. Let us help.' Her heart was truly thrumming now, a counterpoint to the low rumble all around, the smashing and clanging.

'Skye, Shelley. We have to join. Like Cordy showed us.'

Eloise's eyes snapped to the witches, their movement bringing them closer to her. A dish erupted from the side table against the wall and hit Shelley in the head.

'Shelley!'

'No!' Adam roared, leaping to Shelley's side.

'I'm okay.' Shelley pushed Adam away as she regained her feet. There was a trickle of blood on her brow.

A pulse of rage came down the pack bond as Adam's gaze

snapped to the blood. Iain tried to move to stop his packmate, but only made it another step forward as Adam growled, 'We have to stop her.'

The room shook violently, the light above swinging wildly. With a loud snap, the fixture broke away from the ceiling and the heavy light crashed to the floor. Glass shards sprayed them. Little nicks and cuts stung Iain's arms and face, but they just made him more desperate to get to Eloise. To help. He continued to battle with the thick air that trapped him, his attention on Eloise, her pale face, wide, horrified eyes, the shaking that seemed like it might tear her apart if it became any more violent. 'Adam! Don't antagonise her,' River cried out.

'Antagonise her! I don't plan to antagonise her.'

'Adam, no!'

Jason reached for his brother, trying to stop him, but it was too late, he'd already leapt forward.

Eloise raised her hands as if to ward him off. Adam was pushed back by a punch of power Iain could feel. His packmate flew through the air, smashed through the plate-glass window and hit the patio tiles with a dull crunch.

'Adam!' four voices screamed.

'No!' Eyes wide and full of fear, Eloise's hands fluttered up to her mouth, yellow-green flames flickering around their tips. 'What have I done? What have you made me do?'

Iain stumbled forward as the thick air around him became thin again, Eloise's shock loosing her control. Jason raced past him and out the patio doors. Bron's tense voice carried over the noise of rumbling and crashing, instructing Shelley and Skye to join hands. They were going to try to contain Eloise as Cordy had shown them. But deep inside, he knew it wouldn't work. Eloise wasn't one of them —not yet. Her magic was alien, her powers not linked to theirs in any way. Eloise's powers were taking her over, pushed by whatever was manipulating her aura, speaking in her mind. If they didn't find a channel, she would explode, taking all of them with her.

There was only one thing he could think of doing. It was crazy— he had no reason to believe it would work. He was certain it would.

There was a connection between them. He'd felt it from the first. Now he had to see if it would be enough.

Seconds ticked by with agonising slowness as he stumbled drunkenly across the floor, his progress impeded by the belching, shaking floor. Finally, he made it to Eloise's side—she was still facing the smashed patio window, watching Jason bend over the still body of his brother, her body shaking so violently now that her teeth snapped in time to the shaking of the room. He grabbed her shoulders and spun her to face him.

'Iain, no!' Bron cried out.

'It's what I have to do.' He cupped Eloise's face in his hands and looked down into her beautiful eyes. 'Pour it into me.'

She stilled. Everything stilled, the silence deafening. Then she jerked, her hands coming up to hold his wrists. Fire flamed all around him—golden-green flames. He tensed, waiting for the burning pain to shred him from the outside in. It didn't come. Instead, glorious warmth, like sunrise over the mountains, raced over his skin, sinking through his pores, into his mouth, through his eyes, into his lungs and heart and soul. His wolf howled inside him and before he could control it, burst forward.

The flames gave way to the rainbow glow of transformation. As it spilled over Eloise, the sound of her heartbeat slowed down to match his. He kept focused on her, staring into her eyes, knowing the moment she was no longer in danger as her power syphoned safely into him. Then the rainbow glow faded and he was on all fours, looking up at her.

She opened her mouth. A whimpering sound escaped, all colour washed from her face. Her eyes filled with something—joy and fear combined. Then with a sigh, she crumpled to the floor.

4

'*It's what I have to do.*'

The words echoed in Bridgette's mind as she released the power gifted to her by the Goddess and sent the Darkness surrounding the Alpha in front of her into oblivion.

Exhausted but exhilarated—she'd banished the Darkness that kept the Were slaves to the moon—she met his eyes, lightning blue eyes that bored into her with an ecstatic joy. Tears stung, tightened her throat. Blood—her blood—covered his lips. Blood he'd taken from her in an invitation to create the bond between them. He howled to the night, a howl echoed by the others all around. Light exploded from him, rainbow hued and so bright it was blinding. Then the wolf was a man. He laughed and reached out to her. But rather than shout his joy as she could see he longed to do, he held himself together to finish the words of the binding.

'You are marked.' He took the athamé from the altar and cut open his palm. Stepping closer, he covered the wound on her neck with his palm. She jerked as the blood merged, sizzling on her skin and into her body with the power of the spell she had just invoked. His eyes flared as the power of the blood bonding took hold, but he stood steady. After a moment, he withdrew his hand, touched a finger to the centre of his palm and used the mixed blood to draw a crescent shape on his chest, then on hers. 'As we are marked together.'

She held out her hands, gripped his. Together they chanted:

'Our blood bound together with the force of our need
Family and Pack in fact and deed
No longer tied to the moon, but freed
To share in the magic of the Goddess, we bleed
Three times three times three times three
So we say, so mote it be.'

A wild wind whipped up, whirling outside the Dance, then inside, coming closer, closer, sucked in by the vortex of power she'd created. He lifted his head and howled to the night sky.

The wind tore around them, sending dirt and leaf debris into the air, its violence frightening. Oh, Goddess! What had she done? The magic might have been blood magic, but her intent had not been dark. She hadn't thought the pull on nature would be so strong. Had the Darkness returned? She couldn't fight it off again tonight.

'It is all right, my daughter. You are safe. Mother Nature is simply reminding you of your solemn vow: though it harm none.'

She nodded and whispered, 'though it harm none.'

The wind died. Ioan, the Alpha of Pack McVale, embraced her, picked her up and swung her around, howling his joy and relief. He pulled her to the edge of the Dance so the others could touch her, affirm the pack bond that had just winked into existence. She endured it to strengthen the bond, though every touch hurt. The magic had taken more from her than she'd ever imagined. But it had been worth it to see the joy of hope she'd given these Were. And her brethren. She had only to find the energy to perform this spell over and over again until all the covens were bound to all the Were: safe.

She stood firm as the Were drifted away to spread the word. Naked and wrung out, she held her back rigid, strong as she watched them depart. She couldn't show weakness. Not with so much riding on this show of her strength. Her promises. Her mad scheme.

Mad it may be, but she would not see her children sucked into the same path of insanity and destruction as their father, her once-beloved Griffydd Brynn. Once the best among them—so talented, he had dazzled her with all he could do. So dazzled, she hadn't noticed what that power was doing to him. She'd tried to save him with this mad scheme, despite the distance grown between them, but it had been much too late. He'd disappeared a year ago—she'd thought him dead. Then one awful night, he'd returned.

She touched her stomach. His babe lay there. The babe he'd seeded in her by force just before running out into the night, dying in an explosion of magic that had taken three of their coven's elders with him. Two months gone and the brilliant light of his suffering still played on the back of her eyes, burned into them forever more.

She clenched her jaw. She would not grieve for him. He had done things she could not countenance, things that had torn her ability to love from her, but she did grieve for what could have been. He had loved her once, as she had loved him. Darkness and a lust for power had torn that from them. She was determined that tragedy would never be repeated. Her children, her people—none of them would suffer the madness, the darkness and shame. Especially not this babe. Created in violence, she may have been, but Bridgette would leave a legacy of light for her and the rest of her children. They would not be lost in dreams of evil and a burst of flame like their father.

This had to work. She would make it work.

Ignoring the pain from the bite in her neck, she staggered across the Dance to the altar stone where she'd draped her robe. Hands shaking, she pulled it over her shoulders, wincing at the encroaching stiffness in ligament and bone. The simple task of dressing was too much and, exhausted, she leaned against the altar stone.

She'd used too much power because of the unexpected banishment. The Darkness had risen from Ioan McVale half way through the ritual, surprising her, but not the Goddess. She'd immediately spoken through Bridgette, helping to banish it. But even with her help, reserves of power and energy had been used and she had nothing to bolster herself for the walk back to her horse. Her gentle Nessie and the nourishment that was in the saddlebags slung over her withers were down in the valley, far away from where the scent of the Were could spook her.

She breathed deeply, willing herself to stand straight. The neck of her robe clung to the blood that trickled from the bonding wound down her back and shoulder. Picking up her athamé, she tore a strip from the hem and padded it up, laying it over the wound, then pulled the robe down tight to hold the pad of material in place. It would have to do until she got back to Nessie and the supplies. Her head spun and she leaned against the altar again, the cold stone a balm to her overheated skin. The burn of too much power always took her this way. She would stand here a moment and get her breath back. There was no need to hurry.

A prickle chased down her spine. Someone was still there. Watching.

Bridgette spun around. The wild movement overwhelmed her. The heavens swirled above her and she clung to the rock, desperate to keep her feet. Fear chased along her spine. She had no energy or power left to fight with. No energy even to call on her Goddess. She was alone. All alone.

In the shadows on the other side of the dance, she heard movement, the merest sifting sigh, like dry leaves brushed along by a gentle breeze. Then in the shadows she saw the glint of amber with flecks of emerald green.

The two glowing orbs that were his eyes watched her from the shadows of the trees. She gripped her robe around her neck, pulling the belt tight around her still narrow waist. If this was one of the Were, she was not in danger—Ioan had promised she would be safe and no Were in his pack or the packs aligned to his would foreswear his promise.

Even so, her voice trembled as she called out, 'What do you here, Were-male?'

'I have brought yer horse and supplies, my lady.'

'My horse? She would not have come to you. She—' The words caught in her throat as he led Nessie forward. The mare, who was gentle for her, was never so placid for others, especially men, and certainly not for one of the Were. Horses smelled the hunter in them.

'How are you doing that?'

'Nessie is a bonnie lass and gracious at that. She wasna fussed by me wild scent.'

'No, you misunderstand. She usually comes to no man.'

'Oh, but ye see, I'm no' a man.' The voice was deep, husky, tinged with a light Scot's bur and a faint ironic humour.

It was a pleasant voice and yet it sent a shiver through her, though she knew not why. He was most likely here at the beckoning of Ioan, so he was no threat. He would not even enter the Dance, stopping with Nessie on the edge of the stones. Forcing her mouth into a smile she hoped didn't show her unease, she said, 'Then, please, send my thanks to Ioan, but tell him it was unnecessary.'

'It wasna Ioan who saw the need. I own I thought the use of yer magic may ha' exhausted ye, my lady, and I ken I was right. Ye look as if the merest puff of breeze might blow ye down.'

'I am not so weak as that.'

'Aye. Ye have a strength inside that is rare to see. Though I expect some of yer strength comes from yer need to protect the bairn growing inside ye.'

Bridgette gasped, her hand clenching over her flat stomach. 'How ... how did you know about my babe?'

'The Were can sense many things, my lady.' His mouth curled up at the corner, teasing, mysterious, eyes glinting in the dark. 'However, my ma is Pack Healer. I have been brought up learnin' at her knee. I ken how to spot a woman with bairn.' He held up his hands. 'There isna a need to fear me, my lady. I mean ye no harm.'

'I know.' She swallowed hard. 'You simply caught me off-guard. And as you say, I am tired.' She clutched at the altar stone. She'd have to go to him—no Were would enter the Dance. Ioan had only done so because it was necessary for her to tear the Darkness from him and cement the bond. But it had taken everything in him to do so. She couldn't expect that effort of anyone but an Alpha. Not until there was more trust between their people.

She let go of the stone and took a step forward, swayed. The world tipped.

Arms wrapped around her, stopping her fall. She looked up into his glowing eyes. 'You entered the Dance.'

'I couldna let ye fall.'

Nessie nickered nervously and butted his shoulder. He shushed her, his hand coming up to cover her nose. The horse sniffed and settled. 'Yer lady is fine, bonnie lass. She only wants fer food and rest.' He lifted Bridgette up with an ease that stole her breath and sat her so she could lean against the altar stone. When she was settled, he fetched the wine skin and satchel from Nessie. 'Bread and cheese,' he said as he opened the cloth on the stone beside her. He cut a slab of cheese and tore off a piece of bread, handing her both. 'Eat.'

She took it gratefully and took a bite, watching him as he packed her things into the saddlebags. He was obviously nervous and mistrustful of the Dance and the power held within its circle, and yet he had entered to help her. How had he found the strength to do so? And why?

Why did this Were help her when every other Were had left, leaving her to take care of herself?

His eyes met hers, the shadow of deep emotion there. It caught at her heart, pulled at her soul, but it was gone before she could understand what it meant, a shutter coming down on those deep, amber-flecked spring-green wells. She shivered as if doused in cold water.

'Are ye cold, my lady?' He pulled her travelling cloak from Nessie and placed it around her before she had chance to answer.

His hands lingered on her shoulders as he settled the cloak around her. She looked up at him, her voice a breath in her mouth. 'Why are you here?'

'I am here for ye, my lady. I am Sgàth. Yer Shadow. Aye, from this day forth, where ye go, I go too. Now, let us get ye home. Ye need to rest.'

She knew she should deny his words—she needed no guard—but the words locked in her throat. So, instead, she simply nodded and let him lift her to Nessie's back. She thought he intended to walk, but before she could blink, he swung up behind her, taking the reins in his hands. She stiffened, even though the warmth of him at her back was more than welcome. 'I can ride without help.'

His chuckle vibrated through her. 'No doubt ye can, my lady, but the journey to yer home isna a short one, and ye need to rest. This way ye can doze without the chance of fallin' off this bonnie lass.'

'You are too heavy for Nessie,' she protested.

'Nessie is strong. She can carry us both, canna ye lass?'

Nessie—traitor that she was tonight—whickered and trotted forward, head held high.

'I will not sleep with your arms banded about me so tightly.'

The breath of his chuckle brushed past her cheek as the vibration of it soothed something deep inside her. 'We will see.'

Soon they left the Dance far behind. Bridgette tried to sit upright and keep herself aware and awake. She tried with all her might. But the night's magic, the rocking of Nessie's movement and the soothing warmth of the Were-male at her back soon lulled her into a deep sleep.

As she settled back against him, Malcolm smiled and breathed in deeply of the scent that had captured his attention earlier that day. She might not know it yet, this witch with flames for hair and the crackle of burning power surrounding her, but she was going to be his.

5

She was going to be his.

'*No! Eloise. Don't let them take your power. Don't let them—*'

She sat up with a gasp, the sense of warmth—a warmth that stroked intimate places deep inside her heart—fading with the images in her head before she could make sense of them. Tears burned her eyes at the loss, but she didn't let them fall. She'd never let them fall since the time her mother caught her crying after one of her dreams.

'*Crying over a dream. Whoever heard of such a thing! Dreams will never bring anything but disappointment and dissatisfaction. Face reality and grow up.*'

The slap of her mother's sharp words rang in her head even though she would never have to worry about being judged by her mother again.

Her eyes prickled harder. *Don't feel sorry for yourself, Eloise. You chose this. Face up to the reality of that.* She gripped the bedclothes tight and pushed them back. Then froze.

Bed. What was she doing in bed? She'd been up, had gotten ready to meet with Jason and Skye and then ...

She gasped as it all came flooding back.

Anger, confusion, fear. The world shaking. More than shaking. Shaking that had come from her. She'd done other things too—the image of Iain caught on the spot, struggling to get to her; of Adam as he flew through the plate-glass window with just a flick of her hand; the flames flaring bright around her that should have burned her to cinders.

She lifted her hands, forced herself to look at them—they were perfectly normal. Not even a blemish. They should have been burned to a crisp by the flames that had encompassed them.

The flames. They were from the power that had been simmering inside her all this time—at least, that's what Bron said. Repressed by Morrigan for some reason, it had begun to leak out of her during the coma.

That's why they'd put the dampening bracelet on her.

Bron, River, Iain—they'd all tried to tell her, but she hadn't believed them. Couldn't believe them. It seemed so impossible. Even when the bracelet failed and they were trying to calm her because they knew what was coming, she still hadn't believed them. How could she? She'd been told all her life how useless she was to her coven—a waste of space and energy until she'd become useful to Morrigan because she could shift her form into a cat. And now to discover that she'd been filled with a power to rival Cain's?

Cain! He'd been there too somehow. Goading her to let go.

Her fingers tingled, trembling with the immense power she had inside her.

Fear shot through her and she clenched them, closed her eyes, unable to look at them again. Was she about to overload? Was that to be her end here—a fiery ball of destruction? Had that been Morrigan's plan all along? To send her off, her powers a hidden bomb, hoping she would explode and take them all with her? Was that what Cain had been encouraging her to do? She wasn't sure. He'd certainly wanted her to use it against the Were. Eviscerate them, he'd said.

Goddess! She couldn't do that. She'd already been responsible for hurting these kind, generous people in a way that could never be truly forgiven—not by her at least. And she couldn't do it again. She had to get out of here.

'You are no danger to them.'

The older, female voice whispered in her mind. The same voice as the one in her dreams. But she couldn't believe it. She'd believed blindly the things she'd been told all her life—why would she believe some voice that spoke in her mind? It was probably just her subconscious desire to stay, to belong somewhere. But she didn't belong here. She belonged nowhere. Hated by her coven, a danger to those who had given her shelter, she was alone.

A harsh laugh escaped her. She'd always been alone. She'd just never faced the reality of it before.

She pushed herself out of bed, stumbling as she tried to stand. Her muscles trembled with the strain. She was weak. Her powers had taken too much out of her. But she couldn't let that stop her. She wobbled over to the table where a teapot stood. There was still some of the herbal brew of Bron's. She sipped, making a face—it tasted better hot. No matter. She sculled it down, wiped her mouth. The magic in the drink tingled through her and she had a moment of worry that she'd just done something stupid, adding more magic to her already unstable system. She clenched her fingers and then made herself look at them. No flame. But they still tingled. She stared at them, breath held, waiting for something terrible to happen, unable to move even though she knew she must. She couldn't explode here.

Couldn't burn down their Packhouse. She wouldn't do that.

She turned, took a step and realised something had changed. The tingle turned to a pleasant warmth. Her muscles had stopped trembling.

The drink must have helped her retain control, not made things worse.

A rush of breath left her and she shook her head at her stupidity. Bron wouldn't have left the drink for her if she'd thought it would do anything but help. She was a Healer after all.

How long would the effect last? She didn't know. Couldn't trust that it would be long given how massive and uncontrolled her power had proved to be.

So ... she had to go before Iain came back. He always seemed to know when she was awake and would be here soon, no doubt. She had to go now, slip away without being stopped.

She wished she could remember what had happened after she'd lost control and thrown Adam through the window. Or maybe she didn't want to know. She remembered Iain reaching her, Bron yelling at him, his hands on her face, the warmth of them sizzling through her. The shock of his touch had made everything stop and then ...

She rubbed her head, unable to remember past that point. Maybe Bron and Skye and Shelley had managed to finish their spell and rope her back in. Yes, that's what must have happened. She obviously hadn't exploded. The house and grounds were still here.

And it felt peaceful. Quiet. Too quiet.

Oh Goddess! Had she killed them? What of Adam? Had he survived the impact with the window? And Shelley—she had been hit by a flying plate. What if she'd also hurt the rest? Her fingers tightened on the curtain as she tried to remember, her gaze skating over the room, landing on the bed.

She'd woken up in bed. Someone must have carried her back in here and tucked her in—she couldn't remember doing it herself. There was also evidence someone else had been in here with her. River's book was on the chair in the corner and there was a blanket thrown over the back of the armchair—it hadn't been there when she'd got up that morning. One of the others wouldn't have been sitting in here with her, reading, if she'd killed or injured their Packmates. She'd be dead too.

Her chest burned. She was holding onto her breath. She released it, long and slow, breathed in shakily. Took another. 'Okay. Time to stop dawdling. You have to go. Now.'

She threw on a light jacket and put her sandshoes on. The new shoe didn't quite fit her twisted foot properly and would rub, but she wasn't going to worry about that now. As quietly as she could, she slipped out the door.

The floorboard half way down the hallway creaked despite her light tread. Crap! She wished she could turn into the cat. While the cat still had the gammy foot, it did move with more speed and silence. But the inhibitor cuff was still on her wrist, so she couldn't shift. She'd have to find some way of getting it off when she escaped. She'd never survive if she couldn't turn into her cat.

Quiet voices drifted up the hallway from the kitchen. She stopped. Held her breath. Listened.

'She's still asleep.' That was Bron.

'Where's Iain?' That sounded like Adam—she leaned against the wall, grateful to know he obviously wasn't too hurt from what she'd done.

'I told him to go for a run. He needs to get rid of all that energy somehow otherwise he'll be bouncing off the walls and shifting at the drop of a hat for days.'

'He was pretty happy.' That was Shelley.

There was a groan, followed by, 'Obnoxiously so. I don't know what you're all smiling about. I don't see it as a good thing. She almost killed us.'

'But she didn't. She didn't even hurt us.'

'Speak for yourself.'

There was a gentle laugh—Bron. 'You're no worse for wear, Adam.'

'Tell that to my aching head and bruised ego. And my back—ow! That hurts.'

'You began to heal over the glass before I could get it out.'

'Maybe changing into my wolf would help.'

'I don't think it would.'

'Changing always helps us heal.'

'Not when you've got glass embedded in your back, it won't.' His only answer was a growl, followed by a husky laugh.

'It's not funny, Kitten.'

'It's always funny when you get knocked on your arse.'

'So, what are we going to do?'

'We'll let her sleep it off and then we'll see how she feels.'

'She needs to go in the caves,' Adam said, his voice harsher than she'd ever heard it.

'No. That's not a good idea.'

'Why not? If she deserves to be anywhere, it's with—'

'I'm not having this discussion again. If today showed us anything, it's that she belongs with us.'

The argument kept on, but Eloise didn't stay to listen to more. She'd heard enough. Adam was right. She had to go. She was a bomb waiting to go off. Cain had encouraged her to use her powers, to let go. This must be the reason Morrigan had let her go last year. She had known Eloise would go to the Were. Had known about the power inside her, that it would grow until she exploded, killing everyone around her, because she didn't know it was there, didn't know how to control it. Her ex-mistress must be disappointed it hadn't happened yet—which was why she'd sent Cain to egg her on.

Tears in her eyes, she ran back down the hall to her room. She'd climb out the window. She should have done that first, except she wanted to check everyone was okay.

She pushed the heavy brocade curtains aside, blinking rapidly as light flooded over her. The late-afternoon sun was turning the orchards and vineyards beyond into a glory of gold and red and orange. Summer was gone and autumn was already stamping the hills with its distinctive colours. Normally she would have stood there and breathed in the beauty of it, but she didn't have time.

The window was old and stuck, but after a good shove she got the sash up. Thankfully her room was on the ground floor and she didn't have to worry about jumping or climbing down a drainpipe. Her cat might have managed it, but as a human, she wasn't what anyone would call nimble, especially with her bad foot. Nor was she exactly back in peak form. It was still a bit of a drop. The ground sloped away from the house at this point and she'd have to be careful not to twist her ankle. She clambered out of the window and let herself down gently onto the garden bed. She crushed a gardenia and winced— River would hate her for damaging a plant, but it couldn't be helped.

Crouching where she landed, she looked around. There was

nobody in sight—thank goodness—but she hadn't been outside before and didn't know which way to go.

An orchard spread out in front of her, running down the hill towards the valley floor. There was some kind of walled garden to her left surrounded by a huge hedge and then there was the house garden to her right. She wouldn't go that way—there was evidence that there was some landscaping going on and while there were large bushes and trees she could hide behind, it looked like the paths meandered all over the place, so there wouldn't be a clear way to go. The walled garden probably wasn't a good idea. She'd seen it through the patio doors when she'd been in the kitchen, so knew those sitting in there talking would see if she headed that way. She had no idea if the drive led to the front of the house or wrapped around behind it because the walled garden hid it from sight—she didn't want to come out on the drive. There would undoubtedly be sentries there.

So, there really was only one choice. She had to go for the orchard even though she remembered seeing part of it from the kitchen as well—the patio spread across the back of the house, separated from the inside by a wall of glass. The Were loved their open spaces, it seemed.

Not so great when you wanted to slink away.

She'd have to stay low as she ran over the grass that lay before it. There were a few trees on the edge of the grass that shaded the slope. If she kept close to them she might just escape the notice of anyone who happened to glance out the patio doors. It wasn't a great option, but it was the best one she had.

Breath in her throat, she took off as fast as her deformed foot would allow. Everything seemed heightened—the light of the late-afternoon sun around her as if she were in a spotlight; the sound of her feet slapping on the hard turf a thunder roll in her ears; the pull of her muscles as they strained to keep going—she'd barely walked in the last few weeks, let alone run pell-mell—her breath, harsh and grating, hurt her throat. The breeze carried every scent to her in a muddle so that she couldn't make sense of any of it. Her skin was hot.

Her fingers tingled. There was a shout. She turned, saw nothing, kept running.

She was halfway to the orchard when rainbow-bright colours flashed before her eyes. Oh Goddess! It was happening again. She closed her eyes against the sign that she was about to lose control, stumbled, caught herself, kept running. She couldn't stop. Couldn't stop. She had to get far away from those people who cared so much about her that they were waiting for her to wake up so they could bring her into the fold. It was all she'd ever wanted, but she couldn't have it.

Why had Morrigan done this to her? Used her in this way? She had loved her; had been so loyal. All she'd done was try to live by Morrigan's rule that blood was everything. And to reward her for that, Morrigan had turned on her, had tried to kill her, had pushed her to become a weapon.

She wished her ex-mistress was here right now so she could run up to her, wrap her arms around her and whisper in her ear, 'Fuck you, Morrigan', just before her power turned to flame and them both into ash. That would be justice. But she didn't have that. All she had was herself, her deformed foot slowing her down, and a determination to get as far from everyone as possible.

'You can't do it, Eloise. Not alone. You're too weak. Find me and we'll destroy them together.'

'No, Cain! I won't hurt them.'

'Why not? They deserve it.'

'No, they don't. I'm not listening to you.'

'If you don't listen to me, you'll die alone.'

'Then I'll die alone!'

She pushed at his presence with her mind, willing him gone. There was a grunt and then the press of him disappeared. Tears streamed down her face, breath a slicing gasp in her throat, legs wobbling like jelly. The trees of the orchard were only a few metres away.

Almost there. Almost there. She stumbled. Her muscles weren't used to this much work yet. She'd not had enough time to build up her strength. Oh, Goddess. She was going to fail. She wouldn't be able to get away and all because she was too weak.

'No. No,' she gasped. She was almost at the trees. A few more stumbling steps, that's all, and then she could lean against one of them, hide behind the trunk, get her breath back.

Just a few more steps.

A big black wolf leapt in front of her, snarling, raised teeth gleaming.

She jerked to a stop, then backing up, screamed, 'Get away from me. I'll hurt you.'

A second wolf, silver and black, leapt out of the trees to her right and bowled into the black wolf with a snap of teeth, stopping its advance. The black wolf rolled to its feet, snarled at the other wolf. The silver and black wolf made a strange growling sound, as if it was trying to get a point across. The black wolf backed off. Its eyes were still pinned on Eloise though, but it no longer looked like it was going to attack. The silver and black wolf edged forward, towards Eloise.

She held her hands out, backed away. 'No! Don't come near me.'

Rainbow light cascaded around it and then it was on two legs, hand stretched out as he drew closer one careful step at a time. It was Iain.

'It's okay. You're okay. We won't hurt you. Will we, Adam? You're safe.'

Safe? Oh Goddess. She was anything but safe. She stumbled back a step.

'Eloise?'

He reached for her.

'No! Stay away from me.'

'I'm not going to hurt you, Little Bird.'

He thought she was worried about that? She shook her head, still backing away. 'I know. But I'll hurt you if I stay. You have to let me go. I have to go away.'

'What are you talking about?'

'My power. It exploded. I hurt Adam.' The other wolf growled, making her tremble and flinch. 'I'm so sorry,' she said to the wolf that

Iain had indicated was Adam. 'I didn't mean to do it. Didn't even know I could.' He didn't seem to accept her apology, his lips rolling up into a horrific snarl.

'Adam!' Iain's voice was sharp, the sound pulsing in her head with a sickening throb.

Covering her wince, she said, 'No, he has a right to snarl at me. I hurt him. And I could have hurt you all.'

'But you didn't. And Adam is just grumpy you got the jump on him.' He turned back to the other wolf. 'I've got this. Thanks for stopping her. Now go snarl at Shelley. That at least will make you feel better.'

Adam threw him what Eloise could only call a sardonic look and barked.

'I'll join you later,' Iain said. 'I want to make sure Eloise is okay.'

Adam didn't look convinced, but after another snarling bark, he pivoted and took off up the sloping grass towards the garden on the other side of the house.

Eloise couldn't help but stare at him as he ran. He was so powerful. So big. He could tear her to shreds with a couple of well-aimed swipes of his claws. Morrigan had always said the Were were animals, that they were vicious and dangerous. But Eloise was seeing every day that even though that was true, it wasn't the entire truth. Adam could have attacked her—he'd had the upper hand. Even Iain wouldn't have been able to stop him—but he hadn't. He'd listened. He'd backed off because Iain had asked. He'd almost talked with his expressions, his growls and barks. They weren't simply animals. They were sentient beings with a strong sense of pack, family and friendship. They understood those things, understood loyalty more fully than her coven ever had.

She couldn't ever have a part in destroying them.

'Eloise. It's okay. He won't hurt you.'

She'd almost forgotten Iain was there, she'd been staring so hard after Adam. She turned to face him as he moved closer and had a sudden flash of him pushing through the barrier she'd created with her unexpected power, reaching for her, touching her. He'd stiffened and then ... That was all she could remember. 'I ... I think I hurt you.' She looked at him. He wasn't hurt.

He was completely naked though.

Her mind stumbled over the fact, surprised she hadn't noticed before now. She should look away but he was so beautiful. Leonardo DaVinci would have loved to paint him as a study subject—the definition of muscle, the broad shoulders, the long lines of arms and legs, the V that pointed down to the ... Her breath hitched. Crap! She was staring at his penis. She should be embarrassed but ... Oh, Goddess! She had no idea they were like that. So big. So ... so ... upright. 'Eloise?'

'Here, put this on. I can't talk to you when you're standing there like ... that.' She took off her light jacket and handed it to him.

With a knowing smile, he wrapped it around his hips. 'Better?'

It was marginally better—although she could still see too much of him.

'Eloise?'

He reached as if to take her hand. She stumbled back, her gaze snapping to his face. 'No. You can't touch me. It's dangerous.'

A smile flitted on his face. 'Touching you isn't dangerous, Eloise. Not in the way you think.'

'But my power ... it exploded.'

She stared at him, confusion and something like desire in her eyes. His cock twitched. Her gaze arrowed in on the movement before flickering away. Iain tried to ignore what was happening to his body —usually he was completely fine about being naked, but right now, with this woman, having this conversation, it put him at a disadvantage. Particularly after she'd looked at him like she had, staring at his body, her gaze raking down to his cock and staying there for too long. The look on her face told him she'd never seen one before. He cursed the upbringing that had meant this sensual, beautiful woman had never been with a man in that way. Or maybe she just preferred women.

His wolf growled at that thought and he almost smiled. No, the way she'd looked at him, at his cock, she was attracted to men. Just a pity she'd discovered that fact right now.

Dragging his thoughts away from how he'd love to be the one she shared herself with for the first time, he tried to remember what he'd been about to say, but instead, her words suddenly registered. 'Don't you remember what happened yesterday when I touched you?'

She flinched. 'Yesterday?' She shook her head. 'It doesn't matter. I'm a bomb. Morrigan made me into a bomb. You have to let me go.'

'Ahh.' Now it made sense. It had been obvious she'd been trying to escape—the thought had made him furious when he'd seen her. Just by running over the uneven ground the way she'd been, she could have hurt herself, passed out, put her recovery back weeks. However it wasn't fear of them that made her do it. It was fear *for* them. She wanted to protect them. He wanted nothing more than to reach for her, hold her in his arms and comfort her, but she was still so on edge. And he was virtually buck naked. So despite the fact that his wolf was lunging at his skin and howling for her touch, he made himself stay still. She looked at him, a thousand questions in her beautiful eyes.

'You aren't a bomb. That might have been what Morrigan intended, but it isn't what you are. You are a gift.'

She was shaking now, but still he didn't move towards her. 'I don't understand.' She glanced away, eyes raking over the house. 'My powers ... they were so violent. I tossed Adam through the window with barely a thought.'

'You were protecting yourself.'

She shook her head, eyes meeting his. 'It wasn't like that. I didn't know what I was doing. I'm dangerous. I'm not sure how I didn't explode, but I could go off at any moment. I can't control it. You need to let me go.'

'No!' She jumped, looking as if she was about to bolt again. She was still skittish. His heart ached to see it. 'No, don't run. I didn't mean that to sound so harsh. It's just ... you belong with us and I desperately want you to know it.'

'Saying I belong with you doesn't make it so.'

'I know. I know. But it's not just me saying it. It's fact. It's based on what happened yesterday.'

'I almost killed you yesterday,' she said, her voice a horrified whisper.

'No. You didn't.' He was unable to help a smile from touching his lips. 'I don't know why you can't remember, but it was the most remarkable thing. You have no ties to us, and yet, when I touched you, your powers channelled into me and enabled my wolf to soak them in. The same as it would if you'd been a Pack Witch bonded to our pack.'

'You changed?'

'I changed. It was amazing. I've never felt anything so pure and golden before. It was like being covered in ambrosia. I felt like a God.'

She stared, blinked, then whispered, 'It's not possible.'

'I know. It shouldn't be possible for an unaligned witch to channel her powers into one of the Were, but you did it. Bron thinks maybe somewhere in your witch ancestry, you were tied to a pack. And when push came to shove, your powers followed the ancient link and saved us all. Either that or you're that one-in-a-million witch the ancient stories speak of— one who can channel her powers into any living thing, even to reach into the aether to manipulate the power there.'

Eloise stared at him for a moment and then snorted. 'Well, that's hardly likely.'

'Why do you say that?'

'I've never managed anything more spectacular than a basic healing charm.'

'You can't still think you have no power.'

She blanched. 'No. I don't think that. But it's hardly likely I'd be this mysterious witch with amazing powers. There is nothing amazing or special about me.'

He shook his head sadly. 'You don't see yourself clearly.'

Her lips wobbled as tears brimmed in her eyes, but she blinked them away. 'I see myself fine.'

'No, you don't. Morrigan really did a number on you.' His fists clenched at his sides. 'If I could get my hands on that bitch right now, I'd tear her to shreds for that alone.'

'Get in line.'

Iain laughed appreciatively at the viciousness in her tone. 'The little bird is growing up to be a hawk.'

Eloise's lips twisted bitterly. 'I'm not a little bird. But I do have claws.'

'So I see.' He loved the fire in her eyes, the colour it brought to her pale face. The fear and uncertainty were still there, but she wasn't overwhelmed now and she was listening to him rather than concentrating on finding the best way to leave. 'You really do belong with us, you know. This only proves it.'

'What do you mean?'

'Your powers—they didn't destroy, they fed into me, just like a Pack Witch's power.' He couldn't stop the joy from spreading on his face. 'I've been so full of energy in fact, I've hardly been able to sit still. I've been able to change into my wolf without losing any of that energy. It's as if your power was made to align itself to ours. That alone means you belong with us. But this ...' He gestured towards her, the upright stance, the fire in her eyes. 'You have a fire inside you. The fire the Were have always had that allowed us to fight all those years ago, and with Bridgette Colliere's help, change our destiny. You can change your destiny too. Learn with our Pack Witches—they want to help you discover who you were meant to be. You can feed your power into us when it gets too much so you're safe. And I can help you discover your shifter side, maybe even find out where you are truly from. If you leave now, you'll be on your own, a possible danger to everyone you get near. Definitely a danger to yourself.' He took a step closer, but kept his hands at his side, not wanting to have her back away again. 'Stay. Let us help you learn everything you need to know to be the powerful witch and shifter you are capable of being.'

Her gaze skated over his face, searching for something there he could only guess at.

'Will you let me leave if I want to?'

'You are not our prisoner.' He met her gaze. 'But please, don't go.

You need help. You need to let yourself get strong again—we need to keep up your physical therapy. But more than all of that, you have proved you belong with us and we fight for what is ours. We'll fight for you, Eloise. If you let us.'

Her mouth worked and she looked away, eyes scouring the landscape, breathing as fast as if she'd run a race. Finally, when he couldn't stand the silence a moment longer, she turned back and with a curt nod, said, 'I'll stay.'

He let out the breath he didn't realise he was holding. 'Good.'

She held up her hand. 'Not so fast. You have to promise that if I can't control my power, you'll let me go.' He began to shake his head. 'No arguments or I go now. I've been used by Morrigan for too long. I won't be her tool anymore. I will not be responsible for hurting any more of your pack.'

'You're pack too, now.'

An expression crossed her face, one of painful longing, and then she smiled sadly. 'That remains to be seen.'

'Come inside. Talk to the others. You'll soon see I'm right.' He held out his hand. She stared at it for a long moment and then reached out to take it, her movement hesitant, as if she fought herself. When their hands met, there was a zing, like electricity if it was made of warm water. She jolted and pulled her hand out of his.

'Are you okay?' he asked.

'Was that my power?' She looked up at him, eyes wide.

'Maybe,' he lied. It hadn't felt like her power at all, but it had been just as earth shatteringly good. 'Come inside.' He held his hand out.

She shook her head. 'I better not.' Her gaze flickered over him, then her eyes widened and met his before darting away. Cheeks flushed, she looked everywhere but at him. 'I think you need to go and put some actual clothes on. My jacket isn't really sufficient.' Her blush deepened.

He found it charming. Unable to hide his smile, he said gently, 'Were don't have the same hang-ups about nudity that the rest of society has. You'll get used to it—just like you would have if you'd been brought up with your shifter family.'

She swallowed hard. 'I'm not sure I'll ever get used to that.'

He led her to the patio but left her to climb the steps to go inside alone. She looked over her shoulder.

'Go on. I'll put some clothes on.'

She smiled, the barest lifting of her lips at the corner, and then skittered up the stairs and disappeared inside.

Iain bunched the jacket in his hand and lifted it to his nose. It smelled of her. Fruity, fresh wildness of spring cherry blossoms and the deep warmth of a full-bodied shiraz. That smell filled his chest, warmed his heart.

She'd given him her scent.

She might not know what it meant to a Were, to give them your scent, but it was the ultimate act of trust. One he wasn't going to jeopardise. Smiling, he loped around to the side door. He'd go and put some clothes on for her, if only to have her turn those beautiful eyes on him again. There was no other reason. There could be no other reason. He was a Lone Wolf. He didn't have a right to wish for more from someone like her. She was forever and he could never give that to her.

But he could look. And he could enjoy her looking back.

6

'What happened, Cain?'

The voice slapped at him. Somewhere below him, on the human plane, his body twitched in response. The sensation would normally have made him smile, made him feel alive—good or bad, Eloise and Morrigan were the only ones who could make him feel anything. However, he felt nothing. He'd been too long in the aether tracking his twin, trying to make her do the right thing. 'Cain!'

The slap of her power was even stronger this time. The welcome pain of it ricocheted down the link to his body. He gasped as his body began to convulse. From far away the sound of voices whispered to him, the sensation of hands holding, a needle being pushed into his arm, the rush of something sedating covering him like a blanket. All of it he felt and heard, but it was almost like it was happening to someone else, his senses dulled by long exposure to the aether. If he didn't get back into his body soon, he would be lost.

He had to give Morrigan her report and then fly back to his body. 'It didn't work, Mistress.'

'I felt her power gather.'

'It did, but then, it just ...' He wasn't certain how to explain it. '... died away.'

'So they're still alive.'

'Yes.'

'And so is she.'

'Yes.' That word brought such relief, even though he knew it shouldn't.

'Are you still with her?'

'No, she pushed me away and now I can't get back in. I've been here too long. I'm tired.'

Seething fury raged over him and he tumbled backwards in its wake. Panic took over—his tether was too weak to withstand the cutting power of such a negative emotion. But then the fury died away. 'Mistress?'

A sigh. 'I don't blame you, Cain. It's your bitch of a sister I'm furious with. Have they cast her out?'

'No. They are keeping her. They think they can help her control her power.'

'More fool them. But that could work in our favour.'

'In what way, Mistress?'

Silence. The tether pulled at him—he really had to get back to his body, but he couldn't go without permission. 'I have been gone too long, Mistress. It took me too long to contact you.'

'That's because of the drugs they're pumping through you.'

'If you allowed me to heal myself fully, then I might be able—'

'No. You are more use to me in this state. The coma allows you easy access to the aether. You can spy on them without them knowing.'

'My tether is weak.'

'That might be to our advantage.'

A bewildering sensation struck him—he thought it might be sadness. 'You want me to die?'

A gentle caress on the astral spirit version of his cheek, the ice-cold touch of Darkness that was Morrigan.

'Never. You are mine. I would never wish you harm.'

'Then what are you suggesting?'

'It's just a thought. Where are the others?'

'In the caves on Packland.'

'Can you get to them?'

'Through the aether—yes.'

'Then this is what we will do.'

As Morrigan laid out her plan, Cain began to grin.

He would get Eloise back. He'd never meant to destroy her. She belonged to him—like an arm or a leg belonged to him. And just as he didn't want to lose a limb, he didn't want to lose her either. Just like he didn't want to lose the Darkness that touched them both. Her from birth, him by choice. It bonded them more firmly than even their blood tie did.

His sister was meant for bigger things. He would have destroyed her in his anger though, for Morrigan, and learned to live with it. But this was so much better. This way, the Were would be destroyed and Eloise would be at the centre of it, finally made aware of the true magnificence of her purpose.

Once done, she would come back to him and this time, she would never get away.

7

'Ow, that hurts!'

Shelley pulled the needle back as Adam jerked out of her reach. 'I haven't even touched you yet.'

'Just moving hurts. It feels like the glass is scratching against my nerves.'

She rolled her eyes. 'Bron told you not to change until she had all the glass out, but you didn't listen, did you? You just had to go running off to stop Eloise when Iain was quite capable of doing so. Now you just have to suffer the extra pain.'

'I don't understand why Bron can't heal me,' he grumbled, glaring down at her. 'She could have gotten this glass out of my back by now.'

'Excuse me for only being a lowly nurse and not a Pack Healer.'

'I didn't mean to say—'

Shelley flicked her hand at him, irritated with herself as much as him. 'I know you didn't. But you're not the only one who wishes I had another talent that would prove more useful.' She glowered at the spirits who were hovering around. There were a bunch of ancient Healers who'd gathered and she'd been trying to ignore their attempts to give advice as she tended to Adam. 'No, a poultice will not help to draw out the glass,' she said to one particular pushy spirit.

'And yes, I do have to cut him open with this.' She waved the scalpel at them and almost smiled as they cringed back from it. 'It can't cut you,' she snorted, turning back to Adam. The smile died on her face.

A deep frown creased his brow as he stared at her. 'You see them all the time now?'

She shrugged, not liking the pity in his voice. 'Cordy has helped me to block them out better. Times like this though, when the interfering buzzards think they know better than me,' she said pointedly, looking back at the poultice-pushing ancient crone, 'they become more persistent.'

'If they're hurting you—' He stepped closer.

'I'm fine.' She waved the scalpel. 'But you won't be if I don't get that glass out. Come sit down here. I'll numb the area with this,' she indicated the needle, 'and the glass will be out in no time and then you can change and heal properly.'

He eyed the needle, blanching. 'Perhaps I'll wait until Bron gets back.'

A bark of laughter exploded from her. 'Don't tell me you're afraid of a little needle?'

His mouth twisted. 'Well, I—'

'I don't believe this. You're a big bad wolf. You ran at a witch whose power was about to explode, and that is the least crazy thing you've done. How can you be afraid of this?' She waved the needle.

'I just am. Bron doesn't need the needles.'

'Yes, well, as we've already said, Bron is a powerful Healer and I'm not, and as you well know, Bron is in no fit state to heal you after dealing with Eloise and our prisoners yesterday and again this morning. And I'm telling you, if we don't get that glass out now, it could cause permanent damage. So sit down, put on your big-boy pants, and just grin and bear it.'

His mouth widened into that grin she found way too appealing. 'Maybe you can take my mind off it by giving me a kiss, Kitten.'

She tried to ignore the tingle in her skin. 'How about I leave you to suffer?' She slammed her hand down on the bench. 'I mean, it's your stupid fault it got this bad in the first place. I can't believe you changed when you were told not to. How stupid could you be?'

'Apparently very.' He had the audacity to smile.

She threw her arms up. 'Well I give up on all you stupid, stubborn testosterone-driven Were. You can just deal with this yourself. Or wait until Bron isn't so tired.' She threw the needle and scalpel down on the table and turned to leave.

'Shelley. I'm sorry. Please stay.'

His fingers twined around her wrist, stopping her. She almost groaned at the warmth that shot through her. She hated that warmth and how it made her long for things that could never be hers. She turned, intending to tell him to go fuck himself, but he was looking at her with an expression of pleading contrition, pain a shadow in his amber eyes. Something inside her melted. Not that she could let him know that. 'Fine.' She held up a finger. 'But not another word. Lie down on this bench and let me do my job, okay?'

He winced as he lowered himself onto the bench.

She almost wished he hadn't. Faced with the glorious spread of his muscled back, she tried to ignore the desire to spread her palm in the centre and brush it across the muscles, feel his strength. Instead, she concentrated on the areas that were still showing signs of trauma. It was hard to believe his skin had been shredded only yesterday. When Eloise had thrown him through the window with her powers, they hadn't realised how much damage had been done to his back because of the head wound he'd sustained—he had no idea how close he'd come to dying—and by the time they did notice his back, Bron was too exhausted to deal with pulling glass out of skin that had already begun to heal over the shards.

Shelley had been prepared to take on the task herself, but before she collapsed Bron told them his body couldn't take any more trauma at that point. 'We can wait until tomorrow when I've got my powers back. As long as he lies still, he shouldn't heal over too much.'

If only he'd done what he'd been told. But no, he'd gone running off before they were done and now she was stuck with the task of pulling glass that was even more deeply embedded from the idiot man's stupidly sexy back.

Her fingers made a fist around the needle and she had to take a deep breath before injecting him to numb the affected area. She gripped the scalpel, ignoring the itch under her skin to stroke, and cut into his skin.

Finally, the last piece of glass removed, she sat back, ripped her gloves off and wiped the sweat from her lip. 'You should change again. The wounds will heal properly this time.'

He sat up, wincing a little. 'Want to see me naked, do you?'

'I didn't mean right here.' She turned away so he couldn't see the flush on her skin. It was bad enough to have his broad back on display, but seeing his chest made her insides twitch. All that delicious defined muscle under bronzed skin. It was obscene how much she wanted to touch it. She coughed. 'I'll just tidy up here. You go off and have a run.' She busied herself with wrapping up all the sharps and putting them in the sharps bin.

'I might catch up with Jason first. Try to talk him out of this terrible idea about training the shifter.'

'Her name is Eloise.' She turned to face him again and was grateful to see he'd shrugged on his T-shirt. Not that the T-shirt hid much. It was so fine and tight, she could still see every muscle delineated, the outline of his nipples.

'He's a handsome man. I'd take him for a test run if I was still alive. I don't know why you don't.'

Shelley threw Adeline a 'shut up' look. Bronwyn's dead grandmother, a spirit who'd had no compunction in the past in taking over Shelley's body so she could talk to her granddaughter, just raised her brow and returned to staring at Adam. Shelley shook her head. Adeline had always been incorrigible when alive. Now she was worse.

'I don't care what her name is. She needs to be sent back to the bitch who turned her into a bomb before she hurts anyone here. At least she'd be of some use that way.'

'You don't mean that, Adam.'

'She's dangerous.'

'You know that's not true.'

He frowned. 'No, I don't. You all think I don't know how bad I was, but I do. How could I not?' he said when she couldn't hide her surprise. 'I can feel all of your concern pressing at me. Just like I feel the fact they're worried about the shifter.'

'Iain's not.'

'Iain's not thinking straight. He calls her "Little Bird" for Goddess' sake.'

'He's grateful to her for what she did for him and Gareth and River. And he likes her.'

He shook his head. 'No. It's more than that. She has him twisted around and he doesn't know which way is up. And this idea of his to teach her how to shift into other things ...' he shook his head. 'That's not going to end well for anyone, least of all him.'

'You can't know that for certain.'

He blew out an exasperated breath. 'I can't prove it, but I know it.' He pressed his knuckles to his chest. 'I feel it here.'

Shelley licked suddenly dry lips. 'The spirits are telling me it's necessary.'

'And of course they know better than the stupid Trickster.' Adam's mouth twisted into an unpleasant smile. 'I'm just being my usual idiotic self. Don't listen to me. Nobody else does.'

'Don't talk about yourself like that.'

'Why not? I'm not saying anything new. I'm the Trickster. I'm good for jokes and not much else. Instincts are not my strong point.'

'You're wrong.' Shelley reached out and grabbed his arm.

He jerked then looked down at her hand.

Her fingers tingled where they touched his bare skin. But she couldn't make herself snatch her hand back as she usually did. Not now, when he was hurting in a way that went bone deep. 'Adam?'

He looked up slowly, his amber eyes glowing with something she didn't want to understand. His brow cocked, and his lips twisted into a more difficult smile. 'Don't feel sorry for me, Kitten.'

She hissed out a breath and snatched back her hand. 'I'm not feeling sorry for you, you idiot. But the Trickster ... Jason asked me to research it, to find out more.'

'You found something?'

She bit her lip. 'Not much. But what I have found indicates the Trickster is all about instinct and emotion.' She took a deep breath. 'So, if you're saying this isn't a good idea, then I'm listening.'

His eyes widened and the twist of his smile gentled. 'I'm touched, Kitten.'

She stepped back. 'Don't be. I'm only being sensible. We'd be stupid if we didn't take everything we can into account. Besides, I'm not the only one who thinks that. Jason listens to you. He always has.'

Adam's lips widened into a soft smile that did something twisty to her insides. 'Yeah. My big bro has always been good that way.'

'Go talk to him. See what he says.'

'He won't change his mind.' He touched his finger to her lips when she opened them to protest. 'I never expected him to. It's the right thing to do. The only thing to do.'

She pulled back from his touch, more disturbed by it than she had any right to be. 'But you still need to tell him how you feel.'

'If you say I should, I will.'

It shouldn't matter to him what she thought. She didn't want it to matter to him. 'Do whatever you feel is right.'

He stared at her for a moment and then chuckled. 'I always do, Kitten. I always do.' And with that, he walked out, the impact of dealing with him leaving her breathless and confused, like she'd been tossed up by a wave and smashed back down onto the hard sand.

She took a shuddering breath, let it out slowly.

'Watch yourself with that one, Michellene. He's not as tough-skinned as you think.'

'Go away, Adeline and tell your stories to someone who cares.'

Adeline chuckled. *'Oohoo. Who took their bitter pills today?'*

Shelley picked her things up and turned to leave, but Adeline and the other ghosts moved to block her path.

'He's only going to put up with your wall for so long before he either

walks away or knocks it down. The question you have to ask yourself is, which one do you want it to be?'

Shelley gritted her teeth. 'I don't want it to be anything. There's nothing going on here.'

Adeline chuckled. *'Now who's making up stories?'*

'I've got things to do.'

'Yes, you do. Iain and Bron will need some help with the shifter. And you know what you need to study up on to help him.'

'I know, I know. Witches that could connect to a pack who weren't bonded to one. But I have time. Iain has to help Eloise learn to shift properly first.'

'Don't dismiss this, Shelley. If you don't learn to understand it all in time, then Adam's feelings will not just be feelings—they will come to pass.'

'Then you need to get out of my way and let me get on with it.' Despite the cold chill she knew she'd get, Shelley walked right through the spirits standing in front of her, scattering them to the wind.

ELOISE SUCKED in a breath as Shelley walked out the French doors, mind whirling after what she'd overheard. She hadn't meant to eavesdrop but hadn't been able to make her presence known when she'd heard her name. Especially given what they were talking about.

'Okay. Are you ready?'

Eloise jumped and turned around. She'd been so preoccupied with her thoughts, she hadn't even noticed Iain as he came up to her.

'What?'

'Why so jumpy, Little Bird?'

She shrugged her shoulders, irritated with herself and with him. 'I just didn't hear you, that's all. What did you say?'

'I just wanted to know if you were ready.'

She wanted to tell him that she wasn't ready, was so afraid he was wrong and she was right and wouldn't be able to do this—especially after what she'd just heard. But Bron and Cordelia and the others had been so certain that this was the only way forward. That she could help them as much as they could help her. She knew Bron. Knew Iain. She didn't know Adam or Shelley at all. She couldn't let their doubts affect her. She'd struck an agreement. She had to keep her word. She had to open up to her shifting power fully before she'd have a hope of controlling her witch power. Cordy had told Bron that changing would channel that power into a positive outlet and help her stop it from building to dangerous levels.

Her stomach curdled at the thought, nerves as sparky as if she'd been hit by lightning. But given she didn't really want to implode or explode from a build-up of unused powers, this was something she had to do.

So, instead of speaking all her doubts, she tried a small smile. 'As ready as I'll ever be.'

He grinned—her insides did a little leap and rolled over. 'That's the glowing endorsement I wanted to hear.'

'Are you making fun of me?'

The grin widened. 'Only a little bit.'

'That's not nice.'

'No, it isn't. But this should make up for it.' He leaned forward and for a heart-stopping moment, she thought he was going to kiss her, but all he did was reach for her wrist.

'What are you doing?' She tried not to tremble as his warm fingers slid over her wrist, turning it so he could fit a key to the lock on the magical cuff that bound her.

'I have to remove this.'

'With a key?'

He glanced up, a smile in his eyes. 'Oh, but it's a magic key.'

She smiled—she couldn't help it. 'A magic key, huh? And I suppose you know all about those?'

He laughed. 'Are you questioning my sexual prowess?'

She blanched. That hadn't been what she meant at all. When she didn't answer, he looked up from what he was doing. His fingers stilled on her wrist. 'I'm sorry. I didn't mean to make you uncomfortable. I know you're not used to being teased. Forgive me?'

She nodded.

'Good.' He kissed her.

It started as a brush, the kind of thing she'd seen other Were give fellow packmates when she'd been watching them the year before, but when she didn't pull back, when she moved her lips under his, moving into the caress, it became something else. His lips lingered on hers, pressing more firmly, seeking, asking, wanting.

The earth shifted. Not moved. Simply slipped sideways and left her freefalling in endless space, caught in a moment of time that never seemed to end. She made a strange noise in her throat.

He broke the contact, halting centimetres from her mouth for long, endless seconds, eyes wide. 'Well.' His breath puffed over her face—minty and fresh and a little faster than normal.

Was it possible he'd felt something too?

She sucked in a breath. Her lungs filled with the scent of him. His gaze dipped down to her lips. She swayed forward. So did he. Her lips were almost against his again when he shifted away, bending his attention to the cuff.

She blinked, stiffened at the rejection. Which was ridiculous. She shouldn't feel rejected; she had no right to want a kiss, or more, from anyone. But she did. She wanted his lips on hers again more than she wanted to breathe. 'Iain?' His name a breathless, needy sound. She had no idea she could sound like that.

He stilled and then slowly, too slowly, met her gaze. His eyes burned with something that made her shiver. 'Sorry. I shouldn't have done that.'

'Why?' Now her voice sounded full of tears. She cleared her throat.

'I keep forgetting who you are. Where you've come from.'

She stiffened. 'No kissing the enemy, right?'

The shock on his face was almost comical. 'That's not what I meant. You're not the enemy. I thought you'd know by now I don't see you that way. I never did.'

Now she felt a different kind of shit. 'I know.' She looked down at her hands, picking at the cuticle on her thumb. 'Sorry.'

'Shit.' He reached out, took her hand. 'Don't apologise. You have nothing to apologise for. I'm the one who did something wrong. I keep forgetting that you're not used to physical contact—not like we are.'

She nodded, whispered, 'It was nice for a first kiss, though.'

'Your first kiss?' He looked so shocked.

Oh Goddess. Why had she admitted that? Heat flooded her face. 'Yes.'

'Shit.' He raked his hand through his hair. Why did he look so appealing when he was dishevelled? 'I'm so sorry. I shouldn't have kissed you. Not like that. You deserve better than that.'

'I didn't mind.' And wasn't that the understatement of the year? For a first kiss it had been pretty wonderful, although too brief. He'd left her with the scent of him in her nose, the taste of him on her lips. A wave of warmth had washed over her, caressing her skin and sending little shockwaves through her middle right to her core.

The imprint of the touch still burned on her lips. Just as she'd burned when she'd seen him naked, the long, muscled length of him —an image that had featured in her dreams last night, leaving her hot and sweaty with a needy pull between her legs. The same burn that occurred every time he touched her—and he'd been touching her more and more since she'd woken up. In physical therapy to start off with, but then little gentling strokes on her hand, a squeeze on her shoulder, a hug. She'd tried not to think anything of those touches, because that's just what the Were did. They touched. Just because she wasn't used to it didn't mean it was special. But this had felt different. 'I didn't mind,' she repeated again.

His lips flashed into a grin. 'Neither did I. There's a part of me that would like to do it again. Properly.'

'You would?' She had been so afraid she'd misread his reaction, that it had been a friendly caress of one packmate to another and not more. A little sun burst to life in her chest.

'Except ...'

The sun dimmed. 'Except?'

He glanced down at the hand he still held in his, his fingers brushing over the magical cuff stopping her from shifting and, supposedly, keeping her magic in check. 'We need to get this off you and start your training right now. We can get back to the kiss later.' He looked up at her, his head angling on the side in that animalistic way the Were had. 'Are you okay with that?'

'You're asking for a raincheck on kissing me?'

He laughed. 'When you put it like that, it sounds awful, but yes, I suppose I am.' He leaned closer, gaze burning into hers. 'I want to kiss you again. Properly. And I don't want to be somewhere we can be interrupted. I want to take my time. Okay?'

She took an unsteady breath. 'Okay.' The sun was blazing again.

'So, let's get this cuff off.' He bent to the task again, fiddling with the key that looked so ridiculously small in his big hands. 'Ah-ha!' he said as there was a light click. A buzz ran over her and then coolness on her wrist where he'd been holding her.

She shivered.

'Are you okay, Eloise?'

'Yes. That was strange.'

'It was your magic settling.'

'Yes.' She could feel it. But that wasn't the reason she shivered. She wanted him to touch her again. Ached for it. She shivered again.

'Bron said that might happen, remember?'

She cleared her throat. 'So, what do I do?' He was trying to be professional. So would she.

'Let's go out into the garden for this. Were and shifters are happier outside in nature.'

Her eyes widened. She'd always felt that way, but her life with Morrigan had meant spending more time hidden away than enjoying the wide-open spaces. She'd always thought there was something wrong with her that she'd felt stifled. She was learning so much from the Were about who she really was.

'Come on.'

She stumbled along beside Iain as he walked outside.

'I'll lead you through a few focusing exercises we do with our young, and then we'll see what you can do.'

She nodded and followed him down the patio stairs into River's magical garden. The breeze was full of the scent of sun-warmed grass and the mixed smells of flowers and herbs that seemed to pervade all the gardens he created. Iain led her over to a strange wooden chair that looked as if it had grown, rather than been made. She ran her hands over the silky wood as he gestured for her to take a seat. It was large enough that she could cross her legs or pull them up in front of her as she liked to do. 'This is amazing. Who built this?'

'Me.'

'You?' She knew she was gaping. 'I thought you were a sommelier or something.' She'd heard him talking about it the year before with River.

'I am. But I also love to work with my hands. I do some carpentry and I sculpt.'

'Wow.'

'Why so surprised?'

'You all have hobbies and full lives ... I just never knew that was possible. I always assumed the pack structure would be like it was for us in the coven.'

He frowned. 'Surely you were allowed to have hobbies in your coven?'

She shrugged. 'Not really. Nothing that wasn't seen as useful for the group as a whole. I did well with schoolwork and wanted to be an engineer, but Morrigan didn't have a use for that. I was allowed to help my Pa with the cars sometimes, though.' Her mouth twisted as she remembered working in comfortable silence with the man she had always believed wanted the best for her. Now she had to wonder if those feelings had ever been real. Not that she could ask. He and her 'mother' were long dead.

'It made you happy?'

'Yes.' It had made her happy at the time.

'That's how I feel when I make something like this.' He gestured at the chair. 'Actually, I made it for you.'

'For me?' Her skin had to look like she had been horribly sunburned by now. She wasn't quite sure where to look. The fact that he'd made something for her touched her even more deeply than the kiss had.

'Yes, for you.'

'Why?'

'Because I wanted to.'

He made it sound so simple; as if men made chairs for her every day. She ran her hand over the satin smoothness of the grey wood, a strange lump rising up her throat. 'Nobody's ever done anything like that for me before.' She blinked back the tears in her eyes. 'Thank you.'

The sound was a whisper on the breeze, but with that keen Were hearing, she knew he heard it. 'It was my absolute pleasure.'

She looked up at him. Could he truly mean that? He looked sincere. They stared at each other for long, slow seconds. She wished he'd kiss her again. But then he broke the tension building between them by sucking in a sharp breath and clapping his hands together. 'I think we should get started.'

'Yes,' she croaked. He might want to kiss her again, he might have made this wonderful chair for her, but that didn't mean he felt anything more for her than something fleeting. He was a Were and she was ... Well, she didn't know what she was.

It was time she found out. 'Let's get started,' she said, her voice firm this time.

8

'Okay.' Iain couldn't help the smile that bloomed on his face as he gestured her to follow him over to a patch of nearby grass. He shouldn't have kissed her like that, so casually, but he was glad he had.

Something had shifted between them. And like a drug addict, he wanted more. Wanted to help her open herself up fully to what the world had to offer. However, the best way he could do that right now was to help her understand her shifter side, not kiss her again.

He pushed down the urge and sat on the grass. 'We have to centre ourselves, enhance our link to nature.' He crossed his legs and gestured for her to sit opposite. She did so, copying how he sat, the backs of her hands resting on her knees.

'This is how we teach our young to control their change. For Were, our wolf is always inside. In the past, when we were bound to the moon, the wolf was rabid, scratching to get out, howling to be heard. Now, since the Were-Witch Pact gave our wolves freedom, we live in harmony with the other side of ourselves. Our wolves are our friends.'

'Morrigan always talked about your wolves like they were evil animals. I couldn't help but think that changing into my cat form meant I was a little like that too.'

'We're not evil, and neither are you.' Inside him, his wolf growled.

She jerked back, eyes wide. 'What was that?'

Iain stilled even though his heart beat wildly against his ribs. 'You heard that?' She nodded. 'That's ... strange.'

'Strange? What was it? It sounded like you growled.'

'I didn't growl. My wolf did.'

'You mean through your throat?'

'No. Inside me. In my mind, in that space he occupies. There was nothing physical about the growl.' Usually only other Were or a mate could hear the wolf when it was locked inside.

She is your mate. The memory of the dream he'd had where he wasn't himself—a memory he'd been doing his best to forget, even though it was a dream that was taking over from the horrible nightmares of torture and death he'd had since Yule—pushed to the fore.

But no. It couldn't be true. It was impossible.

Her eyes widened, her hands twisting white in her lap. 'How could I hear your wolf?'

He wasn't sure. 'Maybe because you shared your powers with me when you were about to explode with them?'

'A link formed?'

'Perhaps. I don't know. Maybe it's simply because my wolf is very close to the surface—that's part of what makes me a Lone Wolf.'

'Is that ... hard?'

He smiled. 'Yes. In the dark years, before the Pact, Lone Wolves often went rabid and had to be taken down by the Hunter of the pack.'

'Oh ... that's horrible.' Eyes wide, hand trembling against her lip, she said, 'That ... that doesn't happen now, does it?'

He smiled gently. 'No. Not since the Pact. But it does take extra work to keep the wolf from taking over. Especially given how close we came to having the Pact destroyed by Morghanna's ancient Curse.'

'What do you mean?'

He paused, swallowed hard. 'When Skye was taken by her maternal grandmother without our knowledge, the Curse began to enact on us. Twenty years of slowly losing contact and control over our wolves. It was a creeping inexorable slide into hell that gave me a thorough glimpse of what it must have been like for my Lone Wolf ancestors.'

'Why did it take so long?'

'Skye wasn't dead, and despite what her grandmother did when she supressed Skye's powers, they were still strong enough to seep out a little and feed the link between her and us. It was a tenuous link, but enough to keep all of us going for that long.'

'It must have been horrible.'

'It was. The worst of it was losing that close link with my wolf. He'd always been a friend, an ally. But over those twenty years, I heard him less and when I did, he was frustrated and angry.'

'And that seeped into you?'

'Absolutely. What he feels, I feel. The worst thing was feeling his pain at not being able to come out and run free and being helpless to do anything about it.'

'How awful.'

Her hand covered his, her empathy a warm wash that helped to lessen the agony of remembering that time. 'It was worse than awful. The anger of its incarceration built inside me until it was all I could think about.' He unclenched his jaw, tried to soften his tone. 'It's what helped me truly understand the madness that drove my ancestors centuries ago, turning them into vicious killers on the nights of the moon. The wolf was always there but could never get out except for three nights a month. Years of that drove the wolf insane until all it wanted was revenge—and it didn't matter who was in the way of its need. They came to think that was the way it had always been, but we've recently found ancient parchments that suggest that wasn't true. Something separated us from our wolves.'

'The Darkness Bron talks about that was in River?'

'I don't know. Shelley says the parchments don't say. There's just a reference to the time of freedom before the period they called the "locked moon". It's doubtful we'll ever know the truth of what happened then. Although, it would be good to know so we could make certain it never happens again.' His eyes met hers. 'We never want to become the murdering monsters we once were.'

'You aren't murderers or monsters.' Her hand clutched over his.

'If not for Jason's strength buoying us all through the worst of that time, that would have been my fate.'

She shook her head, gaze intent on his. 'No. I don't think that's true. Not just Jason's strength kept you from that. Your strength. The strength of your beautiful wolf. The strength of your beautiful soul.'

As her words rang around them, warming him in a way words had never warmed him, he turned his hand in hers and squeezed. 'Thank you for thinking that, although, I'm not sure it's true.'

'It is,' she said vehemently. 'Your wolf is beautiful. You are beautiful.'

The warm sensation increased, tingling through him.

She sucked in a breath, her cheeks flaming red, and pulled her hand from his, shoving it in her lap. 'I didn't mean ... I shouldn't have said—'

'My wolf thinks he's beautiful too,' he said, chuckling a little to try to alleviate her embarrassment. 'In fact, he's pushing to get out and show you his handsome self again.'

She met his gaze briefly, smiled shyly. 'Maybe later?'

'Definitely later.' His smile widened. 'Maybe you have a beautiful wolf inside you too, howling to get out.'

'There's only ever been the cat—and she doesn't howl. Nor does she push to get out.'

He tipped his head to the side. 'I'm not sure that's completely true.' He held his hand up as she went to protest. 'I'm not calling you a liar, but I think you've been conditioned not to acknowledge what's happening inside you.'

'What do you mean?'

'I know it's a little different for the shifters I've met from what we Were experience, but not completely different. There's a need inside them to transform, to bond with nature on a different level, discover the world from a different perspective.'

Goddess! He was telling her things she'd felt only in her deepest soul—things she'd never been able to voice before because if she had, it would have only pointed out how she didn't belong with the others in her coven.

'They often have a form that's a favourite,' Iain continued. 'But they can transform into any animal as long as they have seen it in the flesh. Didn't you feel a certain amount of peace and freedom when you transformed into Bluebelle?'

'Yes.' It was astonishing how he understood and accepted things as normal that she had long thought signs of an evil canker at the core of her soul. 'I used to sometimes transform into Bluebelle and escape outside when I couldn't stand being with my fam ... being inside anymore.'

'You didn't want to be with your family even then?' Anger filled his eyes. 'I knew they used you, but I didn't realise they were abusive.'

'No. They weren't abusive.' She swallowed. 'My mum and dad were firm but kind. They just didn't love me.' She knew now it was one of the reasons she'd been so quick to believe Morrigan when she elevated her to a position as spy and asked her to do things she knew were wrong. 'And as for the coven. Some were always nice to me, but I knew I wasn't truly one of them.'

Sorrow and pity replaced the anger on his face.

'Don't feel sorry for me. I had Cain. He always loved me. Protected me.' Her voice choked on the last because it wasn't true anymore. She turned her mind away from that thought, the pain too much to bear in this moment when she was supposed to be starting anew. 'Tell me more about the change.'

He did, telling her about the shifters he'd worked with in Europe. Many of them were farmers and vintners, using their natural affinity for nature in toiling the land, growing things, just like the Were did. He told her of how he saw one turn into a hawk so he could oversee the fields that were in his care, the golden glow of change shifting over him like folding water. 'I saw that same farmer turn into a dog who ran after wayward sheep and brought them back home. He was laughing as he changed back into his human form and dared me to race him.' He smiled, as if savouring a wonderful memory. A slash of jealousy shot through her.

'You make it sound so simple.' Her voice was choked. 'But it's never been like that for me. Changing into Bluebelle and back was always painful. And I could never change successfully into anything else.'

'That's probably because you were led to believe it was wrong.'

That was true. The fact that Cain wasn't capable of changing confirmed everything the others told her about her natural ability to do so. But now she'd seen Skye and River—one a witch, one a Were—she realised that their difference was a natural split of the genes they got from their parents. She said as much to Iain now.

He sighed heavily. 'Shifters are a little different from Were in that they can carry both witch and shifter genes inside them as you do. Cain would have been the unusual one in your pack for his inability to change and the fact he could only do magic. You would have known that if you hadn't been stolen from your family.' He reached out and took her hand, holding it in the warm safety of his. 'You say your coven didn't abuse you, but they did, by not sharing that truth with you. By not allowing you to be the person you are supposed to be.'

'Maybe they didn't know.'

'Oh, they knew. At least, Morrigan knew.'

That knowledge was a punch to the gut, but still she said, 'Perhaps they were afraid.'

'And their fear poisoned your joy. Don't let them have that control over you anymore, Eloise. The change is pain, but it is also wonder and delight and freedom. Once you allow yourself to feel that, you'll be able to change into anything you want.'

'You sound so certain.'

'I am.'

Her breath was tight in her chest as she watched him, watched his expression, his absolute certainty. Adam's words flittered through her mind and she couldn't help voicing them. 'What if this is wrong? What if this is part of Morrigan's plans and it's what sets me off?'

'What if the moon crashes into the earth? What if the earth quakes and swallows us whole?'

She snorted. 'You're being ridiculous.'

'So are you. Stop finding excuses because you're afraid.'

'They're not excuses. I heard Adam express his doubts to Shelley. She didn't think they were so silly.'

'Adam doesn't know you.'

'And you do?'

'Yes. And I trust this is the right thing. I trust you.'

'Why? Why do you trust me?'

His amber gaze held hers. 'Because you saved us last year even though it nearly cost you your life. You left everything behind, gave up everything you knew, to do the right thing. Besides, I watched you sleeping for months. There is no artifice in a sleeping person—you can see their truth reflected on their face. And what I saw told me that you are a good person.'

'How? How do you know?'

'Because your expression when you were asleep is the same as now. Except now you are full of curiosity.' He smiled. 'I know your face and your expressions almost as well as I know my own. You are uncomfortable with artifice and you are one of the worst liars I have ever come across. Even last year when you were Bluebelle, I could tell you were uncomfortable with what you were doing. It was a curious thing to feel from a cat.'

She let out a long slow breath. Goddess! He did know her. Knew her better than anyone else ever had. Even Cain. That trust, his trust, it touched her to her core.

But it wasn't just his trust. He was her ... friend.

She couldn't stop herself reaching for that friendship and trust. She needed them like she needed air to breathe, water to drink, like she needed the warmth of the sun on her face. She took in a deep, shuddering breath. 'I trust you, too.'

'Good.' His smile was so bright, she didn't need the sun. 'Now, let's continue. We'll start with the basics. You need to learn that the shift doesn't have to be painful. That it is about wonder and love. I want you to close your eyes and think of something joyful. Concentrate on it until the joy of that fills every part of you.'

She closed her eyes. She didn't have many joyful things to think about, and every single one of them seemed to centre on Iain. Picking the most recent one, she filled herself up with how it had felt when he'd told her he'd made that chair for her.

'Good.' His voice weaved its way to her through the flood of golden warmth of emotion thinking about his gift gave her. 'Now, keep that feeling inside you and shift into your cat.'

She frowned. She couldn't believe that shifting wouldn't hurt and she didn't want to let go of this wonderful feeling, but she had said she trusted him. Thinking of her cat form—a form she'd moulded after a stray her mother had kept and lavished attention on when she was little—she changed.

As the tingling prickle of pain began to shoot through her, she struggled to keep hold of the feeling of joy inside her. 'It hurts.'

'Don't change then. Let it go and start again.'

She did as he suggested, gave herself a little shake and started the process again. The pain gripped her faster this time. She gritted her teeth, concentrating completely on the memory of joy when he'd given her the chair, but she just couldn't seem to fold the joy around her. 'It's no good. I can't do it. Maybe it's always meant to be painful for me.'

'No. I know that's not true. Try again.'

She glowered at him. 'What if I don't want to? I'm tired.'

'Excuses.'

'What?'

'You're making excuses because you're afraid you'll fail.'

'I am failing!'

'That's because you're telling yourself it's impossible.'

'Because it is impossible,' she snapped. She didn't need this. It was supposed to help, but it was making her feel worse. Her fingers were tingling—the first sign of her power rising. A sob rose in her throat and she moved to push herself to her feet.

His hand on her arm stopped her. 'Don't give up. I know you can do this. You've just got to believe in yourself.'

'I don't know how.'

'Yes you do.' He gripped her hand, pulled her closer until their knees touched. Her skin tingled, but not with power—with something far warmer and more dangerous. She shivered. 'Do you trust me?'

Her gaze flickered to his. She hadn't lied before. She did trust him. She didn't know when or why or how, but she trusted him better than she'd ever trusted anyone, including herself. 'Yes.'

'Then listen to me. Shifting is pain, but it's also pleasure as we release part of our essence into the world. All you need to do is find something joyful to fill yourself with and wrap yourself in it as you change. After a while, it will be the change itself that brings you joy.'

She huffed out a laugh. 'I can't imagine that could ever be true.'

'It's how I feel. It's how every Were and shifter feels. I know you can feel it too. You just have to trust yourself. I do.'

There it was again. His trust in her, warming her from the inside like a bonfire blaze just lit. That was her joy—his trust.

'You've found something good, haven't you?'

'Yes.'

'Then use that. Use it now and change.'

She concentrated on the blaze of warmth his trust created in her, let it wrap around her and then pulled the image of Bluebelle up in her mind, letting the essence of the cat sink into her skin, her muscles, her ligaments, her bones. Then she let it sink into her mind —the final process before the change began—keeping the warmth of Iain's trust, his voice, wrapped around her like a blanket.

She let the change fold around her.

It happened so quickly. One moment she was looking out of human eyes, and the next she was staring up at him through eyes that tilted the world at a different angle.

Shock shivered through her, alongside the most incredible sensation of fulfilment. She'd forgotten how wonderful it was to be in another form. Or maybe she'd never truly felt it. Not this sense of unutterable rightness.

'Your change is so beautiful. Like molten gold in sunlight.' He was staring at her, awe in his tone and expression.

She purred, basking in his affirmation.

A smile broke out on his handsome face. 'Feels good, doesn't it?'

Yes, it did. More than good. For the first time ever, the change hadn't been pure pain. It had been a marvel; uncomfortable as her cells shifted and rearranged themselves into something else, but full of golden, honeyed warmth that filled her with energy. Unable to help herself, she bounded in a circle, and then to the sound of his laughter, pounced over to him, the pull of her deformed foot not as bad in cat form, and rubbed her head on his knee. His eyes full of joy, he stroked her from head to tail. She purred loudly.

'Hello, Little Bird.'

His low laugh lit the air again as she nipped at his hand in remonstrance, as if to say, 'I'm a cat, idiot!'

He seemed to understand. 'A cat for now, but always my Little Bird.'

The words were a warm blanket over her shivering soul. She rubbed harder against him, trying with everything in her to say the same back to him through touch. She'd never be able to tell him with words what his trust and friendship meant, but she could show him in other ways. She climbed into his lap and with her paws on his chest, licked his chin.

'That tickles.' He chuckled, grabbing her with his large hands and holding her still so he could look in her eyes. 'Remarkable. Even in this form your eyes are still the same.' She tried to shift her head, embarrassed—she'd always hated her eyes. They seemed somehow less than human, a constant reminder that she was different from all those around her. Even Cain didn't have her eyes—his were a deep green, without the golden yellow tinge of hers, and they weren't slanted as hers were.

'Your eyes are beautiful, Eloise.' His breath brushed over her fur like a caress and she stopped struggling. 'I noticed them when I saw you as Bluebelle and thought them remarkable, but they are even more so in your human face.' He tipped his head to the side again as if considering something. 'I wonder if they are the same when you're a different animal.' His grin widened as he put her down. 'Shall we see?'

His enthusiasm was catching and she meowed a yes. He seemed to understand. 'Watch me change and then see if you can mimic it. And don't forget to fill your mind with something joyful.'

She didn't have any problems doing that. Not with him standing there, smiling down at her, sharing what seemed suddenly so intimate—the ability to change.

With open wonder, she watched as the rainbow glow of Were change wrapped around him. It was so bright, almost blinding, and yet she couldn't look away. And then there was a big black and silver wolf with Iain's amber eyes standing in front of her. A few months earlier, she would have been frightened out of her wits, but now ... She walked over to him and rubbed herself against him—except he was too tall and she could only wind around his legs. He made a noise that sounded like a chuckle and lowered his head so she could rub against his snout.

If anyone were to walk into this scene now, they would stare in wonder—a huge wolf allowing a little tawny cat to use him as a rubbing post. But that person watching wouldn't even know the true wonder; that for the first time ever, she thought she actually could do whatever she wanted.

Standing back from him, she stared at his form. He'd told her shifters could change into any animal they'd seen. But she didn't want to turn into him. She wanted another form.

An image came into her head of a snowy wolf she'd once seen in a documentary Morrigan had made them watch in an effort to understand the animal nature of the Were and their need for pack. All she'd seen was how almost human the wolves had been with each other—not that she'd ever admitted that fact to anyone in her coven. It had just served to make her feel even more wrong because they all came away from that documentary talking about the vicious nature of the animals they had to fight.

But she'd never been able to forget the snowy wolves, especially the beautiful female with the wolf cubs.

With that image in her mind and the thought of joy bubbling in her heart, she pulled on the feeling of change inside her and wrapped herself in it. A prickling sensation, more joy than pain, swept over her as gold of change tinged her vision, and then it was gone and she was staring the big black and silver wolf in the eyes, barely having to look up at all.

And in those eyes was the reflection of herself—the snowy wolf she'd envisioned.

She'd done it!

A wolf-bark escaped her mouth. Shocked, she skittered back and then barked again. She'd never known how freeing it could be to bark, to shout, to give free rein to every emotion inside.

The big black and silver wolf—Iain—woofed back at her, the sound full of encouragement and pride. He'd told her she could do this and he was right. She barked at him again and spun in a circle, bouncing on legs that were strong and agile, despite the tightness of her deformed paw. With a sudden burst of speed, she raced to the edge of the grass area, turned and raced back to him. He nipped playfully at her and nudged her with his big, handsome head, eyes sparking with fun and laughter. In her mind was a voice, an echo that sounded like 'let's run!', and before she could think twice about what that voice was or where it had come from, she took off, Iain at her side.

They ran through the garden and into the orchards, paws pounding on the hard dirt, flying past the trees at a speed she'd never dreamed of racing at before. Her deformed paw held her up, but only a little, and she pushed herself harder, faster. They burst out into an open field, the long grass warmed by the sun, whipping against her fur as they pounded, side by side.

Sooner than she liked, she began to feel the pull of muscles, her breath an ache in her chest. She'd run further and faster than she'd ever done before, so she shouldn't feel so sad, but she did. She couldn't keep running. Couldn't keep this magical moment from ending.

As if he could hear her thoughts, Iain barked, slowed his pace and began to swing left.

She followed.

They broke out of the long grass and trees. The ocean spread before them, the sparkling blue-green deepening into the distance until it melted into the powder-blue sky. They ran to the edge of the cliff and stopped. The breeze had picked up. Spray hit her face—the salty-wet smell of the water and the briny tang of seaweed tumbled on the golden sand below filled her nose. The sun was hot, but the breeze held a hint of coolness as it ruffled through her fur.

If she were to die tomorrow, she would die happy to have experienced such a perfectly wonderful moment as this.

Iain stood beside her, a silent sentinel, seeming to understand her need to just be.

How long she stood there she didn't know, but then the urge to run rose in her again and, with a woof at Iain, she took off and down the steep path cut into the cliff that led to the beach. Her deformed paw made her stumble a bit, but she was used to that. She just kept on going.

They ran and played chasey with each other and with the waves until she was panting. Tongue lolling out of the side of her mouth, she flopped onto the warm rocks, letting the sun seep into her wind-ruffled fur. Iain lay close beside her.

The sun was high over their heads when her stomach grumbled and Iain signalled it was time to return. Exhausted and resigned that her day playing in the sun was over, she followed him back up the steep path. They didn't run back this time, just content to trot side by side to the house. When they got there, Bron was waiting for them at the back door, a huge grin on her face.

'Oh, Eloise, you're beautiful.'

She yipped her happiness at Bron, whose burbling laughter joined her wolfy noises. Eloise couldn't help it. She loped up the steps, and rearing up, put her paws on Bron's shoulders and licked up the side of her face.

'Alright, alright.' Bron's shoulders shook as she took Eloise's face in her hands, ruffling the hair around her ears. 'I'm glad you've had a lovely time. Iain's a good teacher. But you've been out long enough and I can tell you're exhausted. And famished. Come inside, change, have a shower and then once you're done, you can tell us all about it over some lunch.'

Eloise woofed her agreement and lowered back down onto all fours. But just before she trotted inside after Bron, she turned back to Iain and nuzzled her head against his in thanks. In her head, she thought she heard that strange echo again, a voice that said, 'My pleasure.' But before she could think anything about it, he'd turned and trotted away.

Half an hour later, she came out of the bathroom. Bron had kindly brought her a long, flowing dress made of some soft material in a fresh, spring green—her clothes had dissolved when she'd changed. She spun, enjoying the way the skirt of the dress flowed around her bare legs, when there was a knock on the door—probably Bron calling her for lunch. 'Come in.'

The door swung open.

Iain.

Dressed in a blue T-shirt and board shorts, a bottle in his hand, he smiled wide. 'You look pretty.'

She blushed. If she looked pretty it was all because of him. The joy she'd felt earlier, her thankfulness to him for giving her the gift of her natural self, rushed up and over her.

She raced over to him and flung her arms around his neck, hugging him. 'Thank you. Thank you.'

His answering smile when she pulled back filled her with a warmth that touched the very centre of who she was. Deep inside, there was a vibration as something long dormant unfurled, like the frond of a fern waking to the sun. It was such a sweet sensation, an astonished bubble of laughter escaped her lips.

Iain's answering smile washed over her. Acting on impulse, she leaned forward and pressed her lips against his.

He jerked and a low growl rumbled in his throat.

She stilled. Goddess—had she stepped over some essential boundary she hadn't understood? She went to pull back when his hands cupped her face, and his mouth opened, tongue sweeping across her lips.

Heat shot through her veins. A gasp shocked from her.

He pulled back, the flash of something heated in his eyes. His fingers tightened on her cheeks as he searched her eyes for one heart-stopping moment. 'Rain check over,' he growled. Then his lips were on hers again. Clinging. Hungry. Demanding.

The unfurling thing inside her opened with a sharp snap. The heat that had shot through her at the touch of his tongue on her lips burst into a raging blaze. It swept through her, cauterising any thought she had of pulling back. In one part of her mind she knew she should be frightened by the sudden intensity of rightness that swept through her, but she didn't listen to that part. Only listened to the blaze as it turned her into an inferno of need. Her fingers shot into his hair, pulling him closer.

'Finally. My love.'

The voice was only a whisper in her mind, but it vibrated through her to her very core.

It frightened her. The longing in it. The need.

But it wouldn't let her pull away. *'Closer. We need to get closer.'*

She couldn't deny the need. It was too strong, too woven into the fabric of her being. With a cry, she pushed forward, one hand a fist in his hair, the other pulling at his shoulders, gripping the strength of the muscles straining in his back as he endeavoured to be gentle. 'Touch me. I need your hands on me.'

9

er voice. It touched something deep inside Iain, overrode the shock of her mouth on his. Her fingers buried in his hair, pressed to his scalp, drove his desire higher. It wrested control out of his hands. Iain had no choice but to do as she asked.

Angling his mouth, he sucked on her lower lip, pulling it into his, nipping. He growled in satisfaction as she jerked in his arms. One hand dug into the glorious mane of tawny hair, still damp from her shower, the other dropped to her waist, hauling her closer. He angled her head so that he could deepen the kiss, his tongue tangling with the sweet taste of hers.

Her heart beat frantically, the wild sound music in his ears. He pulled her even closer, growling as she rubbed her breasts against his T-shirt-clad chest. Sweeping his hand up, he closed it over one ripe firm breast. The hard peak of her nipple pressed into his palm through the thin material of her dress. He groaned at the exquisite sensation. More. He wanted to give more. To take more. He left her lips and closed his mouth over the frantic beat of her pulse in her neck. She stilled under his proprietary touch, but he didn't let go, her desire thick in the air around him telling him she liked what he was doing.

'Bite me. Mark me.'

Her whisper was an unsteady caress, but more perfect than anything he'd ever heard. Even so, he didn't immediately do as she asked. He'd wanted this ever since he'd stopped her from running away. Standing naked before her, her eyes running over him in a way that made him hungry for more than the touch of her gaze, he'd known this was coming. He hadn't intended to, had tried to ignore the desire he'd seen in her eyes. But at the same time, some demon inside him pushed her, teased her, sought that desire out. Then he'd kissed her before their session and all pretence was over. The moment his lips had met hers, even in that faux-friendly kiss, he knew this was going to happen.

Just like he knew he shouldn't have promised a rain check, should stop this right now. He was a Lone Wolf for fuck's sake. He had nothing to give her beyond the passion in the moment. But God help him, he couldn't stop. Couldn't make himself do the right thing and walk away. It was more likely that Morrigan would turn into a saint than him being able to walk away from Eloise right now.

He licked the salty, fragrant skin over her pulse.

She tipped her head, baring her neck. 'Please. I need to feel you.'

Her words were a stroke over his sensitised skin. His wolf lunged to do as she asked. 'Do you know what you ask?' Even through the passion-hazed fog, he knew marking her in such a way would create a bond he wasn't sure either of them were ready for.

Her hand brushed over his cheek, fingers curling in his hair, pressing him closer as she rubbed against him. 'Please.'

The desire-laden word snapped his control and he could no more deny her than he could stop the breath in his lungs, the beat of his heart.

He sank his teeth into her throat.

She jerked.

He swept his tongue over the small sting of pain, then did it again, her pulse a living entity under his fingers, in his mouth. It was strong and bright and sweet; oh so sweet. It pulsed in time with the blood that pumped through his veins. That pulse thrummed through him, a painful beat in his suddenly rigid cock. A cock that was on fire with the need to be inside the slick heat of her; a heat he could scent all around him, drugging him, driving him insane. Insane enough that he ignored the voice screaming a warning in his head.

She was still so young, so naive and innocent; certainly wasn't ready for the demands of his ravening wolf. But he couldn't ignore its demands.

It wanted to take. More, it growled. And Dark Moon damn him, he wanted the same.

'Kiss me.'

Releasing her pulse point, a slave to her desires, he kissed up her neck, enjoying the little sounds she made deep in her throat as he nipped and licked the sweet saltiness of her skin. His lips found hers —home. He was home.

Her fingers gripped his hair, clung to his shoulders. Her fingernails bit into his skin as she kissed him with a desperation that would normally have had warning sirens going off in his head. But with her tongue a wet glide against his, her breath in his mouth, the cool silk of her hair in his hands, the satin smoothness of her skin against the roughness of his fingers, his lips, he couldn't make himself move away.

He needed.

She needed.

That was all that mattered.

If this was insanity, then bring it on. When she'd pressed her lips to his, opening herself to his touch, to his caring, it was like he'd woken with a start and seen the world for the first time. A world that would never be whole or full of colour without her at the centre of it.

His hands moved over her, pulling her closer, moulding her slight frame to his muscular one.

She was his. His.

Then he scented it. The sting of fear. Her fear. It was the only thing that could have driven him to his senses in that moment.

Gentling her as she tried to cling to him, he pulled back, his thumbs sweeping over her cheekbones, brushing back the mess he'd made of her hair. She trembled all over, her breath coming in shallow little gasps. There was a fine layer of perspiration on her skin. She whimpered and turned her head to try to capture his thumb with her seeking lips, but he held her firm. 'Shh, Eloise. Shh. We don't have to rush. It's okay.'

She opened her eyes. They were swirling gold mist.

The sight shocked him out of the euphoric, desire-laden state. 'Eloise?' Fear trembled through him.

'Not Eloise, my love.' The voice was deeper, slightly accented. He should have noticed the change when she'd spoken earlier, but he'd been too caught up in what she'd been doing with her tongue, with her body, to have taken it in.

'Who are you?'

'One who has waited an eternity for this.'

'Morrigan?'

She laughed, the swirling gold mist in her eyes glinting. 'She cannot have you. You are mine.'

'Who are you, then? Tell me your name.'

She frowned, the gold flickered with black. 'You do not know me, my love?'

'Eloise. I only know Eloise.'

'Do you love her?'

'I barely know her.'

'Then why would you kiss her like you did?'

'I—' There was no answer. He had no clue why he'd let an innocent kiss escalate like he had. 'You did something.'

Tears welled in Eloise's eyes. 'Nothing you did not want me to do.' Her hand dropped to his chest, her palm pressed to the muscle over his heart. 'Listen to the beat and you will know I speak truth.'

'I don't want truth from you. I want you to release Eloise. Give her back to me.'

Her lips trembled and she nodded. 'Your will is mine, my love.'

She jerked. The gold flickered to black then flickered to gold, which swirled away like fog at sunrise. She blinked up at him.

'Eloise?'

'Iain.' Her eyes rolled up in her head and she collapsed into his arms.

He picked her up, swivelled around and took a seat on the armchair, her slight body cradled in his arms. Her breath was a welcome puff of warmth against his aching skin, her heart a steady thump-thump in her chest. He held her close, rocking back and forth. 'Fuck, fuck,' he murmured, trying to come to terms with what had just happened.

But he couldn't. How could he? It was beyond his experience.

Was it beyond hers? Had this happened to her before? He brushed her hair from her cheeks, kissed her sweaty brow, lips lingering on flesh that still smelled of desire and need.

'Come on, Eloise. Wake up. Don't leave me to figure this out alone. Please, come back to me.'

His mind spun with questions. Who had just taken over her body? It said it wasn't Morrigan, but did it mean them ill? It had called him "my love". But he'd never loved anyone—not like the presence had implied —and none of his lovers had died or possessed the kind of magic you'd need to take over another person. Besides, he refused to believe that presence had been here for him. He was nothing. A Lone Wolf. He may have been a lieutenant in the McVale Pack, but he had no real power in the scheme of things. What use could he be to anyone, let alone a person with the kind of power to take over a witch-shifter's body so completely?

His fingers tightened on her arm. Yeah. He had questions and hopefully Eloise could answer at least some of them. 'Come on, Eloise. Wake up. I need you to wake up.'

Eloise moaned and pushed against him, her head lolling against his shoulder. He cupped her cheek and tipped her face up so he could look in her eyes. 'Eloise. Come back to me. Come back to me.'

Her eyes flickered open. Green-gold eyes. He breathed a sigh of relief.

'Iain?' She tried to sit up but then clutched her head, collapsing back against his shoulder.

'What happened? Why are you holding me?'

'You passed out.'

'Really?'

'You can't remember what happened?'

She squeezed her eyes shut. 'I remember coming out of the bathroom.' Her frown deepened. 'You came in to get me for lunch and then—' She gasped, her eyes snapping open, going to his lips. It felt like a caress. 'I kissed you.'

Her hand rose, shakily, touched her lips. 'Oh, Goddess. I kissed you.'

A hazy memory rose in her mind—of her leaning forward and pressing her lips against his, just like he'd done with her earlier. The rain-check kiss. Except it had felt nothing like the previous kiss. The gentle tingle of passion had been engulfed in demanding, hungering flame and she'd been lost. 'Oh.' Slowly, she looked at him. 'Was it bad?' She slapped her hand over her mouth. Why had she asked that question?

'It was ... amazing.'

'Yes,' she breathed. Cheeks ablaze, the memory of her lips pressed against his, clinging, opening, rushed over her. Her veins throbbed with liquid heat that made her want to run from the room and rub herself all over him at the same time. It hadn't felt bad to her. Exquisite. Perfect. Except, somehow the kiss didn't seem to belong to her. Perhaps at the start but not what it had become.

'It wasn't you,' he said, seeming to read her mind.

'No. It wasn't me.' The half-lie bit at the back of her throat. It had started out being her—but she didn't have to admit that.

'It's gone, whatever it was.'

She flexed her fingers, realised they were gripping his T-shirt, pressing against his hard chest. It was so tempting to stroke, to shape the vivid line of muscle under that thin material. Her fingers tingled with the knowledge of something just beyond her grasp. With a gasp, she thrust away from him and stood up so fast she stumbled, would have fallen over, except Iain steadied her. His touch stoked the heat flaming through her body. 'Please. Don't touch me right now. I ... I don't seem to have full control and I don't know what I'm going to do.'

He looked at her and then slowly let go. 'You should sit down.'

She wanted to argue, but her legs didn't agree. They were shaking, hard. She plonked down on the bed, her legs sprawling gracelessly in front of her.

'Has this happened to you before?'

'What? Blacking out and kissing men I hardly know? Oh, all the time.' His eyes widened as the words tumbled out. The look on his face was even more priceless and she couldn't help but laugh, a snorting, almost hysterical sound.

'How can you joke about this?'

'Hysteria?'

His lips twitched but he didn't laugh as their gazes met, held. Something soft and wondering swirled inside her as she stared into those too familiar eyes. He shouldn't be so familiar given how little time she'd actually known him. He shouldn't feel like coming home, but he did. She had no idea when she'd begun to feel like that. Right now, she was glad of it.

'We'll get to the bottom of this, Eloise. I promise.'

His voice was soft, slightly rough, but it broke into the moment and she was able to blink, look away. 'Of course. You need to make sure whatever took me over is no danger to the pack.'

He came out of the armchair and down on his knees in front of her, took her hand in his, held on even when she would have pulled away. 'No. For you. Only for you.'

Her throat was suddenly too thick to speak, so she nodded, blinking fast.

'We need to tell Bron and the others. Maybe get Cordy in on this too. They'll know how to figure it all out.'

'Sure,' she managed.

'Lie down. I'll go get Bron.'

'Okay.' He helped her lay down on the bed and then left. She wanted to ask him to stay, but that would be cowardly, and too needy.

She closed her eyes, breathing in deep. His scent was all around her. She licked her lips. She could still taste him.

Soft black swirled behind her eyelids in a stroking wave and she tried to remember the kiss, the strength of his muscled body pressed against hers, his desire. The memory wove around her, caressing her, making her soften into the bed. Sink through it. Falling. She was falling.

She opened her mouth to scream, but only laughter came out as she landed on a bed of softest feathers, the hard muscled warmth of a masculine body following her down, pressing her into the mattress. Strong arms banded around her as plump lips met hers and inside her head, a voice whispered, *'Home. My beloved. He is home.'*

Yes. He was home.

Giving in to the dream, she floated away.

WHEN IAIN, Bron and River rushed into the room, they found Eloise fast asleep. Obviously loathe to wake her, Bron simply checked her aura and then pulled the two men out into the hall behind her, leaving the door partially open.

'She seems fine now and is sleeping peacefully. Tell me exactly what happened.'

Never a man who talked about his private life, Iain was even more reticent to talk about what he'd just experienced with Eloise, but he had no choice. He couldn't tell Bron about the presence without telling her about how it had manifested.

After he finished, Bron regarded him for long, untenable seconds, arms crossed, teeth biting into her lip. 'I've never heard of anything like it. The closest thing to possession we've seen is when Morrigan took over Skye's grandmother's body, but that was different. Morrigan overrode the soul, killing it, and took over the body.'

'What about when Harrison and Adeline took over Shelley,' River added. 'Could it be something like that?'

Bron rubbed her brow. 'Yes, the effect on her aura is more like what Shelley's looked like after that, but not quite.' She looked at Iain. 'You say that Eloise remembered what happened to her?' He nodded. 'And the entity spoke to you?'

'It called me "my beloved" and seemed upset I didn't know who it was.'

Bron tapped on her bottom lip as she thought. 'It could be a past-life regression thing.'

Iain snorted, but Bron arched her brow. 'After everything we've seen, I can't believe you're sceptical about that. I mean, you're a Werewolf and I'm a witch and some kind of Darkness tried to possess River last year, turning him and his wolf into a Beast that tried to kill me. I think past-life regression is tame on the paranormal reality scale compared to that.'

'Could the Darkness have tried to possess her?' River asked, face paling.

Iain stilled, River's words cutting into him. By the Moon, no!

'No. It wasn't the Darkness,' Bron said.

'How do you know?'

'Apart from the fact I can see no evidence of it on her aura, I don't think its tactic is to kiss us to death.'

The humour in her tone, and her words, were equally comforting. 'If it wasn't that kind of possession, if it was a past-life regression, then why did it respond to me?'

'Because you could be someone from her past life that was important to her.'

'How do you know it was a her?' River asked.

Iain shrugged. 'I suppose I don't. All I can say is the presence felt like a woman. That's why I thought it was Morrigan at first. But as Bron so rightly pointed out about the Darkness, Morrigan wouldn't kiss one of us either.'

'Then we're left with a mystery,' River said.

'We can't leave this mystery unsolved. You didn't see her face when she realised what she'd done.'

'I know how you love puzzles, Iain.' River gripped his shoulder. 'I'm sure you'll figure it out.'

'I don't know if I'm up to this task.' Iain scraped his fingers over his stubble-roughened jaw. 'You have no idea what it was like when she was kissing me. It was so …'

'Familiar?' Bron said.

'Right?' River suggested.

He couldn't deny their words. 'This is so fucked.' He raked his hand through his hair. 'What are we supposed to do now?'

'Well, if it's a past-life regression, there's not much we can do aside from help her explore what it is if she wants to control it. The thing is though, it might never happen again, so we might be opening an unnecessary can of worms.'

'And if it happens again?'

Bron said, 'There's no sign of anything wrong with her aura—and there would be if the presence was dangerous to her. Strangely enough, her aura is looking better than it has since she came to us.'

'Wow, it just goes to show that old adage is actually true,' River said.

'What adage?'

'That a kiss can make everything better.' He turned to Iain. 'Although yours must pack a pretty powerful punch to heal an aura.' Iain punched him on the shoulder. 'Ow!'

'This is serious, you idiot!'

'I love you too, man.'

Iain nodded, gaze meeting in deeper understanding than words could ever express.

The River of the past would never have been able to joke like that.

'While you two have bro-mance time, I'm going to contact Skye, Shelley and Cordy. Cordy will know what our next step should be if it's a regression we're talking about.'

'And Shelley might have read something in the diaries, given she's read more of them than the rest of us' River finished for her. 'I'll come with you.'

'I'll stay with Eloise.' He longed to get back into that room, to be near her.

Bron didn't argue. 'Call us if she wakes.' She touched his cheek with a soft caress. 'Do what you've been doing. She needs that the most.'

Iain's skin prickled as they walked away to make their calls. There was something behind her words he couldn't figure out. But River was right—he was good at puzzles. He would figure it out. Just like he would make sure they figured out what the hell had just happened to Eloise.

He had to. It couldn't happen again. Soon, his wolf would make it impossible for him to stay and he couldn't be bound in any way to Eloise when that happened.

He was a Lone Wolf, and Lone Wolves walked paths that could never be walked with others. Especially a shifter-witch who obviously longed for a home.

10

Eloise gritted her teeth, frustration streaming through her in a torrent so violent she thought she would scream if she didn't get it out. But screaming would do nothing more than make the Were hovering behind her treat her with even softer kid gloves. She'd never been treated so carefully as she had in the week since her 'episode'. They were all doing it, but Iain was the worst. It made her teeth ache with wanting to snap at him.

But how could you snap at someone when they were being so horribly nice? On top of everything else, she didn't want to seem like she had a screw loose. Or was ungrateful.

'Try it again, Eloise.'

'You just need to concentrate.'

'You can do it.'

She wanted to glare at Bron for her cheerful encouragement, slap Shelley for saying the obvious and throw the computer against a tree. Cordelia O'Brien's knowing smile as she looked out from the computer made her want to scream. How could the witch look so content, so pleased with what was happening? There was nothing pleasing about these sessions she'd video conferenced in on every day for the last week. Sessions Eloise had nicknamed 'magic for dummies'.

But instead of doing any of those things, she closed her eyes and tried again.

All she could see behind her eyelids was the dappled shadow of the sun shining through the trees above.

This was nothing like those exercises Iain had her do to tap into her shifter ability. They were a whole other kettle of fish that she couldn't seem to grasp. Secretly, she'd tried using what Iain had taught her, but unfortunately, what worked for those abilities didn't seem to work for her witch ones.

The other witches assured her these would work as soon as she gave herself over to them. But how could she do that when she was afraid of the dark she needed to sink into to reach the meditative state that would allow her to tap into the power that they insisted was at her core? Not to mention, nobody could explain what the presence that had taken her over was. All they were certain of was that she needed to learn control of her powers. Maybe, if she did that, she'd be able to explore what had happened, figure it all out and control it.

And there was the other major problem. She wasn't sure she wanted to figure it out. The strength of emotion felt by that presence had overwhelmed her. And her dreams had been full of scenes she knew she'd never experienced. It was frightening and quite frankly, she didn't want to think about it now.

However, they were right about one part of the need for her to learn control. She didn't want to be taken over again. She wanted to know that what she felt was hers and not some unknown presence. So, she did need to control her powers. Which meant she had to get this right because she couldn't rely on her shifting abilities to keep the dangerous build of power at bay.

At least the daily shifting lessons with Iain were helping to make her feel more centred—she'd managed to turn into a horse she'd seen in a neighbouring paddock the day before. She just wished that something about them could help her now.

Birds chattered in the pine trees behind her, their cheeping so happy and welcoming, she wanted to join them. Could she turn into a bird? Fly away from her problems to soar in the endless, open blue?

The tingle of change began in her fingers without her thinking about it any further.

Iain squeezed her shoulder. 'Concentrate on this. We'll play with your shifting later.'

He was right, damn him! She let the sensation slide away and focused again on that black spot in her mind.

The warm breeze fluttered the hair on her nape, whispering of secrets to be discovered if only she would follow the trail of scent it left for her. The trickling of the water in the fountain, which she was supposed to be using as a sensory guide, sounded like someone was laughing at her for being such a magic dunce. Not to mention she was too aware of the Were standing at her back, her literal and figurative Shadow. He wasn't touching her anymore, but the imprint of the hand that had squeezed her shoulder still tingled with his gentle warmth. Just like she could still feel the imprint of his lips on hers, the sweep of his tongue inside her mouth, the warm pine and ocean scent of his skin, the brush of his silky hair through her fingers ...

Breathe. Just breathe.

She couldn't allow herself to think about The Kiss. It short-circuited her concentration every time.

Breathe. Just breathe.

The reminder didn't help to settle her. Her skin was itchy with the need for something and with all the stimulation, it was too hard to ignore.

'Ask the Goddess for help,' Cordy's smooth, calm voice suggested. 'She's there to guide you. Feel her warmth in the sun, hear her voice in the breeze, breathe in her scent carried on the air. And if you can't hear or feel her there, look within. She's in your thoughts. In the beat of your heart. The rush of your blood. The warmth in your breath. If you open yourself to her even a little, you'll find her there, waiting for you. She's part of everything around you. She comes in the quiet of the night, speaks to you in your dreams.'

Her dreams? She'd heard a voice in her dreams throughout her childhood. It had stopped for many years, but recently, it had come back.

Ever since she'd come in contact with the Were.

Was that voice the Goddess? There was no way to know. But it had never sought to harm her. It had even encouraged her to open her eyes and accept what she was seeing of the Were. At the time, she'd ignored the voice—it went against everything she believed. But now, she wondered if that had been the Goddess trying to make her see the truth: that what she was doing was wrong.

'I think I've heard her.'

'You see,' Bron said. 'I told you she comes to us all.'

'But I'm no-one special.'

'You are exactly who you are supposed to be,' came from behind her.

Iain. His voice a stroke on her senses, his approbation warming her deep inside. Just like his kiss had warmed her. She may have started that kiss, but he'd kissed her back well before the presence had taken over. And the memory of that was a blissful madness. She wanted to experience the bliss of that madness again. And worse ... she wanted to experience more. With him.

'Eloise?' She jumped as Bron said her name. 'Are you okay?'

'She's tired. She should probably rest.'

She glanced back at Iain and scowled at him—she couldn't let her feelings show. And she absolutely couldn't let him get away with treating her like she was made of fragile Murano glass. 'I'm fine. Stop treating me like I'm going to break.'

'I'm not.'

'Yes you are, and it's making me feel even more frustrated with how stupid I am at this stuff.'

'Hey. Don't talk like that.'

'Why not? It's true.'

He hunkered down beside the chair she sat on. The chair he'd made for her. His fingers were almost on her cheek before he jerked back, his hand spread across the weathered wood of the chair, right next to hers, but not touching. Even so, she could feel the heat of him.

Wanted it so badly she had to stop herself from leaning into it by moving her hands to grip the wood beside her legs.

'You have to stop with the "magic for dummies" thing. You aren't stupid.' His voice was a rough caress. 'You've just never been trained. And you're doing really well, isn't she?' He looked up for confirmation.

Bron and Shelley nodded.

Cordelia said, 'Absolutely. Novices take years to get this right.'

'But I don't have time to be a novice. I have to learn this or I could explode, right? I could hurt others, kill them even, if that happened.' None of them answered, but they didn't have to. 'Then, I better get this right.'

'Perhaps we should try another spot?' Shelley suggested. 'I prefer a quiet room and Skye found success in the backyard where she could hear the children playing in the distance. And we all know Bron loves to meditate and commune with the Goddess in the gardens River creates for her.'

'We all love to do that.' Bron's eyes glowed with warmth.

'Yeah, but it doesn't work quite as well for us there as it does for you.'

'Do you want to try somewhere else, Eloise? Is there somewhere that speaks to you more than here?' Cordy asked.

'No.' She gripped the chair tighter. She loved this spot in the garden with the hill falling away towards the orchard to reveal a glimpse of the folding green, ruby and gold of the hills in the distance. And she loved this chair. 'I feel safe here.'

'Good. Then let's try it again,' Bron said.

Cordy nodded from the computer. 'Concentrate on the moon. It's almost full, heralding a very powerful time of the year. Easter is almost upon us. The time we celebrate the power of Ostara—a Quarter Day. It's a time ripe for learning.'

'I know.' Morrigan might have kept much from her, but not the basics of witch and Wiccan lore. Ostara—or Oestra as Morrigan called it—was the first day of the Vernal Equinox, celebrated as the first day of the year on the Zodiac calendar. It was a potent time. Four days of growing power, made even more so by the advent of a full moon. Given what Morrigan had done at the last time of power growth, Eloise shuddered to think what evil her old Mistress was planning for this Quarter Day. She wished she knew what it was so that she could be of some help to the Were and their witches in stopping Morrigan, but she had no idea.

At least they knew what Morrigan was capable of now and Iain had told her they were all working towards finding out what her plan might be. The only thing in their favour was that while the Quarter Day might give Morrigan power, it also gave the same to the Pack Witches. Even more if she could just figure out how to help them by adding hers to the mix.

Taking a deep breath, she closed her eyes and settled into the hated dark. To distract herself from her fear, she reached out and tried to feel the vibrations of power from the coming Quarter. A tingle slipped through her and away before she could gather it. Cursing, she gritted her teeth, took a deep breath and tried again. She could do this. She *would* do this. She must.

Unclenching her hands, she placed them palm up on her knees and pictured the faint whitish blue of the moon above and the elements of nature all about her. The warmth of the sun on her skin. The brush of the wind through her hair. The way the scents of the afternoon wove through her mind. She couldn't help but notice Iain's scent mingled with them. It tugged at her memories, made her think of laughter and sunshine, lying curled up in the long grass on the dunes, listening to the waves crashing on the hard-pressed sand as a storm roiled in the distance; the endless seeking, longing of it.

The sound came to her now, the thunder of the waves an echo in the distance. There was an arctic tang of lightning on the air. The whispered promise of something more, something bigger, on the wind as it brushed over her body, tangled in her hair.

'*Eloise.*'

'Shh. I'm trying to concentrate.'

'*Eloise. You need to listen.*'

'I am listening. To the wind and the rain and the thunder.'

'Can you hear the sound of my words in them?'

'No. I can only hear ... your words?' She sat up, looked around to see an empty beach, the grass swaying in the wild wind. What the hell? She looked around frantically. Iain was nowhere in sight. Neither was Bron or Shelley or the computer with Cordy's smiling face on it. 'Where am I?'

'You're where you took yourself to commune with me.'

'What? I can't do that.'

'Oh, but you did. And I'm so glad you did. I've been calling to you for years but you have been unable to hear me.'

'Goddess?' She scrambled to her feet—it seemed rude to sit in the presence of a Goddess.

'Who else would it be?'

'I didn't mean to bring myself here.' Eloise shook her head, unable to comprehend that she'd actually not only succeeded in tapping into her essence but was now talking to the Goddess. 'How? Why?'

'You are more than you think.'

She jerked as the words pulled at her. 'That's what Iain keeps saying,' she said, hesitant.

'He is a smart male.'

She let that digest for a moment before asking, 'What should I call you?'

'I am known by many names, but for the purposes of today, you may call me Arianrhod.'

'Arianrhod,' she breathed. It was strange and beautiful all at once.

'You have a question for me, I think.'

Eloise nodded. She was meant to learn about her witch magic, and who better to ask than the Goddess from whom all power sprung. She opened her mouth but there were too many questions, all vying for attention: how she could have had power all these years and not known; who her people were and where were they now; what her main talent was; how she could control it. As was the way of things, the only question that blurted from her lips was the one she really didn't want the answer to. 'Bron and Cordy think I know Iain from a past life. But that's not possible, is it?' Her question was answered with silence. A part of her was relieved, but another part annoyed. Why bring her here if not to answer her questions? 'Aren't you going to even help me understand this?'

'I wish to help you, Eloise, but there is no help in giving answers to puzzles already solved.'

'Do you have to speak in riddles?'

The waves laughed at her, a bubble of warm, welcoming sound. *'I speak as I must. There are rules that even I must follow.'*

'Rules? But who gives rules to a Goddess?'

Silence.

Eloise ground her foot into the sand, trying to find some patience. She may not have meant to come here, but she had to be here for a reason. She couldn't lose herself in frustration. 'Okay, so the puzzle might already be solved, but not by me. How do I find these already given answers?'

A bubble of amusement again on the waves. *'You are learning well, my child. Bron and Cordy have the right of it. You have an old soul, as does your Were.'*

'He isn't my Were.'

'Are you certain of that? A past self cannot take over a body unwilling.'

The crackle of electrified warmth shot through her as she remembered how Iain had kissed her and how it had made her feel suddenly, shockingly alive. Desire, so fierce she trembled with it, had shot through her and she'd been helpless in the wake of it. 'Oh,' she breathed.

'This is a question important to you, but it is not why I have come to you today. You have come so far, do not falter now out of fear.'

Eloise's eyes prickled. 'I am afraid.'

'Of course you are afraid—you would be foolish to be unaffected by what has come to pass; and what is to come. There is a nameless Darkness out there that I have spent an eon fighting. For an endless time, it seemed I must do this alone, but then warriors were sent to help me in my task. You are one of those warriors, Eloise.'

Eloise's entire frame shook with the enormity of the Goddess' words and she collapsed back down onto the sand. 'I don't feel like a warrior,' she whispered. 'I feel like nothing.'

A soft caress of breeze on her face. *I know, my child. But that is a borrowed feeling, swollen by fear. You were taught to doubt, but now you are learning a more positive lesson.'*

'I'm afraid it's all going to be taken away if I cherish it too much.' The words were rough, torn from the heart of her.

'If you allow that fear to grow, you will never be who you are meant to be. You will never become the warrior you were born to be.'

'I don't want to let you down. Or Iain ... I mean the Were and their coven. They've been so good to me.'

'And they will continue to be good to you regardless of what you learn. But their wishes and desires are unimportant, as are mine. Believe in yourself. Live your life. Embrace all it has to offer and do not allow fear to rule your existence. Fear is a tool, no more. Learn from it but then cast it aside.'

Eloise pulled her knees up in front of her, wrapping her arms around them, rocking slightly back and forth. 'But I don't know how to do that.'

'You will find a way.'

'With Iain and his pack and their coven?'

'That is up to you.'

She made an exasperated sound. 'You know, you're very annoying to talk to.'

Laughing bubbled from the waves again. *'I've been told that before.'* The laughter died away. *'What in my answer frustrates you?'*

'I wanted you to say yes, or no.'

'How can I say either of those things when ultimately you are the only one who can answer that question? Especially when you already know the answer.'

Eloise blushed. She did know the answer.

She would stay with Iain. Would fight to do so. He felt like home.

She'd never felt that before, not even with her brother.

Thinking of Cain, she blurted out, 'How is Cain my brother but not a shifter too? Is it like River and Skye—one's a witch and one's a Were?'

'No. Unlike Skye and River you are not equal and opposite with your twin. Both of you have equal power.'

'Then why can't he shift?'

The wind sighed around her for a long moment and she thought the Goddess wasn't going to answer her.

'Cain cannot shift because his ability was subsumed by you when you came into being in the womb. You are by far the stronger.'

'What? But that's not true. He's always been stronger than me.'

'That is a lie told to you by Morrigan and her followers for reasons of their own. They sought to control you, to have you help feed the lie by allowing Cain to leech power from you. But the moment you broke from him, from them, the lie was shown and you took back what was always yours.'

'It's no wonder he hates me.'

'He doesn't hate you for that, child.'

'Then why did he follow Morrigan against me so easily? Why believe her over me?'

'Because she filled him with fear.'

'Of me?' She couldn't believe that. Who would be afraid of her? 'Is this because of that warrior thing you said that I was? And how am I a warrior and Cain isn't? He's more powerful than me.'

'As I said before, Cain is not the stronger—you are. But that is not the point. You are not a warrior because of the strength of your power. You are a warrior because you are strong in ways Cain will never be. You are good and kind and thoughtful. You have empathy. You think of the good of others. Cain thinks only of himself.'

'He wasn't always like that.'

'Your loyalty to him does you credit, but it also blinds you to the truth.'

'Which is?'

'Cain and Morrigan fear you because you are a Nexus.'

'A Nexus?'

'Yes. A Nexus. You and your power are at the centre of things. It has been at the centre of things for a very long time.'

'My past life?'

'Yes. Morrigan found you and took you because of this. She sought to *use that to her advantage by trying to damage you beyond repair, using magic to syphon your magic to your brother and then twisting you to her needs.'*

'She didn't succeed.'

'That is yet to be seen. There are changes coming, choices to be made, it will be up to you to decide which direction the path will continue along for us all.'

Eloise shivered, suddenly icy cold.

In the distance, the sea changed. Waves thundered across the horizon, surging closer. Dark sickly green-grey clouds above turned the sapphire blue to a deep, ominous, swirling green that was so dark it looked black. Eloise wrapped her arms around her knees and hugged tight. 'But that's not fair. How can everything come down to a decision I make?'

'Because you are a Nexus, my child. You always have been.'

Eloise hissed in frustration. 'I don't understand.'

'You will.'

'But how?'

'Find answers in the past to help you navigate your future.'

'That makes no sense.'

'It makes the only sense worth having. I must go now.' The Goddess's voice began to fade. *'Trust in what you feel, my child. Discover your history—both of them. In those you will find your truth. For now, we must return from whence we came. You have been here too long. As have I. I cannot let the Darkness find me here with you. It will retaliate.'*

'No. Don't go. I need help. I can't do this on my own.'

'You are strong enough to fight the coming storm, Eloise, but I assure you, you are never alone.'

The words echoed into silence.

Eloise sprang to her feet, panic rising to squeeze her chest. The Goddess had lied. She was alone. Now more than ever. 'Come back. Come back. Don't leave me here by myself. I don't know how to get back! I don't know how to fight the coming storm.'

The world turned wild around her, as if thinking of the storm had brought it into reality. Bright sun turned to the eerie black-green of a coming thunderstorm. Lighting flashed, closer, closer. Thunder rumbled louder. The wind turned cold and bitter, pulling at her hair, tearing at her clothes. The rich scents of sun and sand and surf overcome with the nasty miasma of rotten seaweed and too much salt.

Icy cold rain poured over the water, up the beach, drenching her in a few seconds. Wind buffeted her, making her stumble. The roiling mass of waves smashed up the beach towards her. The dark waves licked at her toes, the ice of them a spear through her maimed foot.

A shard of pain shot up her leg and into her spine, forcing a short scream from her lips as she struggled to back away from that violent oily-dark froth.

'Eloise. Seek the truth in me.' The dark whisper came from the black waves at her feet, from the cold rain and buffeting wind pressing into her skin. *'I will give you all the answers. I will not fill your mind with useless riddles. Come into my arms. Join your coven once again and be strong.'*

'No. No.' She shook her head, backing away as fast as she could, but the waves kept coming, the wind smacking at her, shoving her back towards the waves. 'They want to kill me.'

'Not if you come willingly. Not if you help us. You must release them from captivity. You must free my servant, Cain, from his bonds. Then we will forgive all transgressions. Come to us, Eloise. Come now and you will never be alone.'

Oh Goddess! The Darkness had found her.

She needed to get out of here. But how? Why hadn't the Goddess told her how to leave?

She backed up, smacking into the cliff behind her, feet scrabbling to find purchase on ice-slicked rock. She didn't want to fall back into the claustrophobic embrace of Morrigan's coven. She didn't belong there with them, surrounded by hatred. She didn't want that. She wanted warmth and strength and acceptance and love. She wanted ... 'Iain! Iain!' she screamed into the enclosing dark.

'I'm here, Eloise.' Strong fingers gripped her hand, held on.

But she couldn't seem to rise out of the dark. She'd always been frightened of it and now ... it froze her in place. 'I can't make it. It won't let me,' she cried, voice rough with fear and desperation.

'I've got you, Eloise.' Warmth wrapped around her. The soft press of lips warming the chill skin on her forehead, her cheeks, her eyelids, her lips. 'I've got you. Just open your eyes and see.'

Her eyes were closed?

Was she doing this to herself?

No, that couldn't be the case. Even so, she shuddered.

'Open your eyes, Eloise. Come back to me.'

Iain's warmth surrounded her, his scent filling her nose, lighting the way. Slowly, with difficulty, she forced her eyes open and looked up.

And into a gaze she trusted more than she trusted herself.

'You've got me.'

'I've got you.'

The fear fell away and there was only his smile.

11

Eloise woke from sleep, a warm muzzy feeling stealing over her. Soft sunlight tangled in her lashes as she rolled over and almost slipped off the couch.

'Oops!' she laughed, catching herself. How had she gotten on the couch? She'd been outside in the garden, trying to commune with the Goddess when ...

'Oh!' Her vision. She sat bolt upright, swaying slightly as the room spun around her.

'Steady there,' Iain said, catching her before she truly did fall off the couch.

His arms were warm around her, and she wanted to sink into them. Being held by him forever sounded like a brilliant idea. That way she'd never have to face what she'd found out in the vision. When he began to pull away, she held onto him, fingers digging into his warm flesh. 'Don't go.'

'I won't.' He stared into her upturned face, his expression inscrutable. Then, with a soft groan, he cupped her face and kissed her trembling lips. The kiss was soft, short, barely a brush of skin against skin, but the power of it sent shockwaves through her.

'Why did you do that?' she whispered as he pulled back to look at her again.

'Because you needed it.'

'Oh.' Her fingers loosened on his shirt as disappointment sank deep into her stomach.

'And because I wanted to.'

'Oh.' Her fingers flexed, tightened. Words bubbled up inside her, words she couldn't hold back. 'I want to kiss you too.'

His breath puffed against her face as the golden-amber of his gaze heated, deepened. But he didn't try to kiss her again. Instead, he peered into her eyes. 'Is that you saying that? Or the other person?'

Her gaze flickered from his eyes to his mouth and back again. 'Me. I think.'

He swallowed, nodded, his thumbs stroking her face. 'Well, until we're certain, I think we maybe shouldn't do it again.'

Her gaze flickered to his lips. His fingers tightened on her face, thumbs sweeping close to the edges of her mouth. She swept her tongue out and touched one of his thumbs.

He jerked. 'Eloise. Stop that.'

'No.' She repeated the action, licking at his other thumb, her gaze firmly on his mouth.

'Eloise,' he groaned.

'Kiss me.'

He groaned again, but his fingers loosened, like he was about to pull away. She grabbed his wrists, holding his hands to her face, her gaze snapping to his eyes. 'Kiss me, Iain. Me. Eloise. This is definitely me asking. I need you to kiss me.'

His gaze flickered from her eyes to her mouth.

Her lungs burned as she waited for him to pull away—she was certain he wasn't going to give in. But then his fingers flexed and with a groan, he pulled her to him.

His mouth pressed more firmly against hers this time, demanding. She demanded back.

A low growl rumbled in his throat. He swept his tongue across the seam of her lips. Everything in her jerked to life and she opened her mouth, letting him in. Their tongues tangled, the sensation like liquid fire racing through her veins. A sound like a purr rumbled in her throat.

'Little cat,' he smiled against her lips.

'I thought I was your Little Bird.'

'You are.' His tongue tangled with hers again, forcing that sound from her throat again. 'And so much more.'

She lost herself to the sensation of his lips moving on hers, breaths mingled, tongues dancing. She didn't want this to ever stop.

Iain knew he should stop. For his sanity and hers, he'd not kissed her since the presence had taken her over a week earlier, but it had been one of the hardest things he'd ever done. He shouldn't have given in now, but when she'd looked at him like that, his control had gone up in a conflagration of withheld desire. He'd wanted to ravage her mouth all week—and now he was, he wanted more. He wanted to run his lips down her throat, to bite down gently on the pulse banging away at the base of her neck under his palms. Wanted to strip her naked and take her in every way possible.

His wolf howled inside him, urging him to do it; mine, it declared. Mine. It urged him to run his hand down her throat and hold her in that possessive grip, to mark her like a Were marked his mate.

He jerked back.

Mate?

No.

She couldn't be his mate. Lone Wolves didn't have mates. Certainly not him. He had more reason than any before him to know that was true. What happened to his parents had almost tipped him over the edge. But Luke McVale had pulled him back from the edge, tying him to his son, Jason. Even so, his wolf constantly walked that tightrope, closer to going rabid than any other. Luke had seen the truth of that, as did Jason now. That's why they gave him permission to roam so long and so wide. Why they had always given him every-thing he needed to assuage his need for touch; a need that could never be truly fulfilled because those he had loved deepest had been stolen away from him at too young an age and made him responsible for a brother equally traumatised.

A mate for him was an impossibility. Even if he wasn't a Lone Wolf with their low rate of mating, he was far too broken to ever be tied down in the way a mate would tie him down.

This with Eloise, it had to be something else. And yet, he'd never felt anything quite like it before. The voracious need to take, to possess and yet to give and protect, was stronger than he'd ever felt about anything or anyone, including pack. But a mate ...

No. It couldn't be.

He realised then she was staring at him, her fingers clenching on his shoulders, her body trembling, her luminous eyes full of tears.

'Iain?' Breath shuddered out of her. 'You don't want to kiss me.' A tear tumbled down her cheek, caught on her lip.

'Shh.' How could she have known what he was thinking? Nobody had ever read him so easily. Although she hadn't quite got it right. He did want to kiss her, more than he wanted to breathe, it was just that he shouldn't. But looking into her beautiful unique eyes, hurt beginning to shadow the passion and desire blazing in their depths, he couldn't make himself listen to his better instincts.

He pressed his lips against hers again, tasting the salty bitterness of her tears. 'Shh.' And again. He held her face so he could look into those luminous, desire-laden eyes. 'I want you.' Another kiss. 'By the Moon, how I want you.' He ran his lips along her jaw, nipped her ear, made her jerk and moan as he sucked the lobe into his mouth, swirled his tongue over the delicate shell and then back to her mouth. 'Do you believe me?'

She breathed a soft sigh of contentment into his mouth that sent golden warmth through his heart. So trusting. How could she be so trusting after what she'd been through?

He wanted to ravage her, to take anything she was willing to give. But her trust made him realise he couldn't do that to her. Instead, he gave her soft, settling kisses, his fingers brushing through her hair. He kissed her eyes, kissed the tears from her cheeks, nipped the pulse in her throat where he desperately wanted to mark her more deeply, but before he could, he made his way up her throat, back to her lips.

'Iain,' she breathed as he covered her lips with his. He tried to keep it soft, but her kisses demanded, pulled at him, taunted him to let go, to give in to the urge to take, to ravage, to taste every part of her, to take her over the edge and make her scream his name as she came and then do it all over again until his scent was embedded in her skin and his in hers so nobody could mistake her as his and he was hers.

But he didn't.

Couldn't.

She meshed her lips with his again, pressed her breasts in that thin T-shirt against his chest. By the Moon he longed to feel the softness of that flesh against the hardness of his own.

No! Don't think of her naked body. He had to pull back. Had to be sensible here.

'We can't do this now. Not yet. It isn't the right time.' Doubt flooded her eyes again and he couldn't help but take her mouth in a ravaging kiss that had to make her understand that he didn't want to pull back, but he had to. Pulling away before he lost control, he leaned his forehead against hers, their panting breaths mingling. 'I can't take advantage of you right now. Not while you're still trying to come to terms with everything.' Not while there were still secrets between them.

'I want you to.' She pushed her fingers into his hair, tipped her face back, lips parted in invitation. 'I need you to.'

He groaned. 'You'll be the death of me, Eloise.'

'And you'll be the death of her if you don't give in.'

He pulled away. Her eyes were swirling with gold again. 'You!'

She smiled up at him, her lips an open invitation. 'I am so glad to see you, beloved. Are you not glad to see me?'

'Give me back Eloise.'

'She is here.' She settled back against the couch, a smile that was hers but not hers curving her lips. 'Why don't you want her now?'

'I want her. I don't want you.'

'We are one and the same.'

'No. You're not.'

'You talk as if you think me evil.'

'For all I know, you are.'

'You know I am not. I could not reside inside such goodness without tainting it if I were evil. But that is not the point. Why will you not give in, beloved? I know you want to. I know you feel she is your mate.'

'I am a Lone Wolf. I cannot have a mate.'

A sound hissed out of her lips. 'My beloved was a Lone Wolf too. Yet he gave in to the urge of the mate-bond.'

'With you?' That was highly unlikely. She was lying—although, why would she lie?

'With me. Only me. Forever me.'

'And who are you?'

'Wouldn't you like to know.' She blew a kiss and smiled, a mischievous smile that looked at home on Eloise's face.

'Why are you here?'

'To try to finish what was started many moons ago. To right a great injustice.'

'Why do you need Eloise to do it?'

'Because we are the Nexus.'

'What's a Nexus?'

'Eloise will tell you.'

'She knows?'

'The Goddess spoke to her of things she needs to be aware of. But as with all things, it will take time for her to understand. Why should you know before she does?'

Iain growled at the circular answer and tried another tack. 'Why now?'

'I can only rise to the surface for short periods of time during extreme emotional turbulence.' The smile widened into something he could only describe as wolfish as her gaze raked up and down his body. 'And you, beloved, cause her extreme emotional turbulence.'

'Me? Or the male I once was?'

'She does not respond to anyone but you. It is only I who see in you the male you once were.' She closed her eyes. 'This is tiring. She is rising to the surface again, and I cannot fight her.' Those glowing golden eyes opened again, making him shiver as they stared at him with an intensity that stroked him all the way to his soul. 'Watch over us, beloved, and think on what I have said.'

And then she was gone and Eloise slumped back on the couch. He caught her up, afraid to lose her again. 'Eloise?'

'Hmm?' She blinked up at him. 'You stopped kissing me.'

He brushed his fingers over her cheek and she rubbed against them, just like a cat. Tenderness swept through him, a tenderness completely at odds with the ferocity of his wolf, and yet perfectly right. 'The presence took over again.'

'I know. She interrupted our kissing. She shouldn't have done that.'

'Oh good, you're awake.'

Iain swung around to see Bron, River, Shelley and Adam striding in the back door.

'Are you ready to tell us what happened in your vision yet?'

'Adam!'

The Trickster ignored Shelley's slap, just leaned against the kitchen counter facing them, arms crossed. 'Well?'

'No. She's not bloody ready. The presence just took over her again. And you were right, Bron. It was a past-life presence.'

'You spoke to it?'

'Her. I spoke to her.'

'Why does she only speak to you?'

'She says I was her mate in a past life.'

'Really?' Bron's eyes lit with interest.

'That's not important right now.' He sent her a stern look. She smiled, a knowing look in her eyes he didn't like.

'So, what else did the presence say?' Shelley asked.

'She said I was the Nexus,' Eloise whispered. 'It's exactly what the Goddess said.'

'The Goddess? She spoke to you?'

'In my vision.'

Bron sat next to her on the couch. 'Can you tell us?'

Eloise frowned and told them everything she could remember from the vision.

Once she was done, Bron blew out a breath. 'Well, for a first-time vision quest, that was pretty impressive.'

'I've never managed a full-blown vision like that,' Shelley said. 'Must be something different in her power from ours.'

'When the Goddess said I was the Nexus, I didn't want to believe it was true. But the way the Darkness came after me when the Goddess left, its desperation to have me back ...' She shuddered. Iain put his arm around her. She smiled up at him, gratefully before turning back to Bron. 'I still don't want to believe it, but now my past-life self says the same thing, I can't deny it must be true. But I still don't know what it means. Do you?'

'No. I don't,' Bron said, visibly shaken. 'But whatever it means, it's something significant. You're important, Eloise. More important than any of us ever guessed. We thought luck had brought you to us.' She looked around at the others. 'Maybe it was fate.'

'What else did the presence say?'

Iain shrugged. 'Nothing else important.'

Eloise knew that wasn't true—it had said they were soulmates—but she wasn't going to bring that up in front of everyone. So she said, 'There was something else the Darkness said.' She looked down at her hands, picking at her fingernails. 'I'm sure it was a lie, but it told me you have Cain and other coven members. Why would it say that?'

Iain stiffened. She felt the significant looks pass over her head without having to see them. Looking up, her skin prickled with cold at Bron's guilty expression, Shelley's shock and Adam's furious scowl. Slowly, she turned to Iain. 'You have my brother? My friends?'

'Yes.'

'Iain!' Adam growled. 'What the fuck are you doing?'

'The cat's kind of out of the bag, Adam.' He grasped her hand.

She pulled away. 'Cain's here?' Her gaze skated around the room, to beyond the windows. A moment ago the light had been golden and now everything looked so dark.

Oh, Goddess. That's why he could get to her so easily in her dreams. Her gaze arrowed back on Iain. 'Why didn't you tell me?'

'It wasn't his fault, Eloise.' Bron's tone was soft, pleading. 'Jason ordered him not to. And once the Alpha gives an Alpha order, none of the pack can disobey. Even the witches are bound by it, although we can break the order if we need. But now that you know, if you want to see him, we can take you to him.'

'No we bloody can't.' Adam moved to stand between them. 'We can't take her anywhere near him.'

Eloise's face prickled. Her heart thumped painfully in her chest. 'Adam's right. You can't take me to see him.'

'You're agreeing with him? Don't you want to see your brother?'

'Of course she doesn't want to see him. He tried to kill her,' River said.

'No, that's not it.' Iain's voice was a soft, slow rumble beside her. She turned to face him, finding a strange understanding in his eyes. 'What haven't you told us, Eloise?'

She sucked in a breath. She didn't want to answer that question. She didn't want them to know she'd been keeping things from them after everything they'd done for her. But they had to know the truth if she wanted them to share their truths with her.

The light seemed to darken as she stared down at her hands. 'Cain's been trying to speak to me in my dreams.'

'What?' Shelley asked.

'Hell,' River said.

'Oh, Eloise, no.'

'Fuck!' Adam said. 'I told you she couldn't be trusted.'

The voices tumbled one over the top of another until they were almost a shriek in Eloise's head.

'No! Hang on!' Iain's voice cut across all of them. 'You said, "trying", Eloise.'

She nodded. 'I didn't want to talk to him, even in my dreams. He was filled with so much hatred the last time I saw him. I was afraid if I let him in like I used to, his hatred would spill over into me.' She swallowed hard. 'Besides, I thought maybe I was imagining it. His presence was different somehow and I kind of thought,' she glanced up, her gaze skating from one to the other, 'that you might have killed him that night and what I was sensing was his loss, like a person still feels a severed limb.'

'Oh, Eloise.' Bron's hand slipped over hers. 'Why didn't you ask us?'

'I didn't want to know if he was dead or alive. If I didn't know, he could be neither, and that seemed almost more comforting than knowing for certain he was dead and gone forever, or alive and still hating me, wishing me dead.'

Shelley hunkered down in front of Eloise. 'Can you tell us what he's been saying to you?'

She shook her head. 'I never heard words until the day I almost blew up. He was just egging me on, making me angrier.' She pressed her fingers against her lips, trying to stop them from wobbling. It still hurt to think her twin wanted her dead. 'Before that, it was just his presence pushing at me.'

'How did you know it was him?'

'He used to do it when we were little. Not so much in recent years. The closer he got to Morrigan, the further away from me he seemed. Also, proximity helps. When he's close, he can speak in my mind with much greater clarity. When I came to live with Bron last year as Bluebelle, being so distant from him, it made it harder for him to reach me. Only Morrigan spoke to me.'

'Has she spoken to you since you woke?'

'No. I've only heard Cain.'

'That makes no sense,' Adam scoffed. 'Your precious brother was moved away from here when you woke. If proximity helps, then how can you hear him now?'

Eyes widening, she looked around at the caring, eager faces around her. 'I don't know. You said he was here.'

'No. We said we held him captive. As we do the others. But he's nowhere near. So how is he doing it? Are you inviting him in?'

'No. I wouldn't do that. I don't know how he's doing it if he's not near.' If what they said was true, Cain was more powerful than she knew him to be. How could she fight him if that were true? Her breath shuddered in and out in hard, sharp gasps.

Iain's hand tightened around hers. 'Stop it, Adam. You're frightening her.'

'Maybe she needs to be frightened.'

'Adam!' Bron snapped. 'That's enough. Eloise saved River and Iain and Gareth. She saved all of us with her actions. She even tried to save us when she thought she was a bomb from Morrigan. For those actions alone she deserves our help and respect. Then there's the fact her power syphoned into Iain. We all know what that means. She deserves our allegiance. You know that's true.'

Adam's jaw squared, then he dipped his head, stared at the floor. 'I know. I'm sorry.' He looked up, gaze boring into hers. 'But something about her screams danger to my wolf and I can't help but respond to it.'

'Then perhaps you need to leave.'

Adam bristled, but Shelley stepped in front of him. 'Adam. I need to go back to Melbourne. I want to return to my research. There might be something in the diaries about this Nexus thing the Goddess spoke about. I need you to come with me.' Shelley touched his shoulder, stroked down his arm, the gesture tentative, uncertain. Adam stilled at the touch, and it was as if the air itself held its breath, waiting for him to respond. Then finally, he looked down at her. She jerked, as if struck, but then continued on in the same calm voice. 'Jason will want a direct report and then you can help me.' She moved her hand away.

He captured it. 'You need me. Ah, Kitten, I never thought I'd hear you say those words.' His tone was playful, teasing, and while the tension was still there, the violence, it was tempered with something else. Something softer, giving. Something Eloise recognised. Had seen in Iain's eyes when he looked at her.

'Don't let it go to your head,' Shelley said on a snort, breaking into Eloise's tumbling thoughts. She pulled her hand away from Adam's. 'You're just good at reading between the lines.'

Adam stared at her for a moment longer and then with a gusty sigh, nodded. 'Okay. Let's go.'

Shelley turned back to the others. 'Let us know how it goes.'

'Of course.'

She walked out of the room. Adam followed close in her wake.

Silence fell.

'Where is Cain?' Eloise asked into the silence. He had to be nearer than they were intimating. He had to be.

Iain's arm curled around her. 'He's in a safe place far from here. We thought it best to keep him well away from you.'

Okay. That wasn't what she was hoping for. Even so, she couldn't help asking, 'What happened to him? Is he okay?'

'He's in a coma, like you were. Although unlike you, he has not woken and nothing we've done has changed that state for him. But he is being given the best of care.'

'Thank you.' Despite what he'd done, she didn't want Cain to be in pain. She also didn't want to see him but a knowing struck her that sometime soon, she would have to. She knew it like she knew she was a Nexus, even though she didn't understand either of those things. But she didn't want to think of that now. 'And my coven mates?'

'They are nearby.'

'They are? Are they okay?'

Iain glanced at Bron, as if he didn't want to answer.

Bron took her hand and said, 'Maybe it's time that you come and see them. I can tell you about them on the way.'

Eloise's heart leapt into her throat at Bron's words. 'Why, what's wrong with them? Are they in comas too?'

'Not precisely.'

12

Eloise stared at Bron. 'What do you mean?'

'Things have been difficult for them. They were all injured on the night you helped River.'

'Don't sugar-coat it, Bronwyn,' River said, his mouth twisting. 'I hurt them.'

'No, not you.' Bron captured his hand, held it against her chest over her heart. 'The Beast driven by the Darkness was responsible.' She touched his face, then turned back to Eloise. 'When we arrived, Morrigan and most of the coven were gone. All that were left were those who couldn't walk, and Iain and Gareth, who were both unconscious in that room with the moon door.'

Eloise shifted, uncomfortable with remembering how Iain and his friend had been tortured that night and how little she'd done to help them. 'Are they okay now?'

'Their injuries have healed. But being left behind by Morrigan did something to them. It's as if her abandonment sucked all the spirit out of them. They walk, dress and toilet themselves, eat if we make them, but apart from that, they're listless. They haven't responded to treatment and I don't know what else to do.' She nodded at Eloise. 'Your presence might help them in a way we've been unable to.'

Eloise snorted. 'I doubt that. I'm hardly a Healer. Besides, as far as they're concerned, I'm a traitor.' Iain's arm tightened around her and she drew from the strength that was innately him, the steadiness at his core.

'I think you underestimate yourself, Little Bird.'

She smiled shyly at his complement and said to her lap, 'If you think it might help, I'm happy to try.' Iain might see her with rose-coloured glasses on, but in a way he was right. She might be a traitor, but she didn't want to be a coward. 'Can we go now?' She might not be a coward, but if she waited, she was afraid she'd lose her courage to look her old coven mates in the face.

'Okay.'

Bron stood. River's phone rang just as they walked out onto the patio. 'Just a sec,' he said, answering it. He listened and then said, 'Okay, I'll be right there.' Hanging up, he turned to Bron. 'Stu needs my help with Elsie. The calf's a breech and he needs me to calm her while he turns it and gets it out or he might lose both of them.'

'Go. Meet us later if you can.'

He gave her a quick, hard kiss, and then loped off the other side of the patio and disappeared around the corner of the house.

'Elsie?' Eloise asked as they walked across the patio and down the stairs onto the sloping grass.

'She's Stuart's prize cow.'

'You have cows?'

'Not on this property, but on another close by,' Iain said. 'Our interests are wide and varied and all of our people have multiple talents. River happens to be particularly good with animals.'

Eloise wasn't surprised. He'd been the first one of them she'd felt comfortable with when she'd been masquerading as Bluebelle.

Despite her tension about seeing her coven mates, Eloise felt better as they walked towards the huge hedge that bounded the secret garden—she knew now her love of the outdoors was because she was a shifter. There was a certain freedom in that knowledge. Like she could be close to understanding herself someday soon.

Bron led them through the beautiful carved wooden door—nymphs and fairies peeked out between twining vines on its surface—and into the secret garden. Iain had brought her here a few days earlier to run through the meandering paths and secret nooks in first her cat form, then as her wolf. She'd had such a lovely day that day, exploring. There had been beauty in sights and scents and sounds to discover in every step.

There was no exploring today, however. They headed somewhere else, somewhere hidden. Her delight in the masterpiece of land-scaping faded.

They walked along a path that bounded the edges of the garden and out through another door in the hedge that angled off to the right. Beyond the hedge was another orchard. The tree branches drooped with late summer fruit, their leaves turned a golden-green under the constant heat of the sun.

Despite the beauty of the walk, she began to tremble. She wished Iain was walking in front of her. She'd much prefer to ogle at his muscled back then concentrate on this ever-growing sense of dread inside her.

'We're almost there.' Bron's smile was soft, almost as if she understood the anxiety gnawing at Eloise. She could probably feel it without even looking at her aura, given the strength of her Healer powers. It was nice to be understood, but it didn't help alleviate the sensation of rising fear and panic.

Iain captured her hand in his. She gasped at the exquisite warmth, the steady strength of his touch, marvelling at how with such a simple gesture, he did what Bron's empathetic smile hadn't. The fear and panic didn't go away, but it did settle to the point she could breathe again.

She glanced at him, wanting to say thank you, but couldn't find the words. He smiled, seeming to understand anyway.

They exited the orchard and headed down a narrow path cut into the side of a steep hill masquerading as a cliff. Eloise peered over the edge. If someone was pushed over, their body would certainly never be found in the brush and scrub on the valley floor.

'I won't let you fall,' Iain said.

Eloise swallowed hard and gripped his hand as if it was the only thing between her and a plummet to certain death.

With Bron in front of her and Iain just behind, they descended into the green heart of a wilderness that spread from the base of the cliff to the steady rise of rolling hills a kilometre or more away.

They finished their descent and began to walk down a dirt path that meandered through a forest of gum trees. The fallen bark from the ghostly gums created a soft, slightly crunchy carpet under foot. 'Is this still Packland?'

'Yes.' Iain's deep voice soothed the rawness in her belly. 'Our Packlands are extensive. We are made up of many families, many of whom live here.' He slanted a smile at her. 'You didn't imagine we would all fit in the main house, did you?'

'I suppose I didn't really think about it.'

They walked out of the dim shadows cast by the arcing branches of the gums around them and into a large clearing at the centre of the valley.

Eloise gasped as she caught sight of the house at the centre of the clearing. It looked like something from a fairy tale; a house that grew from its surrounds and was part of them. It was made out of a mixture of the same slate and red-tinged rock as the cliff at her back and the silken, sunset-tinged wood of the ghost gums that surrounded it. In places angular, in other places rounded to follow the arcing lines of the hills that rose behind it, it was at once modern and timeless.

And more beautiful than any house had the right to be.

'Do you like it?' Iain asked, his eyes feasting on it in the same way hers were.

'Like it?' Eloise breathed. 'It's remarkable.'

'Iain designed it,' Bron said.

Eloise almost choked on her surprise. 'You did?'

He nodded, pride in the movement. 'I dabble in architecture too.'

She stared at him then gestured at the house. 'You do so much. You're so talented. Why are you here, Shadowing me?'

'Because I was called. And because I need to.' He shrugged. 'Besides, none of us are bound to one role.'

'I noticed that about the Pack Witches when I was watching you all last year. We'd always been told they were bonded in servitude, having no choice but to be a Pack Witch and give up half their power to the animals that are the Were. But if that was true, Skye wouldn't have her childcare centre and Shelley wouldn't still be nursing. And you wouldn't have your business,' she said, nodding at Bron. 'It was so confusing. I couldn't understand why it was allowed. I mean, we were allowed to work outside the coven, but only if it benefited the coven. I thought at first that must be the case with all of you, but your earnings never went to the Pack as far as I could see and none of the Were came to your work for a Healing except for River. No pack members had children at Skye's childcare centre except for Jason and Adam's nephew, Tom, and that seemed mostly because Skye thought he should be there. And the Were could never go to the hospital Shelley worked at. I realised then that you did those things for yourselves.' She looked at Iain. 'I didn't think that would extend to every pack member, but it does, doesn't it?'

'Pack comes first, but within that, we are all encouraged to be who we are. We would weaken if we didn't. Strong individuals make a stronger whole.'

She shook her head, awed and also disgusted with herself for the lies she'd once believed. 'It makes so much sense. We never had anything like that in the coven.'

'That's because Morrigan was keeping you tethered to her, never allowing any of you to become truly powerful so that you might challenge her. She kept you subservient through fear and lies.' He nodded to the house. 'That's what it smells like over there. Fear and lies.'

Bron tapped her finger against her lips and frowned as she stared at the building in front of them.

'What is it?' Iain asked.

'That might explain why Eloise's coven mates are dying, despite everything we've done to prove we mean them no harm. They truly believe the Were will use them and their powers and kill them when they're of no more use.' She turned to Eloise. 'That's what you were taught, wasn't it?'

Eloise nodded, so ashamed of what she had once believed to be true.

Bron touched her shoulder. 'You didn't know any better. How could you?'

'I should have seen. We all should have seen.'

Bron's expression filled with an age of sadness. 'We all fill our lives with lies we think are necessary to survive. At one time, what Morrigan gave your family and those other families that made up your coven, was absolutely necessary to their survival. What we've learned from the older diaries is not every witch or Wiccan coven was included in Bridgette's Pact, and many were left to fend for themselves. It was the major flaw in her plan, one I'm certain she meant to remedy but that never eventuated for some reason.' Her expression cleared as she looked at Eloise. 'What's remarkable is that you opened your eyes and saw outside the boundaries of the lies you were brought up to believe.'

'It's not remarkable. I simply did the right thing.'

'And that's what makes it, makes you, so remarkable,' Iain said, his grip tightening on her hand as if he would never let her go.

She didn't want him to.

Bron gestured towards the building that rose before them. 'Shall we?'

13

Eloise had to unlock her knees and force herself to move. The dread began to chew on her insides again at the thought of what awaited her in the house: the hatred of her coven mates; her guilt.

Iain's hand tightened around hers.

She glanced at him. He smiled and nodded.

He believed in her. She needed to believe in herself.

She smiled at him and nodded her readiness. She could do this. She had to do this. She had to prove to herself that she could face up to her past and walk away with the strength she'd learned with the Were and their coven. With the male at her side.

Iain pressed his thumb against a security panel next to the front door. A woman's face appeared on the screen next to the pad, her smile widening as she saw who stood there.

'Iain, love. Aren't you a sight for sore eyes?'

Love? She called him love? Who was this woman?

Her gaze darted to Iain. His face broke into a warm smile as he said, 'Hey Gabs. Nice to see you, too.'

'I heard I missed you last night. Pity. I've been lonely and could have done with some stimulating company.'

Something in Eloise's stomach began to churn.

'I don't know that I qualify now,' Iain said evenly.

Gabbie chuckled. 'After Portofino, you would always qualify.'

Was it okay that she wanted to slap this woman and the way she talked so openly, so intimately, to Iain? Not that he seemed to mind. Or did he? His smile wasn't so easy now as he glanced down at Eloise, his fingers tightening on hers a little. To give her courage? To tell her there was no point being jealous because she could never match up?

Just then, Bron stepped in front of Iain and waved cheerily at the woman on the other end of the communications panel. 'Hi Gabbie. Sorry to interrupt, but we're not here to socialise.'

Gabbie sighed. 'Nobody ever is these days. It's always work, work, work.' She leaned sideways and Eloise heard a loud click. 'Come on in. I'll meet you at the door.'

'This isn't the door?' Eloise asked as Iain pushed the left-hand side of the huge wood and metal double doors open.

'Nope. This is just the outer gate to the upper section of the compound.' Eloise looked up at the two-storied building before her. 'Upper section?'

'Think of this like the tip on an iceberg,' Bron said as she disappeared inside.

Iain turned to Eloise. 'You okay?' he whispered.

'I'm fine.'

He nodded, but the nod was a distinct, "We'll talk later" kind of nod. Then he said, 'After you.'

Sighing loudly, she limped forward. Her shoulder brushed his chest. She shivered. He took in a sudden breath.

She stopped, looked up, saw something raw and unbidden in his eyes as he looked down at her. He was holding himself still, unnaturally still, trying not to move or touch her further. She swayed towards him.

'Not now,' he muttered.

Sucking in a sharp breath, she nodded and trembling, moved into the room beyond and stopped. 'Oh Goddess. That's beautiful.'

She moved as if in a dream, the woman forgotten—everything

forgotten—her feet making a soft, uneven swoosh across the slate tiles. In her peripheral vision she was aware of eggshell white walls, the glistening chestnut of silken wood, a circular sweep of stairs leading up, a fall of coloured glass shapes glinting above their heads and the fresh green of pot plants dotted around the space, but she couldn't take her eyes off the doors in front of her.

They were huge. A masterwork of metal—all sorts of metals in different shapes and textures—curved across its surface in a twisting, twining pattern that she recognised as a tree. On the right-hand door, beneath the tree, stood two wolves howling up at the moon above, and hovering between the tree and the moon and the stars was a woman, her full figure naked and glorious, her long, copper hair moving in a breeze that Eloise could almost feel. On the left-hand door, the image was of the tree again, but this time the woman stood, clothed, between the two Were caught in transformation from wolf to human, her arms stretched out to welcome and encompass them.

A tear slid down her face. She knew the story—the story of how the Were-Witch Pact came into existence—but she had never seen it depicted like this, with such love and humility and joy. The feeling of loneliness and desolation coming from each figure in the right-hand door was so tangible, it was an empty ache around her heart. The sense of completion in the left-hand door filled that empty space with so much light and life and laughter, it was a warm breath on her face, moving her hair, lifting her up until she was light as air.

She brushed her fingers over the surface—the metal was warm. 'Oh,' she breathed.

'It has that effect on everyone when they first see it.' Bron placed her hand beside Eloise's, running it along the flow of metal of the half-transformed creature in front of her, her mouth curved in a soft smile. 'Iain and his brother, Patrick, made them. Patrick is actually the pack's Lore Keeper in training. He recently graduated as a lawyer to help with that work, but he does sculpture in his spare time. He works with metal and glass every chance he gets.' She waved at the chandelier above their heads. 'It's such a gift.'

'Yep. That's my bro. Gifted.' Iain closed the front door behind him, sealing them in.

'You made this?' She looked back at the door. 'Huh. I don't know why I'm surprised. I thought you were a sommelier and a carpenter in your spare time. Now I find out you design buildings and sculpt as well. Is there anything you can't do?'

'Plenty. But I'm good with my hands, sculpting, carving, drawing, painting. My wolf craves the tactile sensation. It settles him.'

'It hasn't helped with the nightmares though.'

He shot a quick look at Bron. 'They're not so bad.' His gaze slid to Eloise. 'Not anymore.'

'What nightmares?' Eloise asked, concerned.

'It doesn't matter,' he said, his smile a little forced.

Eloise went to object, but Bron touched her shoulder, leaned in and said in a whisper that Eloise knew Iain could hear, 'Don't expect him to tell you about a weakness. He's too much a Lone Wolf. They're convinced they don't need anyone.'

That explanation didn't help. 'What exactly is a Lone Wolf? I don't really know Were terminology.'

Iain's frown faded. 'It surprises me you don't know.'

'It wasn't something Morrigan made us learn about.'

'Of course.'

'Can you tell me?'

'Yes, although, it's kind of hard to explain, other than to say my wolf is wilder than other wolves and needs a lot of alone time, otherwise it goes a little crazy.' His sexy chocolate eyes didn't leave hers. 'It also means I can be a little intense and that I need more visceral stimulation than other wolves.'

She nodded. 'You need to touch things.'

'Some things more than others.' His fingers ran across her cheek, brushing a stray strand of hair behind her ear. She wanted to tell him to never stop touching her, but he dropped his hand to his side, frowning. She wanted to kiss the frown from his brow, to ask him what was wrong; to assure him she wanted his touch. Longed for it in fact. She should be frightened of the need, but she wasn't. Maybe, like him, she needed tactile stimulation due to her shifter genes? Did they have Lone Shifters? Another thing she'd have to find out about.

Although, maybe it was just that she'd been starved of touch all her life. She never wanted to be starved of it again.

'What took you so long?' The doors swung open and Gabbie sauntered in.

'I didn't know we were in a rush,' Iain said.

The tall, voluptuous Amazon of a woman, who looked even better in the flesh than she did on the monitor, brushed past Eloise and wrapped her arms around Iain. 'Maybe I was.' Her hands slipped up his back and into his hair, and before Eloise could take another breath, Gabbie plastered her lips to Iain's.

The heat of the kiss chased over Eloise, tingling her skin, fanning the anger that had been warring with fear and worry in her chest ever since she'd heard about Cain and the others.

Her vision shifted, everything seeming too large and yet small at the same time as she watched Gabbie's body melt into Iain, her plump breasts pushing into his firm chest, nestling just under his pecs as if finding the spot that was designed for them to mesh with.

Her fingers twined in his hair, one leg pushing between his.

Fingers tingling, a strange sound rumbled in Eloise's throat as part of her longed to lunge forward and tear the other woman from Iain's arms.

'Are they upsetting you? You should slash her throat,' Cain's voice whispered in her ear. *'Or if you won't, I will. I'll kill them both.'*

'You wouldn't. You couldn't.'

Laughing answered her and then faded away as she realised the others were all looking at her.

'Eloise? Are you okay?'

She looked up into Iain's worried gaze. 'Fine. I'm fine.'

'You don't look fine. Was it Gabbie kissing me? Gabbie didn't mean anything by it. She doesn't know about ... well, she doesn't know that you're not used to casual intimacy.'

Her face heated as she looked at the others, understanding dawning in their eyes. Oh Goddess! They thought her jealous—

which she was of course, no matter how stupid or absurd it was to be jealous of a man she had no claim over. But she couldn't let them know that. 'It wasn't that.'

Iain's gaze intensified, his nostrils flaring a little. He could scent her lie.

Shit. 'Well, maybe it did shock me a little. But it wasn't that. I just ... it was just ... I heard Cain.' The last was a harsh whisper. 'In my head.'

Iain gripped her shoulders. The elation he'd felt at her show of jealousy was torn to shreds at her words. Not that he wanted her to be jealous. He'd never wanted to pull away from someone as much as he'd wanted to when Gabbie kissed him, but he couldn't extricate himself from her quickly without hurting her. Thankfully, Eloise had cried out, breaking the uncomfortable moment. It was natural to think it had been jealousy. He'd been absurdly aware of Eloise—the way she'd stiffened outside at the sensuous females insinuations; the shortening of her breath and the thunder of her heart; the snarly noise she'd made just now when Gabbie had shifted closer to Iain, rubbing against him; the dangerous prickle of her power in the air.

But now, where a moment ago his wolf was howling in triumph that their witch-shifter had been jealous, it was now howling in distress. 'You heard Cain?' She nodded. 'Fuck.' His gaze went to Bron. She stroked his back as she turned to Eloise, but it didn't stop his wolf from emitting a low hum of aggravation.

'What did he say?' Bron asked softly.

Eloise's throat moved as if she were choking down something distasteful. 'That he wanted to kill Iain. And Gabbie.'

'That's nothing new,' Gabbie said. 'But hang on. What do you mean you heard Cain? He's in a coma, isn't he?' She looked a question at Bron.

Bron shrugged. 'He is. But it appears he's able to communicate with his sister. I don't know how. According to Eloise, he shouldn't be able to do it across so great a distance. Of course, I'm new to a lot of this and as we've been discovering, there's a lot of ancient lore lost to us that might explain how he's doing it.'

'Is he a danger to anyone?'

'I don't think so. But once again, I don't truly know.'

Iain had been looking at Eloise through this discussion, saw the moment her face paled. 'What is it?' Iain took her hand in his, holding it against his chest. 'What have you remembered?'

Her fingers flexed against his as she spoke. 'I don't know. It could be nothing. But ... what if he's a Shade?'

Bron frowned. 'A Shade?'

Eloise looked stunned. 'You don't know about Shades?'

'As I said, I'm new to a lot of this. What are they?'

'I don't know how to describe it.' Her brow furrowed as she struggled to find the right words. Iain gripped her hand tighter, thumb brushing over her wrist, her pulse thrumming as fast as a bird's under the silky skin. 'It's kind of like a lost soul. When someone separates their astral self from their body.'

'That can only happen in death,' Bron said.

'No. It can be done by the person wilfully. Or by someone else.'

'That's a violent act against nature.' Bron looked horrified. 'Surely it would kill the soul?'

'The Shade can live for some time unconnected from the body, but yes, it will eventually wither and die. Although, that is a slow process as long as the body is alive.'

'But without the soul, wouldn't the body die quickly?'

She nodded. 'And the Shade would be no more. It dies when the body does as nothing can truly exist in a vacuum. But there are ways to keep a body alive for some time now that there weren't before.'

'How do you know this?'

She blinked, her eyes wet and wide. 'It's happened in the coven, most recently to my adoptive grandfather. At Morghanna's behest. She needed him to kill someone for her that she couldn't get to. He volunteered. He went into the astral sleep and then she cut the tether tying his soul to his body. He found the person as a Shade and killed them.'

'I don't understand,' Bron said, rubbing her forehead. 'How could he touch anything? The astral soul isn't a physical thing. It couldn't effect any physical act.'

'Shades can. They suck the life force energy out of people.'

'Like a wraith? But they're myths,' Gabbie said.

'Most myths are based on reality of some sort,' Bron said, frown deepening. 'Perhaps that's where the idea of the wraith came from?'

Eloise shook her head. 'I don't know. All I know is that my grandfather killed a man at Morrigan's behest and he did it as a Shade. And then Morrigan had my adoptive father bring him back with dark blood magic.'

'It could just be a tale.'

'It isn't. We all had to learn the incantations to bring a person back from Shadehood to their body before they died. It's part of our basic training. Even those without enough power to actually enact it are taught the spell.'

'Would there be any signs that he's done such a thing, if it is possible?'

'I don't know.' She rubbed her knuckle against her forehead. 'My grandfather's heart stopped for a moment when Morrigan did it to him. My father also mentioned something about there being a fading, although I'm not sure what he meant.'

Iain looked at Bron, who shrugged. 'Perhaps he meant that the body began to die.'

'You could be right. I didn't know him before it happened, but there was something not quite right about him the few times I saw him before he died.'

'What do you mean?'

'It was like he was alive, but not really there. Like his soul never fully made it back to his body; he couldn't truly engage with the world around him.' She shuddered.

'Ugh.' Gabbie shivered. 'I'm glad I came up to hear this fairy tale.'

'I'm sorry. But you did ask.'

Gabbie grimaced. 'I wish I hadn't.'

'Cain's not a Shade though now, is he?'

'No. I don't know. It would explain how he's able to speak to me in my mind if he's far away. Although, I would have thought I should see him as well.'

'Why would you see him?'

'Because we're connected by blood.'

'Could anyone else see him?' Iain asked.

She shook her head. 'The stories I heard said that was what made them so deadly. They can only be seen by blood relatives.'

'Are you certain?'

'I don't know. I'm just telling you what I've been told. There hasn't been another Shade created since my grandfather, so I don't have any actual experience of one. It could all simply be a story told to frighten the young into doing as they're told.'

Iain breathed in deeply. 'Okay. Let's assume it is possible. Then I suppose the question is—is your brother likely to ever do such a thing?'

'I have no idea. I hope not. Although, for Morrigan, he might just do anything.'

'Even become like the living dead?'

She grimaced. 'I ... don't know. He always feared death. He said he didn't want to become nothing.' She shivered and Iain had a hard time not pulling her into his arms and keeping her there, safe from anything that would frighten or upset her. But he couldn't. Not without destroying the slowly building confidence in herself. He clenched his fingers into his palms, trying to ignore the itching surge of his wolf to break free and comfort her.

'I would hope that fear might give him pause at least. The spell to bring the Shade back ... it's a difficult one with horrible consequences if not done under the right circumstances. I don't think Morrigan's got anyone strong enough to do it, aside from herself. And she's not his blood relation, so she wouldn't be able to bring him back.'

'Blood relative? Do you mean a blood relative has to do the spell?' Bron asked.

'Yes. Anyone can do the initial spell, but to entice the Shade back to the body, there needs to be a strong tie. A blood tie. Or the Shade won't come back. It's best if the spell is done on the full moon too, but even then, it's dangerous.'

'In what way?'

'It uses a huge amount of power. My father brought my grandfather back, but it used all of their magic and they could never truly use their powers again.'

'That's a relief.'

Eloise looked at Gabbie.

'Well,' she said, gesturing at Eloise. 'You and your twin were adopted. So, there isn't another blood relation in the rogue coven who could bring Cain back, is there? So, he wouldn't be able to do it, even if Morrigan asked him to. Because he wouldn't be able to be brought back.'

'She's right,' Bron said, rubbing Eloise's shoulder. 'As you've said, Cain wouldn't risk it, especially if he couldn't be brought back. So there must be another reason for why he's able to contact you.'

'I guess so.'

'You don't sound convinced,' Iain said.

'I am. You're right. He wouldn't do it. Not if he couldn't be brought back.' She shifted, shoulders tense. 'And he loves having power too much to ever risk losing it. I don't know why I didn't see it before it was too late.' A terrible sorrow darkened her bright eyes.

'There's nothing you could have done, even if you had seen it.' Iain's hands itched to stroke down her shoulders, hold her close, especially when she looked up at him with those sorrow-drenched eyes. 'Sometimes, it doesn't matter how much we love, how much we care, we can't save a person when they don't want to be saved.'

The question in her eyes made him realise he'd said too much; given away too much. He cleared his throat.

'So, we don't have to worry about Shades for now,' Gabbie said. 'That's good. I hate creepy unnatural stuff like that.'

'Yes because packs of Were and covens of witches are just so normal in this world,' Bron said, lips quirked.

Gabbie smiled at her. 'Maybe not what the humans would call normal, but we're certainly natural.' She clapped her hands together.

'Shall we get down there? I for one would like to get this over and done with. I've got places to be. An accommodating Were to find.' She cocked her brow at Iain.

He shook his head. His wolf growled as it slunk deeper inside. It had enjoyed playing with Gabbie and her wolf in the past, but like him, his wolf couldn't think of touching another woman now. Not since touching Eloise.

'You should have told me you were in heat,' Bron said as Gabbie moved past Iain and Eloise to the door. 'We would have sent someone to relieve you so you could get out and play for a bit.'

Gabbie stood taller. 'I know. But it's not that bad yet. My shift ends tonight. I can hold out until then.' She turned back suddenly in one of those lightning-fast moves the Were were capable of, her gaze pinned on Eloise this time. 'I'm sorry if I made you uncomfortable.' She put her hand out.

Eloise looked uncertain for a moment, but then did something she wouldn't have done a few weeks earlier. She stopped wringing her fingers, shoved her hand out and took Gabbie's hand in a rough, quick shake. 'It's okay. I suppose I have to get used to stuff like this if I'm going to be around you all for a while.'

Gabbie's smile was a friendly flash of delight. 'I hope you will.' Eloise looked questioningly at her. 'It will be nice to have another woman to talk to around here.'

Eloise's expression became even more confused. 'Why? Aren't there many female Were in your pack?'

Gabbie laughed. 'Of course there are. But there are not many who are soldiers like you and me. It's mostly the Maternals who live on pack land. It will be nice to have someone to talk to who understands what it's like to be out in the field. As a woman. And maybe I can help you understand more about the pack.'

'I'm not a soldier.'

'Of course you are. You have the scent of a warrior all over you.'

'I—'

'Eloise, what is it?' Iain tightened his grip on her hand.

She frowned. 'The Goddess called me her warrior, but it's ridiculous. I'm not a warrior.'

'Yes you are. It's coming off you in waves,' Gabbie said.

'Gabbie is a sensitive. She is able to sense those with special aptitudes. If anyone would know, she would,' Bron said.

'Right.' Eloise bit her lip, then looking around her, said, 'Morrigan better watch out then, right?'

'Right.' Iain couldn't help the pride that surged through him at her tone. Weeks ago, she wouldn't have been so accepting. Or so defiant. Determined. He just hoped she could see the changes the rest of them were seeing in her. They were remarkable.

She was remarkable.

Gabbie touched Eloise's arm. 'We'll talk later, okay?' She punched in a code next to the door and it opened. 'Do you want me to come down with you?'

Iain looked questioningly at Eloise.

'I don't want an audience for this,' she said to him, her voice an apology.

'You're right.' He looked up at Gabbie. 'You go upstairs and watch on the monitors. We'll call you if we need you.'

'Okeydokey.' Gabbie's smile flashed. 'Catch you later.' She nodded to Bron, her gaze lingering on Iain for a moment, as if to apologise. He nodded, then she smiled and disappeared up the stairs that led to the upper level.

'She seems ... nice,' Eloise said into the silence.

'She is. You'll like her. She's really quite stable and sensitive when she's not in heat.'

Eloise coughed. 'That's a problem, is it? For the Were females?'

'Not a problem, no. Except Gabbie's line of work can make it difficult at times.'

'Line of work?'

'As she said. She's a pack soldier. Probably will become a lieutenant in a few years.'

'Like you?'

'Yes. Like me.'

'She's also a physical therapist,' Bron said. 'She works with the young and the old in the pack, keeping them fit and healthy, as well as working with those recovering from injury. She was one of those who worked alongside me and Iain when you were in your coma, working your limbs so your muscles didn't atrophy. We weren't sure how long you were going to be out.'

'I ... I'll have to thank her.'

Iain wished he could crawl inside her head and see what she was thinking in that moment. She was usually easy to read, but right now her expression was inscrutable and too much of an enigma for him to be comfortable with. But he didn't get a chance to delve any further into her emotions or thoughts, because Bron ushered her forward and they descended the stairs into the underground compound.

As they exited the hall at the base of the steps and entered the main cavern, Eloise gasped. Natural light fell around them, enhancing the size and openness of the cave to maximum effect.

'It's wonderful, isn't it?' Bron gestured at the large space, the tangle of greenery that was a garden you could spend days exploring in one corner, the carpet of grass expanding across the middle of it with benches and play equipment—some that was designed for children, but other pieces that were part of a circuit track for exercise and training purposes—the droop of willows that shaded a hollow where what had once been a trickle of water that seeped through the walls from an underground spring had been turned into a clever water feature that burbled and fell over rocks to a clear pool below, steam rising from its sparkling surface. It always beckoned to Iain to strip and plunge into its warm depths, and he wondered if it had the same effect on Eloise as her gaze took it in.

'This is amazing. How do you get so much light down here—it feels like I'm outside.'

Iain shoved his hands in his pockets in an attempt not to reach out and touch her, feel the glory of her wonder with his fingertips. He pointed to the ceiling. 'There are vents up there big enough to let natural light in, although the passages down from those vents aren't straight. So we put mirrors in.'

He watched as realisation dawned. 'Like that scene in *The Mummy* when they go into the caves of the sunken city and use the mirrors for light?'

'You've seen *The Mummy?*'

She nodded. 'The older one with Brendan Fraser. It's one of my favourite older adventure movies along with Indiana Jones—they have everything. Romance, a bit of scare, lots of humour.'

'I'm surprised Morrigan let you watch movies.'

Her smile dimmed a little and he was sorry he'd mentioned the mad bitch's name.

'We didn't go out to the movies, but we weren't completely cut off from the world. We used to have movie nights once a month where a different coven member picked the movies. Cain and I always picked the adventure-type movies my dad had.' She looked down at the floor. 'It was something I had in common with them.'

He moved over to her, took her hands. 'I do too.' She looked up at him, confused. 'Love that kind of movie. The Mummy movies are some of my favourites. And Indiana Jones—well, the first three. The last one I don't count.' A small smile bloomed on her face. 'It wasn't that bad.'

'It wasn't that good, either.'

'No.'

They stared at each other, the feel of her hands in his, the glow of her beautiful green-gold eyes, holding him captive.

'Are you two finished reminiscing about movies?'

Eloise jumped and snatched her hands back to her sides. The loss of her touch was like a blow to the chest. But he covered quickly, turning to walk with her into the cavern. 'I studied ancient architecture to find the best ways of using mirrors to light underground areas for the majority of the day—the Egyptians were ingenious bastards—and came up with this.' He gestured at the light about them.

'It's magical.' Wonder had filled her face again as she looked around, taking in what he'd done, except this time the wonder was replaced with an edginess he wished he could rid her of.

'It also has the added benefit of making the caves seem more spacious,' Bron added.

'Is that important?'

'Uh-huh. Were aren't comfortable if they feel hemmed in.'

'Why wouldn't they stay above ground then?' She pointed at the ceiling. 'The house looked huge. Surely it would have lots of rooms and common spaces.'

'It does. But these caverns are even more expansive and can fit the entire pack if need be. The caves are safe like above ground isn't. Were also need to feel safe.'

'And do you? Feel safe down here?'

'We once did.' He didn't need to say Morrigan's name—it was like a wall between them. A wall he wanted to knock down. 'We're building ourselves back up again. Now that the Curse is broken and we have not only our Pack Witch back, but others making us stronger, we have a chance to take back what's been lost.' He brushed her chin with his finger, making her look up at him. 'You are part of that, too.'

She swallowed hard and looked away. Once again, Iain wished he knew what she was thinking, because he couldn't make out what her expression meant.

'How big is the McVale Pack?' she asked as she continued to follow Bron.

'We're the second largest pack in the southern hemisphere next to the McClunes. They have four hundred core families. We dropped down to two hundred but are slowly building that back up again. We used to expand across Europe with many places just like this at capacity. Most aren't as large though, and only some still have pack-mates living in them— most are used for storage.'

'Why would you keep them, then?'

'They're ours. Besides, they come in handy. During wartime, we used them to keep our people safe. In the last world war we also extended their use to the Underground to help Jews and other fugitives escape the Nazis.'

'That's amazing.'

He shrugged. 'It is what it is. Our pack is old. This place is brand new in comparison to the European bases. The caves were found when the pack moved here from Scotland over one hundred and fifty years ago. It's been expanded on over the years as the pack grew.'

'The house above looks new.'

'It was finished a few years ago—although there was always a house there.' She looked up at him, curious. 'We have to have a blind. People don't ask questions if they see us going into a house. They do if they see you disappear into the earth.'

'I had no idea places like this could exist. It's so big.'

'Yes,' Bron agreed as she began to walk across the grass. 'It's one of the reasons we decided this would be the best place for your friends, especially given you were last living in caves. They have free run of these lower caves and we've limited interaction with the pack, using mostly female Were to bring the things they need, so they'd feel less intimidated. We've been observing them through monitors in the security room in the house above, rather than setting sentries and guards down here. Many of the lounge areas and sleeping quarters are set up with similar natural light displays and an open feel to them we thought would help provide them with a sense of comfort and space. We couldn't let them go, but we also didn't want them to feel imprisoned. But I'm afraid it's made no difference.'

Iain hugged Bron to his side. 'You're doing your best for them. Nobody could ask you to do more.'

'But it hasn't been enough. They're still dying. Everything they believed in has dissolved into nothing. They were left for dead. Abandoned. They're too far gone to even be afraid of us anymore.' Desperation clouded her eyes as she looked at Eloise. 'I'm hoping that seeing you will give them something to live for.'

Eloise nodded. 'I hope so too.'

14

Iain frowned. There was something in her voice that whispered of doubt. He wished he could wipe away that doubt, but knew she had a right to it. He understood her worry. That's why he was here, watching over her. Despite their near catatonic state, he didn't trust her old coven mates. They could respond negatively to her presence and she knew it.

Despite that worry, she followed Bron towards the other side of the cavern, chin held high, the only sign of her nervousness the fact her limp was more pronounced.

Brave. She was so fucking brave.

'They mostly stay through here,' Bron said as they entered a dimly lit corridor. 'We've tried to encourage them to use the garden, but they don't and we won't force them.'

A shadowy figure moved across the light down the end of the corridor, paused, and then moved away.

'I thought you said they were almost comatose,' Eloise said in a harsh whisper.

'They are.'

'Maybe they're feeling better,' Bron said, her voice falsely bright.

They continued on and entered the room.

The room was depressingly quiet with a sense of darkness, like a fog settling over the room despite the light coming from above. Even the fresh green paint on the walls and splashes of scenery in the paintings and depth of textures in the tapestries didn't help to lift the sensation that he was walking into a morgue.

Eloise's face paled, her hand covering her mouth.

Iain edged up behind her. 'Are you okay?'

She didn't look back at him, her eyes seemingly unable to divorce themselves from the sight of the dozen people in the room lolling dispiritedly on lounges, chairs and even the floor, staring blankly.

They had to be starving and thirsty and yet the platter of muffins and cookies was untouched, the water jug full. They were showered and wore clean clothes, but there was a definite air of dereliction about them—like they'd lost all hope.

He wished they'd never brought Eloise here. She didn't need to see this. He reached out, intending to turn her back the way they came and escort her out, when she stepped towards one of the men sitting on the floor, his legs splayed out in front of him, his chin on his chest.

'Andrew?' She went down on her knees beside him and took his hand in hers, clutching it to her chest. 'Andy? It's me. Eloise.'

He lifted his head and looked at her, eyes glazed.

'Andy? What's happened here? This isn't like you. Andy. Please. Tell me what's wrong?'

For a brief moment a light of recognition flared in his eyes. 'Eloise?' His lips began to twitch into a smile and then the smile stiffened as shock widened his eyes. 'El, you have to get ou—' His teeth clamped together on the word and he stiffened then began to shake.

Spittle frothed, spilling over his lips as his head rapped hard against the wall.

'Oh my god. Andy? What's wrong? Andy!'

Iain grabbed Andy, pulled him away from the wall to lie on the floor. Bron knelt down next to him, her hands extended, a golden glow shining from them.

After a long, tense moment, Andy went limp.

'Roll him onto his side,' Bron instructed.

Iain rolled him as gently as possible into the recovery position and then stayed by his head to monitor his breathing.

'This isn't right,' Eloise said.

'I know it's a shock to see him in this condition. But now I know he's epileptic, I can get some medication—'

'He doesn't suffer from epilepsy.' She was shaking, hard. 'This isn't like Andy. You don't know him. He was the most open minded, forward thinking of all of us. He wouldn't starve himself just because he was in your care. He'd take it as an opportunity to learn.' She looked around her. 'As would Dora and Frankie and Margot. I get why Morrigan would leave them all behind because all of them had questioned her at some time or other. Talked about leaving her recently after Alfrere died and she came back with a different face. None of them would do this.'

She pushed to her feet, moving slowly and steadily around the room, looking at all the faces, staring into their eyes, calling their names. Not one of them acknowledged her in any way, just stared apathetically at nothing. 'This is wrong. There's something wrong here.' She ran over to the table and, picking up a jug of juice, poured a glass then returned to Andy's side, pulling him up to lean against her chest. 'Come on, Andy,' she said, trying to make him hold onto the glass. 'You need to drink something.'

Ian's wolf's hackles rose as it sensed danger growing. Except, nothing in the room moved except for them.

Bron must have sensed it too, because she whispered in Iain's ear, 'Keep an eye on Eloise while I check something.' She closed her eyes and breathed in deeply.

Iain stood by her side, keeping guard. Eloise held the glass to Andy's lips, trying to get him to swallow. Orange juice ran down his chin. 'Andy. Please. Drink. Please.'

His eyes snapped open. 'Traitor!'

Eloise scrambled back as he sat up, the glass smashing on the floor, orange juice flying everywhere.

'Eloise!' Iain reached for her.

Andy turned. There was a zap, like lightning, and Eloise flew across the floor, smashing up against the far wall.

'Eloise!' Bron cried out.

Andy raised his hands, black lightning zapping between his fingers as he pointed them at Eloise. With a snarl, Iain leapt at Andy, punching him square in the jaw. The warlock slumped unconscious on the floor. The black lightning disappeared with a fizzing pop.

'Iain! What did you do?' Eloise pushed upright from the wall, took a step, winced and crashed to the floor.

Iain wasn't quick enough to catch her, but he was at her side an instant later. 'You're hurt.'

She shook her head. 'It's just my foot. I twisted it.'

'Let me look.'

'No!' she cried, pulling her leg out of his grasp. 'You need to check on Andy. I thought I heard something break when you hit him. Why did you hit him like that?'

'He attacked you. Was about to shoot black lightning at you. It was the only way I could stop him.'

'But that's not possible. That's not one of his talents.'

'It is now.'

'No. You don't understand. He didn't have that kind of power. In fact, his power was all in his memory. His ability to retain anything he'd ever read and repeat it verbatim. He was training as our coven librarian. He was so gentle, one of the few who was always nice to me. He couldn't do this.'

She tried to gain her feet, but she couldn't seem to put any weight on her injured foot, so she began to hop. Cursing under his breath, Iain scooped her into his arms.

'No! You have to let me see Andy.'

'Bron has to check you over first. You could have broken something.'

'Umm, Iain? I think we've got bigger problems than that.'

He turned to see what Bron meant. Half of the inhabitants of the room were now standing up, facing Eloise, glaring hatred in their eyes.

'Traitor,' they intoned as one, their voices a cruel snarl. 'Traitor.'

'Fuck.' There was a buzzing sound of electricity that made his hair stand up all over his body. 'Run!'

Bron got to the door before them. A bolt of lightning hit the archway to their left. He ducked. Kept running. Another blast. Plaster and rocks sprayed around them.

Bron looked over her shoulder behind them as they ran. 'Faster. They're coming after us.' She ran faster. Iain stayed right on her tail.

They raced out into the bright light of the cavern, across the grass and over to the door that led to the stairs. It opened just as they got to it.

'What the fuck was that?' Gabbie asked, eyes widening as she looked beyond them. He glanced back. Half a dozen members of Eloise's old coven lurched into the light of the room.

'Fuck!' He grabbed Bron, yanking her into the corridor ahead of him and turned to close the door, Eloise still in his arms.

'Stop!' Eloise's eyes were wide and bright with tears as she looked across the grassy expanse they'd just crossed. 'Look.'

Every single one of the coven members had stopped a few paces into the cavern, vibrating in place, their faces lifted to the source of the light like moths caught in a bug catcher. Then one by one, they all fell to the ground, twitched and went deathly still.

'Oh, God.' Eloise's gasp was a torture of pain-filled grief. 'What have I done? I've killed them.'

'I'll check them.'

'Bron, no!' He grabbed for the Healer, but she was too quick when he was already burdened by holding Eloise up. She darted out the door, racing back into the cavern and over to the bodies lying unnaturally still on the ground.

'I want to go, too,' Eloise said as he placed her gently down near the panel that opened the door. She took a step forward, winced and fell back against the wall.

'No.' Iain pointed his finger at Gabbie. 'Stay here with her. If she moves, close this door.'

'But what about you and Bron?'

'We can take care of ourselves. Besides, they weren't after us.'

Eloise winced at his words, but her eyes were blazing as she glared at him. 'I want to help.'

She was so fucking brave. And strong. His wolf growled its agreement. But he couldn't let her know he thought that—it would just egg her on. 'Your presence might make them worse. Stay here.'

Her shocked breath followed him as he ran across to where Bron was kneeling on the grass. He was sorry he'd caused Eloise pain, but couldn't take those words back, not when he needed her to stay put.

He was at Bron's side in a flash, swinging her away from the body she was examining, putting him between her and danger.

'Iain!' She tried to push him out of the way. 'They're unconscious. They can't hurt me. Besides, I don't think that was ever their intent.'

His gaze darted back to where he could see Eloise using Gabbie to help balance and support her as she hopped through the door. 'Damn it. Why can't women ever do as they're told?'

Bron made a choking sound. 'I'm sorry, Mr Misogynist. What century are you living in?'

He rolled his eyes at her. 'You know what I mean.'

'I'm afraid you're going to have to explain it to me.' She tapped her fingers against her arm, looking at his hands that were still holding her in place.

'I meant witches, not women.'

'And that makes it better, does it?'

'I'd do the same if you were a Pack Warlock and you were putting yourself in danger. It would be my duty to pull you out of it and put myself between you and said danger.'

'Right. So this was equal opportunity man-handling?'

'You betcha.'

She snorted. 'Well, I'm a Healer and it's my job to look after people, so suck it up and deal with it, because I'm going to check on my patients.'

He looked down at the half dozen people on the floor. They still hadn't moved. 'Are they dead?'

Bron's lips pressed in a grim line. 'No. But they're not in a good state. They certainly won't be attacking again anytime soon.' She edged towards the nearest body. 'Whatever energy they used is long gone, and even if they came back to consciousness, they wouldn't be able to use any powers again for a while. Especially seeing they've not eaten or drunk anything for a few days.'

'So how did they manage to do that? According to Eloise they don't have that power.'

'Yes. Siobhan, the McClunes' Healer, told me that too when she came to see if she could help. She couldn't feel any significant power in any of them.'

'Eloise said that bloke is a librarian.'

'Patrick's like a librarian and he's as dangerous as they come.'

'That's not my point.'

'What is your point?' Eloise asked as she joined them.

He glared at Gabbie. 'I thought I told you to keep her away.'

Gabbie let out a short bark of laughter. 'Good luck with that. She's a warrior, Iain. Not a dog. She's hardly going to stay away from the danger just because you tell her to.'

'Yeah,' Eloise said, smiling at the Were-female supporting her. 'Besides, you heard Bron. They can't be a danger now.'

'How do you know? You just told us none of them had any powers of significance and yet your buddy over there managed to summon warlock-lightning. How do either of you know they're not a danger now?'

'I don't know how they did this or how they hid this kind of power from Siobhan,' Bron said, worry and confusion playing on her face. 'But I do know my own art and what I'm seeing in their auras now tells me they are out for the count and their power is completely exhausted.'

'Will they recover?'

'I don't know. I've never seen anything like this before. Have you?'

Eloise's mouth twisted, eyes stark with pain as she took in her felled friends. 'No. But I knew deep inside,' her hand clenched against her chest, 'that I shouldn't have come here.' She looked up at

Iain. 'You were right before. This is my fault. I did this to them. I shouldn't have come.'

'I didn't mean—'

'Yes you did.'

'Iain, what did you say?' Bron looked between the two of them, but Iain didn't answer. He couldn't. He was so afraid he'd ruined something special growing between him and Eloise, and he had no idea how to fix it, or why he wanted to.

He should let the rift widen. It was best for Eloise. Best for him.

Eloise took a stumbling step back from him and winced, her lips a thin line as pain whitened her face.

'You shouldn't be walking.' Iain reached out to help, but she shoved away his hands.

'I'm not helpless.'

'Nobody ever said you were. But you are injured, so don't act like a stubborn idiot.' Her face hardened and she opened her mouth to retort when a groan stopped her. Turning in a wobbly spin, she glanced down at the woman to her left and stopped with a gasp.

The woman's eyes were open, her gaze pinned on Eloise.

'Marcy? Oh, my Goddess, Marcy. Are you okay?'

The woman screamed.

'Marcy!' Eloise cried, pushing away from Gabbie, past Iain. He grabbed her arm before she could get any closer. 'Let me go,' she yelled at him.

The woman she'd called Marcy screamed again, but the cry petered out on a sob. 'He's in my mind,' she whimpered. 'Get him out. Get him out.' She began to scrabble at her head, nails raking at her skin. Eloise pulled on her arm again. Iain didn't let go but supported her as she limped towards her friend.

When they got there, she dropped to her knees, grabbing Marcy's hands, trying to stop her from clawing at herself. 'Marcy, stop it. You're hurting yourself.'

'I ... can't ... stop ... him.'

'Who?'

'*Him*. He's in my head. He's in my head. It hurts. I can't ... fight him.'

'Who are you talking about?'

'Cain.'

Eloise paled at the sound of her brother's name. 'What do you mean? Cain can't be in your head.'

'He is. He is,' her friend cried. 'He's in my head. He's making me —' The words choked off on a strangled cry.

'Gabbie,' he said over his shoulder. 'Go call for help. We'll need Cordy and her coven.' He didn't have to look to know the Were-female had done as he bid.

Marcy screamed—a piercing sound that made all of them wince.

'Marcy. Marcy.' Eloise held on tighter as Marcy began to struggle against her hold, but Marcy got loose. Fingers arced like talons, slicing across Eloise's forearm.

Iain grabbed the woman's arms and slammed them to the ground. 'Please, don't hurt her.'

'I'm trying not to but she's not making it easy,' Iain said as he leaned across the woman, keeping her pinned. He looked over his shoulder at Eloise, gaze going to her injured arm. 'Are you okay?'

'It's only a scratch.' Her voice hitched and she turned to Bron, almost as if she didn't want him to see the lie in her eyes. 'You have to help her.'

Marcy bucked, her mouth twisted as she groaned.

'Fuck. She's strong.' Iain grimaced as Marcy almost escaped his grip.

'Iain, try to keep her still.' Bron knelt on Marcy's other side. 'I can't use my power on her while she's moving so violently.'

He nodded, shifting to hold the woman's hands in one of his, using his other arm as a bar across her chest. He tried to hold her as firmly as possible without hurting her—which was difficult as she thrashed and jerked beneath him. And every moment he was aware of how close Eloise was as she knelt beside him, her focus on her friend.

His wolf growled his displeasure that she was too close to danger.

Her long, tawny hair brushed against his arm as she shifted to lean against her friend's legs. He had to fight the urge to push her back, pick her up, carry her away. His wolf growled louder, scratching at his skin, pushing to get out, to protect, to save.

Stop. She doesn't want to go and we can't force her. We're not her mate. His wolf growled a denial in his mind—a denial Iain couldn't delve into now. He couldn't let it through. To protect Eloise, the wolf just might kill all her coven mates. Pushing down on his wolf like he'd never done before, he forced it back. It howled, lunging against the cage of his mind again and again, causing a pain like a bruise to bloom in Iain's head. *Please,* Iain said to the wolf, trying to make it understand before it damaged them both in some permanent way. He'd never been so at odds with his wolf. It hurt. *I promise, I'll let you out later. I'll ask her to change to her wolf. You can play and cover yourself in her scent then, but for now, this human form will help her more than the wolf. I know you see that. I know you understand.*

The wolf growled, and he thought it was going to ignore him and burst through his skin. *Please. For Eloise.* The wolf whimpered and then backed away. *Thank you.* The wolf snarled and Iain almost smiled—he understood the trust his wolf half was giving to his human half in this moment. It was a huge thing. A gift.

He wouldn't let either of them down. He would see to Eloise's safety if it killed him.

The wolf hummed its approval of this thought and contented itself with prowling in the corner of his mind.

Then suddenly, the golden warmth of Bron's presence filtered over him, through him, steadying him and his wolf with her mental caress.

He relaxed against that caress, needing it more than he could express.

Bron nodded, then turned back to her patient and closed her eyes.

He glanced at Eloise to see if she had seen or sensed any of what had just happened. Thankfully her attention was centred on her friend who had ceased her struggling but was muttering under her breath, her face a mask of pain and fear.

'Is she okay? What's going on?'

Marcy's eyes slipped closed, her face relaxing with sleep. Bron blew out a heavy breath and leaned back on her haunches. 'Right. I've put her to sleep. That should stop her from hurting herself at least.'

'Thank you,' Eloise said.

'What about the rest of them?' Iain asked. He gestured to the others and it was only then he noticed that every single one of the coven faced Eloise, their eyes open, staring hatred and accusation and ... longing? It was a look so cold it burned. His wolf growled and its hackles rose, a ridge he felt all the way down his spine. He sprang into a crouch. 'Why are they doing that?'

'It's Cain.'

'You can't believe what Marcy said. She's out of her mind.'

Eloise's eyes pinned him to the spot, fear and horror trembling in their depths. 'I know. It should be impossible if he's as far away as you said he was but ...' She shook her head. 'The black lightning. The eyes ... It's Cain.' Her nostrils flared as if scenting something. 'It even smells like him; like his magic. It's him. Oh Goddess. You lied, didn't you? About where he is? He's here, isn't he? He has to be here. It's the only thing that makes sense.'

'No!' Iain shot Bron a look. 'He was moved to McClune lands when you woke. He's not here.'

'But he is. He is.' She stood, trembling, took a stumbling step. 'I have to get out of here. Now. He'll leave them alone if I go.' She began to hobble towards the door.

With a growl, Iain bent to pick her up.

'What are you doing?' She said, slapping his hands away, sounding more affronted than he'd ever heard her.

'Getting you out of here.'

'I can walk.'

'Not quickly.' She opened her mouth to argue further, but there wasn't time for her pride. 'I thought you said you needed to get out of here now."

'I do.'

'Then let me help you do that.'

Her mouth twisted. 'I'm not a sick bird you need to rescue.'

By the Moon, he loved her strength. 'I know,' he said with pride he didn't have a right to feel. She wasn't his mate after all. 'This isn't about that. It's about getting you out of here now. Just like you said.'

She stared at him then nodded. It was all he needed. He scooped her into his arms and said to Bron. 'We're going. Now.'

'I can't leave them alone like this.' She looked down at the bodies on the ground. Their eyes were glowing red with hatred. Blood red. As in actual blood was now dripping from their eyes. Then it started to drip from their noses, mouths, ears, creating vivid trails on pale skin as it ran across their faces to pool on the green grass.

'Get me out of here or he'll kill them,' Eloise whispered, her voice pained, haunted.

But he couldn't just run out with her, no matter how much he wanted to, and leave Bron here. 'Bron. You have to come now.'

'I can't leave them.'

'You have to,' he said, begging her to understand the predicament she was putting him in with the look in his eyes. 'You can watch them from the monitors. If there's no change, you can call River and some of the others and come back down here.'

Thankfully, understanding lit Bron's eyes as her gaze ran between him and Eloise. She shook her head a little, sighed then said, 'Okay.'

He gestured for her to go first. Giving him a look that let him know she wasn't happy, she took off in front of them. Iain followed.

Bron broke off and went up the stairs when they got to the main entrance, but he didn't follow. She knew what she was doing. And so did he. He pushed open the front doors, desperate to give Eloise sunshine and light after the darkness of what they'd just witnessed.

He placed her down gently on a seat that had been carved out of the stump of a fallen tree at the edge of the clearing just outside the house.

She dropped her head into her hands. 'Shit. Shit. This is all my fault.' She looked up at him, gaze bleak. 'They're going to die, aren't they?'

'Not if we can help it.' He sat down next to her, took her hand. She gripped him tight. 'Bron will contact Jason and keep an eye on your friends through the monitors. I'm sure River will be down soon and then she can go back in. And Gabbie is contacting Cordy. They'll do everything they can to help your friends.'

She rubbed her hand across her eyes. 'Why would Cain do that to them? It's not like him. Not the boy I grew up with.'

'He tried to kill you, Eloise. He's changed. Been completely taken over by Morrigan.'

'I—' She sucked in a breath. 'You're right. He's been getting closer and closer to her and pulling further and further away from me for a couple of years now. It got worse last year after Alfrere died. She began to teach him things she'd never taught the rest of us. Things Alfrere had known. Dark things.' She swallowed hard, her expression bleak. 'The Cain I grew up with would never have tried to kill me. He wouldn't have done *that*,' she said, pointing towards the caves, hand shaking, 'in there, to those who were once friends. But I know it was him. I know that magic; could taste the flavour of it. The evil in it might have made it bitter, but it was still familiar.' She swallowed hard. 'It was like Cain, but with a hint of Morrigan.'

'Do you know her magic that well?'

Her expression became bleaker. 'More than anyone else in the coven, I know the bitter tang, the whipping feel of it. This was that and yet more—' She frowned. 'More familial. Like my own magic but with a stinging caress.' She shuddered. 'And to be able to do that from wherever he is. He's so powerful. I never knew he was so powerful.'

'It makes sense. You're powerful too.'

'Not like that.'

He took her hand again, brushing his thumb over the back of it. 'No. Never like that. You would never use your powers to hurt and maim. To kill.'

She closed her eyes, lashes trembling against her cheeks. 'He hates me.' Her breath hitched. 'I never let myself believe it before, but he truly hates me. He wants me dead.'

A tear traced an aching path down her cheek. He wiped it with his thumb. 'I won't let that happen. *You* won't let that happen.'

'How can you be so certain of me?' she whispered, her beautiful eyes full of tears.

He cupped her face, stroked his thumbs across her cheekbones. 'Because I look into your eyes and see beauty and strength and truth.'

'Truth? After I spied on you all for so long? How do you know it's truth?'

'Your eyes are so expressive—I don't think you could lie even if you tried. Although, I suspect, it isn't in you to try.'

She laughed, a breathy, trembling sound that stroked over his skin. 'Are you calling me a bad liar?'

'Yes. But in a good way.'

Her hiccough of laughter brushed over him. His wolf hummed in pleasure. His fingers firmed on her face and he leaned forward, kissed her brow. 'I think it hurt you to be deceitful.'

'How can you know me so well when I don't even know myself?'

He kissed her nose. 'I see you.' Her eyelids fluttered closed. He kissed one. 'I see you more clearly than I've ever seen anyone else.' He kissed her other eyelid. 'I think in the same way you seem to see me.' His lips hovered over hers.

'Iain?' Her eyes opened—drenched pools of golden-green fire.

'Shh,' he said and pressed his lips to hers. He meant it as a soft kiss of encouragement, of understanding, but her lips moved hungrily against his, clinging, nipping, sucking. Fire sprang to immediate life, blasting away his good intentions. For a blissful moment he gave in to it, meeting her tongue as she thrust it into his mouth, sucking her lip, never wanting to let go. A burning pain started to grow in his chest and he realised he needed to breathe. So did she. Her breaths were coming in little gasps as she clung to his shoulders, meeting his hunger with one just as insatiable.

His wolf surged to the fore, mingling with the man. They wanted to take, to ravage, to make her theirs. Forever.

Fuck!

He pulled back with a gasp. Forever? Where had that come from? Not to mention he shouldn't be doing this. Not now, after what happened. Not until he knew the source of this hunger—was it their own or was it fuelled by the past-life presence?

She swayed towards him, lips searching for just one more kiss, fingers digging into his shoulders, pulling him back to her.

He couldn't let her take what she wanted. Not until he was certain it was what she truly wanted.

Gripping her hands, he pulled them from his shoulders and moved back as gently as he could. She blinked up at him, confusion and lust sparking in her eyes. 'We can't do this now,' he said, voice shaky.

'You're right.' She shifted away from him. 'I don't deserve joy given what I've caused.'

He sucked in a breath. 'You can't blame yourself for that?'

She glanced back towards the house. 'In part. If I hadn't been so blinded by my need to be loved, I would have seen Morrigan for who and what she is. I wouldn't have done what she asked and caused so much pain.' Her voice faltered, but she lifted her chin, hands clasped steadily in her lap. 'But there's little point wasting time with what ifs, is there?'

She fucking took his breath away with the strength of her. 'No,' he finally managed to say around the lump firmly wedged in his throat. 'We need to focus on the now.'

'And the future.' She faced him, her eyes fierce. 'I can't allow Cain and Morrigan to do what they will. There has to be a way to stop them.'

'And we'll find it. I promise.'

She breathed in deeply and nodded. Such a simple thing but her trust filled him with such heat, he thought he might burn up from the force of it.

They sat there for a moment, gazes linked, an unspoken promise in the air.

He would not fail her.

With that promise ringing in his mind, he asked, 'You think Cain could be linked to Morrigan?'

'Yes.'

'So she could be using him to get to you?'

Her eyes blazed with something he didn't understand. 'It's possible. I just don't know. I don't know what her plan is. I know that she hates the Were and that hatred has been passed down to her followers.' She looked away, but not before he saw the bleakness in her eyes. 'It was so easy to believe her because she played on our fear and ignorance.'

'If you could learn not to fear, to see us for who we are, then maybe the others can too.'

'Maybe.' She frowned.

'What's wrong?'

'I don't think it's that simple. I think because of what I am it made it easier to see the Were for who you truly are. I mean, there's a part of you that's in me too. I couldn't keep being afraid of myself. It's unnatural. The others though—' She tightened her hands over her knees. 'They don't have that. And I don't know how to give that to them.'

'That's not your responsibility.'

'Isn't it?' Her back stiffened and her fingers trembled. Then she gripped her knees so tightly veins could be seen through the white. 'I'm supposedly some Nexus and have great power. I should be able to do something, to create change, but I have no idea what being the Nexus means let alone how to use the power that's inside me. How can I help anyone when I can't even figure that out about myself?'

He grabbed her hands again, held strong when she went to pull away, forcing her to look at him with the power of his will, his belief in her. 'We'll find out together. I promise.'

She looked at him, eyes swimming with emotions deeper than any ocean he'd ever come across. 'What if it's not quick enough? What if they get to me first? They want me dead. What if I don't have time?'

A wolf growl in his throat, he pulled her into his arms. 'I won't let Morrigan or Cain or any of the others hurt you.'

She wrapped her arms around him, her hands trembling on his back. 'How can you stop him?'

'Yes, how can he stop me?'

16

Eloise stiffened at the sound of that voice. Cain's voice.

Familiar laughter echoed around her.

Heart beating an unsyncopated rhythm in her chest, she jerked out of Iain's arms, eyes darting around. It had been bright earlier, but now a pall had fallen over everything. The leaves on the trees, the grass, the flowers, even the blue of the sky was dimmed. 'Cain?'

'Cain's here?' Iain moved with lightning speed to stand in front of her, protective. His gaze darted around the clearing. 'What are you seeing, Eloise?'

Cain's laugh came closer. Panic squeezed her lungs, her breath sharp gasps slashing at her throat. Her brother's presence was a cold inside her as surely as Iain's warmth pressed against her side. 'Where are you? Show yourself.'

A slightly man-shaped shadow loomed up out of the shade of the trees. A pearlescent shadow just like the one she'd seen in the caves. A shadow that had made her coven mates attack. 'Cain?'

Iain stepped in front of her, his body perched over the balls of his feet, growling.

She'd never heard anything so protective yet threatening at the same time. 'Can you see him?'

'No.' The growling became louder. 'But I can sense him. It's like lightning in the air—but wrong somehow.'

The shadow shuddered, then disappeared. An icy crawl, like the pinprick of a thousand insect feet, traced up the back of Eloise's neck. 'Maybe he's gone.'

'No. He's still here.'

Laughter again. Behind her. She spun around, gasped. The shadow was on the path at the edge of the clearing that led back to the cliff stairs.

Iain moved, herding her behind him, ready to push her out of harm's way. The shadow flickered and disappeared.

'Where is he now?'

She shook her head. 'I can't see him.'

'Fuck.'

That same sensation crawled up her spine and gripped her neck. Slowly, ever so slowly, she turned.

Cain stood an arm's reach away, his features clear to her now even though he was almost translucent. He was smiling, enjoying her fear; enjoying the fact that she couldn't touch him; enjoying the moment she realised what he was.

He wasn't just a shadow or a spirit or even a ghost. He was a Shade. She'd thought it impossible, that he'd never do such a thing but ... 'Oh Goddess, Cain. What have you done?' But she knew what he'd done. Morrigan had made him do what she'd made no-one do since her grandfather. She'd torn his soul from his body. And he'd let her knowing the consequences. 'Cain. Cain. Why?' she said on a sob.

'What? What is it?' Iain asked, gaze frantic as he looked around, trying to see what she saw.

'Cain. He's a Shade.'

'I thought you said he wouldn't do that.'

'I was wrong.' She sucked in a pained breath. 'Goddess, Cain. Do you know what this means?'

He leaned close to her, eyes like blue coals. *'Of course I do, little sister. I have damned myself, because of you.'*

'Why did you let Morrigan do this to you?'

'She didn't do anything. I was the one who suggested it.'

'But why?'

'It was the only way to reach you.'

'There were other ways. There are always other ways.'

'Not with the animals in the way!' Cain's eyes blazed, the blue subsumed by glowing red. *'You are mine! Not theirs. Mine!'* He reached for her.

She jerked back, stumbling, his grasping hands just missing her.

Iain's strong arms bounded around her, holding her steady. 'What is it, Eloise? What's he saying?'

Cain's gaze snapped to him, something colder than rage and hatred burning in their depths. She moved in front of Iain, hands raised, drawing her brother's attention back to her. 'You have my attention now. You don't have to hurt anyone. Just tell me what you want.'

He chuckled nastily. *'Silly sister. Hurting someone and what I want are the same thing.'* He grabbed her wrist, jerked her forward. His touch was an ice-burn slicing through her skin. She screamed.

Iain swiped out with his clawed hand, hissed as he made contact with the Shade he couldn't see. Cain's form wavered for a moment and then became more vivid. *'Mmm. That felt good. Do it again.'*

'Don't touch him,' Eloise said to Iain as he went to swipe out again. 'Every time you touch him he can pull on your life energy.'

Iain instantly backed up, herding her behind him, protective. 'What about you? What happens when he touches you? Is he taking your life energy too?'

'Oh, I'm taking more than that. See.' Cain darted forward and touched her on the shoulder. Eloise screamed. The touch arced through her, skin, muscles, nerves, the ache in her deformed foot a sudden tearing pain. Her joints locked—the only thing stopping her from collapsing on the leaf-strewn ground.

'Where the hell is he?' Iain pinned her to his side, turned in a circle, every muscle tensed.

Cain's smile grew impossibly wider, making him look like a funhouse clown. *'This is fun.'* His arm snaked out again, slicing an arc of fire through her leg. She tried not to scream, gritted her teeth against the pain, but a whimper of sound made it out of her lips as she clutched at the agony in her leg. It felt like something was ripping and tearing its way through her nerves, growing, surging.

'I'm sick of this. I can't fight what I can't see. I know you like to move under your own steam, but you're hurting and I have to get you out of here.' Iain picked her up, backed away from where she'd last indicated Cain was standing.

Cain materialised in front of them. *'If he takes you away from here, I'll kill the others.'*

'Iain no! He's going to kill them if I don't listen.'

Iain hesitated. 'Can he do that?'

'I told you before. Shades can kill. It's why Morrigan uses them. He can do whatever he likes while still on this plane.'

'But why is he hurting you? Aren't you the only one who can save him?'

'Yes. But Shades also take power from those they're blood bound to. It keeps them more strongly on this plane.'

'And I'm blood bound to Morrigan too. Which makes me even more powerful.'

'Oh Goddess!'

'What? What did he say?'

She told him. 'With both me and Morrigan to pull from and his own power, he could last for months as a Shade.'

'Uh-uh-uh. No telling our secrets to the beasts.' Cain made another pass, his fingers glancing across her throat.

Cold seared into her chest, threatening to stop her lungs. She gasped for air that was suddenly too thick and cold to breathe. She bit her lip against the scream, the tang of copper live in her mouth.

'Eloise!' Iain swung around, his wolf in his eyes. 'He's killing you.'

His arms tightened around her and he began to run towards the path that led out of the clearing.

'Try to leave, and I'll kill him.'

'No! Iain, please stop.' Thankfully Iain listened to her, stopping immediately. 'Put me down. You can't take me anywhere.'

Iain did as she asked but stayed on alert as he stepped in front of her, arms out to protect. 'Where is he?'

'There. By those trees.'

Iain swung around, claws elongating from the ends of his fingers. 'What do you want of her? Of us?'

'Aww, he's so protective, isn't he? It's so cute, given how quickly I could kill him.'

'Do that and I won't help you. I won't bring you back. That's what you want, isn't it? That's why you keep coming to find me.'

There was a pause and then, *'Yes. That's exactly what I want. You will come to me. You will do the ceremony, bring me back to my body, and then you will do exactly what I say until your debt has been repaid.'*

'So you are my brother? My true brother.'

'Of course I am, you little fool. We are bound, you and I, blood and bone and sinew. What made you think otherwise?'

Laughter rose in her, bitter as bile that she swallowed back. 'Just a wish I had.'

'No matter how much you wish it, you'll never be free of me, Little Bit.'

She jerked, the use of his pet-name for her a punch in her chest. She lifted her chin. 'I'll bring you back to your body then, but I won't let you do anything else.'

His laughter was a wild shriek in her head. *'And how are you going to stop me?'*

'The Were will stop you. I'll help them.'

'You'll help the Were?' He cackled wildly, head lifted to the sky.

'They're powerful. So am I.'

'Yes.' His gaze returned to hers, the black of them slick and shiny. She shuddered. *'You are. But your power is not for them to use. It's for me. And Morrigan.'*

'Iain. Eloise!' Gabbie ran into the little clearing, claws out, eyes wolf bright, glancing around to figure out the threat.

Cain's lips widened. *'Ooh, a present. Thanks Little Bit. I was getting hungry.'*

'Gabbie. Run!' Eloise screamed. But it was too late. Cain was already at Gabbie's side, his hands curling around her throat.

The Were-female cried out, a choked sound, as she tried to slash with her hands. But it was no use. The more she touched the Shade, the quicker he drained the life from her. With every second she grew weaker, while he grew more vibrant, less a shadow and more a shimmering imprint of colour against the greens and browns of the surrounding woods.

Horror clawing at her throat, Eloise could do nothing but stare.

'Gabbie!' Iain moved as if to go to his friend's rescue, but Eloise grabbed his arm, holding on tight, stopping him.

'No. He'll kill you too.'

'I have to help her.' He pulled easily away and leapt at the shimmering thing wrapped around Gabbie. He struck at it, trying to tear it off, but every time he touched it, he gave it more energy.

Cain laughed.

Iain kept fighting despite the fact that he was weakening. Eloise grabbed at his arm, was able to pull him away despite his greater power and strength.

'No! I have to save her.'

'You can't. You can't.' She pulled him back further, towards the path.

Cain turned his head. *'Uh-uh-uh, Little Bit. Not so fast. I want his power too.'* Tendrils of shimmering shadow curled out, wrapped around Iain. The big Were she'd come to care for so deeply trembled, swung drunkenly at the tendrils wrapping more tightly around him with every second. She tried to pull him away, clenching her teeth against the pain as the tendrils touched her, biting into her skin with a pain so cold it burned. But Cain had him, just as he had Gabbie. He was killing them. All to prove a point he didn't need to prove.

'Cain. Stop. Please stop.'

Her brother just laughed, gripped tighter.

Iain groaned and crashed to his knees, taking her with him. 'Run,' he said, his eyes wide with pain. 'Leave me. Get to safety.'

'No. No. I'm not leaving you.'

'How touching. How pathetic.' Cain's mouth pulled into a hateful sneer.

'Cain, stop.' They were barely words, mostly a hacking, sobbing sound. 'Please stop. You've proved your point. Please. Don't kill him. Don't kill them.'

Cain tipped his head, looking at her for a moment as if she were a curiosity. *'Okay.'*

Iain slumped into her arms with a groan, the heavy weight of him almost too much for her. She lowered him to the ground, cradling his head in her lap. He was so weak. Too weak? She didn't know. Didn't know how much Cain had taken from him. Looking up, she saw Gabbie was still upright, neck clenched in Cain's hands.

'Her too.'

Cain looked at Gabbie as if he'd forgotten he was holding her. *'Oops. Too late.'* He let go. The Were-female crashed to the ground.

Eloise stared, unable at first to comprehend the blank glaze of Gabbie's eyes. 'You killed her,' she whispered after a moment.

'No. You killed her. You did this, all this, you traitorous bitch, when you allowed them and their Goddess to touch you.'

She blinked rapidly, dug her fingernails into her leg trying to suppress the tears that threatened. She couldn't let Cain know just how much he'd hurt her or he'd do it more. Kill more. So she took a steadying breath and asked, 'But why do this to them? It's me you hate. Me you want to punish. Leave them alone. Take me.'

'But this is your punishment for your betrayal and intransigence.'

'They don't deserve this.' She pressed her fingernails in harder. 'They never did anything to you.'

'Yes they did!' His eyes flashed red as he screamed. *'They betrayed that which kept them succoured for so long. I can feel the pain of that in him living in me.'*

'Him? What are you talking about?'

'You'll understand when you come back to us. When you embrace the Darkness within you. When you become like us.'

'I will never become like you.'

'Yes you will. You will. You're mine!'

'How is it I never realised just how insane she's made you?'

His eyes glowed coal red and black as he looked down at her. *'Not insane. Enlightened. As you will be enlightened when you come back into the fold.'* He smiled, his expression benevolent, almost kind, just like he used to look when he was trying to protect her. *'You belong with me, sister dear. You know you do. Not with these savages.'*

Her arms tightened around Iain, eyes burning with the effort not to cry. 'He's not a savage. You don't know them. They're good, Cain. They want to help us, not hurt us.'

'They're abominations, every last one.'

'No, Morrigan was wrong about that. River and Skye are her family. They're blood. If you'd only listen to me, get to know them ...'

'Lies! All lies. You are filled with their lies. You need to come back to us. You need to rid yourself of the poison they have filled you with.'

'I'm not filled with their poison. Morrigan is the poisonous one. She's turned you into a killer.' Her eyes blurred as her gaze skated over Gabbie, a still, crumpled heap on the ground.

'You've been tainted by them. Come back with me and I will see you cleansed.'

'I never want to be cleansed if it means becoming like you! I won't be responsible for killing my friends.'

He pointed down at Gabbie. *'They might as well be dead already, like this one. Your presence here among them will only bring death faster. The question is, do you want to save the lives of those in the caves? If you come to me and do as I say, I will save them. I will save you.'*

Her eyes hazed over with tears. This Shade wore her brother's face, but it wasn't Cain. Not the boy she'd grown up with. Not the teenager who'd always protected her, who'd held her when she cried, who had always been there for her. Morrigan had poisoned the boy who'd been her brother leaving someone she didn't recognise in his place. 'Why are you doing this?'

His lips curved but lacked the warmth of a true smile. *'You could say I saw the light.'*

She wanted to hit him, but she had to try to reason with him. To make him see. She knew it was pointless to talk to him about the Were, but maybe ... 'What light would lead you to harm our coven mates? Morrigan still has their allegiance.'

'They are tainted by their proximity to the Were and by the fact that they gave themselves up. They are of no use to us now. Their lives are meaningless. However, I will allow them to live only if you do as I say.'

Iain groaned. Cain's gaze snapped to him, a sneer ruining his handsome face. 'And I will let you have him for a little longer. But if you dally, my dearest twin, he will be the first to go.'

Her arms tightened around Iain. 'I will come.'

'As I knew you would.' Cain smiled and faded away into the darkening woods.

'Eloise?' Iain's eyes flickered open.

'Iain?' She ran a trembling hand down his cheek as her eyes starred with the tears that now came in a flood. 'Are you okay?'

He reached up, fingers trembling, touched her cheek. 'You're crying.'

She tried to speak past the horrible lump clogging her throat, swallowed, tried again. 'I'm sorry. I'm so sorry. This is all my fault. If I'd—'

His fingers over her lips stopped the words. 'It's not your fault.'

'But he hurt you, to get to me. To make me agree. He ki ...' She choked on the word. It was too hard to say. Instead, her gaze skittered over to Gabbie's lifeless body a few metres away. Iain's gaze followed.

'Gabbie?' There was a moment's horrible pause as his gaze fixed on his dead friend, then he was on his feet, stumbling over the rough ground towards her.

Eloise could say nothing around the terrible tightness that filled her chest, constricted her throat. All she could do was cry harder as Iain grabbed Gabbie up in his arms and keened to the night sky, the sound an aching torrent of grief.

Howls sounded in the distance—other members of the pack

hearing him, or maybe already feeling Gabbie's loss through the Packbond. She could only imagine the depth of their loss. The only person she'd had that kind of close bond with was Cain, and he'd torn that to shreds when he'd turned on her and tried to kill her; whatever had been left of that was now obliterated by what he'd just done.

The thought made the pain inside her throb. She swiped the tears from her face and wrapped her arms around her knees, trying to stay still, trying not to call attention to herself, trying to be the nothing she'd always been.

The keening sound stopped and Iain spun abruptly to face her, eyes pain-ravaged pools in his pale face. 'What are you doing?'

'I'm sorry. I don't mean to distract you. I was trying to be quiet.' She skittered to her feet. 'I'll just go ... get out of your way. You don't need me here.'

'No!'

The force of that word held her still for long enough for him to gently lay Gabbie back on the ground and stagger over to her. Just before he got to her, she came to her senses and turned, about to flee. He must want her out of his sight. He must hate her ...

'Stop it.' His arms bounded around her, turning her, hands cupping her face, forcing her to look up at him. 'Whatever you're doing, stop it.'

She blinked up at him, surprise taking her voice. 'I ... I ... thought you would want me gone.'

'Let's get one thing clear, Little Bird. I never want you gone. But I wasn't talking about your need to leave right now. I get why you might want to do that. I was talking about what you did just before. The way you began to disappear.'

She shook her head. 'I don't know what you mean.'

His thumbs swept over her cheeks in that way that always made her stomach curl with warmth, her legs to weaken. 'You do. You were willing yourself to be nothing. To not be here.'

'How do you know that?'

'I felt it. You became smaller, quieter, in my mind. It was like you were fading. My wolf felt it too, like you were going away, willing yourself to not be here with us. You can't do that, Eloise. Not ever. Do you understand?'

She shook her head slowly, hardly able to make sense of his words. 'I thought you wouldn't want to see me here, not after what Cain did. I was just doing what I used to do in the coven when I didn't think anyone wanted to see me. I tried to become as small as I could, so they wouldn't notice me. Wouldn't blame me for things that weren't my fault. I got so good at it, I could go unnoticed for days, weeks. I had no idea I did anything physical, or mental, to myself.'

'By the Moon, Eloise!' He pulled her to him, stroked her hair. 'You taught yourself to disappear.' There was a low rumble in his chest. 'I want to kill them for making you feel like you had to do that.' He pulled away from her, cupped her face in his hands again, looking deep into her eyes, his full of desperate worry. 'But you can't do that again, Eloise. Not ever. With your power ...' His words choked off. There was struggle in his eyes, in his expression, as he tried not to give in to his anger, his terror, and yet his hands remained gentle, giving, as he cupped her face. 'With your power, you could do something horrible to yourself. Do you understand? There is no longer any need to disappear. You are stronger than that. Stronger than you've ever been. Promise me you won't do that again. You can't go away. You can't.'

'I won't,' she said, voice a mere whisper. 'I promise.'

His gaze chased over her face and then his lips were on hers, hard and clinging, as if he wanted to drink her up, become part of her. He hauled her closer so she could feel every inch of his hard frame pressed into her, muscles vibrating as their tongues tasted, teeth nipped, every breath a gasp as if it were the last.

She could taste his grief for Gabbie, his fear for her, but there was something else there too, something challenging and deep with a slight dark edge, something that burned with fire and passion and desire. She recognised it. Felt it in herself. It was dangerous, yet life affirming. And rather than be scared of it like she would have been in the past, she wanted it. She wanted it more than she'd wanted anything in her life. She wanted to be more than she'd ever been. She wanted to be the powerful woman they'd all been telling her she was, but she'd been too caught up in the past to realise they weren't selling her a dream. It was the truth.

Iain saw her as she truly was. It was the most remarkable gift. She wanted to give him an equal one. The only one she had to give.

The only question was, would he value it?

'If you allow that fear to grow, you will never be who you are meant to be. You will never become the warrior you were born to be.' The Goddess's words came back to her, and she knew that it didn't matter if Iain valued her gift to him or not. What mattered was that she give it with her whole heart and be brave enough to face whatever outcome came to pass. She couldn't control what others did to her, but she could control how she responded to it.

Iain was right. She could never disappear again. She was stronger than that. Always had been. It had just taken this tragedy today for her to see it.

With that enlightened thought came the realisation that she couldn't offer herself to Iain yet. She couldn't give him what she'd never given anyone else. Not here. Not beside the scene of such horror and violence and grief. They would have time again later. For now ...

She pulled back, slowly, lips lingering on his, hands stroking, calming, down his face, his neck, shoulders, back.

Iain felt the change in her and roped his desire back under control with sheer, fist clenching force of will. His lips left hers for the last time, her breath brushing over his face, panting, as his was doing over hers.

Fuck! He couldn't believe he'd just lost himself to his passion, here, now, in this place of fear and death. She'd think him an animal.

Or would she? Had it been Eloise returning his passion kiss for drugging kiss, or the past-life presence?

She was looking up at him, her hands stroking down his back and he breathed out a sigh of relief to see her eyes were her own green-gold. 'Iain?'

'Sorry. I'm so sorry.' He forced his fingers to unclench, sliding them from her hips, from her nape where he'd wound them into her hair. 'I don't know what I was thinking.'

She smiled at him—actually smiled. That smile made the clenching worry in his chest loosen a little. 'I don't think either of us was thinking just then.' Her smile softened. 'And don't be sorry. I'm not.' Her gaze slid behind him. 'It's just ... Gabbie. We need to take care of Gabbie.'

'Fuck.' For one wild, desperate moment, he'd forgotten the reality of her death. Fear and then passion had numbed the tearing wound that was her absence in the Packbond. But Gabbie deserved better than that from him. So did Eloise. He opened his mouth to say so when he felt the vibration along the Packbond. 'The others. They're coming.'

She stepped back from him. 'I'll leave you and them alone to deal with her.'

'No.' He grasped her hand, pulled her closer, but didn't allow himself to hold her again—just her hand. Only her hand. 'You are part of us. You belong here.' She still seemed uncertain. '*I* need you here.'

'Okay.' Her eyes glowed with tears, but she didn't let them spill, simply stood at his side as two pack members ran into the clearing. One look at Gabbie and they lifted their heads and howled. She shivered, clenched his hand tighter.

River, Bron at his side, ran into the clearing after the first two, his howl short and sharp, the sound of a torn heart. Bron ran over to Gabbie.

'She's gone,' Iain said, voice choked as Bron knelt by her side.

'I know. I just need to—' A sob caught her words, tears pouring down her face.

River went down beside his mate and hugged her to his side. 'I'll help.'

She nodded, wiped the tears from her cheeks. 'She was taken with such violence. I just have to gentle her human and wolf souls into passing.' Her hands glided over Gabbie's pale form, settling her limbs, closing her eyes. River's hands echoed Bron's movements, smoothing Gabbie's clothing, brushing her hair to fall in waves around her face. Together they settled her, hands folded over her chest, Bron whispering words under her breath, the sound a hum that tingled on Iain's skin.

Eloise shuddered at his side. 'It's working. I can feel it. The violence is going.'

'I am bringing her back to nature,' Bron whispered. 'It is what all our souls crave—to return to what we came from. Violent deaths make it impossible for us to do this unless certain rites are performed.' Tears tumbled down her face, but this time she didn't swipe them away. On her, they weren't a sign of weakness—they were a strength. 'In the end, this peace is all we have to give to departing souls.'

Eloise trembled again. 'You are so lucky to have each other.'

Iain tightened his hand around hers. 'Yes.'

17

It seemed like a dream; a horrible, sad, dream. But it wasn't. The pain and grief around her told her it was too viscerally real, an aching bruise that wouldn't heal.

When Bron and River finished settling Gabbie's body, Iain and the others knelt by Gabbie's sides, running their hands over her, touching, petting. Iain waved her down next to him, encouraged her to follow their lead. 'It helps the soul to let go, to move on.'

It felt strange, but right at the same time, to touch the dead woman.

Once they were done, Iain let go of her hand, and with River and the other two Were, picked Gabbie up and carried her to the Pack-house where she was laid on a large flat-topped stone in the garden surrounded by a ring of other rough-hewn stones. A Dance. They had their own Dance!

She'd never been to this area in the garden before. No surprise given they wouldn't want to advertise they had their own Dance. It made it even more special now that they allowed her to see it; to stand here with them in this place of power.

Even so, she couldn't help glancing around, watching for Jason and Skye or Adam and Shelley to arrive. She needed to tell them all about Cain, his threat, what he wanted to do. But should she let them grieve first and then tell them, or should she grab them as soon as they got here? And how could she possibly tell them that she was the reason their packmate was now dead?

'You are not to blame,' Iain whispered in her ear.

She glanced up at him. 'How did you know—'

'I just did.' He squeezed her hand. 'As for the rest, we must grieve first. We will tell them later. Together.'

Others began to arrive then and her attention was torn from future worries to the present.

Every new arrival stopped on entering the clearing and howled to the sky as they saw Gabbie laid out. She hadn't noticed when River slipped away, but then he was there, arms full of flowers and blossoms from his garden. Bron helped him lay them around Gabbie's body. The last ones, a few stems of kangaroo paw, he placed on her chest, folding her hands over them. 'They were her favourite,' he said.

Once that was done, Bron and River backed away to stand under a ghost gum. Iain led Eloise to stand beside them.

Every Were who arrived howled to the sky then walked to Gabbie to touch her. Once done, they joined the growing group, creating a series of circles around the fallen. They held hands, stroked arms, rubbed backs, nuzzled. Touching. Always touching.

Iain never let go of Eloise's hand.

Finally, as the sun was setting with a blaze of furious crimson and purple, Jason, Skye, Adam and Shelley arrived, a little boy, Jason and Adam's nephew Thomas, holding his uncles' hands. She'd met him only briefly when she'd been taken to the Packhouse last year for healing when she'd hurt herself in her Bluebelle form.

The moment Jason stepped into the clearing, it was like everyone breathed again, his presence a soothing balm. She'd never really understood the link between an Alpha and his pack, couldn't quite comprehended the impact of it on every aspect of a Were's psyche, but in that moment, she felt it as certainly as she felt Iain's hand in hers.

One side of the concentric circles opened, letting him and the other through. He walked stiffly, Skye clutching his hand, the little boy his other, gaze on Gabbie and nothing else.

Adam and Shelley waked to the other side of the stone Gabbie lay on then as if on a silent command, they ran their hands over Gabbie, encouraging the little boy to do so as well, helping to soothe her soul to its final resting place.

After a few minutes, Adam and Shelley came around and took the young boy's hands—the little fellow was so stoic, it made her want to cry anew—and moved to the side. Jason stood for a moment, running his hand over the Gabbie's hair, then bent to place a kiss on her lips, whispering something before he stood upright.

Then he turned to face his pack.

The look on his face stole Eloise's breath. There was grief there. A fury savage in its quiet certainty that this death would be avenged. But alongside that was warmth. Comfort. Power. Bound with a sense of familial love so strong it could never be broken. It tugged at her, threading through her deepest soul, winding itself into her heart, and she knew she could never do without this feeling.

That if it was ever broken, she would not survive.

Iain's fingers clenched tighter around hers. She looked up at him. His lips curled into a soft smile, just for her. 'You are one of us.'

She smiled back at him. 'I know.'

'She will be avenged,' Jason said quietly, his voice carrying across the Dance. 'But tonight, we grieve. Tonight we celebrate Gabbie as she deserves to be celebrated. For now, finish saying your goodbyes.'

Jason moved through the circles of Were with Skye at his side, Adam and Shelley taking care of the little boy, walking behind them. As he passed by everyone, they touched him and he touched them in turn, sometimes a rub of a shoulder, a slap on the back, a hug, a touch to the cheek. As others continued to arrive, he kept moving around, doing the same thing then letting the newcomers go to the bier to say goodbye.

Finally, they came to stand in the outer circle with Iain, Eloise, Bron and River. Adam and Shelley, the little boy between them, took up position on the other side of Iain.

The little boy turned to Adam, who swept him up into his arms, holding him close as the boy sobbed into his shoulder.

'Why is Gabbie gone?' His voice carried clearly through the silence.

Adam's face stiffened, but his voice was full of love and quiet warmth as he stroked the boy's back and said, 'Only the Goddess knows. But now she can look after all of us.'

'I want her to be here.'

'So do we, T-man. So do we.' Adam kissed the boy's cheek and continued to stroke his back as the boy settled against him, face turned towards the middle of the Dance. Shelley briefly touched Adam's shoulder before she stared off into the distance, a pinched expression on her face.

Eloise leaned into Iain, nuzzled her face against his arm. He slipped his arm around her, holding her close, chin brushing against her hair in a soothing rhythm.

Soon there were no more newcomers.

Silence fell. They remained that way, standing silent guard, until the moon had risen in the sky, the silver orb of it casting a bright light on Gabbie. Then, on some unuttered signal, they all lifted their heads and howled up at the moon, Were and Pack Witch alike. Driven by some instinct she'd never felt before, Eloise joined them.

The sound was haunting, sad and joyful all at once. And as it reached its peak, Skye, Bron and Shelley raised their hands, the lightning of their power—blue, orange and purple— arced out, engulfing Gabbie's body on the bench.

Instinct rose in Eloise again, and she let go of Iain to raise her hands. Power, a green spark of lightning, flew from her fingers and joined the blue, orange and purple display arcing over and around Gabbie. The howls of all the Were turned into a hum as each one lowered their gazes to watch the display of power dancing around their packmate. The hum rose in volume, higher and higher, matching the power as it danced brighter and brighter over, around and through Gabbie. Slowly, her body rose from the stone bier, the power lifting it into the glow of moonlight. The hum hit an ear-splitting crescendo as the magical lightning flared out in a tight little explosion.

Eloise stumbled back at its force, her arms dropping to her side. Silence rang in her ears. She blinked the aura of bright light from her eyes and stared at the now empty stone bier.

Gabbie was gone. Swallowed by their power in the moonlight.

'A send-off befitting a warrior born,' Jason said, his voice echoing around the Dance. 'Be at peace, Gabriella Siobhan McVey. Guard over our pack from the arms of the Goddess and in the light of the moon.'

'In the light of the moon,' the Were repeated.

And then they began to slide away into the night.

Without a word, Iain led Eloise away from the Dance.

'That was ... beautiful.'

'It was. Thank you.'

'For what?'

'Helping Skye, Shelley and Bron release Gabbie's soul from her body and send her to the Goddess.' He touched her cheek. 'How did you know to do that?'

'It felt right.'

'Your power is beautiful.'

She grimaced. 'And frightening. We made her body disintegrate.'

'The Goddess took her. It's the most wonderful end any of us could hope for.'

She didn't know what to say to that. Iain took her hand again and they continued to walk in silence through the garden. After a while though, Eloise knew she needed to say something about what had happened, but it was so hard to come up with the words. 'I ... I'm so sorry for your loss.'

His head dipped. 'Gabbie was good to me at a time when I felt most alone. I'll miss her.'

'She didn't deserve to die like that.'

'Nobody does.' He began to walk faster. 'Come on.' He towed her forward, towards the path they'd taken the first day she'd managed to change into a wolf. She knew without asking where he was heading. Wanted nothing more than to go with him to the beach, to feel the wind and the salt spray on her face, in her wolf fur, to chase him along the sand in the moonlight. But she couldn't. There was too much to say. She pulled him to a stop. 'Iain. We need to talk about Cain. About what he wants me to do. And we need to tell the others.'

Iain sighed, looking around then back at her. 'Will he be able to do anything further tonight?'

'I don't know. Probably not. What he did would have used a lot of energy, if what I've been told is right.'

'Okay. So we have time. The others will be setting up the life celebration. Jason and Skye will be busy with the pack. There is time.'

'For what?'

'I just need to run for a little while. With you. Can we just do that?'

She knew she should argue, insist they talk now so she could make him understand the full depth of what Cain wanted her to do, but his need sang to her, through her, and she couldn't deny it, or him, what he needed to help come to terms with his grief; with feeling so helpless when Cain had taken hold of him.

Taking his hand again, she said, 'Okay,' and with his need a glow inside, she envisioned the white wolf. The change tingled through her, the golden glow of it flashing bright in the dark of the night. A moment later, his change aura lit the night and then he stood in front of her, eyes an amber glow, the silver in his fur shining in the moonlight.

'*Let's go,*' she heard in her mind. Then they were off.

She wasn't as fast as him, her bad leg, even in this form, holding her back from giving full rein to her need to run fast and hard. He stayed with her, even though she could feel his need pushing at him to go faster, to let go, to feel nothing but the pound of grass and dirt and leaf beneath his paws, the brush becoming a blur. There was a greater need inside him—she sensed it more and more every day—to stay by her side, to keep her safe, to ensure she was happy, fulfilled.

She knew that need. It echoed the one in her for him.

They ran to the cliffs and down the path onto the beach. It was there she slowed, trotted to a rocky outcrop, urged him with a bark and words in her mind she somehow knew he could hear, to run out his need. *'I'll wait here,'* she thought to him.

He nudged his head against hers and then spun, a whir of black and silver in the night.

She leapt up the rocks to stand guard over the empty beach and breathed in the salt air. The foam of waves crested in the moonlight, frothy and glistening with silver, and spilled onto the pale stretch of sand. The fishy-salty scents and the low rumbling crash of it was soothing in its predictability, the sound and smell a constant. The air was cooler than it had been in recent weeks. The summer had been long, but now, this was the first night autumn's haunting notes made themselves known in the air; the first sign that winter was on its way in a month or so. It was almost Easter.

Oestra.

Rebirth and awakening. She'd done both, here. With Bron.

And Iain.

She huffed. Who was she kidding? It was mostly Iain. He'd given her so much and she'd brought him nothing but worry and grief. Yet, on this night, when he should want her far from him so that he could grieve alone for the woman he'd once shared himself with, he insisted she be with him. Took comfort from her presence. He was a remarkable male. One she'd almost lost tonight. Could still lose if she didn't do what Cain wanted her to do.

She couldn't let that happen. She had to find the strength to make them all see that doing the blood spell to bring Cain back to his body was the only thing she could do. If she didn't do it, he could kill so many of them before the sustaining power he gained from Morrigan and from her disappeared and he finally faded away. She had to make them see this wasn't about saving Cain—her brother was already dead. The Cain she knew and loved wouldn't have done what that monster had done today, no matter how much he hated someone.

No, what had to be done was about saving them. Saving Iain. He had to live. Had to live in the familial warmth of his pack. She could give that to him. Only her. The knowledge was powerful. Filled her with energy for life. She wanted to share it with him. Share herself with him.

It hadn't been time before. Now it was.

18

ith a wild yelp, she jumped off the rock and onto the sand and raced along the beach towards where Iain chased the waves.

He met her half way, and almost as if he could sense her need, led the way up the path, across the fields and back to the house.

A glow of a bonfire rose above the other side of the house, the sound of a party in process echoing in the night. Gabbie's wake.

They should go join the pack, but one look at Iain's eyes and she knew that wasn't what he needed. But he didn't push. He left the decision to her.

With a smile curling her lips and a warm glow in her chest, she led him to her bedroom, still in their wolf forms. She pushed open the door with her paw and trotted in, turned to see him paused in the door.

'Are you sure?' she heard in her mind.

She answered him by changing back into her human form. Naked, she stood before him, meeting his amber gaze, breath a fast push in her chest. If he denied her, if he turned away now, she didn't know what she would do.

'There will be pain, but you will survive.' The voice, the past presence, was a whisper in her mind. She knew it spoke the truth. She would survive. She hadn't known herself capable of it in the past, but she knew that about herself now. She would survive. But without this, without him, without pack, without their purpose? She didn't know. Didn't know enough about herself yet to know if she would want to bear the pain of loss once again.

'He loves you. There is no need to worry.'

She didn't know if that was true. His hesitation was too long. He was ...

Prowling towards her, changing as he walked, so that by the time he reached her, it was a man's arms that pulled her against a hard, male chest, male lips that captured hers in a hot, wet kiss. He pulled back, his breath a hard pant against her face, his gaze capturing hers for a searing search that touched her deepest soul. And then his lips were on hers again, demanding, taking, giving.

His erection pressed hard and heavy against her stomach. Heavy warmth sank inside her, swirling, tightening her lower abdomen, between her legs. She gasped, grasping his shoulders, pushing urgently against him. He backed her up against the bed and lowered her, coming down on top of her, his weight pushing her into the mattress, thrilling, making her want more. But he pulled back from her, fingers brushing her cheeks, her hair.

'Are you really sure you want this? I don't want you doing something you're not ready for simply because you think this is what I need.'

A sound of frustration escaped her. He raised himself further back, as if he was going to leave her. She moved, rolling over, hands on his shoulders pushing him back so that their positions were reversed, him underneath, her on top. 'I do feel your need. I won't lie. But it's my need too. I can't deny it anymore. I always felt something missing inside me, and since being here with you, your pack, I've realised it was the need for touch. To belong, truly belong. Today, Cain almost took that from me. Almost took you from me. And I realised I couldn't do without it. I can't do without this,' she ran her hands over his chest, 'this feeling you create inside me when you touch me and let me touch you.'

He opened his mouth to say something but she put her fingers over his lips, silencing him. 'I've learned so much about myself with your help. I know I've got so much more to learn. But the one thing I do know is this isn't about me feeling thankful. It's not even about what the past presence inside me feels. She just brought this to my attention. Helped to break down some barriers that would have broken down with time anyway. This is about me. About what I have to give. And what I want.' She bent down, lips lingering over his before she leaned back again. 'And what I want right now is to share myself with you. If you want that too.'

'If I want that too?' His eyes blazed with heat as his gaze swept over her, his hands gliding down her back to press her more firmly against him. 'I don't think I've ever wanted anything more in my life.'

'Really?'

His erection grew, flexing against her, his gaze deepening. She laughed, thrilling to the sensation of what she did to him.

Then his lips were on hers again, swallowing her laughter. With a sigh, she gave herself up to the sensation of skin against skin, hardness against her softness, the spicy taste of him filling her mouth, the heady fresh scent of him filling her senses. She wanted to fill herself up on the taste and feel of him and hold onto it forever.

His mouth left hers and went exploring. She whimpered but the whimper quickly turned into a murmur of approval as he nipped and sucked and licked his way down her throat, skating along her collarbone. He sucked on her shoulder, his fingers chasing fire up and down her arms and along her sides. He shifted, flipped her over onto her back, his gaze raking over her.

'Beautiful,' he breathed, fingers brushing across her ribs to cup and circle her breasts. Her breath caught in her throat. She'd thought it had felt good when he'd touched her through her clothes the few times they'd kissed—but this was so much better, so much more. In fact, she wasn't sure she could take all the more it was.

His lips ran along her chest, down her sternum and across to the mound of her breast. Fireflies danced in her eyes as the sensation of his lips on her skin set off multiple explosions inside like the pop and fizz of fireworks building to a crescendo. She thought she would die from the pleasure of it.

Then his lips covered her nipple, his tongue flicking the tip just as his fingers had done earlier. The wet slip and glide of it intensified the sensation. She cried out, her back arching off the bed, hands digging into his hair, clutching—whether to pull him closer or push him away, she didn't know. Thankfully he didn't stop. Just sank his teeth in, marking her again, then kissed and licked the little pain away before transferring his attentions to her other breast.

His fingers played with the wet nipple as he lovingly sucked and nipped at the other one, then his fingers dipped down her stomach, making her muscles jump and quiver, and speared through the hair covering her core.

'Iain!' she cried.

He looked up at her briefly, a wicked smile on his lips, before returning to her breast, his gaze capturing and holding hers as his fingers found and rubbed the nub of her clit. Then slowly, he made his way down her stomach. Before she realised what he was going to do, he put his mouth where his fingers had been and licked.

'Mmm, delicious.'

She had no idea what he was talking about because there was a roaring in her ears as he licked and nipped and sucked. She knew she was whimpering, could feel the vibration of it in her throat even if she couldn't hear the sound through the roar in her ears, but she didn't care. Her entire being became centred on the little nub of nerves at her core and when he sucked it into his mouth at the same time he thrust his fingers inside her, pumping once, twice, there was no more build. She just exploded.

'Yes, Little Bird. Come for me.'

She couldn't reply. Could only ride the waves of sensation as they rippled through her, over her, carried her away.

Long minutes later, her scream still ringing in her ears, her skin wet with perspiration, she looked down her body. He looked up from between her legs, watching her, a look of male satisfaction on his face that made him all the more handsome and sexy.

She wanted him inside her more than she'd ever wanted anything in her life. She grasped his shoulders and said, 'Please'.

Rising, his body covered hers, thighs nudging hers apart. The tip of his erection brushed against her curls. 'Once we do this, Little Bird, there's no going back. Even though Lone Wolves don't mate, I know myself too well to think I could let you go after you give yourself to me in this way.'

She touched his cheek, met his gaze. 'What makes you think I'd leave even if you wanted me to go?'

He barked out a laugh. 'My stubborn Little Bird.'

'My equally stubborn Shadow.'

His eyes blazed and then his lips were on hers and with a flex of his hips, he was inside her.

She tensed as a tearing pain shot through her.

He stilled. 'Shh, shh,' he murmured, stroking her hair back from her face, then stroking down her arms to tangle his fingers with hers. 'It will be gone in a moment. Do you trust me?'

'Always.' Moving her hips up, she urged him to slide deeper.

And Goddess, he did!

The slow slide in and out filled her with so much pleasure, it was almost torture. She could hardly take it. She needed him to move faster. Needed more of him. All of him. Tilting her hips higher, she wrapped her legs around his waist, let go of his hands and grabbed his hips, urging him to move faster. He moaned into her mouth as he obliged her urging.

His chest hairs rubbed against her sensitised breasts, lightly at first, then harder as he wrapped an arm around her and lifted her up so they were sitting, him on his haunches, her with her legs wrapped around him, his cock buried even deeper inside her than before. His mouth captured her scream, holding her tight as he encouraged her to move, riding him, their bodies pressed so closely together it was difficult to know where she ended and he began.

His pace sped up, then she was on her back again, his hands

tilting her hips, giving him even deeper access. She moaned as he pressed deeper and deeper inside her.

'Oh ... My ... God ... dess,' she cried out as he pounded faster and faster into her. 'Iain. Iain. Iain!'

The last was said on a scream as the orgasm ripped through her. In some distant place, she heard Iain cry out her name before he collapsed on top of her, his heart thundering against her chest, his breath a harsh pant against her ear.

When neurons began to spark in her brain some time later, she couldn't help but smile. She was thoroughly and utterly taken. He had blown her mind—twice. Her first experience had been more than she could have ever hoped for.

Despite the fact that her bones had turned to mush, she managed to wrap her arms around him, hold on tight and kiss his neck.

She never wanted to let him go. Never wanted this to end.

But it had to.

The sobering thought made her shiver, her grip on him slipping. Tears pricked her eyes, but she couldn't let him see them, so she turned her head, biting her lip, hoping she would be able to pull it together before he recovered.

As the thought circled in her mind, he lifted his head. 'Hey! What's this?' He touched her cheek.

She should have known he'd recover quickly—he was a Were after all. 'Nothing,' she sniffed.

'Did I hurt you? I know it was your first time. I shouldn't have been so rough.'

'Oh, Goddess no!' She brushed her thumb over his lips, a bubbling laugh escaping as he chased it playfully to give it a little nip. 'It was perfect.'

His grin was lopsided, his gaze filled with pleasure. 'It was for me too.'

'Really?'

'Really.' He kissed her nose, her forehead, her eyes, her lips. 'You are truly amazing, Eloise.'

'I think that's my line.'

He chuckled. 'It's both our lines.'

He was still inside her, still so large. She frowned. 'Didn't you ... you know ...?'

His lips twitched. 'I think if you've experienced it twice you can say the word, Little Bird.'

'Smug!' She slapped his arm. 'I wanted to know if you came too.'

His smug smile disappeared as he touched his forehead to hers, his breath a warm puff against her face. 'Oh, I came. Didn't you hear me?'

'I heard you roar my name.' Her skin heated. 'But I don't know ... that could have been a Were thing.'

'No. That was an "Eloise, you blow my mind and make me come like I've never come before" kind of thing.'

She tried to stop the smile from breaking out but couldn't. 'Really?'

'Really.'

She bit the corner of her lip, uncertain how to ask. 'Then why ... how are you ... I mean I can feel—' She waved her hand towards where they were still joined so intimately.

He chuckled. 'Now, that *is* a Were thing. It happens when we have mind-blowing sex and is the first step in the ma—' A strange expression crossed his face. 'No. It's not possible,' he whispered.

'What's not possible?' she said, shifting a little under him, aware that, despite his consternation, he had suddenly grown bigger inside her. He blinked and looked down at her, the expression in his eyes one of wonder and unutterable joy. It was a look that made her feel treasured and special and she couldn't help but smile back at him in the face of it. 'Iain?'

'It's not possible. Unless—' His gaze raked over her face. 'Can we have been wrong?'

He kissed her, stealing her breath, making her jerk beneath him as something powerful and golden tugged deep inside her heart. It squeezed, spread, wrapped around her, fired all her nerve endings, but before she could even gasp, it was gone.

No. Not gone.

But it didn't hurt anymore. It just was. 'What was that?'

'Something miraculous.' His words whispered across her lips and then he was kissing her again, the heated passion of it stealing her breath, her words, her thoughts as she lost herself in sensation once more.

19

Sometime later, after they'd made love again and he'd held her for what seemed like minutes but could have been hours, he lifted his head, thumbs making lazy circles on her cheeks. 'You should sleep. It's been a long, hard day.'

'Shouldn't we go join the wake?'

He glanced at the clock. 'It would be over by now.'

'Then we should go and tell the others about what Cain said.'

'Jason and Skye will be with Gabbie's family right now. The others are probably asleep.'

She sighed. She wished she could sleep, but Cain was out there, waiting for her to do as he wished and there was a time constraint on her doing just that.

Oestra. The full moon. It was tonight. If she didn't move soon, Cain would come looking for her and she knew what he'd do if he found her here, in Iain's arms. She shuddered.

'Cold?'

He reached for her but she shifted away. 'No.' She pushed up onto her elbows, brushed her fingers over his forehead. 'It's not that. And I can't sleep, not now. Not until after I've done what needs to be done tonight.'

'What are you talking about?'

She clutched the sheet to her breasts as she sat up, face stiff with the knowledge she was about to tear the beautiful feeling rising between them to shreds. 'I have to tell at least you what happened with Cain.'

His jaw tensed, lips thinning into a tight line. 'I know what happened with Cain. The bastard killed Gabbie. Tried to kill me, too.' His gaze burned with violence as he looked at her. 'I want to kill him.'

'No! You can't.' She tried to swallow down the panic in her throat, but the look in his eyes wedged it there.

'I know he's your brother, Eloise, but he's a murdering psychopath and deserves to die.' He sat up, swung his legs over the edge of the bed, back to her. She wanted to reach out, stroke the long, muscled length of his spine, but the warmth between them had become some brittle, tenuous thing at the mention of her brother. As she knew it would.

As she wrapped her arms around her knees, her instinct was to press into the corner, to shrink away from the violence and hatred emanating off him in waves. But she'd come too far to react like she used to. Couldn't let a lifetime of repression take over when she needed to stick to her guns, to act, to ensure what needed to be done was done before anyone else was hurt. Or killed.

Fingers gripping into her skin through the sheet, she forced herself to speak. 'I don't want to save Cain because he's my brother. I know he deserves to die. I wish we could go right now and put him out of his misery.'

He peered at her over his shoulder. 'You're just saying that because you think it's what I want to hear.'

She flinched. Couldn't help it. His words hurt. 'I thought you knew me better than that.' She scrambled past him off the end of the bed, losing the sheet in her effort.

'Eloise. I'm sorry. Eloise!' He grabbed her before she'd made it halfway across the room to the ensuite. She fought him when he tried to turn her around, desperate for him not to see her tears, so he pulled her back against him. His warmth, his strength, seeping into her back, drew all the fight right out of her.

'I'm sorry.' His apology was a warm breath across her ear. 'I shouldn't have said that. I'm just so angry. My wolf … I … am grieving. He … we, lashed out. I'm sorry. I do know you. I know you're in pain too over what your twin did.'

'My twin is dead. That thing out there today is some creation of Morrigan's. I don't know who he is.'

'I know. I know.' His lips brushed over her shoulder. Up her neck. 'Forgive me. Please forgive me.' He took her earlobe between his teeth, sucking gently. She moaned, leaned back against him.

'I should be asking your forgiveness. If it wasn't for me, Gabbie would still be alive.'

'No. Don't think that. Don't let my stupid words make you ever think that.' He gripped her shoulders and she turned then, needing to see his face, to read the truth of his feelings in his eyes, to see that the lash of his anger wasn't aimed at her.

He cupped her face, his gaze telling her she was everything precious and wonderful to him. 'You are not responsible for what Cain did.'

'I know.'

He smiled, a breath of relief brushing over her face. 'Then why did you say that?'

'I just meant that if I hadn't gone down there, he wouldn't have done what he did.'

'I think he would have done it anywhere, no matter where you were.'

He was right. She knew he was right.

'So why did he do it? What do you need to tell me?'

'Can I get dressed first?' She couldn't have this conversation with both of them naked. There was too much of what they'd just shared still between them, and she didn't want Cain there too, the evilness of him touching places only Iain had ever touched.

'Okay.'

They dressed in silence and when she was finally done, she sat on the armchair in the corner, Iain perched opposite on the bed, a careful expression on his face, gaze boring into hers. Goddess. What was he going to say? She wished she didn't have to tell him.

'Eloise? What did you agree to?'

She flinched at the worry in his tone. 'How do you know I agreed to anything?'

'Because he didn't kill me. He could have, but he didn't. I know that's because you agreed to do what he wanted. So what was that?'

'He won't attack.' Her voice sounded so far away it was a mere echo of who she once was. 'He won't attack if I do as he says.'

'And what does he want?'

'Cain can only do what he's doing at the moment because he's split his soul from his body. He's incredibly dangerous as a Shade. You saw what he did ... felt it. He'll do that to as many of the Were as he can get to for the time he has remaining as a Shade. Unless I heal him, bring soul and body back together.' She glanced up at him, away. 'If I do it, he'll be less of a threat.'

'We should just kill him.'

'No! That won't work. He's blood bound with Morrigan, drawing from her. And from me. If you kill him, it means he could stay a Shade for months, in which time he could travel where he likes and do what he likes given there would be no tether to his body at all. And what he likes is to kill everyone. Not only that, he'd drain me and Morrigan to do it. And you wouldn't be able to stop him.'

He was suddenly across the room, kneeling in front of her, hands on her shoulders, forcing her to meet his gaze. 'Could he kill you if he drained you too much?'

She shrugged. 'Possibly. But I don't care about that.'

'No you wouldn't. But I do.' He drove his fingers through his hair. 'Fuck!'

She grabbed his hand, held it still. 'Iain, I'm not worried about what he can do to me because before things even get to a point where he might drain me of life, he could do untold damage to your pack.

To my friends. To you.' Her voice broke, but she kept on; had to make him see. 'He'd do it just to teach me a lesson. But if I bring his soul back to his body, he won't be able to go where he likes. You'll have him as prisoner and under your control. You can limit his magic by putting one of those magical restriction cuffs on him.'

'He's already wearing one.'

'That's why he did this,' she said, the full horror of it overwhelming her. 'He needed his magic and you'd cut him off from it.' She looked up at him, pushed her emotions down—they had no place in this. 'We have to return him to his body. It's the only way to keep everyone safe.'

'But if you do that, can't he just become a Shade again if we don't let him go and stop him from using his magic?'

'No. You can only do what he's done once. If you do it again, there is no coming back.'

'Won't he try to kill you himself when he wakes up?'

She shook her head, unsure of how she was able to keep talking. 'He says I belong to him. He apologised for trying to kill me.'

'And you believe him?'

'Yes. You didn't hear him. He truly thinks I belong to him. He doesn't want me dead if there's another alternative. Besides, you'll be there to stop him if he tries anything.'

'You're bloody right I will. And a dozen other soldiers as well.' He ran his hands down her arms, gripping her hands. 'He won't harm you again. I won't allow it.'

She looked at his large hands enveloping hers, their strength, their warmth. The burning cold wasn't as bad when he touched her and, even though she knew it was wrong to fall into the trap of needing him, she couldn't bring herself to break away. 'I won't allow him to hurt you either. I won't allow him to hurt anyone else.'

His gaze held hers for a moment and then he was kissing her, fierce, possessive, desperate. She kissed him back, no less fierce, no less possessive, no less desperate. This might be the last moment they had together because she had no idea if she was truly strong enough to survive what she had to do tonight.

But that didn't matter. The pack mattered. Most of all, Iain mattered. She would die before she let any harm come to him or those he loved.

She gave herself to the kiss for as long as she dared, but before it could turn into something more, something she ached for, she pulled away. Breath mingling with his, she held his face in her hands. 'Call Jason and the others. Marcus and Cordy too. We have to tell them what Cain wants.'

'They won't want to agree. They'll think killing him the better option.'

'We'll make them see it's not.'

'Yes. We will.' He paced over to the bedside table, picked up his phone and began to make calls.

Warmth chased the cold of apprehension from her body at his absolute trust in her; at the way he backed her, no question. She'd never had that. Ever. Not from her parents, or Morrigan or even Cain, truth be told.

She knew now why that was; that she was a fool to ever have expected it from them given she had never been theirs. They'd only managed to love Cain because he was what they'd always wanted—a powerful male witch in the family. But she—she was too different. Something they feared as much as hated because of her difference. Because she was reminder of the evil they'd done. They'd fooled her into thinking their lack of love for her was her fault. But the truth was far worse. Morrigan, her parents, the coven, had been her kidnappers. She knew enough about shifters now to know that like the Were, they would never give up their young freely. No, she and Cain had been taken by bloody force and all these years she'd been made to feel less, to feel worthless, because of it.

Despite all this, because of her innate need to belong, a need she was only now coming to understand, she'd come to love the liars even though they'd never loved her; believed in them even though they'd never believed in her; believed their truths were her truths even though they were lies. She'd been brainwashed by them. She'd been their fool.

She wouldn't be their fool anymore.

Cain thought her weak and unable to think for herself. He thought she would allow him to commit genocide. He didn't know her at all.

So where did that leave her?

A witch without a coven. A shifter without a pack or pride or family or whatever they called themselves. Fuck, she didn't even know that. But she was going to find out. Just like she was going to find out where she did come from, right after she'd thought of a way to stop Cain from doing something that would destroy his soul and hers along with it if he succeeded, murdering a whole lot of innocent people along the way. She wouldn't let him do that. She wouldn't let him darken his soul any further.

She wanted to believe there was some way back for him, even though there probably wasn't. Something had taken him over. The same evil that was inside Morrigan. She had no idea if there was a way to exorcise it and stop insanity from unfolding; but there had to be.

It couldn't end like this.

Perhaps that's what she'd do after she'd finished tonight. Figure out the origin of the Darkness in Morrigan, what it ultimately wanted. Maybe being the Nexus meant she could stop it.

The thought made her breathless. Could she? She had no idea. There was a lot of ground to cover before then. So much to learn. It made her sick to think of it. Sick and small.

No! That wasn't who she was anymore. She was someone who acted. Who wasn't afraid of the long term or the bigger picture. She would convince Jason and the others that she had to do what Cain wanted. There was no other choice.

'It's going to be okay, Eloise.' Iain had put down the phone, his eyes a hot, amber blaze in the semi-dark as he stared at her from across the room.

'I know.'

He strode to her then pulled her up from the chair and into his arms. 'You believe me?'

'Yes. But more importantly, I believe in me.'

A smile broke out over his face that felt like the sun. 'Let's go tell them how it's going to be then.'

'Let's go.' She took his outstretched hand and let him lead her out the bedroom door. She'd expected him to lead her to the kitchen to meet with the others, but they headed out the front door and to the right of the house. 'Where are we going?'

Iain gestured at a large barn sitting at the far side of the home paddock. 'Jason and the others returned to Melbourne last night after the wake—he wanted to give us privacy for our night together.'

'Oh. He knows?'

'Jason's my Alpha. He knows most of what goes on in the pack. And what he knows, his senior people know.'

'Okay. Still, I didn't expect them to leave after what happened.'

'They know that.' He smiled down at her. 'Living in a pack can be full-on, but we do respect a pack member's right to privacy. There are still Were on the property looking after the farm and your coven-mates, but the rest returned to where they're needed most.'

She nodded, grateful nobody was here last night to hear her enthusiasm for what had happened between her and Iain. What was between them was still too intimate and new to share with anyone else like that. 'So only a few of them know then.'

He looked a bit self-conscious. 'Actually, even with the distance, it's hard to hide from the pack something like what we shared last night. They would have felt the excess of positive emotion emanating from me through the Packbond and, while they wouldn't exactly know the cause, many of them know me well enough to guess.'

'Oh.' She cleared her throat, her face and neck unbearably hot. 'So everyone knows we ... we made love.'

'Yes, and everyone will be thrilled.'

'Why?'

'Because you made me happy. And you gave something positive to the pack.'

'I did?' She grimaced. 'I expect they'll want me to talk about it.'

'Not if you don't want to.'

'Good. What was between us is mine ... and yours. It's ours.'

'Damn right it is.' He laughed, a short sharp joyful bark of sound, and kissed her head. 'I know it's all strange, but I promise you will get used to it. You'll have to if you're going to be with me.'

Going to be with him? Oh Goddess. She longed for that more than she'd ever longed for anything, but was it possible? Could they overcome all the obstacles in their way and become truly partnered? And did he want the same?

It was a sobering, aching thought. She stopped walking.

He stopped and turned, pulling her gently to face him, fingers brushing her cheek in that way that made her heart race and ache with warmth. 'Eloise? What's wrong?'

'Can we? Be together? I mean, Bron has told me a little about what it is to be a Lone Wolf. I know you feel something deep for me, something that confuses you as much as it confuses me, but feels right at the same time ...' He nodded, encouraging her to go on. 'But Lone Wolves, by nature, long to be alone. So can we truly be together? I know you don't mate. I can accept that.' She shrugged, smiled. 'I don't know if I can mate with anyone anyway. There's so much I don't know about myself. I don't even know what the future might hold after tonight. I don't even know why I'm thinking about any of this, why it matters, with Cain and Morrigan out there determined to destroy everything important to me.' She raked her hand through her hair. 'I'm not even making sense to myself, so how can you figure out what I'm trying to say?'

He made a huffing sound. 'I know what you're trying to say, Little Bird, because the same thought worries me too.'

'It does?'

'Yes. You deserve every good thing in life there is to experience and I worry that I can never be that, not truly, for you. But what I do know is, I have never felt like this before about anyone else and my wolf feels connected with you in a way that has never happened before. Not even with our Alpha. I'm not sure what that means or if it will last forever, but what I know is that even the Lone Wolf needs a place to call home; something to come back to. My pack has always been that for me, always there to support me and take me in, no matter how long I wander alone. I think, perhaps, you are becoming that for me too. That without you to come home to, my wolf would go rabid, just as it would have gone rabid in the past without my pack. A part of me belongs to you. I want you to know that.'

Oh, his words thrummed through her, an ache she never wanted to be rid of. Perhaps she was an idiot, standing here, talking about belonging when there was so much at stake, but she needed those words. Needed to have them twine with her soul, to strengthen the beat of her heart. And Iain knew it. Knew exactly the right thing to say. How did he know her so well?

My beloved.

The voice was a mere breath in her head, but it shuddered through her, making her gasp.

'Eloise?'

She met his gaze. 'I feel the same about you, Iain. There's a part of me that will always belong to you.'

He cupped her face, eyes blazing with heated passion, but his lips met hers with the lightest of caresses. She whimpered as he pulled away and his lips twitched into a satisfied smile. 'No matter how much I want to explore this and what it means, we have to go. Jason and the others will be waiting.'

'Yes. Of course.' She forced herself to step back, to move to the door. 'So what's in the barn?'

His smile widened. 'You're going to like this.' He pulled open a panel in the wall. Behind the panel was a keypad. He pressed a couple of numbers and then put his thumb onto a plate that slid out of the wall. A moment later the large double wooden doors slid open. 'After you.'

She tried not to show her surprise as she stepped inside—she really shouldn't be surprised about anything after what she'd seen and been through in the weeks since she'd woken, especially after what had happened today—but it was difficult when instead of the scent of dry hay she'd expected, there was the sterile scent of cleaning fluids, the slightly sweet scent of wax and a hint of oil. Instead of rotting wooden walls, there was gleaming black polished cement. Along one wall ran a workbench with all the tools a motoring enthusiast could ever need, and at the far end of the barn was a car hoist. Dust motes danced in the stream of sunlight that came in through the dust-covered window set high in the far wall.

The sunlight danced across a line of gleaming cars, each one more expensive than the next.

'Holy shit!'

'I knew you'd like them.'

'Like them?' She took a few steps forward on stiff legs. 'This is something out of a dream.' Her gaze roamed greedily over the ten cars before her. Cars. They weren't just cars.

They were works of art.

'Want to work on them, do you?'

'Oh, Goddess, yes.' She clasped her hands together. 'Although these are nothing like the old cars we had in the coven. My dad used to talk about cars like this when I'd help him with the old Rovers and Holdens we had. He spoke their names in a hushed, reverent tone.' Names like Porsche and Ferrari and BMW and Jaguar. 'Special. Exotic. I never thought I'd get to see one, let alone be close enough to touch.'

'When we're done with Cain and Morrigan, you can do more than touch.'

She spun, breath a clutch in her throat. 'Really?'

Iain touched her cheek. 'Of course. I'm sure Gareth won't mind sharing his domain with you. Not after you helped save him last year.' He looked around, his grin a lopsided slash in his face. 'Besides, I think we're going to have trouble keeping you away from this place now you've seen it.'

'I think you might be right.'

Iain's lips twitched as he walked over to the wall and pressed a switch. Lights came on overhead.

The cars' highly polished duco gleamed like starlight. She knew she should concentrate on getting to Cain, but with such beauty in front of her, it was difficult to focus on anything else. A little dizzy with lust, images of her sitting in those cars, driving them, or bent over the open bonnet, greasy hands inside the darling engines, swept through her.

She pressed her hands tighter against her stomach.

'We'll take my car.' He gestured at a red Ferrari.

'This is yours?' she breathed, moving closer. The dancing horse badge was something she never thought to see up so close. She wanted to touch it. But couldn't. She'd leave a smear on it or something. 'One of these is worth the price of a house.'

'I earn good money.' Iain grinned as he thumbed the keys in his hand. The door nearest them swung up. 'I like to go fast. Do you want to drive?' He held the keys out to her.

Her heart leaped into her throat. That he would trust her that much was a gift beyond words. But she couldn't. Not now. Not with her mind in too many places to take care of such a precious gift and treat it with the homage it deserved. 'Next time?'

He smiled softly, understanding in his eyes. 'Definitely.' He walked her around to the passenger door, opened it up. 'Now in you hop.'

Tentatively, she lowered herself onto the seat, breathing in the scent of leather. Her mouth dried as the door closed with a swish and click.

Then reality pushed forward again, past her awe and the luxury of the car she was in. They were heading to Melbourne and she had to convince the Alphas of two packs that what she had to do tonight was the only way.

Iain slid into the driver's seat, his gaze immediately on her. 'Are you okay?'

'Let's just go.'

His hand curled over hers and she met his amber gaze. 'They'll trust you. Just like I do.'

She managed a small smile. 'I know.'

The question was, would the burgeoning strength she had found inside be enough to gain her what she wanted more than anything else? To belong. To be loved. Her gaze flickered to Iain and then back to the road ahead.

Only time would tell, and right now, time wasn't on her side.

The car started up with a rumbling purr and then they were flying out of the barn and down the driveway to the road beyond.

20

Bridgette stood in front of the altar, perspiration running between her naked breasts, prickling at the base of her spine. Exhaustion made her upraised arms tremble. Her knees locked tight against the quiver she could feel in the marrow of her bones.

She had to keep going only a little while longer. This was the last pack in the Highlands and as of a moment ago, she'd linked them to herself as she had all the covens in the area. She'd repeated this ceremony hundreds of times in the last months since she'd begun her quest to save her race from the destruction of their own power—and of course, to save the Were from the Darkness that had been hellbent on destroying them.

Her best friend, Morghanna Cantrae, the coven's Medium, had spent months contacting as many other covens and packs as she could through the spirits and the aether, to invite them into the fold. She was now travelling to the European nations to join them via the Pact spell in Bridgette's stead. When she returned, she would be linked along with those left of her original coven with the second most powerful pack in the Highlands: the MacCraes.

Bridgette missed her terribly, but it was necessary.

Cecily, their coven's Healer was doing the same essential job in the Baltic States. Connor, a powerful Seer was helping her and trying to find anyone they may have missed and making the offer to them.

And an offer it was. She would not force anyone.

Sadness swept through her at the thought of Morghanna's beloved yet headstrong sister, Morrigan. Morghanna still wept over Morrigan's denial of the need for the Pact. She had railed at Morrigan for her stubbornness—stubbornness that was mystifying given how both their parents had died. One would think Morrigan would side with them in the fight for their people and their survival. But no. She said she would find another way and Bridgette had made Morghanna let her go on her various forays away from the safety of the coven. The young witch was determined to discover another solution to the duel problem of their powers imploding and the need to hide who and what they were from the inquisitors.

Bridgette knew it was a hopeless task, as there was no other way. She had looked into every future, every option, and this had been the only path that had a hope of success. But she would not force Morrigan to accept. The girl would find her way back to them. Of that she was certain. She loved her sister more than life itself. It was that love, that need to protect, that drove her now.

Bridgette just had to hope Morrigan would remain safe while she travelled, not only from the inquisitors, but from the build of her own powers.

She held her head high, face tilted to the moon as she shouted the final words to complete the cycle of binding and rid this pack of their burden of Darkness forever. Her voice was hoarse, but her words still rang with power as she banished the Darkness back to the nether it had come from. It screamed its defiance, but even though it had become more desperate with every purging, it had no power against the combined might of her powers mixed with her beloved Goddess'.

The light spun bright about her. The Were howled to the moonlight as the moondust she'd summoned sifted down on them, releasing them from the cursed torture of their trapped wolves and allowing them to feel a harmony with their animal side they'd never felt before. No longer made rabid from a month-long incarceration inside human flesh, the wolves could live in harmony with their human sides, unfettered and in control of their base nature. No Were would ever rampage through the night, murdering innocents, feeding on human flesh in an orgy of hatred. The Pact would create order from chaos.

The Witch-Were Pact would save them all.

The silver glow that surrounded her flickered out as the last of the Were ran off into the night to rejoice in their ability to change at will. It would only last a few days, a week at most, with the power she'd given them tonight, but it was enough for now. The local coven they would be linked to would give this gift to them when she finished the working. Once the final spell was in place, every witch and warlock who agreed would be bonded to a pack, would be bound to that pack for eternity through their bloodlines, sharing of their power and existing in harmony with those who saved them with their need.

Her arms dropped to her side and her knees buckled.

'I have ye, my lady.'

Bridgette smiled in relief as strong hands caught her, stopping her from crashing to the ground. 'Malcolm.' His name was a mere puff of breath as he covered her in a cloak and swept her into his arms, carrying her from the Dance.

He'd stood just outside the ring of stones as she performed the ritual, just like he'd stood every night as they brought more packs into the fold. He was strong and sure and always at her side looking after her every need. 'How do you always know when I need you most?'

'I am Sgàth, yer Sgàth, my lady.'

'You are.' She tried to make out his face as he carried her through the edge of the wood, but it was difficult as the only source of light was the moon high above, its light flickering through the canopy of trees. She willed him to look at her, but he didn't. She felt the loss of his warm gaze as a shiver through her bones.

'Are ye not well, my lady?'

'I am simply tired.'

'Ye shouldna' have worked yer spell tonight.'

'I had to. The power of my pregnancy married with the power of Oestra on this first night of vernal equinox enabled me to reach all the packs in this area at once. It would have taken much longer if I had not cast out the Darkness tonight and bound them to me with the power of the Goddess's rebirth.'

He sighed but argued no further. 'I built a fire in the shepherd's cottage. It is rough, aye, but there is a pallet of fresh straw. Ye will rest there afore we move on the morrow.'

'That sounds blissful.'

She lay in his arms, head on his shoulder, enjoying the heady sound of his heart beating in his chest and began to doze. She awoke as he laid her down on something soft.

'Where are we?'

'In the cottage. Sleep mo ghrá. Ye are tired.'

He bent over her, laying a blanket over her legs. A fire glowed in the hearth and by its light she could now see his features. Reaching up, she touched his face as he bent over her, wanting him to look at her. 'What about you, my Shadow. Will you not take some rest?'

'Nae. Not yet. I will guard ye.' He straightened.

'What danger can come to me here? The covens and the packs in this area are now our friends. They would not see us harmed.'

'Nae. But they are no' the only ones nearby. There ha' been burnings in this region, and other attacks aside. I wouldna risk yer safety.'

She sighed. 'You are a good Shadow, Malcolm. I will tell the McVale of your devotion to your task.'

Those bright, gold-flecked green eyes pierced her in the semi-dark, something wild and passionate flaming there. 'I do no do it to impress my Alpha.'

Bridgette's throat went dry. 'Then why are you here?'

His gaze bored into her as in a low, husky voice, he said, 'Ye ken why.'

She shook her head.

'Ye do. Dinna tell me ye dinna ken it when ye feel it in every glance atween us.' He cupped her cheek and Goddess help her, she couldn't help but lean into it. 'When ye long fer my touch.' He gripped her hand, held it against his chest. 'When yer heart beats apace with mine. Ye ken.'

She held herself still, her jaw clenched against the desire to admit to him the secret want inside her, marring her soul.

It was impossible. Couldn't he see that? She could not take a lover. She could not love again. Not like that. Not like this. Not like he wanted, needed, deserved. She'd had her chance. She had children already, was pregnant again by the man she'd once loved and lost in the most insidious way. She could not take the chance at such pain of loss ever again.

'Why canna ye admit that you want me?'

Oh, Goddess. Such pain and desire in his voice as to be impossible to deny. *Why must you do this to me? Why now?* she railed silently to her Goddess. She couldn't lose him as her Shadow. Not now. Not when she needed his strength so.

But there was no answer because the only answer could come from inside her. 'I do not want to hurt you, Malcolm, but I cannot give you what you want.'

He growled, the low hum of it vibrating deep inside her, tugging at her desire. 'Ye are my mate.'

'No!' She scrambled up from the pallet, away from him to the other side of the room. 'No.'

But he was at her side in an instant. 'Aye. Ye are my mate.'

'But you're a Lone Wolf.'

'Lone Wolves mate, but only to one who speaks to their soul on every level.'

'You're mistaken.'

'Nae. I am not. Yer very scent is imprinted in my heart.' He leaned forward and dragged his nose across her collarbone. She had to bite her tongue to stop from groaning, but he heard it. She could tell by the smile that curled on his lips that he knew she was weakening to him.

'I belong to nobody but myself.'

'I dinna want to own ye, Bridgette. I wish to share everything I am with ye. Ye are my mate. I kenned it the very first time I saw ye. As ye ken it now, even tho' ye would deny it.'

'No. You imagined it.'

'This isna something I ever imagined. Were never mate with humans, and bonds atween yer kind and mine are almost as unusual. And for a Lone Wolf to find a soulmate—even more impossible. Yet it is so.'

She shook her head, opening her mouth to protest, to stop him from saying what sounded like truth but couldn't be, but he put his fingers over her lips, gaze never leaving hers. 'Aye. I speak truth as ye well know. I could no more deny the bond that sprang into place than I could deny how beautiful ye are. Or how powerful. I ken I shouldna even deign to be in the presence of one such as ye. Our backgrounds are agin' us, but I dinna think ye are one of those highborn women who care about such things and I canna deny how I feel any longer.'

His words were like a warm stroke inside her, his soft Scots burr reshaping her soul. She tried to resist it, resist him, but the longer he stood there this close, his breath brushing over her face, his heat radiating into her in a way that was disturbing her in too many ways to fathom, one hand's fingers circling her wrist, the other stroking her cheek, making shivers cascade all over her body, she knew it was becoming increasingly impossible.

Even so, she had to stop him. Tell him so that he understood. 'I cannot be with you, Malcolm.'

He tensed, his nostrils flaring. 'I am no' good enough for ye. I ken that. But I dinna think it would worry ye so. Mayhap I were wrong.' He let go of her and turned away.

'No!' Her denial was too sharp, almost desperate. 'No,' she said more gently as he turned back to face her. 'You were right. I do not care about status. What matters is what kind of person you are—and Malcolm, you are the best man I have ever met.'

Joy bloomed in his eyes and he took a step towards her again, but before he could come too close, she put her hand out, planting it on his chest. He stopped. His heart beat hard and strong through the swell of his pectoral muscles. One of his nipples was under her palm —it pebbled to her touch. She swallowed hard again, knew she should pull her hand away. But touching him felt so good. He was so good. 'But it doesn't change things.' She cleared her husky throat. 'Because I still cannot be with you in that way.'

'Ye deny ye feel for me?'

She hesitated. She couldn't lie to him. He would know. 'You are more than my Shadow. You have become my friend and confidant. My strength.'

His mouth crooked up at the side as if he found what she said amusing, but there was no amusement in his glowing eyes. 'Friends dinna tremble when they touch.'

'I am not trembling,' she said, her voice a bare husk. He looked down pointedly at her hand, which was still planted on his chest. She swallowed hard.

Before she could pull away, he grasped her wrist, holding her hand there.

Oh Goddess. It was too much. Too much. 'Please, do not do this.'

'Ye feel it.' He inched closer.

'You are incorrect.' Her breath hitched.

He took the step that brought their bodies flush, that trapped her hand against his chest. 'Ye feel it.' His hands slid up her arms to her shoulders.

She shivered, her breath coming hard and fast and hot in her chest. 'I do not.'

'Ye feel it.' His fingers wound into her hair, pulling her face up, lips inches from hers.

'You are wr—'

His lips covered hers.

She stiffened as lights exploded behind her eyes. The sensation of his lips—so firm to look at, but so soft in reality—overwhelmed her senses. A small part of her mind tried to tell her she was exhausted, and that was why she was having this reaction to his kiss. Why she couldn't push away. But as energy shot through her and her power expanded, shimmering from her skin and into him, she knew it for a lie. Something else was happening here and she couldn't control it. Couldn't stop it.

His tongue swept across her lips, cajoling, demanding entrance. On a moan, she opened to him.

He didn't sweep in though like she expected him too. He nipped her bottom lip and then followed the tease by sucking her lip into his mouth. She moaned again, hands sliding up his chest to clutch at his shoulders before diving into his silky dark hair.

It was then and only then his tongue met hers. She welcomed the intimacy as if it were manna from heaven. She'd never felt anything so good as the way Malcolm kissed; with his entire being. He kissed her as if he needed her; truly needed her. As if he could not survive if he did not keep his mouth on hers.

However, if she didn't stop this madness, she would be the one who wouldn't survive. She wrenched away from him, stepped back, tried to create some distance. Her back hit the wall behind her. She blinked up at him. He smiled, stepped closer, pressing against her once more.

She moaned at the delicious sensation of his muscles pressed along the length of her, the friction of her breasts against his hard chest. Without thought, she slid her hands into his hair. She saw his grin just before he bent to take her mouth with his again. The hard length of him ground against her as his tongue played with hers. Her fingers tightened in his hair.

He growled low in his throat. The growl vibrated through her and her womb clenched. *Let go. You must let go. Must stop this.* But she couldn't listen to that last voice of sanity in her head. She couldn't.

His mouth left hers and she whimpered until his hot, hot lips pressed wet kisses down the length of her throat, coming to a stop where her pulse beat wildly against her skin. He bit down lightly. She jerked, but didn't pull away, the building heat inside her tied in some inexplicable way to the sensation of his teeth on her neck.

She wanted more. More.

He cupped her bottom, pulling her even tighter against him. The sensation made her want to scream, but it wasn't enough.

She wasn't close enough. She ground into him.

His cock flexed against her and this time he groaned.

'Bridgette. I need to be inside ye. Now.'

'Yes.' She knew she shouldn't have said it but couldn't stop the word exploding out of her mouth. She was flying, filled with a burning need she hadn't felt for years.

No. That was wrong. She had never felt something that burned this bright, this hot.

His warm breath against her neck, her cheek, her mouth, he lifted her in his arms to lay her down on the pallet once again. His hand swept over her and her gown fell open, baring her to his gaze.

For a brief moment she was cold, alone, vulnerable, but then her gaze met his and the fire of desire blazing there, for her and only her, warmed her from her toes to her head, lingering in swirling pools of tugging heat in her womb, her breasts. Liquid warmth pooled between her thighs and his nostrils flared as the scent of her desire filled the air. He had seen her naked over and over, every time she had performed the ceremony to bond the Were and covens to her and the Goddess. But if he'd looked at her like this then, she'd missed it.

A smile tilted his lips, so sexy it made her womb clench tighter, and he leaned forward, his hand tracing the path his eyes had previously taken. He lingered over the small bulge of the child growing in her womb—a child that was treasured, despite having been begot in violence. The way his hands stroked over her, he treasured the growing soul inside her the same way she did.

'Sex cannot harm the bairn.' His voice was strained, husky with his desire.

'I know.' The way he cared for her and the babe took her breath away.

Then he kissed her again and all thought exploded. His hands moved from her rounded stomach to her breasts. She arched into his touch, trembling, writhing. 'Now, my Shadow. Now.' Material tore as he pulled off his trousers then he was on top of her, his legs, hard and hair-roughened, rubbing in the most delicious way. The tip of his erection pressed against her entrance. She tensed, waiting for him to push inside her like her husband had when the passion took him. But he didn't.

'Open yer eyes.'

She didn't want to. Didn't want to see the look in his eyes that told her this meant so much more than she was ready or willing to accept. She shifted, tried to push up, to force him to enter her, but he pushed her down with his hips.

'Open yer eyes, mo ghrá.'

'Kiss me. Take me now.'

His knuckles brushed over her nipple. She gasped, tensed. 'Not until ye open yer eyes.'

She shook her head.

He sucked her nipple into his mouth. She screamed and arched into him. His tongue twirled around the tight, sensitised bud, then he pulled back. Blew on the sensitised peak before covering it again with his entire mouth as his fingers speared into the wet folds between her legs, stroking, driving her to insanity. She tried to move, but he was merciless, tormenting her with his mouth on her breast and his fingers sliding around that little nub that could bring so much pleasure if only he would touch it.

Goddess! She would surely pass out with the exquisite build of tension winding deep inside her. 'Please. Please. Come inside me. I need it. Now.'

'Open yer eyes.'

She did as he asked, a sob in her throat. His gaze was a thunderstorm, wild and turbulent and so full of his certainty that they were mates, she could almost believe it true.

But it couldn't be true. She couldn't let it. Unable to meet that gaze any longer, she said, 'Kiss me.'

He did as she asked this time, still holding her hips down so she couldn't move up and onto him, his hands cupping her face. His lips moved over hers. She opened to him, brushing her tongue along his, seeking more. Deeper. He moved, brushing kisses along her jaw, her cheek, over her eyes. 'So beautiful.'

He pulled back, the pressure of his gaze like a stroke. She rolled her face to suck his thumb into her mouth, twirling her tongue around the tip.

'Fuck. Ye will be the death of me, mo ghrá.'

'Then take me now before this is the death of both of us.'

He spread his legs, opening hers, flexed his cock so it brushed over her entrance once, twice, then, lips meeting hers in a hot, hard tangle of tongue and teeth, he plunged inside her, swallowing her scream of relief and release.

Legs and arms wrapped around him, Bridgette gave herself over to the sensation of him moving against her, inside her.

She almost sobbed with the joy of it. After her husband had died, she had never thought to do this with anyone again. However, this could never be allowed to happen again after this night. He was mistaken—she wasn't his mate. He was just carried away with caring for her.

But right now, in this moment, she allowed herself to enjoy the feeling of a man, a wonderful man, inside her, making love to her with his body and soul as if she was the only thing in his life that held any importance.

It was a heady feeling.

And the orgasm, when it came, lifted her up and over, flying into the clouds so high she thought she might never come down.

So high, that for a moment, a blissful, delicious moment, she didn't worry about the future and what tomorrow might bring.

21

Eloise woke with a start when they stopped driving, the dream whispering tendrils of fog in her head, her body tingling with expectation. She jumped at Iain's touch.

'Eloise? Are you okay?'

She wasn't sure. Her dream had been so intense and the desire to crawl on top of him and repeat what she'd experienced in the dream was overpowering. Especially now she had first-hand knowledge of exactly what being with him felt like.

He seemed to know what was in her mind as she stared at him, because he frowned and grabbed her shoulders. 'Eloise? Are you there?'

She blinked. Okay, so maybe he didn't know what she was thinking. 'I'm here.'

'But your eyes. They're flashing from green-gold to swirling gold and back again.'

'Are they?'

'Yes. Like when your past-life presence took you over. Except, then your eyes were entirely swirling gold.'

She closed them, rubbed at her lids. 'It must be the dream. I was dreaming of them ... her. She must be close to the surface.'

'So she was making you look at me like that.'

Ah, so he had noticed. She could lie, deny her feelings, her hunger, but she wasn't the same person she'd been when she woke up from the coma. 'No. That was me. The dream made me remember last night. How you made me feel so alive, like I've never felt before. I want to feel that again. With you.'

'Eloise.' He sounded choked.

'What?'

'You undo me.' He reached for her.

She moaned as their lips met, as his tongue slid against hers. Right. So right.

Her mind swirled with images and thoughts and feelings, some which she recognised as hers, some which weren't. But she didn't care. Didn't care as long as he stayed pressed up against her, chest to chest, his lips on hers, drinking her in, echoing her hungry, needy sounds.

A tap sounded behind Iain on the glass and she jumped, face flaring hot as she glanced over Iain's shoulder.

A Were she'd not met peered through the car window looking a little chagrined. 'Sorry for interrupting, but Jason is waiting for you inside.'

Iain cupped her face in that possessive-gentle way she loved, his breath a hot pant against her face as he looked in her eyes as if to check she was alright. When she nodded, he leaned his forehead against hers. 'Later?'

She smiled, pulling back to look in his gorgeous eyes. 'I'll hold you to that.'

Grinning, he hopped out of the car and raced around the hood to open her door. Warm air swirled into the car along with the scents of many Were. Taking a deep breath, she took Iain's extended hand and allowed him to lead her into the house she'd last been in as an injured cat.

The Templestowe Packhouse looked so different from her human height. Bigger and smaller at the same time somehow. Her head span as she tried to rectify the images in her head from Bluebelle's viewpoint and what her human eyes were seeing now. Iain's hand on her arm brought her attention snapping back to him.

'What's wrong?'

She shrugged. 'Nothing. It's just so strange to be here again. It feels kind of wrong, like I shouldn't be. The last time I was here, I was spying on you all.'

'Things have changed. You've changed.'

That was the understatement of the year. Last time she was here, she'd been a spy, betraying the Were's kindness. Now she couldn't allow Cain to make her part of betraying them again. She had to do this. Had to make them let her wake Cain, and then she would make sure that he could never hurt any of them ever again.

Iain led her down the hallway to the lounge room. 'They'll be here soon. Jason and Marcus are just finishing up with a tour of the perimeter and Skye, Cordy and Shelley are finishing up a training session with Adam and River.'

'How do you know that?' He hadn't touched his phone since that one call he'd made before driving up here.

'It's a lieutenant thing.'

She nodded. She'd wondered last year if they had some internal way of communicating with each other. 'Okay.'

There was a shout outside—little-boy joy—and she went over to peer out. Tom was playing with the girl she knew was his nanny—she couldn't remember hearing her name last year when here but knew it was the same girl because she'd come to shepherd Tom away when Shelley had brought her in for healing.

As she watched them, she realised the little boy and his nanny weren't simply playing. They were searching for something.

Seconds later, Tom let out a whoop of excitement and held up a colourful foil-wrapped egg.

'What's he doing?'

Iain stepped up beside her. 'It's an Easter egg hunt.'

'Oh.' She'd read about them, but never experienced one. She wondered if chocolate eggs tasted as good as they sounded.

The little boy's laughter reached out to her, even through the thick glass of the floor-to-ceiling windows. It was amazing how joyful he sounded. He'd been so sad when she'd seen him at the wake the night before. It was a testament to Jason, Adam, Skye and their pack that the little boy was capable of such joy even in times of grief for the pack. Even more remarkable given he'd lost his parents, his grandparents, his other uncles and aunts in one accident—an accident caused by Morrigan and her desire for revenge.

How much more would he lose if she didn't find a way to stop her ex-mistress?

She couldn't stand that she was probably about to play into Morrigan's hand in saving Cain. She had no doubt Morrigan planned for Cain to do something horrifying when he was back in his body. She had to figure out what and stop him before he hurt these good people who had done nothing but be kind and generous to her. Before they destroyed the man who had shown her just how strong she could be and encouraged her to find who she really was.

She couldn't let them hurt him. She couldn't lose Iain just when she realised she loved him.

She gasped, hand to her mouth.

She loved him.

She turned, wanting to shout the words, to let them flow out of her mouth and cover them both with the joy of her discovery.

'Eloise?' he said, reaching for her.

'Iain, I—'

'Iain, mate.'

Her mouth slammed shut as Adam entered the room. Iain frowned a question at her, but she shook her head and took his outstretched hand. She'd tell him, but not now. Not in front of others.

Adam came forward and the two men shook hands. 'So …'

'Yes …'

They slapped each other's shoulders and then Adam grabbed Iain's forearm and pulled him forward to bump chests in a strange version of a hug and then stood back, nodding.

Eloise couldn't help but chuckle, bemused.

'What?' Adam asked.

She gestured between them. 'Other people would have taken a thousand words to get to that level of understanding, but you two did it in two. Plus a handshake-hug-chest-bump thing.'

'Are you dissing us, Little Bird?' Iain pulled her to his side.

'No. I guess I'm just a bit envious of how close you are. That you can communicate in such a simple way.'

Adam's eyes widened as he watched the two of them. She stiffened, getting ready for him to start telling her again he didn't trust her, but then strangely, he only leaned closer, his nostrils twitching as he took in a deep breath. 'It can't be.'

'What can't be, A?'

'Your scent—it's mingled with hers, almost as if—' He shook his head. 'No, it can't be possible.'

'What can't be possible?' Eloise didn't like Adam's tone. He almost sounded ... horrified? No, that wasn't it. But he wasn't pleased.

Adam clenched his jaw and swallowed hard, like he was swallowing bad medicine and had to choke it down. Then after a long moment passed, he said, 'I'm sorry for my rudeness earlier. I hope you can forgive me.'

'Am I hearing things?' Shelley said as she sauntered into the room, Skye beside her. 'Is Adam apologising to you? Next thing you know I'll see a dodo in the backyard.'

Skye snorted. 'Shelley, don't be mean. Adam's realised he was wrong about Eloise. It's a good thing—especially given he's like a weather vane for the pack.' She beamed at Eloise. 'The pack are beginning to trust you like we do.'

Given how Adam was behaving, Eloise didn't think that was it. And from the piercing question in Iain's eyes—a question Adam was studiously ignoring as he looked beyond her and out the window— she didn't think Iain believed it was simple acceptance because of the pack.

Shelley touched her arm. 'Nice to see you again so soon.'

'I wish it could be under better circumstances.'

'It can't be helped.'

'You should have seen the drama when I first came into the pack.'

Skye leaned in and gave her a hug. 'Things will settle down and then we can all truly get to know each other.'

Eloise couldn't help but feel warmed by their welcome. They really wanted her here. If she'd had any doubts left, they were gone now. 'I'd like that. A lot.'

'When are we getting this party started?' Adam asked as he flopped down into one of the cream lounges.

'Marcus is just discussing something with Cordy,' Jason said as he walked into the room. He sat in the lounge next to Skye. Her hand found its way into his immediately and he covered it with both of his. It was natural, protective, and they both seemed to relax a little with the touch. Eloise now understood why. She always felt more centred when Iain was with her, especially when he touched her.

'They won't be long. And River and Bron won't be long. He says she's just on a call to the Peninsula Packlands to check on your coven mates.'

'Oh, how are they?' Eloise asked. Cain said he wouldn't touch them, but she wasn't sure she could trust him about that. 'Have they recovered from what Cain did to them?'

There was a short silence while every eye in the room landed on her.

'Why does that matter? They were all part of what happened to Gabbie. They deserve to die.'

'Adam!' Shelley snapped.

'They had nothing to do with what happened to Gabbie,' Eloise said, voice hoarse with emotion. 'They attacked me. Only me. It was Cain who murdered Gabbie.' Every eye returned to her. Her knees trembled at the impact but she stood strong.

'Cain?' Skye turned to Jason. 'You never said. But how?'

Lips set in a pained grimace, thumb stroking over her hand, he said, 'Iain told me what happened via the Alpha-lieutenant link. I didn't want to worry you all until we'd had a chance to talk to Eloise and plan from there. I wanted her to be able to tell all of us together, rather than reliving that pain over and over.'

Adam seemed to vibrate in his seat and then sprang to his feet.

The motion made Shelley snap her mouth shut, her gaze troubled as she looked between Iain and Eloise's clasped hands and Adam pacing.

'This is bullshit. We should just go and kill the fucker right now and be done with it.'

'Adam!' Shelley tried to grab his arm but he shook her off.

'No. Why are we showing our enemies such mercy when they show us none? If none of the rest of you has the balls to do it, then let me.' He turned and sprang towards the door.

'Adam,' Jason was on his feet and in front of his brother, stopping him dead, before Eloise could even blink. Adam snarled at him, but Jason didn't let go. In fact, he seemed to grow larger, a low growl emitting out of his chest that vibrated through the entire room. The sound made Eloise want to cower, to run and hide. Iain's hand tensed around hers, but when she looked up at him, his eyes were fixed on his Alpha.

Adam fought for a moment longer, but then slumped, as if all the fight drained out of him in less than a blink. He looked up at Jason, eyes awash. 'I'm sorry.'

'I know. You're being ruled by the pack, their grief, anger, fear. But you're stronger than that, Adam. You know you are. Just as you know why we can't behave like our enemies. Mum and Dad taught you better than that.'

Adam dragged his hand across his face, swiping at the tears. 'I know. I know.'

Marcus and Cordy chose that moment to enter the room. Eloise could practically feel Marcus' wolf bristle in response to the tension.

'What's going on?' Cordy asked, eyes wide, stepping past Marcus, even though he was obviously trying to hold her back.

'Nothing.' Jason turned to stand in front of Adam.

'It doesn't feel like nothing,' Marcus growled, his voice a low rasp —honey over gravel—that made Eloise think there was little difference between this man and his wolf.

'We're breaking new ground here with pack relationships,' Skye said, joining Jason. 'Sometimes things get a little ... unexpected.'

Cordy's gaze flickered between Jason, Skye and then Adam, whose head was bowed, not meeting anyone's eyes. 'Trickster stuff?'

'Trickster stuff,' Jason agreed.

Marcus nodded.

Eloise frowned, not understanding what seemed so obvious to everyone else. What the hell was Trickster stuff?

Cordy walked past Jason and touched Adam's arm. 'I think Marcus' nephew might be shaping up to be a Trickster too. Perhaps you could help him.'

Adam looked up. 'I'm not sure I'd be any help.'

'You could chat with him. Tell him what you feel. He's so overwhelmed, and you better than anyone would be able to empathise. Figure things out together, maybe?'

Adam trembled for a moment and then nodded. 'Yeah.' A small smile. 'I think I can do that. I'm still finding out what it all means, but I'll do what I can.'

Marcus simply slapped him on the back. 'I'd appreciate it, mate.'

'What have I missed?' Bron said as she entered the room, River at her side.

'Eloise was just going to tell us about how Gabbie died at the hands of a man who's been in a coma for months.' Adam crossed his arms and leaned against the wall.

Marcus bristled. 'Are you accusing us of not doing our job properly?'

'That's not what is happening here,' Jason said.

'There's no way Cain has escaped.' Marcus stood in front of Cordy, arms crossed, chin squared.

'I'm sure that's not what they meant,' Cordy said, stroking his back. 'Why don't you calm down and let them explain.'

'We know Cain hasn't escaped,' Jason said. 'I brought you into this because I trust you to help keep us all safe. I still do.'

'Then what are you saying?'

Jason looked over at Eloise, brow raised. 'Can you explain exactly what happened?'

She took a steadying breath, and with Iain's hand on her hip, his arm a comforting weight around her waist, she told them about the attack, by her coven mates and then by Cain in his Shade form. She told them what Cain had asked of her and what he'd done to poor Gabbie when she'd refused. 'He would have killed Iain too if I hadn't agreed.' She swiped at the tear that fell down her cheek. 'I'm just so sorry I didn't agree fast enough to save Gabbie too. But I really didn't think he'd kill her.'

Iain held her tighter, hand rubbing up and down her arm. 'There was nothing you could have done to stop him. He wanted to make a point and so he did.'

'Holy fuck!' River said, turning accusing eyes on Bron. 'You didn't tell me that.'

'I didn't know all of it. I just heard that last part myself.'

'Why are we here discussing this?' Adam barked.

'Bloody right.' Marcus pulled his phone out of his pocket. 'That fucker has to die.'

'No!' Eloise put her hand out as if she meant to wrench his phone out of his hand. 'You can't. He'll kill you all.'

There was a snort of derision from Marcus, but Iain said, 'Listen to her.' His voice didn't carry the Alpha command, but silence fell none the less. 'Just listen to her.'

Adam looked as if he was struggling not to say anything more, shifting back and forth as if he wished to pace again, but couldn't. Marcus vibrated with suppressed anger, but when Cordy placed her hand on his arm and said, 'Listen, lover,' he grunted his acquiescence.

'We're listening,' Jason said. 'We're all listening.' The others all nodded.

'Tell them.' Iain's words whispered in her ear. 'Tell them what you told me.'

She took a moment to collect her thoughts. When she spoke, her words were slow but certain, her voice clear and showing none of the tension trembling in her stomach. 'I know waking him is dangerous, but he's in your custody.' Her gaze went from Cordy to Skye to Shelley to Bron. 'I won't lie and tell you I'm not hoping you can help save him. There's an evil in him, an evil that didn't used to be there.

It's in Morrigan too and I'm certain it's making them do things they wouldn't normally do.' Bron's gasp as she grabbed hold of River's hand made her stop. 'You know what I'm talking about?'

'Yes.' She looked at the others. 'We've come across it before. We call it the Darkness. I banished it from River.'

'You did?' Hope rose inside Eloise. It must have shown on her face because Skye sat forward.

'We don't know what it is, though,' she said.

'Bron isn't quite sure how she got rid of it,' Shelley added.

'And getting it out of me almost killed her.' River pulled Bron closer, as if afraid she was in danger again.

'I understand.' She swallowed hard. 'But even if you can't get rid of this Darkness, I think you have ways that can keep Cain contained so he can't hurt anyone else once he's back in his body.' She looked at Cordy, who blanched but nodded.

'I don't understand how letting him live is better than killing him,' Marcus said.

'Because if I don't help him, if we kill him,' she said, her gaze flying to Marcus, to Adam, 'or let him die,' she added, gaze going to Jason and Shelley, 'then while he is a Shade, he can go where he likes, he can take over anybody with a speck of magic, and if he touches you, he will drain the life from you just as he did from Gabbie. As he almost did from Iain.'

'He can't last as a Shade for long,' Cordy said. 'As I understand it, his soul will fly apart without the anchor of his body.'

Eloise swallowed the bitterness in her throat. 'He is able to tap into Morrigan's life force, and mine, so he can last for longer than a normal Shade. Can you take the chance of him roaming free with the power he has? Even if he only had a short time, a few hours, he'd come right for the people in this room and kill you all and there's nothing you could do to stop him. If you touch him, he will drain you. He'd decimate your packs. He'd ensure Morrigan's success.'

'Is this true?' Adam asked Cordy.

She frowned, her expression strained. 'We don't have much lore about Shades, but what we do have suggests it's the darkest of dark magic. There's not much we can do to fight that, not without a lot more research and study.'

'Or without using dark magic ourselves,' Shelley said grimly.

'What would happen if you did that?' River asked.

'The Pact would be broken between the pack and ourselves,' Cordy said quietly. 'And who knows what the Darkness would be able to do then?'

'A lot,' Shelley added. 'It says in the diaries that dark magic is addictive. Seductive. Using it once, even for good intentions, is virtually impossible. We'd be opening ourselves up to the Darkness, inviting it in.'

'Then we don't want you doing that,' Adam said.

Eloise gulped. 'I don't want any of you doing that. Not for me, or my brother.'

'If Cain knows he could cause so much havoc as a Shade, then why does he want you to bring him back to his body?'

Eloise winced but met Jason's question head on. 'Because he knows he'll die if he stays a Shade without access to his own life energies. He can't live off Morrigan and me forever. Despite his wish to kill all of you, he wants to live. He also wants to get back to Morrigan. But you can stop him. You can put one of those bracelets that negate power on him.'

'We have. That didn't stop him from doing this,' Cordy pointed out.

'The fact the bracelet negated the magic in his body wouldn't have stopped him from being able to make himself a Shade.'

'Then what's to stop him from becoming a Shade again when you wake him and he realises his magic is restricted?' Shelley asked.

'He can't become a Shade again without seriously damaging his body and soul. He won't fight the magical restriction in the same way. You can hold him for the rest of his life if needed. But you can't let him continue on how he is. Please, you have to let me do this.'

Silence greeted her plea, sawing on her nerves like an overplayed bow on a violin.

Skye cleared her throat, glanced at her mate before her gaze returned to Eloise. 'You said you've had virtually no training in magic and given you've been concentrating on your shifting, you don't know much more now than you knew when you came to us. How do you know you can reunite his soul with his body?'

'It's something we're all taught. Morrigan has used people in this way before, and so we all need to know how to bring them back.'

'It isn't easy magic,' Cordy said. 'Can one of us help you?'

No! The word almost burst from her, but she managed to hold it back. She couldn't have any of them there. Cain would find some way to hurt them before he returned to his body, she knew he would. Besides, she couldn't let them see what she was really going to do. Shelley had spoken before of dark magic—and that was exactly what this was. 'You can't help. Only someone with a blood tie can perform the ceremony. The fact that he's my twin makes my ability to do the ceremony for Cain even stronger. Also, the power of Oestra will help me, too. But I need to make a move now. Cain has to see that I'm coming. He could be watching right now. If he thinks I'm not coming, he'll do something worse than what he's already done.'

She looked around, unable to read in their grim expressions whether they believed her or not. 'Please. We're running out of time.'

Jason met Marcus' gaze. The other Alpha grimaced but nodded. Jason sighed. 'Okay. I've got to stay here, but Iain will take you.'

'How far away is he?'

'An hour,' Marcus said, his voice a low growl—although she was getting the impression that was just how he spoke, not that he was angry with her. 'He's on McClune Packlands up near Kinglake.'

'Does that give you enough time?' Cordy asked.

She nodded. 'Yes. It's best performed at midnight when the moon is at its zenith.'

'The power of Ostara—or Oestra as you call it—is greatest then too.' Cordy looked at Marcus. 'That gives us a little time to source the materials I'll need to make a stronger magical repression cuff. We can make it back well before midnight and be there for back-up if necessary.' She looked at Eloise. 'Although I won't have the cuff immediately ready. The magic is best done by the light of the full moon at midnight as well.'

'If the stories I've heard are true, he'll be weakened by the spell when I bring him back, so there will be a little time.'

'How much?'

'I'm not certain.'

'Then we'll just have to hold him until you're ready,' Jason said, looking from her and Iain to Skye, Shelley, Adam, Bron and River. They all nodded.

Marcus growled his agreement. 'I'll call our people and let them know you're coming.' He held his hand out for Cordy. 'Let's go and source your things.'

Cordy gave Eloise a hug. 'Be careful,' she whispered, and then, joining Marcus, she left the room.

The other witches followed her lead, leaving with their mates or Shadows.

Relief and fear rose over her at once as she was crazily torn between spinning wildly or running to crouch, cowering, in a corner.

'Are you okay?'

She turned to Iain, a little burble of laughter rising up. 'I thought I'd be in for more of a fight.'

'They know what's at stake. And they trust you.'

'Yes.' It was a heady feeling. One she didn't want to let go of. She only hoped she was strong enough to do what had to be done so she had time to explore all it meant, and more. The thought sobered her, all the joy and relief washing away under the heavy weight of choice and responsibility Cain had laid on her shoulders. 'Let's go,' she croaked.

Iain frowned, questions in his eyes, but he simply nodded and said, 'Let's go'.

22

'**M**istress. I've contacted her. She's coming to me just like you
said.'

'That is excellent, Cain.' Morrigan spoke to the
Shade before her, refusing to allow excitement to rise. Her plans had
so often gone awry. The animal bastards who made up the McVale
Pack always seemed to destroy what had so carefully been wrought.
But no more. There was nothing they could do to stop this from
coming to fruition.

She had out-thought even the Goddess. Nobody would ever have
expected her to make Cain tear his soul from his body so he could
travel the astral at will as a Shade. Not with how important he was to
her, to the Darkness.

If they had thought of it, they would have expected her to use him
to suck the very life from them all. But that would never satisfy her
craving for revenge. Cain would never be able to kill enough of them,
and others would live on, ensuring the survival of the Were and their
abominable Pact that tied them to the witches and warlocks who
should be free.

No. She had to destroy the Pact. She had to tear the Were apart
from the inside out. Had to destroy who they were, like she'd been

destroyed when her beloved sister was so cruelly taken from her because of what those animals had done; because of how little they had cared for the health and safety of those who had given them their freedom back.

She shook off the rage that filled her at the thought. It wasn't time for rage right now. She had to remain clear-headed and calm for this to succeed.

Her plan was a risk. A terrible risk. But, oh, by the Darkness, it had been worth it. The moon was in play again. The surge of power due to the vernal equinox was in her favour.

It was a time of rebirth, and oh what a rebirth it would be for her and her kind.

If only she had Eloise's power to pull on too, everything would be perfect. But Eloise was completely blocked from her. That little shapeshifting bitch had turned out to be far stronger than Morrigan ever gave her credit for. Not even when she was in the coma had Morrigan been able to whisper to her, to pull her back to her side like she'd done to Cain. She had almost given the girl up as a lost cause. But Cain was going to make her useful again, if not in the way originally planned.

Smiling, she said, 'Your sister's sacrifice will auger the coming of the blood moon and then all will fall on their knees before us. Together we will rid the world of the filthy Were.'

Morrigan expected Cain to cheer at her statement, but instead he paused then said, 'What of Skye and River?'

Morrigan snorted. 'You refer to that ridiculous tale about River and Skye being descendants of my beloved sister! It's nothing but rubbish. Morghanna would never have debased herself with one of those animals in the way Bridgette Colliere did.' Besides, she would have known if her sister had been with child. They'd been so close. Morghanna would not have kept such a thing from her even though they'd been at odds those last ten years.

A sick sensation swirled inside; a flicker of doubt within the certainty.

What if she hadn't told her because of what she'd said to

Morghanna the last time they'd spoken not even a year before that horrific night. Her sister had managed to track her down finally and spoken to her through a scrying medium. She'd sought her help and advice, but Morrigan would hear none of it.

'No. I will not come back with you. I will never come back with you. I cannot watch you make yourself less than you were meant to be. The Cantrae sisters were born to do astonishing things together. It was prophesied. If you ally yourself with Bridgette Colliere and the Were, you turn your back on prophecy. You turn your back on me for these last nine years and I can have nothing more to do with you.'

They were words spoken in anger, because of the fear and desperation she'd seen in her sister's eyes. She'd feared she might give in to her sister's needs and to stop that, had uttered words she never should have. She'd regretted those words later, but pride had stopped her from seeking forgiveness, even though she knew Morghanna would give it. Morghanna wouldn't have shunned her. Even at the last, she begged Morrigan for temperance. She'd begged Morrigan to forgive and to live on for the both of them.

If there had been a baby, Morghanna would have told her then.

Yet she'd said nothing.

She stared at the Shade in front of her and said firmly, 'Your sister was wrong. She's been tricked by the Were in an attempt to turn me from the task ahead. But it didn't work. I will not be swayed, not even with tales of blood relations that don't exist.'

Cain nodded. 'As you say, Mistress. They aren't blood. And only blood matters.'

'Yes.' The ties of blood were stronger than anything else on this earth. The Darkness had whispered that to her on the night Morghanna had been slain, building on the fire of her rage, hammering her need for revenge to a fine point. Morrigan had carried those words with her through the centuries. She was doing this for the sake of her blood. 'I know you might be reticent to do what I have asked, Cain, but remember, if you do exactly what I've told you, Eloise will return to us. She is lost to us now, but when her blood is returned to you, we will not only use the power of it for the blood moon, but you will tie her power to you forever. Then she will be redeemed. And you will be responsible. Think only of that.'

'I believe, Mistress.'

'I know you do. You are my saving grace, Cain. Now go. Do as we planned. Eloise's blood will allow us to harness the power of Oestra and create the blood moon, and with it, we will destroy the Were and reclaim what was taken. I will see you when you return to me.'

'Until the blood moon.'

'Until the blood moon, my precious one.'

As he disappeared through the wall, a sense of loss overwhelmed her. For a brief moment, she almost called him back. Almost stopped him. What if something went wrong? What if she lost him like she'd lost so many before? She couldn't stand it. Couldn't stand it.

'Cain,' she cried out.

But he was already gone.

An overwhelming desire to scream, to tear at her clothes, her hair, took over. 'What am I doing?' Morghanna wouldn't like it. She wouldn't approve. 'What have I done? What have I—'

The Darkness curled deep inside her, snapping out like a whip, cutting off her words. *'Calm yourself. Do not forget your purpose, my black heart. Remember your revenge. Our revenge. We will destroy the plague of the Were and the line of witches that tore from both of us that which we once loved.'*

The Darkness. The Darkness was talking to her again. It had been silent for weeks. Knees weak, she sank to the floor. 'Yes, my lord. Yes.'

'Cain knows what to do. You have primed him well, as I instructed. He will not fail you.'

Her lip wobbled. 'How do you know? So many of the others have.'

'Because a little bit of me is inside him too.'

She gasped. 'When?'

'When he was a child. His desire to protect his twin mixed with his jeal-ousy over the abilities she had that he didn't, allowed me entrance. He is one with us in a way his twin never was. He will see this through.'

Yes. He would. He was the noose they would tighten around

Eloise's neck. He would bring her to heel and in so doing, bring the Were to their knees where they belonged; supplicants begging mercy.

Mercy her sister had never received.

Mercy the animals would never get.

'It has begun,' she whispered.

'Yes, my dark heart. It has finally begun.'

23

Iain gripped the wheel tightly as he moved the car smoothly around another corner. The roads through the national park could be treacherous. He needed to concentrate. And yet, he couldn't stop glancing over at Eloise.

She'd been quiet ever since they'd left the Packhouse in Templestowe, her hands clenched in her lap, face white, looking implacably ahead. Her tension was a saw on his nerves, her pain and worry tangible. He wanted to take her hand, to stroke her face, tell her not to worry, soothe the pain away.

Hell, if he was being truthful with himself, he wanted to do more than stroke her skin. He wanted to take her face in his hands and kiss the breath out of her until the strained look in her eyes dissolved under the heat of passion, memories of what they'd shared last night surging forward. It had been the first night for as long as he could remember that he didn't relive the nightmare of his capture and torture by Morrigan and her minions. And it was all because of her.

She brought a peace to his soul he'd never experienced. And a wild passion he wanted to explore.

Mine.

The whisper, a harsh growl of longing and ownership, echoed in his mind, egging on feelings he shouldn't have. Couldn't have. He was a Lone Wolf. Lone Wolves didn't mate.

And yet, when they'd joined last night, his body had responded like it would to a mate. His wolf wanted her in the way a wolf hungered for a mate. Hell, he wanted her more than he'd ever wanted anything in his life, more so now than before last night.

However, the bond wasn't there. He'd looked. It was missing.

So, why did he feel so tied to her?

He returned his gaze to the road, fingers gripping the steering wheel harder. He took a deep breath and almost cursed out loud. The scent of her, the lingering warmth of her wrapped around him and with it, the memory of her pressing up against him, skin to skin, her body wrapped around his, filled his mind with such tearing suddenness, it felt real.

Fuck! He had to stop thinking about sex and Eloise and the roaring ache of his engorged cock pressing against his jeans. He'd never experienced this kind of aggressive sexual need before outside of those dreams he now knew were past-life memories.

He had to control it. This wasn't the time. Gabbie had died. More could follow her if he didn't get Eloise to her brother and help her pull him back to his body. What they'd shared last night would have to be enough until this was over. Eloise didn't need him pawing all over her or acting animalistic and possessive right now. Especially as he couldn't back that possessiveness up with something more long term and respectful. She was a forever kind of girl and despite the bewildering feelings inside him towards her, he was uncertain he could give her forever.

He took in another deep breath. The tyres squealed on the bitumen as he took a corner too hard. Crap! Every breath was full of her. Every little gasp or quiver of her flesh was a turn-on. And he really wished she'd stop biting her lip—such beautiful lips deserved much better care. Or to be bitten by a lover in the midst of passion as he drove into her with his cock and his tongue.

'Iain!'

Her fingers were white on the dash in front of her, eyes fearful as she stared at the road whipping by. He looked at the speedo—they were doing two hundred.

'Sorry.' He shot her a look of chagrin and slowed down. 'I'm just anxious to get there.'

'I'm not,' she whispered.

Her whisper was an ice bath. It reminded him of how this must be for her. She was fearful and unhappy, and here he was thinking of nothing but stopping the car, stripping her naked and entreating her to ride him until they were both nothing more than trembling puddles of spent desire.

Roping back the violence of his need, he concentrated on the winding road, sweat beading his brow as he tried not to breathe in the scent of the female at his side.

Finally, they made it through the tight curves and emerged out of the darker bushland into the open pastures that spread across the valleys and gentle green hills. Ten minutes later, he turned off the road and slowed to cross the cattle grid. As the car rattled over the metal grates, he risked a glance at Eloise.

Her hands were a white knot in her lap; the flush had disappeared from her cheeks, replaced with a pallor like snow.

'We're almost there.'

She nodded, hands wringing tighter. 'Good. I wish it was done already. That everyone was safe and Cain was under control and no danger to anyone.'

'We'll all make sure of it.' He pulled onto a dirt road that led across the paddock. 'But that's not what has you truly worried, is it?'

Her golden-green eyes were pools of worry as she met his gaze. 'The Goddess said I'm a Nexus. That what I decide will shape the future.' Her lips trembled. 'I don't want that on my shoulders.'

'You don't have to make those decisions alone. I'm here for you. We all are.'

Her lips trembled into a tight smile. 'I know.' She bit her lip again. 'But don't you see? That's part of the problem. I now have something to care about. Something to lose. And I don't want to lose it.'

'You won't.' He pulled the car up outside a barn at the far end of the paddock. Then, turning to her, cupped her face. He brushed his thumbs over the smooth silk of her skin, tamping down the absurd desire to lean forward and lick, to savour the spiced-cream taste of her that waited for him. Swallowing hard as he held on to his desire, he said, 'I ... we won't let you go.'

She licked her lips and closed her eyes as his fingers skimmed over her cheek. 'Iain?' Her eyes fluttered open, her lips wet and glistening from the touch of her tongue.

Fuck she was sexy. He cupped her cheek, gaze roving over her face to return to her lips. 'Yes?'

'Kiss me.'

His cock flexed, gaze colliding with hers. Her eyes were swirling pools of gold and green. 'No.'

She edged forward, breath brushing over his face. 'You want to.'

'Fuck yes. But not while she's there, looking at me out of your eyes. When I kiss you, I want to make sure it's you and only you.'

She squeezed her eyes shut. 'I think I need her, though. To do what I have to do tonight. I can't shut her out. Please don't make me.'

'Damn it, Eloise.' His thumbs brushed roughly over her cheeks. He blew out a breath, tried to calm his hammering heart, keep his hands gentle on her face and not pull her towards him like his wolf wanted him to; like he wanted to.

'What? What is it? Is it because you're worried that I'm not making this decision for myself? That it's the presence making me act like this?'

'Yes. No.' His fingers flexed on her face and he tipped her head up, but still she avoided his gaze. 'Look at me, Eloise.' She bit her lip and he groaned, the effort to not lick and kiss away the hurt almost more than he could bear. 'Look at me.'

Her eyes met his in a tentative way that made his wolf whimper.

Voice a rough whisper, he said, 'You tempt me beyond all sense. You make my wolf so crazy he's forever lunging against my skin wanting to lick you up, to take a bite of you, to mark you as his. I want you. All of you. I want to mark you so everyone knows you're mine. The need is a voracious hunger inside that's only been growing with every moment I've known you. I've never felt its like before. It's not something a Lone Wolf should ever feel, but I can't ignore the truth of it. I don't know what that means; I don't know if I can ever give you what you deserve or need from a partner, but I can't deny what I feel.'

'Iain,' she said on a shaky sigh that had pleasure curling around his heart. 'It's like a clawing pain right here.' She pressed her hand against her chest, over her heart. 'A pain that could turn into pleasure with just the touch of your lips.'

'Yes,' he breathed. The truth of her words were a hum inside him. 'But it isn't the bond. I don't know what it is. I don't know what I can promise you.'

'I don't want promises. I know you're a Lone Wolf. I don't care. I don't care about what happens in the future when the now is all I can think of.'

'You *should* care. You deserve so much more than what I have to offer.'

'You're wrong. I don't deserve more than I have if what I have is you.'

They stared at each other, desire a palpable pulse between them. Breath shuddered out of her lips in a rush he found so sexy he thought his cock might break in half as it flexed against his jeans.

Thankfully she broke the stare, looking down, and said, 'But now is not the time for this conversation.' She looked back up at him. 'That's what you're trying to tell me, right?'

'Probably.' He could barely remember anymore when she looked at him like that. His fingers trembled on her face.

She smiled. 'Probably?'

'Yeah. No.' He squeezed his eyes shut, trying to centre his thoughts. 'The point I'm making so badly is—'

Her chuckle brushed over him, broke into his words. 'I don't think you're doing too badly. I think you've made it pretty clear you want me.'

He huffed out a laugh. 'Yeah. But that's also the problem. I can't kiss you right now, because if I do, I'm never going to be able to let you out of this car. My wolf is already struggling against the need to keep you safe and the need to keep the pack safe. I know you're not my mate, but the thought of you doing something that will put you in danger is driving us insane. If we kiss, you and I both know it won't stop there, and if we make love again ...' He shook his head. 'I can't ... I won't be able to ...'

'Shh.' She put her fingers over his lips. 'It's okay. I understand. This is all so confusing.' She rolled her eyes. 'And such bad timing. Which is just me all over, really. I never could get the timing thing right.'

'I think you did pretty okay last night.'

She dipped her head, gaze leaving his, and even in the dark of the car, he could see the deep pink of blush chase across her cheeks. It made him smile.

'I don't want to cause you and your wolf any pain, but I'm not going to lie. I want to share with you again what we shared last night. I want to do that again, and again, with you. But you're right.' She looked up at him. 'Now isn't the time.'

'No. It isn't.' Although, by the Moon he wished it was.

Her pulse fluttered in her neck—he could hear it, see it, smell it, feel it inside him. 'You have to let go. It hurts too much to be this close and no closer.'

'I know,' he said. She went to pull away but he couldn't let her. The wolf was growling loudly under his skin.

'Iain?'

'Just give me a moment.' Touching her might incite his and his wolf's passions, but it also settled them.

Just like a mate would.

The thought flickered through his mind but then was cast away again. His wolf could never mate because it would always be driven by that rage of need burning inside him to be alone, to roam. The one didn't go with the other.

Eloise didn't pull away. Instead, she covered his hands with hers and leaned her forehead against his, instinctively knowing what he needed. Their breaths—panting, hot— mingled, hers caressing his face, across his lips, adding to the sensation of being touched.

After a long moment his wolf settled just enough for him to have control and he was able to pull away. It was a control he had to hold onto. Because she needed him and he would be there for her in the way she needed with no uncertainty. Certainly not the uncertainty of whatever the hell was going on between them. They had to have time to figure it out. And tonight wasn't it.

As he pulled away she shivered and wrapped her arms around her middle.

'Cold?'

He went to pull off his jacket but she shook her head, shifting away from him. 'No.' She broke away from his gaze and stared out the windscreen at the green landscape around them, lush with farm fields spreading towards the blue-ish haze of bush-covered hills in the distance. It was twilight. A time of magic as day dissolved into night. He couldn't believe that only yesterday they'd woken with none of the heaviness of destiny upon them. Gabbie had been alive. Eloise hadn't known Cain was a Shade. She hadn't even known her coven mates were on their lands.

He wished they could go back to that time, save her from all this pain and worry, but that was as impossible as wishing they were actually mates. He watched as she took in their surrounds, registering the barn. 'Is he in there?'

'No. This is only a blind. There's a shaft that leads to old mine tunnels and natural caves deep below the surface. He's being kept in one of those.'

They hopped out of the car and moments later were in the barn. Hay dust rose in the air around them, golden in the shafts of late-afternoon sunlight coming through the door and high windows.

He closed the door behind them then gestured forward. She followed him to the hidden lift at the back. He pressed a panel.

Her brows rose as the wall shifted sideways with a groan and the lift was revealed. 'I wasn't expecting something so mod-conish.'

'We Were love our mod-cons. After you.'

When they were inside, he pushed the button that would take them to the bottom of the mine. The door slid silently closed. She shuffled slightly closer to him, grasped for his hand, gripping tight.

'It's quite safe,' he assured her.

She nodded jerkily. 'I would have thought all the caves would make this area unstable.'

'Not necessarily. It depends on what you're doing to it. How you're treating the land. And if it's one thing Were know, it's how to look after the land.'

'Why is that?'

'It was our only source of survival for a long time.'

Tension vibrated down her arm as the lift jerked, but when he looked at her face, all he saw there was determination. As if sensing his gaze, she glanced up at him, her golden-green eyes almost glowing in the dim light of the lift. 'I have to do this.'

He touched her cheek—couldn't stop himself. 'You are so brave.'

'No. I'm not.'

She licked her lips and he had to hold back a groan. He'd wanted to kiss her in the car, but that need ramped up to a ravaging urge as he looked down at the soft, slightly wet flesh, wanting nothing more than to taste and feel her tongue glide next to his.

But he couldn't. Not now. Not before they saw Cain. He couldn't distract either of them in that way. Her gaze rose to meet his, golden-green eyes glowing in the low light, a look in them that told him she sensed his turmoil and shared it.

He could drown in those eyes.

The lift jerked and shuddered as it reached its destination, the doors opening with a gasp. The sound broke the tension between them and she pulled away from him. He knew he should be relieved that the moment was broken, but he felt lost.

Sighing, he turned to face the gloom of a long horizontal mine-shaft lit only by lamps hung on the rafters. Deep, tangy mineral scents curled around them.

'How far underground are we?' Eloise asked as she ventured into the tunnel.

'Far enough. Most of the structures the McClunes use are closer to the surface, but your brother was a special case, and it was thought best to keep him as secure as possible, far from anyone he might wish to hurt.'

Eloise looked up at Iain, unable to read his expression in the low light, but there was something in his voice that sent a warm glide through her, despite his words. Protective. Of her.

She trembled at the thought of what that might mean. What it promised if only she could be strong enough to reach for it and hold on. The rich, warm scents of him—like a sun-bathed ocean next to a forest—rose around her and she couldn't help breathing it in. Holding that warmth to her like a secret prize that was only hers, a security blanket shielding her from the cold dankness of these tunnels and the bitter edge of the Darkness she could sense up ahead.

'Are you okay?' She nodded. 'Okay, then let me show you around.'

Her steps were jerky, and not simply because of her twisted foot as she followed him down the tunnel. She wished there was some way out of this, but there wasn't. Her fingers tightened against her sides as she hugged her arms around her. She was so afraid that despite everything they'd planned, someone would get hurt. Cain should be weakened and disoriented and no danger to anyone for a short time after the procedure, as she'd told the Were. But there was a creeping feeling at the back of her head that kept whispering questions to her:

Why hadn't Cain demanded to be removed from here to somewhere much easier to escape from? What did he know that she didn't?

She couldn't figure it out. Maybe he was just truly desperate to live and thought he could figure his way out of his incarceration afterwards. Maybe he thought Morrigan had a plan to get him out. She didn't know. Couldn't know. But maybe she could get Cain to tell her.

She stopped. 'Actually, can you take me straight to Cain? I need to see him now. To prepare myself.'

Iain gestured down a side tunnel. 'Follow me.'

She moved more certainly now. She had to see his body. Speak to Cain while touching the flesh that was related to her. They had a twin connection of sorts. Hopefully she'd be able to tap into it through his body and figure out what he had planned.

And when she knew, she could stop him. She hoped.

24

The room Eloise was led into was like a hospital wing—bright white lights, white walls, gleaming concrete floors, beeping machinery. There was a nurse at a desk and a guard on duty. They were chatting quietly and turned at their entrance. They both nodded at Iain, but as their gazes fell to her, their smiles froze, eyes glacial, hostile. In the past that would have made her skitter away, hiding from the hostility. But not now. She was stronger now.

Who knew a little bit of trust and respect would go such a long way?

So instead of cringing, fists at her sides, she simply nodded to them and gestured at the curtain on the far side of the room. 'Is he there?'

'Yes,' the nurse said.

She swallowed hard, hoping none of them could hear how hard and fast her heart was beating. Ignoring the others, she said to Iain, 'I need to see him by myself, first.'

'What if his Shade comes?'

She looked around. 'It's not here now. If it comes, I'll call you.'

He watched her for a moment before nodding. 'I'll chat with Alistair and June, see if they've heard from the others, if Cordy's been able to get what she needs for the binding charm.' He touched her cheek gently before crossing the room to the other Were.

Making her stiff legs move, she limped to the curtain and twitched it aside.

Cain.

He had a face that would make angels weep, especially with that mop of chestnut curls tipped in gold. He almost looked like the boy she'd idolised when she was little; the brother who she'd looked up to, who'd protected her from those who teased her about her leg, her stutter, her shyness and her unpredictable power, always certain about his way forward. She hadn't been surprised when Morrigan picked him out to train. He had always been remarkable in her eyes. Still was. The things he could do ... they'd take her breath away if they didn't make her tremble in fear.

Morrigan had changed him so much. He had always been full of life, so gentle and kind. Now he was lifeless, his bones harsh slashes pressing against too-pale skin, his soul cruel and twisted.

'Oh, Cain.' She stumbled forward, grasped his freezing hand. His chest rose, up, down. Slowly. Too slowly. She didn't need the machine beeping away to tell her his heart was beating—she could see it in the pulse of blue veins on the side of his pale, pale neck. He had once been all sunshine and laughter—in a time so distant it almost seemed another life. That boy was gone and in his place was a man she hardly recognised. A man moulded by Morrigan and the Darkness that infested her. 'What did she do to you? What did she do?'

Bron had done a good job with his injuries. He was fully healed—in body. Bron couldn't heal his soul. Nobody could, except him. But his soul didn't need to be healed to bring it back to his body. It just needed to be pulled to him, the rift sewn up with darkest blood magic.

Breath shuddered in her chest, rattling up her throat, squeezing.

Blood. It always came back to blood.

'How did you do this? How could you?' Hot tears splashed on her hand where it held his.

'*Our Mistress required it of me.*'

She jumped at the whispery echo of his voice in her ear, dropped his hand, backing away from the bed, gaze frantically looking for his Shade. *Please don't let it be here.* She wasn't ready to be bitten by its touch, not again. Not so soon. But there was no sign he was here at all. Then how was he talking to her?

'*We are linked by blood. Besides, you're standing beside my body—that makes it easier. I'm almost disappointed you came—it would have been such fun to play the Shade harbinger of doom. That Were's life energy was so good. I don't think I've ever felt as alive as I did when I was taking hers.*' A sound like a sigh.

She flinched, glanced towards the Were then back at Cain's body before whispering as softly as she could, aware the Were could probably still hear her. 'You took a life. How can you be so cavalier about that?'

'*Easy. It was fun. And I'll take more than one life if you don't do what I ask. I'll even take yours if I have to.*'

'I thought you loved me.'

'*I do. But Morrigan told me the truth when you were playing at being cat. Told me what our blood could do.*'

'And what is that?'

'*It can take over the world. We could control all the witches, destroy the Were, take back what is rightfully ours. And after tonight, that's exactly what we will do and your powers are the thing that will help us do it.*'

'No.' She stumbled back, almost into the curtain. 'I won't do it. I won't help you after I wake you up.'

'*You won't have any choice. You're already linked by a blood-bond to me, Little Bit. After tonight, that bond will be so much deeper. I'll have control over you, over your power. With you by my side, nothing will be able to stand in our way.*'

Horrified, Eloise shook her head. 'You can't. You can't do that.'

'*I can and I will.*'

'I won't let you.'

'*And how will you stop me? You have to bring my soul back to me or I will kill all the Were I can get my hands on before I fade away. And their deaths will be your fault.'*

'No. Please don't.'

'I will make sure they feel every ounce of pain and suffering they can before they die. And I will leave your Shadow for last so he can watch everyone he knows and loves die painfully, knowing that fate is coming his way.'

'No!' She couldn't stand the thought of Iain being hurt, in pain. 'I'll fight you.'

'You won't win. You know I've always been stronger than you.'

'Maybe that's what you wanted me to believe, but now I know that I have power that is stronger than you and Morrigan's combined.'

'True. But you still have no control over your power and no idea how to gain that control. The only person who knows how to use it is Morrigan.'

Goddess, he was right. This is why she'd been kept ignorant for so long and there was no way she could rectify it. Not in a few hours. Even so, she had to try to convince him he couldn't be a part of this scheme. He couldn't do this to her. 'This is wrong,' she hissed, glancing back over her shoulder to see if Iain was looking this way. But he wasn't. Did that mean he couldn't hear this conversation or that he trusted her enough to allow her to handle it.

'This is what Morrigan wants.'

'Morrigan is wrong. She's being controlled by an ancient Darkness that cares about nothing and no-one, not even her.'

'Liar.' She winced as his shriek echoed in her head. *'It loves us. Needs us.'*

'It needs you, but it doesn't love you. It doesn't care about you at all. It even made Morrigan break her own law. Blood matters. It's always been her most sacred tenet and yet she's breaking it even now asking you to force me to do this. By using me in this way.' There was a pause. Was she getting through to him? 'You know I'm right, Cain.'

'No. No. She isn't breaking her laws. She cares about them still. She told me what you said about River and Skye can't be true. That monster isn't related to her. Her sister would never have done such a thing as to mate

with an animal. And who would know better than our mistress? It's the Were who lie.'

'Oh, Cain.' She pressed her hand against her lips to stop them from trembling. 'You've been brainwashed. We all have been. By Morrigan and her need for revenge.' She gestured over her shoulder. 'These are good people. They don't deserve to be destroyed.'

'They aren't people. And the witches who side with them deserve anything and everything our mistress metes out to them.'

She closed her eyes and cried inside for the boy who had been her brother. He was obviously long gone and in his place was this cold, implacable man filled with hatred and a borrowed need for revenge that was based on a lie. The hope she'd held onto that she'd be able to make him see reason was gone. He was so twisted, he would never see the lie.

Sighing, she opened her eyes and, unable to look at his body, stared at the wall. She had to find out why he was so certain he would still be of use to Morrigan after she brought him back to his body. 'It won't matter if you have me or not. The Were will never let you leave here. You are their prisoner.'

'As if they could cage me after I have your power inside me.'

'My power? But if you go through with this, you won't have my power. Morrigan will.'

'True, Little Bit, but not right away. During the blood spell, your power will first come to me. It will make me stronger than ever. I will escape, taking you with me so I can syphon your power from now until the end of time, sharing it with Morrigan. And if you don't want to see your precious Were killed during my escape, I suggest you find some way of getting rid of them so they don't get in my way. One way or another, I'm returning to Morrigan tonight.'

Oh Goddess! She knew their plan had to be bad, but that was worse than she thought. Grasping at straws, she said, 'They won't leave me alone with you. They don't all trust me yet and they most definitely don't trust you.'

'That's your problem, isn't it? I don't know why you're so worried. You know they're going to be killed anyway.'

'No! They'll find a way to stop you. They've done so in the past.'

'That might be true, but their luck can't last forever. Morrigan will find a way. Especially with you on our side.'

'I will never be on your side. Besides, I think you overestimate my power.'

He laughed. *'And you underestimate it. Even Morrigan did until just recently. But we've discovered you're a Nexus. You have unlimited power if only you knew how to use it. And after tonight, it will be mine and Morrigan's to command. I think you'll find that with your power on our side, the Weres' remaining time on this earth will be short.'*

'I won't do it.'

'Then shall I kill them now? I won't get to kill them all before I fade, mores the pity, but I bet I can get every Were on these Packlands and then start on your beloved McVales before I fade into nothing. Let's start with this lot in the tunnels.'

Cain's Shade shimmered to the left of her and then drifted across the space towards where Iain was standing with the two other Were. His arms lifted, reaching for them.

'No! Stop. I'll do it. I'll do it!'

Iain and the other Were snapped around at her cry.

'Eloise? What's wrong?' Iain began to move towards her, but his path put him closer to Cain's Shade.

'No! Don't move. He's here. The Shade is here. You have to go. Get out now. He said he wouldn't hurt you if you got out, but he'll kill you if you stay.'

The guard's gaze darted around the room. 'I can't see anything.'

'Neither can I,' the nurse said.

'Shall I show them, sister dear?'

'No! Leave them alone Cain,' she screamed, flinging herself forward, wincing as she brushed up against him. 'Go. Go now,' she said to Iain. 'You have to get out. He'll kill you.'

Iain didn't question her further, simply turned and growled in a sharp command, 'Out. Do as she says. Now.'

They scrambled out of the room, Eloise right behind them.

'Sister?'

Cain's voice stopped her as she reached the door. She was achingly aware that Iain was waiting just outside the door—too close, too close to danger still—when she turned. Cain stood there, a smile apparent on his Shade's face.

'Be back at midnight, alone. Don't be late.' He began to laugh.

Iain reached for her, pulled her through the door before she could answer and tore back up the hallway, pulling her close as he ran. The door slammed closed with a loud clang behind them, cutting off the sound of Cain's laughter.

They made the lift, joining the other two Were. Iain pressed the button to close the doors—as if that could keep Cain out if he wanted to follow them. She sobbed out a hysterical laugh at the thought as the doors closed too slowly and the lift began to move towards the surface.

'What happened, Eloise?' Iain grabbed her shoulders, spinning her to face him. 'Did he hurt you? What did he do?'

'I can't ... he said ...' She couldn't say the words. Not to him. Not to anyone. Because suddenly she knew what it truly meant. Knew what she had to do.

She had to go through with the ritual, waken Cain with her blood. But she couldn't let him have access to her powers. Couldn't allow him to continue to tap into her life-essence. There was only one way to stop that from happening. In her dreams, the past reincarnation had sacrificed herself to save those she loved. And now, in this life, Eloise had to do the same.

She had to die.

Was this always to be their soul's fate? It seemed it was.

'Eloise? What is it?'

Even through the tears that blurred her vision, Iain's worried gaze blazed down at her.

Oh Goddess! She couldn't let him know. He'd stop her and then Cain would kill him. Better he live with the sadness of her loss than not live at all.

Trying to calm her roiling thoughts and the grief sweeping through her at what she was about to lose, she blinked the tears away, wiping them roughly from her cheeks and took a deep breath. 'He just frightened me, that's all. It's fine. I'm fine.'

'Are you sure? You don't look well.'

'I accidently touched him. I'll be okay. Just hold me. Hold me please.' His arms went around her immediately, pulling her close, tucking her into the comfort of his warmth and strength. She was trembling too hard to do anything more than cling to his shirt; clinging as if the touch of him was the only thing holding her to this earth, to her sanity.

'Hey. It's okay. It's all going to be okay.'

'Does this mean the deal's off?'

She flinched at the harsh voice behind her. She'd forgotten the other two were there. She shifted to look over her shoulder. 'No. He just wanted to make a point.'

'What point?' the guard asked. 'That he's a mad fuck? I think we already know that.'

'No. He just wanted to make sure I did what he wants. He was showing me his superiority. That's all.'

'Scared the crap out of me,' the nurse said, and shuddered.

The doors opened behind them and they all stepped out, Iain's arm tight around her, keeping her against his side.

'What are we supposed to do now?' the nurse asked.

'You go tell Marcus what's happened.'

'Sure. Then we'll come back with reinforcements,' the guard said.

'No!' Eloise cried. 'If you go back there, he'll kill you. He will only let me back inside.'

'That's not going to happen,' the guard said. 'You've got rocks in your head if—'

Iain held up his hand. 'If Eloise says it has to be that way, it will be that way.' He turned to her. 'But we will all be on the other side of the door watching in case anything goes wrong.'

She nodded, knowing that was as good as she was going to get. 'Of course. Cordy and the others will need to be there to cast the spell to keep him bound just after he's woken anyway. But until he is no longer a Shade, nobody can be in the room with me.' She wouldn't be responsible for any more deaths. Except her own, of course.

Iain looked questioningly at the others. They nodded their agreement, although it was obvious the male in particular wasn't happy. 'Go report to Marcus,' Iain said. 'I'll let Jason know what's happened.'

'Marcus won't be happy.'

'He'll get over it.'

The guard grunted, but didn't argue further, simply turned and, with the nurse at his side, left the barn.

As the door slammed shut behind them, Eloise closed her eyes. Icy cold gripped her heart. This was it. She was almost out of time.

She wanted to cry at that cruel, simple fact. A few weeks earlier she'd thought she had all the time in the world to explore the new life she'd made for herself. So many dreams. So many plans, all of which had opened like a flower before her, full of possibility. And for the first time in her life, she'd been ready and willing and able to pick up that flower and leap forward into the possibilities.

But her brother had crushed that flower. In the matter of a few minutes, all the petals of hope she'd held so dear were scattered to the wind and she had nothing but one single course laid out for her to take.

Death. Her death.

Oh Goddess! She didn't want to do it. Didn't want to miss out on the life she could build with the Were. With Iain. A life that was suddenly so full of possibilities she never imagined being hers. She wanted the opportunity to be embraced by Iain, to feel his lips on hers again, to feel his heat and power sweep through her, filling her with that expression of sunshine she'd seen on the faces of Skye and Jason, Bron and River. She wanted the hot, sweaty passion of tangled limbs, of naked skin sliding against naked skin, of him inside her, possessing her as she possessed him.

One.

She almost laughed out loud at the thought. She was dreaming— she knew she was dreaming. Skye and Jason, Bron and River—they had that because they were mated. Iain wasn't her mate. He was a

Lone Wolf and she knew what that meant, no matter how much he wanted her. They had no future. No true future.

But she didn't care. She wanted whatever they could have. Iain had already helped her experience things she'd never thought to experience. He'd already brought her so much ... feeling. It was overwhelming. And frightening. But even so, she wanted it, despite the fact that it could never be hers. She had to die, to save him, to save the others.

But she didn't have to go without taking a little bit of something more for herself, did she? Iain was here with her now. She had until midnight before she had to do what must be done to stop Cain and Morrigan from attaining her power. This time, now, was her last ever chance to be with Iain, to give herself over to the fever of him running through her veins before she consigned herself to oblivion.

Mind ticking over, she moved out of Iain's arms. 'Can we go somewhere? I want to be with you. I need to be with you.'

Iain hesitated for a bare fraction of a second and she held her breath, certain he read on her face what she was truly thinking. But then he pressed a swift kiss to her lips, took her hand and said, 'Follow me.'

Instead of heading outside, he turned to the left and led her up narrow stairs that were tucked into the far corner.

'What's up here?'

'Accommodation for visitors from outside packs. It's hard for two Alphas to stay in the same house together. I've stayed here before with Jason when we were trying to build ties with the McClunes before Skye came back to us. It's simple but clean, and there's a kitchen stocked with food. We can rest and eat before you have to go back down to the caves.'

'Sounds good.' In fact, it sounded perfect.

Upstairs was a corridor and along the corridor were three doors on the left and two on the right and one down the end.

'Food or rest first?'

'I want to go to the bedroom.'

He led her to the middle door on the left, opened it and pulled her through.

Inside was a king-sized bed, a side table with a lamp on it, a small gate-legged table and chairs in the corner and a dresser in the other. A large window was set into the far wall opposite the bed. Moonlight streamed through the glass, lighting the bed as if it were in a spotlight.

She stopped dead, grief cutting through her chest, stealing her breath. This was going to be the last time with Iain. The last time she would ever feel him with every part of her being. The last time she would have a chance to tell him about the joy in her heart.

She loved him. She loved him. She had to tell him. It was her last chance.

She turned to him, mouth dry. 'Iain.'

'Eloise? What is it?'

She looked up into his gorgeous face, those beautiful amber eyes that she could drown in forever, gloried in the caring there, the heat of his passion for her. She opened her mouth but the words she needed to say wedged in her throat.

She couldn't do it. Couldn't tell him she loved him. It was selfish, given what she was about to do, knowing she was going to betray his trust and keep this final, important action from him until it was too late. He cared for her and her betrayal would already hurt him. Knowing of her love would hurt him even more.

Well, if she couldn't say the words, she could show him; could share her joy with him in that final, intimate way. Grasping his hands in hers, trembling, she stepped closer. 'Kiss me.'

His gaze roamed over her face, stopped on her eyes. 'She's with you again.'

'I know.' And she did. She could feel her past self at the back of her mind, whispering her want, her need, her love, her grief, her support. 'She is here. But she's not ruling me. She's simply an echo. She's not me. She feels something for the one who was part of you, it's true. But her need isn't my need. Her passion isn't mine.'

She gripped his hands tighter, moved closer. 'She longs for that other part of you, that ancient part of you, that echo. But that echo is not you, just like the echo of her is not me. She might be here in part, just as she has always been here, but it is not her making me say any of this to you. It is not her asking you to kiss me, undress me and take me in the moonlight. She isn't the one asking to feel your skin against mine, revelling in the warmth. She isn't the reason fire rampages through my nerves and veins, shivering along my skin, tightening my muscles, every time you are near. It's not her lips that move against yours, seeking out the hunger in you, the deep, rich taste of you. She doesn't thrill to the touch of your breath on her face, the scent of you wrapping around her. She doesn't long for your hands to touch where no other hand but mine has touched before. Doesn't revel in the sensation of you all around, the thick length of you inside, pressing deep, bringing me to ecstasy. She doesn't feel this need here,' she pressed one of his hands just under her stomach, 'and here.' She pressed his other hand over her heart. 'All she knows is what I know—that you are the only one who can feed that need, the only one who can fulfil it. So please. Please, don't turn from me. Not now. Not tonight. Not when I need your warmth and hope and joy deep inside me where it can fuel me through what I have to do tonight. I'll beg if I must. I'll—'

He put his finger over her lips. 'No. You never need to beg. You are too strong to beg.'

'Then why aren't you kissing me?'

He shook his head lightly, a small smile on his lips. 'Because you undo me, Little Bird.'

And then his lips were against hers, one hand in her hair, the other pressing her against him.

Warmth. It slid through her with the soft caress then quickly fired to something greater. Something deeper. Something that made her tremble against him, hungering for more. His lips angled over hers, sucking, sipping, teeth nipping, tongue licking.

She gasped.

His tongue slipped into her mouth, sliding along hers. She whimpered. He growled. Pressed her even closer before swinging her around to press her up against the wall.

So tight.

So close.

Not close enough.

She wanted ... she wanted ... she didn't know what she wanted. But her hands clutched at his shirt, the hammering of his heart in his chest thrumming against her fingers, matching the hammering of hers.

She whimpered.

He pulled back. 'I'm sorry. I'm being too rough.'

'No!' She tightened her grip on his shirt. It wasn't enough. She didn't have enough of his heat. She needed the strength of it. Needed more, to help her get through. 'More.'

He growled low again, his wolf in his eyes. In her mind, she heard its howl, its longing for her. She howled back at it through whatever connection allowed her to hear it, wanting it to know she loved it too.

A wave of emotion so strong raced over her, through her, and it was all she could do to hold on as Iain's lips took hers again in a kiss that was all tongue and teeth and longing.

Then his lips left hers and chased down her neck, bringing so much pleasure she trembled with it. She wanted to return the favour. Grabbing his head, she pulled his from her neck, gaze clashing with his. 'My turn,' she said roughly. Then she pressed her mouth against the column of his neck and nipped, teeth sinking into his skin right over his pulse point. He growled, the sound buzzing on her lips. The sensation made her purr low in her throat.

'Fuck.' It was a low, sexy groan.

The sound of it gripped between her legs and stroked. Tremors broke out deep inside, chasing over her skin, filling her with the thrill of an expectation she didn't understand.

She slid her hands up under his shirt, fingers gliding over hot, muscled flesh that trembled under her touch. She nipped his neck again, then licked. His hand was in her hair, gently urging her mouth away from his neck and back to his. Back to where it belonged.

She smiled against his lips then opened to him.

His tongue slipped between hers and stroked deep, sliding and tangling with hers. The wall was hard against her back, but she didn't care. All she could care about was the feel of him pressed against her, the rigid length of his erection pressing into her stomach. She tingled. And writhed. And ached to press her core against that hot, hard length.

He seemed to read her mind because he cupped her bottom and lifted. She wrapped her legs around him and sighed into his mouth at the feel of his rigid length against her core. It felt so right, and yet not enough, not nearly enough.

She wriggled against him. He groaned. She laughed, triumphant that she was capable of causing that pleasure-pain desire in him. The same desire rampaging through her, taking her over, blanking her mind to everything but this moment. To the sensations. To the feeling of utter freedom.

She was flying, her soul singing to the sound of his joy reverberating deep inside.

Home. This was home. She couldn't have it forever like she'd recently come to long for, but she could have it for now and it would see her through to the end.

'I want you inside me now.'

With a moan, he pulled her towards him and covered her lips with his.

25

His mouth was hot and hard on hers and yet she could feel him holding back, holding on. He trembled against her, his need for control warring with the voraciousness of the desire that flared between them, threatening to turn them both into ash.

He was still being careful with her, like he had the first time. But she didn't want him to hold back. She wanted him. All of him. Because this was her last chance. Their last chance. She wanted it to be enough to carry her through the night, to carry him through the future without her. To have this night to remember; a night where they gave everything.

But they couldn't have that if he was being careful.

She held his face in her hands and met his passion-darkened gaze. 'Let go, Iain. Let go.' Then she kissed him, an open-mouthed, tongue-tangling kiss, filling herself with his spicy fresh taste, the pine and ocean scent of him. Heat burst through her—his and hers—as their tongues met and his control slipped a little more. His wolf howled its joy once more in the deep recesses of her mind.

She dug her fingers into his hair and pressed her body harder against his. 'More,' she whispered. 'Touch me.' His hands stayed on her face. 'Touch me.' She bit his lip.

His growl shot right to her core, making her thighs clench, then clench again when his erection flexed against her. She smiled as he pulled her harder against him. She dug her hands under his shirt, the muscles under her fingers trembling. His hair was crisp, his nipples little hard nubs under her palms. She rubbed her hands against them and gloried in his moan.

'Eloise,' he groaned. 'You're going to kill me.'

She threw back her head and laughed, unable to hold in the joy only he could bring her. She'd had such little joy in her life, and to have it in this moment, with this Were, was something truly precious she would remember for as long as she was able to hold onto herself.

His lips found her neck, sucking and licking, and another wildfire burst into life inside her. His hands found the edge of her shirt, fingers gliding underneath. Skin on skin. 'More.' Her voice caught in her throat so it came out as a husky murmur of sound, a sexy purr.

'Yes.' His teeth sank into the place in her neck where her pulse pounded. The bite wasn't gentle—it would leave a mark—but the pleasure of it shot through her nerves, pulling on her core. Something inside her was tightening, tightening.

Any moment now, she might explode.

He licked the bite.

She cried out as the tension inside her pulled tighter, so tight it was almost painful.

'Let go, Little Bird. Let go.' His lips covered hers, his fingers gliding around to her stomach, flicking open the button on her jeans, then they were inside her panties, parting the swollen flesh at the juncture of her thighs, slicking in a wet glide through the folds to her core. She moaned into his mouth as sparking sensations went off inside her like little firecrackers, lights flaring behind her eyelids, the tightening sensation getting even tighter. 'Please, please,' she whimpered into his mouth, her entire frame shuddering and shaking with need.

'Hold onto me, my Little Bird.' His lips left hers again, running hot fire down her throat, back to her pulse. He closed his teeth over it again and pushed his finger inside her, rubbing his thumb against the nub of her clit.

She screamed as everything inside her imploded and exploded at the same time, wave after wave after wave, pounding through her, lifting her up and knocking her flat. Everything flew from her mind, from her grasp, as the most incredible sensation flooded through her.

It was joy. It was bliss.

It was Iain.

She came to, still clinging to him, his arms around her supporting her weight. She smiled up at him. 'Wow. I think you literally blew my mind,' she managed to pant out.

He smiled that smile that made her want to eat him up. 'That was just the warm up.'

Too full of emotion, she kissed him. Didn't stop kissing him when he gathered her closer and carried her across the room to lie her on the soft bed.

Iain came down on top of her, his legs sliding between hers, his chest pressing lightly against her breasts. They kissed for a little longer and then his lips left hers. She made to protest, but he took her earlobe in his teeth and sucked. 'Oh, Goddess!' His tongue dipped into her ear at the same time his hand covered her breast. He brushed his palm over her nipple, back and forth, rubbing her bra against sensitised skin, branding her with need—his, hers, theirs. The sensation was too much and yet not enough. Not nearly enough. Her fingers bunched in his shirt, pulled, ripping his T-shirt from collar to hem.

Her gaze met his. 'Sorry. But I need to touch you.'

'Let me help you with that.' He grinned and shucked off his torn shirt. 'Now my turn.' He pulled her upright and whisked her top over her head, tossing it aside. Muscles rippled on his chest, stomach, arms as he laid her back down then held himself above her, his skin golden in the light, chest hair arrowing down his stomach, pointing to the huge bulge of his erection.

'Oh,' she breathed. Her hand fluttered up to trace over him. Her mouth watered. She wanted to take a bite.

'Go on,' he said, shifting to lay beside her on his back.

Hers. He was saying he was hers.

Her gaze raked over him. She wanted to kiss, to lick, to nip, to suck. But where? What would please him most? His nipple peeked through the dark sprinkle of hair dusting his chest.

She leaned over and touched her tongue to it.

His breath hissed, stomach muscles tensing. Unable to stop herself, she ringed the sensitised nub with her tongue and then bit.

He tensed, a low rumble sounding deep in his throat. Encouraged, she did it again. Kissed her way across the expanse of his chest and did the same to his other nipple. His erection flexed against her stomach and she looked down at it. She wanted to see it. She'd barely got a chance to appreciate it last time, to savour. She wouldn't miss the opportunity now.

She traced her fingers down the muscles of his stomach, dipped into his belly button before settling on the button of his jeans. He jerked as she popped it open and pulled down the zipper. She pulled the flaps apart, exposing his boxer shorts. They were soft blue cotton and fitted him like a second skin—the kind you saw in underwear ads and always seemed to be improbably filled. Those models had nothing on Iain.

She pushed his jeans and boxers down his legs and off, then sat back to appreciate the view.

His penis was huge and erect, glorious and proud and begging to be touched. She ran her finger around the tip, amazed at how it flexed against her hand, at how silky soft the tight skin was. She wrapped her hand around the shaft, exploring the width. Iain hissed, a sound of pleasure. She felt his pleasure deep inside as if it were her own. The tightening began in her core again, panties soaked wet with her desire. His penis would soon press into that soaked flesh, parting her, pushing into her—and she wanted that. Oh Goddess, how she wanted that—but first, she had to taste.

Bending over, hair brushing against his stomach and thighs, she put her mouth to the tip of his penis, tongue circling the rim near the top before she sucked him into her mouth.

'Fuck!' Iain's hands dug into her hair, but she didn't stop. She kept tonguing him, tasting him, taking him into her mouth as far as she could and then sliding out again. He tasted salty and sweet at the same time and she couldn't get enough. Over and over, she slid her mouth down on him, twirling her tongue around the tip, her hand at the base, holding him steady. Then suddenly he reached down and pulled her up across his chest. 'Not yet,' he muttered. 'I don't just want your mouth.'

'Come inside me then.'

'I want you naked first.' He covered her mouth with his again in a drugging kiss that completely took her over. His hands slipped over her shoulders, down her back. He slipped off her bra, then her other clothes and she was lying on him, skin to skin. Rearing up, he held her, chest to chest and then pushed into her in one, glorious stroke.

Her back arched as she took him in, breath a gasp in her throat as he sank right to her core. He kissed her, a tongue-tangling intimate sharing, and then he lifted her hips, showing her the rhythm.

She began to ride him, hard and fast. He sank back on the bed, taking her with him, guiding her hips into a different position, taking him even deeper. Muscles trembled, tightened, tensed as if ready to explode. So close. She was so close. His lips left hers and sucked her nipple into the warmth of his mouth.

She cried out as the orgasm took her, muscles tensing then exploding in a pulsing rhythm against him, around him, and all the time he continued to suck her nipple and move inside her in a way that kept the orgasm cresting over and over.

Finally her muscles quivered to a stop and she flopped down over him, panting, exhausted, replete. 'You've wrung me dry,' she murmured against his chest, a smile etched into her face that felt like it would never disappear.

'I'm not done with you yet.' He flipped her over so she was on her back, and lifting her legs, entered her again and began to move slow and firm against her.

She watched him through slumberous eyes, amazed that she could have orgasmed so hard twice and yet he was building her up again. One of his hands moved from her hip, his thumb brushing over the apex of her sex near where they were joined, touching the nub of pulsing nerves. At the same time, he moved harder into her.

'Oh!' Lights sparked behind her eyes and her inner muscles pulsed and spasmed. 'Do that again.'

'With pleasure.' His thumb moved in circles as he thrust in and out of her.

'Harder. Faster,' she demanded.

His answer was a smile and then his lips were on hers as he moved just like she'd asked.

This time, they reached their peak together, falling over the edge of the abyss to land safely in each other's arms, him still pulsing inside her, long and hard and thick, like he had the night before.

SHE MUST HAVE FALLEN ASLEEP, because some time later, she woke up with a start. 'Goddess! What time is it?'

His lips were instantly on her brow, his fingers stroking down her arm, along her side. 'Shh. It's okay. You have time. We have time.'

He was still inside her, growing larger.

She looked up at him, a smile quirking on her face. 'My, Mr Wolf. What big ...' she let her gaze roam down to his groin and then back up, '... teeth you have.'

He laughed. 'I'll show you how good big teeth are,' he said and then his lips were on hers again, his fingers moving lower, moving seductively against her, and she fell into the madness of passion once again.

She lay in his arms after, the light of the moon crossing the room, rising higher and higher until she could ignore the significance of it no longer. 'It's almost midnight.' She turned and kissed him softly. 'I have to go.'

She ached at the thought. She didn't want to leave this room, leave him, but she had no choice.

At least she had this. She'd wrap the reality of what she'd just shared with Iain around her like a shield. It made her stronger.

Many people never experienced anything even remotely like what she and Iain had shared in the last few days. She would take those memories and smile into the face of Death.

He kissed her one more time, one long, drugging pull of a kiss before he pulled out of her and rolled away.

Cold rushed through her. She hid her shiver as she hastily got up.

'Eloise?' He brushed his hand down her naked back, an intimate caress she would never have imagined sharing with such a man before him. As it always did, his touch left melting warmth in its wake.

'Yes?' She looked over her shoulder and into the warm depths of his chocolate eyes.

'You are mine.'

'I have always been yours.' His smile almost broke her heart.

They dressed quickly and then Iain led her to the kitchen where he made her a cup of tea and scrambled some eggs.

'I'm not really hungry,' she said. 'The tea is enough. Besides, I have to get down there.'

'It's only just past eleven. You have time to eat. You have to keep up your strength.' He placed a large plate of eggs and toast in front of her. 'Please eat. It will make me happier if you do.'

He smiled at her in that way that made her shiver in delicious anticipation. She ate, for him at first, but as the food hit her stomach she was suddenly glad for it. He was right.

Eating food he'd made for her did make her feel stronger.

Once done, he took her hand and led her back down to the lift. He held her hand as they dropped back into the earth, then silently led her down the hall to the door at the end, behind which Cain lay, waiting.

At the door, he stopped, a look on his face that was difficult to define.

'What?'

'I know what you said to the others, but don't ask me to leave your side. I can't do it.' His fingers flexed in hers.

Her lips trembled and she looked away. 'He'll kill you. I won't have you—'

'Let him in, Little Bit. I promise I won't hurt him. Yet.'

She gasped, turning around, trying to find Cain's Shade, ignoring Iain's worried questions.

'Where are you?'

'Near my body. Waiting for you. Let the wolf-man in. He might prove useful later when we want to leave. Maybe I'll even let you bring him along as a plaything. I can see you're fond of him.'

'You just want him there to hurt him, to hurt me. But you won't hurt him,' she said, arms going out in front of Iain. 'I won't let you.'

Cain's laughter shivered around her. *'You're not very trusting, are you? I promise I won't hurt him if he doesn't stop you from doing what you said you would. Cross my heart and hope to die, stick a finger in my eye and all that. Happy?'*

'I'm not anywhere close to happy.'

'What is it, Eloise?' Iain touched her arm, gathering her attention to him; a simple touch that vibrated down to her core. 'What's he saying to you?'

'He wants you to come in. He promises he won't hurt you.'

'Good. I'm coming in anyway.'

'I don't trust him.'

'Neither do I. But I was coming in whether he wanted me there or not.'

'Oh, he's so macho and brave. I almost admire him for that.'

There was one problem with this entire scenario: if he came in, Iain would stop her. He wouldn't be able to help himself. There was no way he was going to let her do what she needed to do for the basic ceremony, let alone what would come after. And while Cain didn't know what she had planned, he had to know Iain wouldn't stand still while she cut herself open and bled to bring him back. He would try to stop her and Cain would kill him.

Eloise squeezed her eyes closed. This was a horrible disaster. But what could she do?

She had to do something.

'What are you waiting for, Little Bit? It's almost time.'

The door opened in front of them, the curtain that surrounded the bed billowing out, as if waving them in.

She had no choice. She had to enter. Iain moved before her, his body shielding hers as if still trying to protect her. She loved him for it, even as she railed at the futility of it.

Nobody could protect her from Cain and what he wanted to do. Nothing could stop him except for death.

Her death.

And there was only one way to stop Iain from meeting his death tonight at Cain's hands.

'Remember, you promised not to hurt him if he doesn't stop me,' she said in her mind to the shadowy form in the corner near the bed. She hadn't wanted to encourage this mind-connection with Cain before now, but she had no choice. She couldn't let Iain hear what she said.

Cain's voice was smug as he replied, *'I know exactly what I promised. I won't go back on my word. Will you?'*

'I'll do what I said I'd do.'

Eloise took in a deep breath, her gaze going unerringly to Iain's as he turned to face her.

'What do you need me to do?'

She held out her hand. He took it. Warmth surged through her, along with sorrow that this was the last time he'd hold onto her and she'd feel it. 'I'm sorry, Iain. Please forgive me.'

Before his face even registered the grief in her voice, she clapped her hand on his shoulder, her fingers squeezing on two points and channelled power through him.

He stiffened as the blow sizzled through him, his gaze shocked. 'Eloise, no!' he gasped and then his eyes rolled up in his head and he fell forward.

26

'This is bullshit. We need to get down there, now.'

'It's not time yet,' Cordy said, shooting Shelley a 'save me from idiot males' look before saying to her mate, 'Cain will know something's going on if we get there too soon. We'll go down just before midnight.'

'But that's more than an hour from now!' Marcus snapped. 'I can't stand around doing fuck all.'

'You're going to have to.' Cordy put her hands on her hips, brows arched at her mate.

Marcus snarled and then turned around, paced, mumbling to Adam as he passed him, 'You try to change her mind. She's not listening to me.'

Adam opened his mouth but Shelley put her hand up. 'Don't. Just don't.' She looked around wildly, head pounding, the spirits yelling at her now, crowding closer and closer. She couldn't take Marcus' and Adam's arguments too. 'I'm getting out of here.'

She turned and marched for the door. There was a commotion behind her, but then only one set of steps followed her.

'Shells, are you okay?'

Cordy. Shelley lifted her hands in despair and turned to face Cordy. 'Why won't they listen?'

'Because they're Were males. It's not in them to stand idly by and wait, even when they know it's the right thing.'

'I don't like waiting either.' They seemed to do nothing but wait. Wait to see what Morrigan was going to do next. Wait to see what new disaster might befall them all. Wait to see what would manifest from these new powers that had been thrust upon them. Although hers weren't so much new, just enhanced and more difficult to ignore. Especially the bloody spirits who just wouldn't leave her alone tonight. She pressed her fingers against her aching head.

Cordy touched her shoulder. 'Leave them to me. Go for a walk and clear your head.'

'Thank you.' She slipped away as Cordy went back into the room and explained again to Adam and Marcus the need to give Eloise space to do the spell. Not to mention the fact that they couldn't bully away Cain's threat to hurt more of them. 'We have to take him seriously.'

As Adam's voice rose again, protesting the witches' trust in what Eloise reported Cain had said, Shelley sighed and raced outside. She supposed she was being a bit unfair, getting pissed off at Adam and Marcus for being who they were—Were males who had worrying about their pack woven into their psyche. It was just that it was the last straw. She'd been trying so desperately to hang on, to ignore the spirits who wouldn't leave her alone, but tonight it was impossible.

'Fuck,' she hissed as the spirits pressed in on her. They were agitated about something, shouting so loudly she couldn't understand. 'Leave me alone.' But of course, they just pressed closer. 'Right. You give me no choice.' She stalked to the dam in the home paddock and, without pausing, waded in.

Water. It was the only place the spirits couldn't reach her. They didn't seem to like the water's energy. It was like the air was thicker, unsteady, always in flux, over water and they couldn't move through it as easily. A few determined spirits did follow her, moving so slowly in the turbulence over the water that they looked like flies caught in amber. 'Leave me alone!' she screamed, the sound pushing them back until they stood, moaning, in a ring around the dam.

She waded in further, the energy of the water dulling the sound of the spirits' wailing. 'Thank the Goddess,' she muttered, coming to a halt in waist-deep water.

She began to shiver—the water was freezing—but she didn't move. Being cold was better than the sensation of implosion that pressed on her constantly. She was sick and tired of being surrounded all the time. Sick of never having a moment's peace. She wanted to be alone. Craved it.

She snorted. At one time, she'd hated being alone. When she was alone, the spirits came to her more readily and she had more trouble fighting them. It's why she'd taken up nursing. It kept her busy and surrounded by the living all the time. She hadn't thought about what happened when someone died. Nor that so many spirits would be roaming around the hospital—you know, you'd think they'd have somewhere better to go than the sterile hallways of the hospital, but apparently not. Apparently it was the place to be if you were dead. There and cemeteries. She shivered. Ugh. She really didn't like ceme-teries. She hadn't set foot inside one of them for years. And after her current tenure was up at the hospital, she planned to never step foot inside a hospital again either.

It was time for her to do something else. Something that took her far away from the dead *and* the living. She had no other choice if she wanted to keep her sanity for as long as possible. She would eventu-ally fall into the insanity that ran in her family—a family of Mediums —but not yet.

The problem was, while she was learning more and more about her 'gift' all the time, she still couldn't control it. The others had no idea how bad it had got for her—she didn't want them to know that with the powers she'd got from Skye last Halloween, she was now open to seeing more than she ever had. Her old blocks just didn't work like they used to. Inviting in Harrison and Adeline the year before to help save River and Skye had opened a Pandora's box of spirits she had no hope of controlling.

They were taking over her life.

She smacked the water with her fist. 'I've had enough, you hear!' she yelled at the sky. She wasn't cut out to be a Pack Witch. She wasn't cut out to be a Medium. She hated everything about it. She only ever saw the horror, not the wonder of it, and she was sick of having her life ruled by something she couldn't truly control. No matter what she did, the spirits were always there, always pressing in on her, and she was fucking well sick of it.

After they were over this crisis, things were going to change. She wasn't sure how, but she wasn't going to use her powers to commune with the dead anymore. She would find some way to shut them down for good.

Then she'd go travelling. Get into some form of research that meant dusty library shelves and no people. She did rather like researching the histories of the Pack Diaries. Maybe that was her path. Pack Librarian, not Pack Medium. Not that. Never again. And if the pack didn't like it, they could just go blow. This was her life and she was finally going to live it. She was sick and tired of trying to live up to other people's expectations of what she was meant to be. Her family, her cheating ex, the pack, even her best friends all expected her to be something she wasn't.

After this, it was going to be Shelley time.

'Kitten. Are you okay?'

Shelley curled her fingers against her side, fighting the sensation that curled through her at the sound of Adam's voice. That sensation irritated her. Her body's reaction to him irritated her. *He* irritated her —beyond measure. And to make matters worse, he wouldn't leave her alone.

Okay, he was her Shadow, but he seemed to stick closer than any of the others who took over from him when he wasn't able to be her Shadow. He was like a cat in that way. She'd always been amused by the way cats homed in on the person who didn't like them and wouldn't leave them alone, twining around their feet, sitting on their lap, purring into their face. It wasn't such a funny trait in a man though.

Adam had actually purred at her the other day when she'd snapped at him about something!

She'd wanted to slap him and kiss him all at the same time—but she'd done neither. She wasn't an emotionally explosive kind of person. Although she did rather feel like a powder keg primed for a spark. She was so sexually frustrated, the itch of it was torment, making her want to scream.

Instead of screaming, she plastered a smile to her lips and turned to face him.

'Finished cock fighting with Marcus have we?'

'That wasn't a cock fight. That was just an airing of frustrations.'

'Can't you go for a run or something?'

'We could, but that was more fun.'

'For whom?'

'Me. Marcus. Even Cordy enjoyed it.'

'I didn't.'

'No.' He stepped up to the water's edge. 'You never enjoy arguing, do you?'

She swallowed hard. 'Not really.'

'You argue with me.'

'That's different.'

He smiled—she wanted to slap him for it. 'I know.'

She blew out a breath and turned back around, staring across the night-shadowed paddocks. 'Go away.'

'Come out of the water.'

'No.'

A sigh. 'Okay then.' The sound of splashing behind her.

She whipped around, staring at him as he waded through the cold water towards her. 'What are you doing?'

'Joining you.'

'Why?'

He waved his hand through the water. 'This appears to be the place to be.'

She almost laughed—almost. 'You are ridiculous.'

'I'm not the one standing in cold water.'

She turned away from him, away from that look that made her feel stripped to the bone. 'It's not so cold.'

'Your teeth are chattering.'

She clamped her jaws together.

'Shelley.' He touched her shoulder.

She jerked away. 'Please, don't.'

'You need to come out of the water. Your teeth *are* chattering and you've got goose bumps so large I could ski through them.'

She shook her head. 'It's more peaceful here. My head is clearer. I can think.'

'The spirits?'

She opened her mouth to deny it, to tell him to go away, but instead whispered, 'They're shouting at me about something, but I can't understand them.'

'You're exhausted. Your concentration is shot. Perhaps if you had some sleep you'd be able to figure it out.'

She whipped around to face him. 'Don't you see? I don't want to figure it out. I don't want any of this. I never did.' Her gaze slid past him, up towards the house. 'It's okay for Cordy and Bron and Skye and the others. They want this—'

'Skye didn't.'

She waved her hand. 'That's just because she was brought up with a lie and believed the wrong thing about herself. Now she knows the truth, she's embraced all this,' she waved her hand around, 'fully. But that was never the case with me. I knew and I didn't want it. My Gran tried to train me so I could follow in her footsteps, despite the fact my aunt was turned insane by the never-ending grind of this "gift". That's what they called it, a gift.' She snorted. 'Even then, I saw it for what it was, and the only reason I went through any training at all was I wanted to learn how to block what I could see, what I could feel, so I wouldn't have to deal with it.'

'Hell, Kitten. Why didn't you tell them?'

She shrugged away his hands as they reached for her again. 'They didn't care that I didn't want my Gramps coming to me telling me I'm with the wrong man and showing me exactly why. They thought it was a wonder that I could see my dead cousin weeping, pleading not to be dead, kept away from her husband and baby. They didn't understand that I didn't want to be touched by the man who got knocked over as he crossed the road, his confusion and grief more painful than his death. That I didn't want to dream of tragedies or people dying especially given they were things I couldn't stop.' She gripped her hair, pulled. 'I don't want all of this ... this ... death and depression and darkness in my head. I just want a normal life. Don't you understand? A normal life. And yet, now I've been tied to the pack, that can never be, can it? Can it?'

Her eyes widened as she realised how much she'd said. She turned away before she could see the look of horror that must be on his face. 'Forget it. Just go away.'

'Shelley.' His hands were on her shoulders again, turning her, the water rippling out around them. 'I'm not going away.'

'I wish you would.'

He cupped her face, forcing her to look up at him. 'No, you don't.'

She shivered, but not from the cold.

His touch. It was too much. And not enough.

She wanted him to go, but a part of her, deep inside, cried out for him to stay. He was the one steady thing in her life right now, the one person who never wanted anything of her except a laugh and a smile. And he always seemed to know when she needed to be pulled from her dark thoughts. Which wasn't a hard thing for him to do. He confused her so much, she could never think straight when he was around.

'Why are you here?' she whispered, voice hoarse.

'Because you need me.'

'I don't need you.' She tried to sound certain, but it came out breathy, a question.

'Yes, you do. You've always needed me, the same as the pack needs me. Maybe even more.' His fingers moved on her face, stroking across sensitive skin, into her hair, holding her still. 'Jason thinks that the Trickster is connected to the pack in a way that no other is. That my wolf allows me to take the emotional temperature of the pack, including our coven, as a whole, as well as the individuals within it. I'm coming to think that's true, because of what I've been feeling, the way I've been behaving, but mostly because I can feel the struggle within you. I can feel your pain as if it's my own.'

'And you think you can fix that with a laugh?'

'No.' His eyes searched hers as his breath brushed over her face. 'But I know I can fix it. I know I have to fix it.'

'Or what?'

'Or we might all be lost forever. *I* might be lost forever.'

'I—' she said, but his words had torn all her thoughts to shreds.

'Don't leave us, Shelley. Don't leave me.'

His thumbs moved on her cheeks, gaze searching hers, understanding in their depths. The heat that had always been there between them, pulled, and suddenly she couldn't stand the distance she'd created. The endless frustration of denying this thing she felt inside whenever he was around.

With a voiceless cry, she surged forward just as he did, their lips meeting in a clash of teeth and tongue. She clutched his shirt, pulling him closer, closer, her breasts squishing against the hard planes of his chest. They fit. She was tall, taller than many men she knew, but he was taller. She never felt 'big' around him, like she was living in the Land of the Giants and she was the giant. Around him, she felt normal sized. Now she felt the right size. For him.

Goddess! How could this be? She was kissing Adam. Annoying Adam. She almost laughed with the ludicrousness of it, except the heated desire surging through every fibre of her being made laughter impossible. She was too hot for laughter. In fact, she was thankful they were standing in icy water, or they might have already combusted on the spot.

She made needy little sounds in her throat as his lips left hers and worked their way down her neck and back up to suck on her ear. She shifted restlessly against him, her hands running up and down his back to settle finally in his hair, fingers curling in the dark threads of silk and pulling him back to her mouth. She needed his lips, his tongue, his teeth. The taste of him filling her up, the scent of him in her nose—citrus and sunshine and laughter all rolled into one. She wasn't sure how someone could smell of sunshine and laughter, but Adam did. He always had. She'd always found it so annoyingly hot.

She gripped him tighter when he began to pull away.

'Shelley.'

Her name was a buzz against her lips but she didn't let go. Didn't want this to stop. For the first time her mind was clear of everything. There was just the heat of him, the scent of him, the humming sound of him harmonising with her needy noises.

Except, how could he be saying her name and making humming noises at the same time?

She blinked, loosening her grip, allowing him to pull back slightly, aware for the first time of the change in his tone as he said her name.

'Kitten? Are you okay? Shelley? Shelley!'

By the way his mouth was moving and the look on his face, he was shouting at her, but his voice was fading away under the humming noise that rose around her.

From her.

She had no idea what it was or why it was, but the humming came from somewhere deep inside. Reaching up and forcing itself out of her against her will.

Her eyes widened in fear as she gripped his shirt, holding onto him as he and everything around her faded away and the world became nothing but the sound.

Then her head fell back, and the scream erupted from her mouth.

'IF YOU DON'T LIE DOWN NOW,' River said, trying to move Bron away from the workbench, 'you're not going to be able to help anyone later.'

'I'll be fine. Truly.'

He didn't return her smile, just shook his head, turning her to face him fully, hands on her shoulders, thumbs stroking her neck.

Warmth shot through her, a heat that only River could spark to life—even when she was completely preoccupied, like now.

'Kiss me.'

He did, but it was no more than a soft press of lip. 'You can smile all you like and pretend exuberance for your work, but I know you. I can feel you inside my heart. I can feel the drag of exhaustion on you, on your power, on the bond.'

'I didn't realise I was pulling on your energy. I'll try to stop.'

'That's not what I mean, and you know it. You need to sleep. You've been on the go for forty-eight hours straight. I really would rather prefer you didn't keel over and damage yourself. I'd be seriously pissed if that were to happen.'

'I can't stop now. I need to do this.' She turned to grab another bunch of lavender.

He put his hand on hers. 'You have the ingredients you need at the shop. I'll call Helen and ask her to put together what you need. Patrick will grab it and bring it over.'

'The shop will need to be resupplied, so I need to make this next batch anyway.' She reached out to grab a beaker, but fumbled, knocking it off the edge of the bench. Instead of the sound of smashed glass on tile, she heard nothing; saw nothing but endless black.

'Bron! Bron!' River's voice came from far away but she couldn't see him, couldn't reach him. All she could do was fall.

River caught her before she hit the ground. She whimpered, her fingernails digging into his arms. 'No. No,' she whispered, her breath coming in painful gasps. Her eyes flickered open—swirling black stared up at him.

'Bron.' He grasped her face in both hands. 'Bron, come back to me. Follow my voice. Don't lose yourself in the vision.'

'Don't let her do it!' she rasped, her voice not her own. 'Stop her. Don't let her do it.'

'Don't let her do what? Who are you talking about?'

Bron snapped upright, her eyes wide open. 'Shelley!' she cried out.

'What is it?' River gripped her shoulders, turned her to face him. 'What's happened to Shelley?'

'The Banshee wail. Death comes.' Her grieved gaze met his. 'We have to get up there now, before it's too late.'

SKYE BRUSHED Tom's hair from his face, kissed his brow. 'Good night,' she whispered. Even though he was sound asleep, she knew somewhere deep inside, the little boy felt her loving touch. That kind of thing counted. She knew that better than anyone. It had been things like this that had carried her through the terrible years after her grandpa died. Her grandmother might not have showed outwardly that she loved Skye, but she'd done it in moments like this, and somehow, deep down, Skye had always known. Just as she knew Tom knew.

Although, Tom never had to wonder if he was loved like she had. He was well and truly surrounded by it through every waking moment. It was a wonder he wasn't spoilt. But he wasn't. He was a wonderful, generous, kind-hearted little boy and he'd grow up into a remarkable man. He would make such a wonderful big brother to a little cousin or surrogate brother or sister.

Unfortunately, that was something she couldn't give him unless she and Jason adopted. And right now, with their lives turned upside-down by Morrigan and her insanity, they could hardly bring another little soul into the crosshairs. No. That would have to wait until all of this was over.

Goddess. She hoped it would be soon.

She bent to give him another kiss but stopped still when a wave of nausea rose up and through her. She stood there, bent over and panting as her skin prickled with sweat. Forcing herself to breathe slowly, she closed her eyes and counted to ten, willing the sensation to pass. She'd been struck with this strange feeling a number of times in the last few days and each time it had taken only a count of ten for it to pass, but not this time. She hit twenty, then twenty-five. She began to panic, but thankfully, as she reached thirty it loosened its grip and slipped away.

She wiped a trembling hand over her brow and forced herself to straighten. She must be coming down with something—although this had been happening for a few days and it hadn't become worse. Except for the length of time it had taken hold of her right now.

Maybe it was just the stress of everything. There certainly was a lot to be stressed about. Yes. That had to be it. She probably just needed to make sure she got a good night's sleep in the next few days and took some time out.

Maybe she'd take Bron up on that massage she kept insisting Skye needed. And she needed to do it before Jason found out about these little bouts of dizziness and nausea. He had enough to worry about. He'd want to roll her up in cotton wool and never let her venture past the front door if he found out. He really did have a habit of being overprotective.

She loved that about him, but it was also frustrating to someone who had been so self-sufficient for so long.

She waited until she was certain she showed no signs of the little bout of whatever it was before she gave Tom one more kiss and silently slipped out of his room.

She wasn't surprised to see Jason waiting for her at the end of the hallway, his hand outstretched—it was eleven, after all and they'd need to leave to get up to the McClunes' lands to help Cordy with the spell to bind Cain. They were just waiting for Bron to finish her preparations.

She took Jason's hand, the warmth of his touch stealing through her. She still couldn't believe he was hers as she was his. It seemed so incredible that she'd only known him for seven months—it felt like she'd known him forever. She couldn't believe she'd fought falling in love with him so hard. It all could have turned out so differently. But it hadn't because he was a stubborn bastard, an Alpha hell-bent on winning his mate, gaining back his Pack Witch and saving his pack.

Thank God for stubborn bastards. They all needed him and his strength, now more than ever. She shivered.

'What's wrong?'

'I'm just worried about Eloise.' She leaned into him, rubbed her head against his shoulder. 'So much is riding on her shoulders.' She shrugged. 'I hate the fact she has to do the spell alone.'

'We'll leave now. We can be there just after midnight to help Cordy with the spell.'

'I thought we were waiting for Bron to finish her herbal preparations.'

'We can go now if it will make you feel better.'

She smiled, stroked his hand. 'You know me so well.' She reached up to cup his face, to seek for a deeper kiss when pain gripped her stomach, then tore through her head.

She clapped her hands over her ears, falling to her knees, unaware of Jason coming down with her, holding her upright. His mouth moved, worry clouding his eyes, but she couldn't hear him. Couldn't hear anything but the screaming in her head.

'Shelley,' she gasped. 'It's Shelley. Death comes.'

ADAM STAGGERED, the scream shoving through his head, tipping the world, spinning it around. His vision darkened as the scream got louder and the pain intensified. Fuck! He was going to pass out again. Pass out and drown in this goddamned dam. What a way to go. He'd never live this down. He began to chuckle, the sound a hiccough in his chest.

Hysterical. He was hysterical. If only he could stop the scream from stabbing at him like a thousand ice picks at once.

He managed to lurch towards Shelley.

Her face was tipped to the night sky, eyes black holes in her head, face paler than a corpse, her features harsher, pulled up, angled somehow, almost like something else had imprinted itself on her features.

He grabbed her, tried to shake her, to shout her name, but there was no sound but the one she made, and no impact from his touch.

She was cold. Freezing cold. And shaking. When the scream stopped, he was afraid she would collapse. And if she did, she would drown. He might have laughed at the thought of his own death in the muddy water of this dam, but there was nothing funny about the thought of her dying here.

He had to get her out of the water. But the world was spinning and everything ached. And the screaming went on and on. His wolf howled inside him, wanting to scamper away, to hide, but needing to see to her safety at the same time. It was as torn as he was. 'Right buddy. Can't let her drown.'

Somehow he managed to pull her behind him—even if he had full control of his body, she was too stiff to lift and sling over his shoulder. He hooked his arms under her armpits and hauled, one painful, jagged step at a time as the screaming went on and on. Somehow, he got them up the bank onto dry grass.

Then the earth smacked against his face, blades of darkened grass obscuring his vision. He tried to move, to see to Shelley, but he couldn't. The scream. It was too much. It was everything. In every cell. Tearing him apart. And it wouldn't stop. His eyes flickered closed and everything became black.

27

Eloise guided Iain down as he crumpled to the floor, tears welling in her eyes as she whispered, 'Please forgive me. I have no choice.'

'*What did you do that for?*'

'You can't hurt him now,' she whispered as she cradled Iain's head in her lap, smoothing his lush dark hair back from his suddenly too-pale face. 'He won't stop me now. You promised you wouldn't hurt him if he didn't try to stop me. Now go back into the aether. I can't do the spell if you're on this plane.'

Cain chuffed out a laugh. '*Well played, Little Bit. Well played. But you need to hurry. Midnight is almost upon us. You've only got forty-five minutes to do the preparation spells.*'

'I know. I'll get it done.'

'*Good. I'll see you in the aether.*' He disappeared.

Eloise barely registered his departure. Her mind echoed with his words and what she'd done to deserve them.

What she'd done to Iain didn't feel well played. It felt like a betrayal.

Her fingers trembled over Iain's face. He had become so dear to her in such a small amount of time. She loved him. He was all she had ever wanted without even knowing she wanted it. The thought that he would never know that was a gaping hole in her chest. She supposed that's what happened when your chest was ripped open and your heart torn out. She hadn't meant to give it to this Were, but she had. And now she was doing the one thing that would guarantee she would never be forgiven—not by him, and not by the others she had come to feel deep friendship for. River. Bron. Skye and Jason. Would they understand, or would they feel betrayed too?

Not that she would even be around to know how they felt—she'd be a withered husk before they even knew what she'd done. Would they think she'd died to help her brother? She hoped not, but there was nothing she could do to change it now. She just had to go forward from here and do what she knew was right. This was the only way she could save them from the person she'd become if Cain and Morrigan had their way.

Leaning forward, she pressed trembling lips to Iain's, tasting the salt of her tears on his lips. 'I'm sorry. I'm so sorry. I love you. I wish I could stay and prove your trust in me, but I can't. I have to do this. I don't expect you to understand, but this is the only way I have of saving you.' She kissed his eyelids, his nose, his cheekbones, the dimple in his chin and then back to his lips, her fingers clenched in the cool silk of his hair. She didn't want to let go, but she had to. 'Please forgive me.'

Teeth gritted with the sheer effort it took to do what she must, she unwound her fingers from his hair, and lying his head back gently on the floor, she stood and turned away, unable to bear seeing him laid out on the concrete floor, vulnerable, his strength and force of will sheered away by the necessity of sacrificing herself to her brother. To save them all.

The first thing she had to do was stop the others from coming in. They'd have felt what she had done to Iain. They'd be down here soon, despite her warning about Cain's threat to kill them if they came inside the room. They'd want to know what she'd done. And why.

She couldn't let them anywhere near her.

She stared down at the keypad. That first. Pulling off the face-plate, she grabbed the wires below and pulled. Sparks shot from the wires and she gasped as little jolts of electricity shot up her arm. Ignoring the small burns—she'd had far worse injuries while working for Morrigan—she looked around for something else to help finish the job.

The Were nurse had left a bottle of water on the desk. She threw the water at the panel. The wires hissed and smoked. She stared at the shorted panel, her gaze going to the streaks of water that darkened the light grey of the wall and the puddle forming on the floor. For a moment, she thought she saw green eyes flash in the puddle, but when she leaned forward and looked straight at it, there was nothing there but the reflection of the darker ceiling and the light above her head.

She dragged the heavy chair the nurse used over to the door and pushed it up under the handle for good measure.

Satisfied the chair and the damaged keypad would give her enough time to finish what she'd come here to do, she walked over to the stainless-steel bench on the right wall. The cabinets and drawers were full of medicines and medical implements. Fingers trembling, she searched for what she needed. Finding it, she tore through the packet to the sterilised implement within. The metal felt warm in her cold hands.

Turning, she made her way back to the curtained alcove, her foot dragging on the floor, increasing the cold burning sensation that had been building there ever since she'd woken from the coma. Before today that pain would have made her wince and falter, but tonight it didn't touch her like it normally would. A strange numbness had settled over her—she wondered if she would even feel it when she slashed her wrists open for the spell.

The hiss of the curtain as she pulled it back was a taunting whisper. Cain lay as still as before, but a dark expectation tinged the air, making her shudder and move slowly forward, as if she walked against an ocean current.

As she looked down at her brother, water splashed on his shoulder. She raised her head to see where the leak was coming from and realised it wasn't water. It was a tear.

Her eyes blurred. She blinked rapidly, trying to steel her composure as the oppressive sensation pushed in tighter around her.

This was it. She had to do it now or face the consequences of her weakness. She put the scalpel down on the bed and, hands raised over Cain's chest, began the incantation that would prepare them both for what was to come.

ADAM MOANED, coming to slowly. Grass tickled his nose. Something wet ran down the side of his face. What the hell? Where was he? What had happened? And what was that high-pitched ringing in his ears? He couldn't hear anything past it.

Memories fluttered then slowly coalesced.

There had been a sound. A horrible scream. It had shattered through him, vibrating in his bones, his nerves, right down to his DNA. It was a noise a human voice box shouldn't be able to make and yet, Shelley had made it. And it had gone on and on until he'd passed out.

Fuck! He'd passed out. For how long?

He tried to lift his head to check the moon but the movement made the high-pitched ringing increase. It hurt. So much. He clapped his hands to his ears but that only made it worse.

Moaning, he rolled over and vomited. The dry retch of his heaving was a low vibration against the high-pitched ringing. But at least it wasn't the scream.

The scream. Shelley's scream. It had stopped.

Shelley? Where was Shelley?

He tried to push himself upright, but his arms were shaking too hard and he felt like he was going to vomit again. So he rolled over instead, onto his back, the movement careful, and gulped in fresh breaths. Out of the corner of his eye he saw a shadow on the grass beside him. He turned his head.

Shelley still lay where he'd dragged her, mouth open on a silent scream, eyes blacker than the night above. 'Shelley!' His voice was dry, sandpaper over gravel. He rolled over, swallowed hard and tried again. 'Shelley! Kitten?' His voice was louder, but she didn't respond. He reached out, the movement shaky, but managed to grip her shoulder, shake her. Nothing. He made himself sit up. The world spun again and pain sliced through his head. He clutched it, feeling the need to hold it where it was, as if it was about to fly off or tear apart. Something warm and wet dripped from his nose, the corner of his eyes, his ears.

Salt and copper. Blood.

Shouting sounded in the distance. The shouting brought his head up again. Shelley still hadn't moved. 'Shelley. Kitten.' Still no response. All right, maybe using her real name, a name he knew she hated, might get a result. 'Michelline?' He dragged himself closer, touched her face. She was cold. Ice cold. Deathly cold. 'Michelline!' Fear gave him strength and he hauled her into his arms. 'Don't leave me, Michelline. Do you hear me? Don't leave me.'

There was a moan and then a faint, 'Don't call me that. I hate that more than I hate Kitten.'

Her breath brushed against his cheek. He barked out a laugh, a note of hysterical relief, and buried his face in her hair. 'You're okay. You're okay.'

'You're crushing me,' she wheezed.

Another huff of laughter and then he pulled back, but didn't let go, holding her, touching her, cupping her face. He brushed her damp hair from too-pale skin.

'What's so funny?'

'Even near death you've still got to tell me off.'

Her lips twitched as she looked up at him, as if she was about to smile, and then her eyes flared and she snapped upright with a gasp, pulling out of his arms. Her gaze roamed wildly over the landscape blindly before landing on him. 'You're bleeding.' She grabbed the hem of her shirt and lifting it, began to wipe away the blood. 'I'm so sorry. I couldn't help it. Couldn't stop it. It just kept coming and coming.' Her voice hitched and she blinked rapidly as if fighting tears. 'It ripped at my insides, and I couldn't stop it.'

'What did?'

'Someone's about to die. Eloise!' She scrambled to her feet. 'It's Eloise.'

Adam staggered to his knees, then to his feet and lunged, grabbing her before she managed to get more than a few wobbly steps up the embankment. 'Eloise?'

'Let me go! I have to go stop her.'

She pulled against his hold but he held on. 'What are you talking about?'

'I saw her. It was there in the scream. She's about to give up her life to bring Cain back. To save us all from him.'

'That's what you saw?'

'Yes.' She looked up at him, horror making her eyes huge. 'But that's not all. I felt what was to come. If she dies, her death will lead to war between us and the rogue coven.'

'We're already at war with them.'

'No. This will be worse. The humans will be brought into it and they won't respond well to the knowledge of us all living in their midst. So many deaths. So much destruction. Everything that's been built will be gone.'

'We have to stop her.'

'That's what I was trying to do before you stopped to ask these idiot questions.'

She pulled out of his grip then and tried to run, but all she could manage was a stagger. He followed, only his longer stride allowing him to keep up as he was staggering worse than she.

Thankfully, as they moved, it got easier, the horizon stayed where it was supposed to, but they were still shaking and breathless, as if they'd run a major marathon, by the time they'd made it the hundred metres or so back to the house. As they rounded the side, heading towards the kitchen entrance, Cordy and Marcus came spilling out of it.

'Shelley, was that you?' Cordy grasped her arms, steadying her.

Shelley nodded, gaze taking in the blood running from Marcus' ears. Had she done that? 'If you mean the scream, yes.'

Cordy's mouth turned grim. 'That wasn't a scream. That was a banshee wail.'

'I thought banshees were a myth.'

'That wasn't a myth that knocked everyone out,' Cordy said. 'The rest are still coming around.' She wrung her hands together, leaning into Marcus as he came up behind her. 'Something terrible is coming.'

'Death,' Adam said, wiping the blood still dripping from his nose. 'Shelley said death.'

Shelley sucked in a breath, her chest burning. 'Eloise. Oh God. How long have we been out?'

'Not long. Half an hour maybe.'

'Fuck.' She looked up at the full moon overhead. It was huge and a ghastly blood red. It was almost midnight. 'I'm afraid it's already too late.' Her lips trembled. 'She's already begun. We'll never get there in time to stop her.'

'We need to call Jason and Skye. And Bron and River. Tell them what's happened.' Marcus' voice was a low growl.

'They'll already know. They couldn't have missed that,' Cordy said.

Shelley turned and stumbled towards the drive where the SUV they'd arrived in a few hours earlier was parked.

'Where are you going?' Marcus asked.

'I know she said we had to stay away because Cain will hurt us, but he'll hurt us more if we don't. We'll need as many powerful witches and Weres as possible here to help, ASAP. And we need to get down there now,' Shelley said, shaking so hard she needed Adam's arm around her to help her into the vehicle.

'Shelley? Are you okay to go?'

'We have to hurry,' she said, dread more than a ball of cold in her chest. It was expanding, rising up to swallow her whole. 'The others are too far away. They're going to be too late. But if we move, we might get there in time to avert disaster.'

'There's something else, isn't there?'

The world spun as the car started up and she had to close her eyes to shut out the horrible dizziness. Taking in a shaking breath, she nodded. 'Somebody is going to die tonight. I can feel it. It can't be escaped. Someone is going to die.'

'Not if we can help it.'

Oh Goddess. She wished that was true but whatever had started up in the mines had already gone too far for them to be able to change anything. It was inevitable. She felt it inside with a part of her she'd only learned existed tonight and wished she could ignore.

But the blood moon was a portent she couldn't ignore. Death was here. It had already put out its hand and it wasn't going to let the night fade without having someone in its grip.

THE PREPARATION SPELLS having been completed, Eloise rolled down the blankets covering Cain. He wore a hospital gown. She picked up the scalpel and used it to cut the front of the gown. Gently, she brushed the tattered flaps aside, exposing his chest. Pale and thin, his skin was perfect except for a half-moon scar on his left breast—a mirror to the same scar she bore on her breast. A tie to their heritage, perhaps? She would never know.

She traced the silvery scar, the salt of her tears flooding her mouth. 'Please, try and find who you used to be when you wake. Don't let Morrigan use you like this.'

She looked upwards. She knew it was useless to plead with the Goddess to help Cain, to make him see how wrong he was and to change his heart. But she could ask one last thing. 'I know this magic is dark and evil, but please, don't let my sacrifice be for nothing. Let my power be strong enough to bring him back to his body and then let it die with me.'

Her hair moved and a warm waft of air caressed her face; the delicate scent of summer grass and the golden warmth of orange blossoms tantalised her for a split second and then was gone. Under her fingers, Cain's skin warmed. Had her plea been heard? She whispered, 'Thank you', just in case.

She took a deep breath, trying to hold on to the memory of that wonderful scent. She smoothed her hand over Cain's chest, lifted the scalpel. She pictured the rune for "returning" in her mind. She had to carve it into Cain's chest.

Blood bloomed in the scalpel's wake, the smell thick and coppery. Her stomach roiled but she forced herself to continue until it was done.

Raising the scalpel again, now glistening with her brother's blood, she lifted her other hand in supplication to the Goddess she would now never serve and never see. She'd never find out if being a Nexus could be a good thing. Never find her true family. Never love Iain again.

With a cry torn from the deepest part of her soul, a cry filled with a grief she could not hide from, Eloise swiped the blade across her wrist.

The metal bit deep, the pain as bright and crimson as the blood that pumped from the severed artery. Swapping the scalpel to her other hand, she repeated the action across the other wrist. The knife slipped in her blood-coated fingers before it did much more than make a scratch. Swearing, she wrapped the knife in the sheet and tried again. It bit deep, slicing through tendon. Her hand flopped, as the burning flare of white-hot pain trembled up her arm.

Horror rose at what she'd done, but she bit it back, clamping her mouth against the bile that rose to choke her. Blood ran in a stream from her wrists across her hands, pumping out of her in a warm gush. The room swayed and she grabbed onto the edge of the bed. Slippery with blood, her one useful hand slid from the rails. She clutched at the sheets, desperate not to fall. She couldn't fall. If she did, she was afraid she'd never get back up.

Desperate, she locked her shaking knees, forced herself upright, to stand steady against the roar of encroaching blackness rushing at her from all sides.

She let go of the linen and held her hands, palm down, hovering a few inches above Cain's chest where she'd carved the rune.

Blood spurted from her wrists onto Cain's chest, running across his skin and down his sides in macabre rivulets. Nausea rose with the black, but she pushed both aside. She had to finish it. She couldn't stop now.

Closing her eyes, she called on her power. It came flooding into her at her call, wrapping around her, weaving into her nerves, tingling across her skin. Light flared behind her eyes and she sucked in a breath at the wonder of it. She'd never seen it like this; never felt it like this. Never imagined it could be this great, even after what the Goddess had told her. She'd doubted, even when Cain told her his plan to use her power, to add it to his for Morrigan's use. Now she didn't doubt. She knew what she planned was right.

They couldn't be allowed to have access to this.

She opened her eyes and focused on the rune beneath her hands, calling its shape and meaning into her mind, filling it with the light. Beneath her hands, the rune began to glow and hum. Despite the thickness of her blood coursing across her palms, she could feel the buzz of power, the rise of heat from the rune as the magic within it was activated by her blood sacrifice. A blood sacrifice that would lead to her death. She had made sure of it. Nobody would come. Nobody would save her. She would die and her power would die with her.

Filled with her own power, she then called on the power of the moon and the power of Oestra. Magic shimmered around her, through her, filling her with an energy she'd never felt before. The ley lines in the earth sang to her and she pulled on those too. She buzzed with the power of the moon and the earth and the Goddess and the tides. It rushed through her, so great, it was almost a burn. It was more power than she'd ever held before—more power than she knew could exist in one person. But it was hers and it felt right.

Trembling, she murmured the words she wished she'd never learned, sealing her fate.

'Return to flesh, use my blood
Separation ends with the red flood

Take my body, steal my breath
I offer myself in trade, to eternal death
Three by three by three by three
My blood is now yours, so mote it be.'

Heat flared from her hands, diving into the rune. A whoosh of blood-orange light encompassed her, expanding out. Her vision wavered and swirled, liquid and viscous, full of all the colours of the spectrum, before settling into a violet blue where shadows whispered and the air vibrated with the deafening melody of life all around. Her head fell back, her mouth falling open and the blood-orange light shot up from her and through the ceiling. Somehow she could see it travel through the rock and soil above her head, up through the roots and greenery of the forest and into the open sky. It shot up to the moon, colouring it in blood.

A beacon.

Aimed at Cain. Drawing him back from the aether where her blood, twin blood, would allow him to re-establish the severed connection with his body. It was why she was the only one who could heal him.

Her blood could bring him home.

———

'Why won't this damn thing go faster,' Shelley said, smashing her hand against the elevator button.

Adam took her hand, held it in both of his. 'Stop it, Kitten.'

She shot him a look but didn't pull away. 'We have to hurry.'

'I know but smashing the button won't make the elevator go any faster.'

She glared at the door. The spirits were swirling around her, their silently screaming faces misting out of the darkness one after the other in a never-ending kaleidoscope. Thank Goddess she couldn't hear the noise they were making. Somehow the banshee scream had silenced them. But the silent screams were creepy, and she wished the banshee scream had banished sight of them as well as sound.

She craved to be alone.

After this was done, she would make sure of it. Except ...

She glanced sideways at the powerful Were standing so staunchly by her side. His kiss was still hot on her lips. Her skin still tingled from his touch. She'd thought her heart was practically a dried husk of nothingness after having been torn apart too many times. Her ex-fiancé cheating on her had been the last straw. Since then, her heart functioned on the bare minimum she needed to stay alive and maintain her friendships with Skye and Bron, and nothing more. She didn't even have anything left to give her family or old coven—had long ago separated herself from everything they were, everything they'd wanted her to be.

But this annoying Were at her side had brought a spark to life in that nearly dead heart, and his kiss had made that spark flare into a small flame that exhilarated and frightened all in one go. She wanted to smother it, to never allow it to grow.

His thumb swept over the back of her hand, and she whimpered as the flame flared.

She had to do something about it before things got out of hand, but she didn't have time.

Not now. Not with all this going on.

Fuck! Death was around the corner. She could practically taste it. So how could she even be thinking about what she wanted to do with Adam? It was insane. And yet her mind pressed her for an answer, almost as if she needed to make a choice. But what choice?

What was the answer? And why was it so important she make that choice now?

'You all right, Kitten?'

Adam's hand swept down her arm, leaving goose bumps in its wake. 'I just need this goddamned elevator to go faster.' The elevator jarred to a halt and the doors slid open. 'Finally!'

Before them, a long corridor stretched out, lit at intervals by lights that gave off a blue glow. Down the end of the corridor was a large steel door with a glass window in it. Two Were stood at the door, banging on it, yelling.

Shelley took off down the hall before the others could say a word, Adam hot on her heels. The two Were turned to face them, looking past Shelley to Marcus.

'Alistair. Jane. What's going on?'

'We came down here as soon as you contacted us, but we can't get in,' Alistair said. 'And Iain is lying on the floor, not responding.'

Shelley pushed past them and peered through the door. She could see Iain lying on the floor, not moving. The curtain around the bed was billowing so she got glimpses of Eloise standing next to the bed, head tipped back, pale face lit by a horrible orange light that seemed to radiate from her to shoot up through the ceiling.

'Cain's killed him,' Jane said.

'Or Eloise did,' Alistair added.

'No. She wouldn't do that,' Shelley said, gaze pinned on the two figures in the room.

'She loves him.'

'How do you know that?' Marcus asked.

'She's his mate,' Adam answered.

'Fucking hell.' Marcus nudged her aside to have a look through the window. 'How the hell did that happen? He's a Lone Wolf.'

'We don't know, but it has. The need began to pull on the Pack-bond in earnest a few days ago, but it strengthened tonight. There's no ignoring it or thinking it's anything else.'

Shelley turned and glared at them. 'Why does that even matter right now? We have to get in there.' Desperation clawed at her. 'We have to stop her. She can't die. We need her. We all need her.'

'What do you mean?'

'Shelley saw it,' Adam answered when she didn't. 'If she dies, there will be war. Not just between us and Morrigan's coven, but the humans will get involved. It will destroy us all.'

'She truly is the Nexus,' Cordy whispered.

Shelley wish they'd all shut up and concentrate on a way in. 'Yes! And she's sacrificing herself so Cain and Morrigan can't use her power. She has to use blood magic, but then she's going to let the blood continue to flow until she's dead.' She rubbed her head. 'The spirits have been trying to tell me all afternoon, but I couldn't hear them. I didn't want to hear them. She's not doing this just to save her coven friends. Or her brother. She's doing it to save us.'

'But Cain's still a danger to us even if he doesn't get her power,' Marcus said.

'Only if he gets back to Morrigan. She knew, by doing this, she was taking their big advantage away. We have to get in there, now, because she's wrong. If she dies, things will be so much worse.' She kneaded her knuckles against her chest, trying to massage out the pain that was pulsing there. 'We have to stop her. We have to get in there, now!'

Marcus reached for the keypad, but Alistair said, 'I've already tried that. She's fried the circuits or something.'

Jane said. 'Smoke came out of it when I opened the panel.'

'Fuck.' He rubbed his hand over his face. 'Right. Then let's find a way in.' He bent down in front of the fried panel and began to pull off the faceplate to expose the wires below.

Cordy turned to the others and gave them instructions to go back up to the surface and get the acetylene torches. 'We might have to cut through the door.'

'Right,' they said and were gone.

Shelley turned back to the door and banged on the glass. 'Iain!' she called out. 'Iain, wake up.'

The curtains around the bed billowed again, showing Eloise, her bloody hands on Cain's bare chest, her head thrown back, white eyes staring up at the ceiling as words whispered from her lips. Shelley didn't need to hear those words to know they were full of power. Even out here in the hall, she could feel the force of that magic skitter up her arms, raising her hairs and electrifying her nerves.

'Eloise! Stop. Pull back. We'll find another way. You don't have to do this. Eloise!'

'It's not working,' Adam said, his head next to hers as he peered through the glass. Maybe if we try a different tack.' His gaze fell to Iain.

Shelley grasped his meaning and tried again. 'Eloise. You have to let us in. Iain's hurt. You need to let us get to him. He may die if you don't let us in.'

The power skittering along her nerves jerked. Eloise's head flopped forward, then she turned to stare at the door with eyes that were no longer pure white. 'Iain,' she mouthed.

She moved, as if to lift her hand from her brother's chest.

'No! I forbid you to stop now.' A voice screamed through the tunnels, making Cordy and Shelley flinch and the Were swear and cover their ears. Eloise jerked, her hand slapping back into place on Cain's chest. Her head tilted back to stare at the ceiling, so far it seemed improbable that anything human could bend like that without snapping their neck. She began to shake. Something dark swirled at her feet, crawling up her leg. She screamed. The agony in the sound made those in the hall flinch again.

Shelley felt wetness on her cheeks—tears. Adam tried to pull her away from the door, but she turned on him, shoving at his chest. 'No! We have to get in there. We have to get in there now.'

He didn't argue, just turned to Marcus and said, 'Let's smash this door.'

Marcus nodded and stood, giving up on the electrics. 'Cordy. Join me.'

'Are you sure?'

He nodded. 'Shelley said we have to get in now. I need your strength to do this.'

'What are you doing?' Shelley asked.

'Something rarely tried,' Marcus said, expression grimmer than usual. Catching Cordy in a rough clasp, he kissed his mate passionately and swiftly, then stood back. 'Now.'

Cordy put her hands on either side of his head, closed her eyes and whispered some words Shelley didn't catch. There was a rush, as if the air had been sucked out of the hall and then power thumped into her, making her stumble back into Adam.

Marcus twitched and seemed to grow larger. His muscles rippled in his arms, his T-shirt stretched to bursting, his eyes snapping with blue lightning in their depths as he growled.

'What did you do?' Adam asked. 'Can you do it to me?'

'I've just brought the strength of his wolf fully to the fore,' Cordy said, as Marcus stretched and growled behind her. 'It's dangerous and will only last for a little while.' She pinned Adam with her stare. 'It will make you incredibly weak and vulnerable after.'

'I don't care. Shelley said we have to get in there.'

Cordy nodded, her face pale. 'Okay.'

Shelley stopped her from raising her hands. 'Have you got energy for this?'

'Just enough.'

'Are you sure?'

'It's the only way. The others are going to take too long to get back with the torch and you don't know the spell.'

'What can I do?'

'Try to get through to Iain. We need him to wake up. I'm afraid he's the only one who'll be able to stop this.'

'I've never tried to contact other members of the pack before through the bond.'

'But you know how?'

Shelley nodded, lips pressed together. She'd never wanted this, never wanted to create more ties—had been happy to pretend connection by burying herself in studying the diaries and learning more so she could simply find a way to stop the hell. But there was no choice. She had to do this. Right now.

Turning back to the door, she stared through the window at Iain, aware of the moment Cordy touched Adam with her power. She felt the kick of it through him, the pained groan as his body was forced to do something that wasn't in its nature to do. Without thinking, she sent power through the bond that linked her to Skye and Jason and from them into Adam. He settled a little. A soothing stroke on her senses through the bond.

Then she turned her attention to Iain. Closing her eyes, she pictured him where he lay on the floor.

'Iain.' She reached down the bond to the spark that was him. 'Iain, wake up. We need you now. Wake up.' Nothing. She didn't give up. Couldn't. 'Iain, Eloise is killing herself. You have to wake up. She's your mate. You have to do this. For her.'

She was aware of being gently moved aside but didn't pull her attention from the spark that was Iain. She was certain it had grown brighter. Certain he was listening.

She kept trying as Marcus began to kick the door with all his Alpha force, Adam adding his strength to the Alpha's.

The screech of metal filled the air.

'Think of what's important to you, Iain. Think of Eloise. Think of how all this began.'

<h1 style="text-align:center">28</h1>

Buzzing filled Iain's head, joining the hammering ache in his skull. The pain was bad enough, but the buzzing—what the fuck was that? He tried swatting at whatever it was but couldn't lift his arm. Then the buzzing coalesced into words. Words that didn't make sense.

'Think of Eloise. Think of how it all began.'

Eloise? How it all began? For him, it had begun when he'd opened bloodshot eyes and seen the brave slip of a woman, beaten and bloody, stand up to her brother and Morrigan and fight for River. For Gareth. For him. For a people she'd been taught to hate. In his pain-glazed eyes, she hadn't seemed insignificant or useless. He couldn't understand why they were talking to her like she was nothing, treating her like garbage. Fury had risen inside him and he'd wanted to lash out at them for daring to touch the angel in their midst.

He should have known then. Should have seen what was so clear to him now.

She was his mate.

There was no stepping back from that. There never had been.

He'd been a fool to think his pack status meant anything in the face of a mating.

His dreams had been trying to tell him that for months now. Because she wasn't just his mate. No. It wasn't as simple as that. She was his throughout time. His soulmate. They were meant to be together. Had always been together.

He remembered now. This had happened before. He'd been a Lone Wolf then too—it seemed that was an indelible part of his essence. But if he was meant to be alone, then why give him someone to be with?

'To challenge us. To make us more.'

The voice of his past came to him. Malcolm's voice. It was a part of him, but not him. He'd struggled against the reality of that presence for so long, determined not to be swayed by it, not to be taken over. But he hadn't understood. Malcolm was only an echo of the past. He had no form or substance on his present. Neither did Bridgette Colliere have anything to do with who Eloise was in the present.

Both she and the ancient witch, the instigator of the Pact, were luminous and brilliant, passionate and unswerving in their beliefs, but Eloise was humble yet fierce in her determination to protect others. She'd been brought up to see herself as plain and unforgettable and unimportant and had only just realised that wasn't true. She was coming to see in herself what he saw—a beautiful, strong woman who had written herself indelibly on his memory and in his heart. His soul.

She was just coming to realise how important she was—everything hinged on the decisions she'd make because she was the Nexus. That's what the Goddess had called her. You couldn't be more essential than that. She was one of the most powerful people he'd ever met and yet she was so humble with it. Such a pure heart. She would always set him straight.

'That's right, Iain. Remember who she is to you and get up. You have to move. You have to try.'

He had no idea what the voice was talking about. Why was it so important he move?

'Eloise has chosen. She is giving her life so Cain and Morrigan can't use her powers. She's doing it to save us all.'

What? No!

She couldn't leave him.

He tried to move, but his limbs wouldn't work. He couldn't seem to roll over, to push himself up. He couldn't even open his eyes.

'Breathe, Iain. Focus on Eloise. Then pull on the pack. We're here for you. Use us.'

It wasn't in his nature to need or rely on anyone. But for Eloise, he would do anything. His wolf howled in agreement, in agony at the thought of losing its mate. The other half of itself. Anything for her.

Anything.

As it had always been. As it always would be. He'd thought he could leave, could live without her, but he'd been fooling himself. She made him whole and he wasn't ever going to be torn from her again.

Iain's eyelids flickered open, and with a teeth-gritting groan, he rolled over, gathering strength from the pack to force him to move.

BRIGHT SHAPES, some golden, some mere wisps of silver-laced shadow, rushed at Eloise, surrounding her.

Spirits.

Their vibrations were like a shouting crowd as they tried to communicate with her, tell her their messages for their loved ones now that she could see them. But she couldn't understand. Their shouting hurt her. The waves of sound raked along her skin. She wanted to protect herself, to cover her ears, but she couldn't move her hands from Cain's chest. They were welded there, her blood a magnet to his, to his flesh.

'Please, stop. Go away. I'm looking for Cain. Only Cain.'

But they crowded in closer. Too much. It was too much. Their touch like a thousand paper cuts. Was this what it was like for Shelley? How could the witch stand it? She was going to pass out. But she couldn't. Not until this was done. 'Go away,' she screamed.

The blood-orange light flared. The spirits fell back, not far, but it was enough.

In the distance, she heard banging and a panicked voice yelling. The name 'Iain' span at her out of the dark again, catching her attention. She wanted to look, but a scream sounded in her head. It shattered through her just like it had before, wrenching a tearing gasp from her throat as that same icy-cold sharp thing with a thousand teeth twisted in her damaged ankle and crawled further up her leg.

The yelling died away as the pain became everything—sight, sound, smell. That old pain. The cankerous Darkness in her ankle that had kept it twisted and deformed throughout the centuries of rebirth. The mark of something horrifying that had touched Bridgette Colliere in the aether and never let go.

She swayed but didn't fall, connected as she was to Cain and the rune. She looked down and her thoughts stuttered, eyes opening wide. The rivers of her blood that had covered Cain's chest, running down the side, pooling into the sheets, now crawled back up, pulled towards the rune. She watched with a kind of numb amazement as it oozed and snaked its way, against all the laws of gravity, mingling with the darker taint of Cain's blood—why was his darker than hers? —and disappeared into the rune, leaving no trace of red in its path.

Blood—her blood—ran from the cuts in her wrists, and straight into the rune. The power of it suckled, like a baby at a teat.

The icy Darkness had reached halfway up her leg. She bit her lips closed to stop screaming from the pain. Her head snapped back against her will and blinded once more, she stared into the abyss of the aether her twin was locked in.

'*Search. Find him.*' The ice-cold voice with a thousand teeth whispered in her ear, shattering her mind. The icy teeth bit deep and rose higher. Pain sliced through her, but it pinched her diaphragm, trapping her scream in her throat as it squeezed and squeezed.

This was it. This was the end. It had been coming for her for centuries and now, in this act, she'd finally unintentionally let it in.

Darkness flooded towards her as her eyes fluttered and her knees weakened. She didn't have much more in her. How was she to fight it off?

The light fluctuated around her. The spirits crowded closer, their roar a crescendo. A sob rose in her chest. It couldn't end like this, but it had to. She wouldn't be used again. Cain would wake, but it would be too late. She had cut too deep, let the blood run too fast, and there was nobody here to save her.

Cain's laugh trembled through her, echoing out of the black. *'You've done well, Little Bit. Soon you will be one of us.'* Coldness touched her shoulder, the icy pain of it slipping down her arm to grip her hand. *'No! What have you done? You're not supposed to die. You're mine. Mine!'*

'I won't be used, Cain. Never again.'

'I won't let you go.'

'It's too late to stop me.'

'No. Darkness, aid me now.'

Then he slipped through her mind, her skin, the cuts on her wrist and was inside her, joining the Darkness, his presence cloying and cold. So cold.

She began to shudder uncontrollably, her teeth snapping together as foam frothed from her mouth. Goddess, no. They couldn't do this. But they were. They worked together to slow the blood loss, pushing power into her life-essence, forcing her to live. She struggled, but they were strong, so strong together, and her control, her will, began to slip.

She wanted to cry, but even that had been taken from her. 'Don't do this to me. I don't want to be used by you.'

'You have no choice. You're mine. Mine and the Darkness'. We won't let you go.' He shifted then, trying to wrap around her heart. They wanted to take that too.

'No!'

The sound tore out of her. They couldn't have her heart. Never her heart. It belonged to herself. To Iain. She wouldn't let them have that.

She grabbed onto every last essence of her will and power and pushed. 'Not my heart. Not my heart,' she muttered, over and over as she fought them. They tried to scrabble at her powers, use them as they'd used them against her before, but she was angry now. Determined. They couldn't have her powers or her heart. In fact, they didn't even deserve her life.

She gritted her teeth, shook with the effort to hold the combined force of them back and stop them from taking control, but even as she did it, she knew she couldn't hold against them forever. Her magic was still too new to her. She didn't have enough control. It slipped from her grasp even as she tried to shore it against them.

She wanted to scream her frustration, her fury. She wouldn't let them touch the beauty that was her love for Iain. Not that. Never that. She had to be braver. Braver than Bridgette Colliere when she'd sacrificed herself to save her loved ones. She wouldn't give up. Wouldn't give in. All she needed was more power. More control.

And suddenly, she knew where to get it.

The bond. It had been growing, filament by filament, ever since she'd woken and seen Iain standing guard over her. But she hadn't wanted to see it. Didn't think she could deserve it. Believed, despite dreams of her past life telling her otherwise, that it wasn't possible. Was afraid to want, to reach for it, afraid to lose it and be outcast again, and in more pain than every other time she'd been outcast. So she'd denied it. Had even denied it when it had strengthened after making love with him. All it needed to snap fully into place was for both of them to accept it. But she couldn't wait for Iain to show his acceptance. She needed to use the strength it gave her now if she was to live.

Without thinking about the consequences of making this decision for him, she grabbed a hold of the bond and wrapped it around her heart, her soul, her essence.

It snapped through her with a sense of rightness that was exhilarating. She cried out in triumph, in joy. Light filled her. A golden light that flowed along the cord that wrapped around her heart and extended out beyond her body, a protective shell, pushing Cain and the Darkness back. They battered at it, but couldn't smash through, no matter how hard they tried.

The Darkness screamed its frustration and wrapped itself fully around Cain's spirit. He tried to fight it as it forced him away, using her blood as a conduit to enter Cain's body, but it was too strong and too much a part of him.

The burn of them was like a surge of something putrid under her skin flowing towards her sliced wrists. Her blood darkened as they finally slipped out of her body and into the rune. It flared, glowing like coal in a fire, searing her fingers where they touched his skin.

She screamed.

'If we can't have you, no-one can!' Cain's screech, a slash of hate-filled venom, punctured the pain. She tried to pull away. Her knees collapsed, but still she hung there, attached. She couldn't free herself. Couldn't move to staunch the bleeding. She was going to bleed out, even though she was free of them.

Panic and grief rose in her; her life was counted in seconds.

No. No. This couldn't be how it was to end.

Her skin prickled. She had to pull away. Had to find the strength. She couldn't let them win. They couldn't take her. Couldn't use her. She wouldn't let them do this to her too. She was stronger than they could ever be. More truly herself than she'd ever been.

There was a banging in the distance, but she could barely hear it over the roaring noise that rose up and engulfed her as she tried to pull on the last vestiges of power left inside her. She had to stay. Had to live. Had to have a chance to tell Iain she loved him; that he was her mate.

The room tipped and swung wildly as she channelled her power down her arms, green flame dancing along her veins, over her skin. She narrowed her eyes, her concentration, trying to make the flame eat at the spell holding her to Cain, burn it away, free her.

At first nothing happened. She concentrated harder, sweat prickling all over her face and neck. She had to do it. Had to ...

One finger shifted. Then another.

Cain screeched in her mind as he fought back, but it only made her concentrate harder. Sweat stung her eyes; damp hair clung to her cheeks, her neck. Three fingers were loose; four. She gritted her teeth, groaned. Her thumb came free and her hand slipped from Cain's chest.

Yes! Yes. But there wasn't time to celebrate. Cain and the Darkness pulled on her power with desperate vigour through the hand still attached to her twin's chest.

She focused entirely on that hand, leaning over the edge of the bed, holding herself upright with sheer force of will.

The green flames of her power danced around her hand as she freed her pinkie. Ring finger. Middle. Pointer. Black hazed her vision, but she didn't stop. Couldn't stop now. She had to save herself. Nobody else was going to do it for her. Her thumb shifted, slid sideways.

She was free.

She stumbled back, the room spinning. She had to get over to the cabinets with the bandages. Stop the bleeding. She stumbled a few steps. The room was so dark. She could barely see past the black hazing her vision. The sound shrieked in her head alongside the slow —too slow—thump of her heartbeat through her veins.

One step. Another. Every part of her cried out with pain. 'Can't stop.' Another step.

Her foot slipped. She began to fall.

Through the black swirl slowly taking over her vision, she saw movement out of the corner of her eye.

Arms wrapped around her before she hit the floor. Warm, strong arms picked her up, held her close. Voices echoed through the noise, sounds she could barely distinguish from the crashing, tearing in her head.

Then one voice made itself heard above the turmoil: The voice of the Goddess. *'Do it, now!'*

Light blinded her. Pain seared through her. She screamed. Red filled her vision, Darkness swirling at its core. A Darkness that terrified. A Darkness that wanted her. She scrabbled away from it, trying to push with everything she had left in her.

'Eloise. Eloise. I've got you. It's going to be all right.'

'Iain. Iain.' She looked up into his beautiful eyes. They were all she could see, except the Darkness which hung over everything.

It reached towards him.

'No!' she screamed, pushing everything she was at it.

There was another scream, echoing hers, and then she was nothing.

STILL UNSTABLE ON HIS FEET, Iain stumbled as Eloise shoved what looked like a ball of sunshine through him and collapsed, a dead weight in his arms. Her scream and the unearthly cry that followed, rang in his ears. A warm trickle ran down his neck. He was bleeding but he didn't care. Not when the blood from Eloise's slashed wrists pooled on the sheets and on the floor beneath Cain's bed—too much blood.

She still bled from the wounds, a slow drizzle that suggested nothing good.

Leaning against the wall, he clutched her to him. 'No! Eloise. Come back. Don't leave me. Don't you dare leave me.'

She was paler than he'd ever seen her. Hanging on by a thread. He reached into his mind for the bond that had so suddenly snapped into place only moments before. It was pulled tight, almost to break-ing. But he could feel her. She was still there, the force of her will to live so strong. 'Stay with me, Little Bird. Stay with me. I love you. I love you.'

He held on tight, curling his body around her as the door smashed open. It came off its hinges and flew across the room to crash against the wall just to his left.

Cain snapped upright in the bed as Marcus and Adam came pounding into the room.

Black lightning crackled in the warlock's eyes and across his skin as he turned to face them.

Before Iain could even take a breath, Cain lifted his hands and screamed, 'Die!' Black lightening shot out of his fingers. It caught Marcus directly in the chest, rammed straight through him and into Adam.

'No!' Iain yelled as Marcus and Adam were flung across the room to hit the wall with a loud crack and thumped to the floor.

Cordy screamed, running forward to collapse next to her mate, her hands shooting out over the gaping hole in his chest. 'No, no,' she cried, over and over as she tried to use her power to heal him.

A choked, breathless feeling scrabbled in Iain's chest as he watched her desperate attempts, her power only coming in pathetic spits and spurts.

Shelley stood, frozen in the doorway, her gaze fixed on something in the middle of the room. 'No. No,' she whispered.

The hairs rose on Iain's skin as the horror in her tone pricked at him. 'Shelley? Help Cordy. Help Adam.'

'It's too late,' she said. 'He's gone. They're gone.'

'And soon, you will all follow.'

Iain's gaze snapped to Cain as he pushed himself from the bed—he'd forgotten all about him in the horror of what he'd just seen. He wanted to move, to protect Shelley from the evil insanity of Eloise's brother, but his mate was lying so still and pale in his arms. He couldn't leave her. 'Shelley, run!'

'You took my sister from me!' Cain screamed over Iain's warning. He raised his hands.

Shelley's gaze snapped to him. Fire sparked in the depths of her eyes as Cain released another bolt of black lightning. She muttered a word, and the bolt shot up to the ceiling, smashing into the rock overhead with a loud bang and a shower of sparks and flame. He shot another at her. She deflected it again, moving into the room, her hair lifting as if caught in some fae wind, a strange amethyst nimbus of light coming from her.

Cain tried again as she took one step after another, getting between him and the bodies on the floor, but the lightning hit a wall, chunks of burning, sizzling plaster raining down on the floor.

'Your spirits can't protect you forever,' Cain snarled.

She didn't seem to pay him any attention, her eyes riveted on Adam where he lay on the floor, a hole burned through the right side of his chest. She muttered something else. Power sparked and air rushed from the room, stealing his breath. Before he could do more than gasp, the air rushed back in. Cain sent more lightning at Shelley who stood between him and Cordy as she knelt on the floor trying futilely to save her dead mate.

Each strike, larger and more powerful than the last, was deflected before it got close to Shelley. He sent a bolt towards Iain and Eloise. Iain rolled to protect Eloise with his body, but the lightning hit some kind of barrier and skittered up to the ceiling.

Shelley was protecting them all. He had no idea she could even do that.

'You'll pay. You'll all pay.' Cain's scream rang around them as he ran past them to the door, shooting bolts that kept skittering away, burning chunks of plaster falling in his wake.

'Don't let him get away,' Iain yelled.

Cordy didn't even look up—she hadn't stopped working on Marcus. Shelley also didn't move, still staring at something in the middle of the room. 'Don't go,' she whispered. 'Don't go.'

Iain knew he should get up, chase Cain down, but he still couldn't leave Eloise. She was his mate. She came first and she needed him to stay. He was the only thing holding her to this earth right now; she held onto the fledgling bond, using his Were strength to keep her alive, and he would do nothing to jeopardise that. He wasn't about to let her go.

Cain's footsteps pounded down the hallway, fading. The warlock had run further into the tunnels. Where did he think he was going? There was no other way out except the lift.

For a few seconds, silence reigned.

Then a sob rent the air. Cordy grabbed Marcus' shirt. 'Marcus. Marcus. Come back to me. Don't you leave me alone! Not like this. Not like this.'

Her agony hurt Iain's ears and his heart, but he couldn't console her. He had to concentrate on keeping his own mate with him.

Eloise's breath had slowed to shallow pants, her heart a fast-paced flutter. But she was still there. He held onto the spark of her in his mind and heart and wound his strength around it. He would keep her alive with the strength of his will if he could. But he couldn't chance that it alone would be enough.

'Shelley.' She didn't move. Still stared at the space in the middle of the room. 'Shelley! You can't help them. They're already gone.' He knew it was harsh—they would mourn the loss of Adam and Marcus later—but he had to slap her out of her shock. 'Eloise is still alive. We have to help her.' She didn't look at him, but there was a flicker of her eyelashes. 'Shelley!'

She blinked and then very slowly turned to look at Cordy, her face creased in a frown. Bending over, she touched the McClunes' Pack Witch on the head and said, 'Sleep'. Cordy slumped over Marcus' body, the absence of sobbing a shocking silence. Shelley nodded slowly. 'I know,' she said. 'Are you sure?' She paused, then nodded. 'I'll tell her later.'

'Who are you talking to?'

She swallowed hard. 'Marcus. He's standing right there. He couldn't bear Cordy's grief and asked me to make her sleep. She'll be no use to us anyway.' Her gaze slipped to the side and then away, as if she was looking at something she'd prefer not to see.

He wondered what Marcus was doing but didn't want to ask. The thought was too raw. The man had just died and caused a tear in his mate's heart and soul that would never heal. Iain didn't even want to contemplate the pain in that thought. That pain was too near. 'We have to help Eloise.'

'Yes.' She blinked again and turned to look at him and the woman in his arms. 'Bron will be here soon.'

'We can't wait for Bron. We have to do something now.'

'You're holding her here.'

He grimaced. 'She's holding herself. She's using the bond and I'm holding her to it, but she's weakening. She's lost too much blood. The bond will tear if we don't do something. Please ... help. You're a nurse. Surely there's something you can do.'

She looked lost for a moment and then her eyes flared wide and she almost snorted out something that sounded like a laugh. He could swear she whispered, 'Shut up you idiot,' but he had to be wrong. Suddenly she was moving, racing over to the bed. She ripped off the bloody sheet. 'Put her up here. We have to stop the blood.'

He levered himself up, his energy almost depleted as he fought to keep Eloise with him. He wasn't going to let go. She was his. She wasn't allowed to leave him. Not again. Not now they'd found each other after all this time. 'Please. Don't let her die.'

'I'll do what I can, but you have to move. I need to get some saline into her. And blood.' She raced to the fridge and yanked upon the door. 'Fuck. They don't have any AB negative.'

'Take mine.'

She glanced at him. 'You're AB negative?'

'No. I'm O negative.'

'That'll do for now. We'll deal with any complications later.'

Iain held onto Eloise's hand as Shelley fetched what she needed. 'Stay with me, Little Bird. Stay with me.'

29

'Are you sure?' Shelley asked Iain, cannula poised over his arm. 'This isn't exactly best practice.'

'I'm sure.' He gripped Eloise's hand tighter, his fingers brushing over the bandages Shelley had bound over the wounds. 'She's my mate. And I can't let her go.'

'No.' Shelley glanced over her shoulder at Marcus and Adam. 'There's already been enough death today.'

Blood flowed from him into Eloise. Iain's wolf growled in satisfaction. The idea of them nourishing their mate in this way pleased the animal heart of him. Eloise had started carrying his scent in the last week or so, but now their scents were wound together in a way they weren't before. She was his. Well and truly his. She had him inside her, just like she was inside him. In his heart. His soul. His mind. His Packbond. She was everything. And he would spend his life making sure she knew it.

His Lone Wolf soul might want him to roam, but never from her. She was his centre. The reason for everything.

'Must get fluids into her,' Shelley mumbled as she set up a saline drip.

In the distance, the lift dinged. Jane and Alistair, and maybe others. They'd have felt it when their Alpha died. They would be vicious in their grief. 'Shelley—'

'I know,' she whispered. 'Marcus will help me deal with them. You can't move.'

Feet pounded down the hall and then Jason and Skye, River and Bron ran into the room—they must have broken speed records to get there. They came to a sudden halt as they took in the scene before them. Alistair and June stumbled in behind them. One look at their Alpha had them falling to their knees, keening their grief to the ceiling.

'Oh my god!' Skye gasped.

'Adam!' Jason shouted, lurching towards his brother. 'Bron! Help.'

'He's gone,' Iain whispered, tears welling in his eyes. 'He's gone. It happened so fast. Cain got them with the same lightning bolt. It went straight through Marcus and hit Adam. They didn't have a chance.'

Bron dropped down on her knees beside Adam, her hands held out over him. Shelley gripped her shoulder. 'Don't. He's gone.'

Bron shook her head. 'No. He's still here. The bolt missed his heart. It's still beating. It's faint but still beating.'

Shelley blinked, then looked beside her. 'That's impossible. I saw —' Her voice died away and she jumped.

'Saw what?'

She blinked again, then shook her head. 'I must have been mistaken,' she whispered.

'Can you heal him?' Jason asked, voice desperate.

'I'm trying. I'm trying.'

'What happened to Cordy?' Skye asked, kneeling beside the other witch who was still slumped across her mate.

'I had to put her to sleep. Her grief was ...' She swallowed, her eyes blinking rapidly. 'The spirits here were going wild.'

'She's alive.'

'Yes. But Marcus is dead.'

Silence. Cordy's grief could fill her completely and then she'd die too—but none of them wanted to face that right now. The situation didn't allow that kind of grief to enter into it—they had to take care of the living and worry about the rest later.

Shelley knelt beside Alistair and June, taking their hands, whispering something to them Iain couldn't hear. They stopped keening, but June still sobbed. Alistair's eyes filled with a fury of grief that burned Iain just looking at it. The McVale Pack had lived through the loss of Luke McVale, their Alpha, and his mate Isla only a few years earlier, the grief still raw inside them. He knew what the McClunes were going through and wished there was something he could do to help them.

'You are so kind.'

The voice fluttered in his mind. It took him a second to understand he'd actually heard it. 'Eloise?' He gripped her hand tighter.

'Yes.'

'Don't leave me.'

'I'm trying not to.'

'Don't stop trying.' He held on tighter, inside his mind, wrapping everything he was around her, around their mating bond, refusing to let go. But she was so weak, so close to death. He didn't know if it would be enough. 'I'm here. I'm here. Don't stop trying.'

'Iain? What is it? Are you hurting?' River knelt beside him, keeping his eyes on his own mate.

'No. It's Eloise. She's in my mind.'

River gripped his shoulder. 'Hold onto her, man.'

'I'll be there as soon as I can,' Bron said, her voice tight with the pain of such a difficult Healing. She winced. 'Oh Goddess, this hurts.' Jason knelt next to her, his hand on her shoulder, feeding her energy, pulling on pack. Iain felt the brush of the request through his Packbond, but of course, Jason didn't ask that of him. He knew. They all knew. Eloise was his. They would help him keep her here. They would not use energy he needed to keep his mate with him.

But not only that, Jason had tied River's energies into him through the Packbond so that he could help him hold on while Bron worked on Adam.

The Healer worked into the night, pulling Adam back from the edge. Shelley got the McClune Were to listen to her, and together they moved Cordy to a gurney and covered Marcus. But once that was done, Alistair called the lieutenants and went hunting, their fury focused for the time being on tracking down Cain.

Once they were gone, Shelley did what she could for Iain and Eloise, stopping the transfusion when she deemed Iain to have given as much blood as he could. River moved between Bron and Iain, giving his energy to both of them, and Skye and Jason stayed with Bron and Adam.

Iain had no idea what was going on in the outside world and he didn't care. All he cared about was the woman whose breathing had deepened slightly, her cheeks still far too pale, milky lids heavy over peridot eyes he loved so much. He could lose himself in those pools of green-gold until the end of time. If only they would open and look at him. Then he'd be able to relax a little and breathe. The bond wasn't as stretched as before, but it was still way too thin.

Eloise's eyes moved under her lids, flickering back and forth. She was dreaming. He wished he knew what she saw. Wished he could tell her she was his mate. That he loved her. He didn't have to ask why she'd tried to sacrifice herself the way she had, but he did want to tell her she couldn't ever do anything like that again. He'd almost lost her.

The thought of that emptiness had panic clawing in his chest.

'People in comas have reported hearing those around them,' River said, reading his thoughts.

Iain didn't know if that was true, but just in case ... 'Eloise, my Little Bird, I love you. Come back to me. You're my mate. My soulmate. I can't live in a world that doesn't include you. Please. Hear me. Follow my voice. Come back to me.'

***

'COME BACK TO ME.'

The voice whispered in Eloise's head. So familiar. So loved. She tried to answer, but the night around her was too thick and the words wouldn't travel. She kept walking through the blackness. It seemed she'd been walking for ages. Time was endless in this dark space.

Nothing to visibly show change. Not even the sound of her feet on the hard ground.

Only the voice. And the feeling she was going in the right direction.

A pinpoint of light became visible, dancing before her eyes so that at first she thought it was a firefly. But then it got larger, the light no longer dancing—it was her movement that created the flicker.

The light shone through the branches surrounding her. Trees.

She was in a forest.

She walked on until she came upon the source of the light. It shone through the window of a cottage set in the heart of a snug clearing. The night sky spread overhead, stars sparkling white and blue and red and green in the velvet black-purple sky. From the other side of the clearing, there came a sound—hooves against hardpacked ground and the rustle of leaves; a wicker and a soft voice urging hurry.

'Almost there, mo ghrá.'

'Do not call me that. I am not your love.'

'Ye are more my love now than ever afore, mo ghrá.'

'I am having my dead husband's child!' the woman argued.

'More reason then to hold ye dear.'

'Argh! You are the most frustrating man I have ever met.'

'I am na fully a man.'

'No, you are a Were.'

'A Were who adores ye, mo ghrá.'

The woman glowered at him and then winced, her face screwing up. The man reached up to rub her back. 'The bairn, mo ghrá?'

The woman nodded, panting, 'It is coming.'

The man lifted her from the horse, handling her as if she were the most delicate, precious thing he'd ever touched and, despite her protests, carried her to the cottage.

His caring brought tears to Eloise's eyes. And as those tears fell, she was pulled forward into the scene.

Pain gripped her stomach, rippling around to her back. She had to stop herself from crying out in agony. Her pain only worried Malcolm—and she didn't want that. Not because she loved Malcolm or thought for one moment he was her mate—because she wasn't and he wasn't—but because he was nice to her and didn't deserve to be worried. He'd made heart-aching love to her in a moment of need and hadn't made her feel anything but precious in the time since. He hadn't pushed to be with her again in that way, which she appreciated, even though a large part of her would have liked it if he had. He had just been her Shadow, taking care of her and her needs, becoming her right hand as the pregnancy progressed and she finished her travels to bind the packs and the covens to the Pact.

The only time he had tried to tell her what to do was before this last trip. Heavily pregnant, she was exhausted from her efforts. Malcolm had wanted to call the final pack to her so she didn't have to travel once more. She would not hear of it. The link would be all the stronger if she used the powers of the Dance in the area near the pack's lands where the coven lived.

She would not allow him to talk her out of it.

That was the first time he'd mentioned his love for her. And he'd done it in such an offhand way, she'd almost missed it.

'My father would be laughing in his grave to see me paired with such an obstinate mate. He always said our men fell in love with women who were born to test us. Aye, and he was right. It is an apt description of ye, mo ghrá.'

She had tried to laugh it off, but the sensations growing inside her —the feelings she didn't want to accept—made that impossible. He wanted her to let the mating bond come fully into being. But she wouldn't do that. She couldn't do that. Because if she did, she'd have to admit she loved him.

Oh, Goddess. She loved Malcolm. Even though she'd sworn she would never love another, she loved him. Longed for him. Wanted to be with him more than anything if she was honest with herself. But she would not be responsible for—

Waters gushed down her leg as he set her on her feet to open the door of the cottage. 'Oh.' She couldn't help the sound of shock escaping her lips. This babe was coming awfully fast. The pains had started not long ago, and yet she wanted to push. None of her other children had come this quickly. Was something wrong?

Malcolm swung her up again into his arms. His lips were tight, skin pale.

'What is wrong,' she managed.

'I smell blood.'

'Oh, Goddess. My baby.' She clutched her stomach. He laid her down on the pallet she'd used last night. The straw was still sweet smelling below the linens and furs, but she barely noticed—all she could think about was the precious life inside her that could even now be fluttering out of existence. 'Don't let my baby die.'

'I willna let that happen, mo ghrá,' he whispered, his Scottish accent made all the stronger by his worry. He cupped her face. 'Ye and the bairn will live if I have to give my life's blood to the Dark One to do it.'

She grabbed his face and looked deep into his eyes. 'Do not make such promises, not even for me.'

'But ye are my mate. I must protect ye.'

'I am not your mate yet. I have not accepted.'

'I know.'

She heard the hidden pain in that simple acceptance. It tugged at something deep within her heart. She was hurting him. She didn't want to hurt him. But she couldn't tell him that, because the pain gripped her again, worse than before, like something was tearing deep inside. She screamed.

'Let me help, mo ghrá.'

She nodded.

Malcolm placed his hands on her stomach, bent over her and listened. He could hear things she could not, things that might help the babe.

'She is breach,' he said after a moment. 'I ken what to do. But dinna push until I say.'

Bridgette nodded as he pushed up her skirts and set to work preparing for the birth. She trusted him, not just with her life, but with her babe's. She'd seen the pack's midwives bring babes into this world when mother and babe should have died. Malcolm's mother had been one of the best. He'd learned by her side and as Lone Wolf, had travelled from pack to pack, to treat the sick and teach where he could.

Many coven Healers could learn from what the wolves knew.

He'd used herb lore he knew to help others as they'd travelled. He traded his herb concoctions and medical treatment for food and shelter. His proficiency had confused her for a time because she'd thought him nothing but a warrior sent to protect her. But she'd come to see he was not one thing. He was a Healer. He was also a warrior, a lieutenant in his pack, a most trusted adviser and her Shadow. He was all of this, but at the heart of him, he was the Lone Wolf. There had been times when she'd caught him looking up into the night sky or out across the expanse of hills they traversed, an expression of desperate longing and need on his face, and she had known he was the Lone Wolf first and everything else second. She could not ask him to change.

'I *am* changed,' he said, breaking into her thoughts.

She gasped, but this time not from the pain. 'What? How could you—'

'How could I know ye and not ken yer worry? I ken why ye havena wanted to commit to the mating, mo ghrá. Ye are concerned that I would leave ye. That I would be driven insane as yer husband was. Ye are worried that the demands of my love for ye and my desire to keep ye safe would make me stay in one place rather than give in to the wanderlust that makes me who I am. But ye dinna ken me, mo ghrá. I am the Lone Wolf no more. I would ha' continued on as the Lone Wolf if not for thee. But I did meet ye and I did change and I wouldna wish it to be any different because for me, ye are the ultimate gift.'

'I never wanted you to change for me.'

'I know. But ye don't understand. Lone Wolves roam because they are forever seeking the missing part of themselves—their soulmate. We can only truly mate if we find that missing part. My missing part is ye.' He rubbed his hands over her stomach, bringing relief to aching muscles. 'This is the change that every Lone Wolf seeks. I niver want to be anywhere ye are not. It will hurt me to do so.'

She gripped his hand tight. 'I wish never to hurt you.'

He held her hands in both of his. 'Mate with me. I canna promise ye a peaceful life or an uneventful one—I may still be restless to travel, to explore, to discover the world and all its wonders. It is part of my life. But given ye are a restless soul yerself, mo ghrá, hungry fer knowledge, we can be restless together.'

She couldn't help but laugh at the cheeky grin on his face, but the laugh quickly turned into a sob. 'My children. I have left them for so long. After this, I cannot leave them for so long again.'

'I wouldna ask ye to.' He stroked his finger down her cheek then kissed her stomach. 'They will explore and discover the world with us when they can, and when they canna, we will stay with them. Truthfully, I dinna need to be anywhere but where ye are. Ye are my world and I will spend a lifetime or more exploring thee.'

Heat rushed through her at the hunger in his eyes—for her and only her. She could no longer deny the answering hunger in herself, but before she could say a word, pain rippled through her again. 'Oh, I need to push.'

He bent over her, cupped her face, brushed back damp strands from her forehead and cheeks, touched her lips with a kiss full of passion and promise. 'Then let's birth this bonnie wee bairn, mo ghrá.'

Malcolm was a skilled midwife and the babe was born with a wild squeal a short time later. A triumphant grin on his face, he held the squalling babe up. Bridgette laughed and cried. Malcolm wiped the babe down and laid her on her mother's chest in the way of his people. After cutting the cord, taking care of the afterbirth and cleaning Bridgette, freshening the furs and straw, he kneeled at her side, his eyes glowing.

'Beautiful, she is, mo ghrá. A bonnie wee lassie. What name will she bear?'

She lifted her eyes from staring at the babe, a babe who despite being created in a moment of violence and terror just before her husband had been destroyed by his power, was so loved. She had thought to name the child after her husband's family, but now she did not want links to that past for the child—it was enough she would carry her father's blood and some of his features. No, she wanted to look to the future and claim the other half of her soul. 'I would like you to name her.'

Malcolm gasped and then shuddered as the bond between them snapped into being, her offering of naming rights the final link, a bond of trust and commitment that she could never step back from. The fury of the sensation took her breath away as everything he was came into sharp focus inside her and the strength of his feelings for her banished all her worries into the dark from whence they came.

He was hers.

She was his.

That was all that mattered.

Malcolm kissed her, wild, unabashed bliss in the touch of his lips and tongue against hers, but too soon he pulled back, ever mindful of the babe. 'Abigail,' he said, touching the babe's back. 'Giving of joy.'

Bridgette smiled. It was perfect. 'Abigail,' she whispered, kissing her daughter's head. She looked up at Malcolm. 'I love you.'

'I know. As I love ye, mo ghrá.' He kissed her daughter and then kissed her briefly before pulling back to cover her with a blanket.

She reached for him again but he pulled back. 'I want to kiss ye more too, but now is no the time. Ye need sleep. Ye and the bairn.'

'You will stay? You will not leave.'

'Nae. Niver. I will sit here and keep guard over ye. I will always be here. I willna leave yer side. Ever.'

Bridgette closed her eyes. Never had she felt so secure and loved. The Darkness had lifted from them all. She had only room for happiness in her heart.

'I LOVE YOU, Eloise. Come back to me.' She was too still for his liking. Her breathing was even, her heart strong, but she should have opened her eyes by now.

'Iain, you should get some rest.' Jason's hand was on his shoulder.

'No. I won't leave her side.'

'You've been up for three days straight.'

He hunched his shoulders, claws slicing out, as he glared at his Alpha. 'Would you leave your mate?'

Jason shook his head as he turned to look at Skye. She was on the other side of the room trying to reach out mentally to Cordy who lay in a stupor, unresponsive to anything. The look on his face as he gripped Iain's shoulder and moved back to his vigil by Adam's bed made Iain's anger slide into guilt. Jason had barely been able to spend time at his brother's side. He'd had to take care of pack matters without two of his most trusted lieutenants. He'd also helped the McClune Pack deal with their loss. He'd been stoic, as a good Alpha always was, holding two packs together despite his own worry and grief. He'd lost an ally and friend three days ago. And he'd almost lost his last remaining brother.

By some miracle, Adam hadn't died from his wounds, but Bron had been unable to fully heal him, despite her remarkable talent. Something about the wound Cain had given him continued to fester and she couldn't get the skin to knit back together. He was breathing though, his heart pumping ever so faintly, machines helping to keep him alive while Bron rested. She'd exhausted herself hours before on Adam and the wounded Were who had come back from chasing Cain before River had dragged her off to bed to rest.

Cain.

The bastard hadn't been caught. Somehow, he'd slipped through their guard—after leaving some deadly traps behind—and managed to get out of the old tunnels and mines. By now, he could be with Morrigan. Who knew what havoc they'd unleash next after almost succeeding in destroying a pack?

Marcus' death had brought his pack to its knees. Cordy's grief wasn't helping. She might be silent, but that silence was a tearing scream. Her pack needed her, but in her current state, she wasn't capable of dealing with their need.

To see such a strong woman brought down …

His fingers clenched on Eloise's hand. Cordy had lost her mate. Nothing would ever be the same for her again. Most Were didn't survive long after the passing of a mate. He knew that from personal experience. Despite the problems his mother and father shared, his mother hadn't lasted long after his father had taken his life. Not even her children could keep her here—and Cordy didn't have children to hold her tight to this world.

Iain had raged at his parents' deaths, but even then, he hadn't felt it like this. Not as close as this. Despite the fact that Eloise had only just accepted their mating—they hadn't had time to fully bind it with the pronouncement in front of pack, or to each other in private. They were connected by the thinnest of threads.

Not that the thinness mattered to him. If she died, so would he. He couldn't live without her. His heart would simply stop beating. So he understood Cordy's agony. Was astonished her heart did still beat. Perhaps it was her strength showing through. Like Malcolm when Bridgette had severed her soul from her body to protect him and her family and coven. He remembered it all now.

The Were who was a part of his soul had wanted to go with his mate, but he hadn't. He'd stayed until the children were old enough to look after themselves. Twenty long, achingly empty years he'd lived after her death and he'd done it to look after those she loved.

Perhaps, like Malcolm, it was the need of her pack that kept Cordy here—the need to be there for those Marcus had loved. Whatever it was, he didn't envy her the life spread before her without her mate.

Empty. Lonely. Endless.

He clenched Eloise's hand again, his thumb sweeping over the back of her palm. She'd lost so much blood. Come so close to death. But he'd held her here with the force of his love; the force of his need and passion for her and the spark of life within her that had become so essential to his own. 'Don't leave me, Little Bird,' he whispered, leaning over to place a kiss on her lips as he'd done a thousand times in the last few days. 'I need to tell you I love you. I need you to believe me and accept that you are my mate. My soul. Come back to me.'

Nothing. As there had been nothing for the last few days. She lay so still, the bandages swathing her wrists hardly whiter than her skin, her fine features as pure as carved porcelain, her tawny hair a halo around her head and shoulders.

If not for the beeping of the machines and the slight rise and fall of her chest, the steady patter of her heart, you could be mistaken for thinking she was dead. But she wasn't dead. He wouldn't allow her to die. Her spark—that unique spark that had drawn him to her from the first—would never extinguish if he had his way. It was there, deep inside him, nestled next to the faint strand that was the mating bond.

'You are mine and I am yours. That is all that matters,' he whispered to her.

There was a change in her heartbeat. A little skip that made his heart hold for a beat.

Her fingers moved slightly against his. Her eyelids fluttered. 'Eloise?'

'Iain.' The merest puff of sound.

'Eloise!' He grabbed both her hands, voice ringing around the usually quiet room.

'Eloise. Can you hear me? Eloise.'

'Iain.' That whisper of sound again, a hint of confusion.

'Yes, Eloise. I'm here.'

'Iain?' He didn't turn at Shelley's question, or the sound of others rushing over to stand at Eloise's bed.

His attention was wholly centred on the woman who stirred on the bed before him. 'Come on, Little Bird. You can do this. Come back to me.'

'Iain? What is it? Is she waking up?' Skye asked.

'Shelley—can you feel anything?' Jason said.

'I think someone should go and get Bron,' Shelley said at the same time.

'I'll go,' Patrick said. Iain hadn't known his brother was there. But then he was gone and it didn't matter. All that mattered was the fact that his precious love's eyes were finally opening.

'Eloise. I'm here. You're safe.'

She winced. 'My head hurts.'

He smiled at the soft complaint. 'Yes. I know.'

'Then stop shouting at me.'

He laughed. He couldn't help it. Just as he couldn't help lifting her into his arms, holding her close, his lips showering kisses across her face as her eyes fluttered open.

'Iain. Be careful of her drip.'

He didn't need them to tell him. He might have been almost dizzy with happiness, but he would never do anything to hurt his precious Eloise. Hands reached in to try to straighten some of the cables, and he let them, but he didn't loosen his grip. He was never going to loosen his grip on this remarkable woman again.

'Iain. You're crushing me.'

Well, maybe just a little. He laughed, pulling away so he could look down at her upturned face. 'You came back to me.'

Her mouth trembled. 'I heard you calling to me.' Her gaze caught his, filled with such grief. 'Oh, Iain. I'm sorry. I'm so sorry. What have I done?'

'It wasn't your fault. It was Cain. You did everything you could.'

'I should have done more. I should have—'

He pressed his lips against hers to stop the words from spilling out of her mouth. 'No,' he said, pulling back when she stilled under him. 'You did everything you could.' He closed his eyes. 'Almost too much. Why did you do that alone?'

Her trembling fingers touched his cheek. 'I didn't want you to be hurt.'

He shook his head. 'Don't you know that if you hurt, I hurt? If you die, I die?'

She nodded, lips trembling. 'I'm sorry.' Her voice was the barest choked whisper, but he heard it.

'Don't be sorry. Just be here.'

She squeezed her eyes shut, lips pressed together, and then nodded again. 'Okay.'

He frowned. Even though she said the words, there was something in them that he didn't believe. Something she was worried about. Something she was hiding. 'Eloise ...'

Her eyes snapped open, her gaze meeting his, unflinching. 'I love you.'

The universe opened up inside him, bright with the lights of a million suns. 'You do?' She nodded, the happiness in her eyes dimming a little. 'But what if it's not enough? I'm still a danger to you and yours. Cain and Morrigan are after me. They want my power. They almost got it.'

'But they didn't. You were too powerful. You drove them away.'

'I did, didn't I?' There was some dawning pride in her voice. 'But I'm not sure how I did that. Or if I could do it again.'

'I am.'

She huffed out a laugh. 'You can't just say that because you wish it to be true.'

'I'm not. I know it's true.'

'But what if Cain is in me? What if he makes me turn on you? I couldn't stand it.'

'Shh,' he said, kissing away her anguish. 'I'm not wrong. He's gone.'

'How can you be certain?'

'Because nothing that dark could live inside something filled with such light.'

She stared up at him. 'I want that to be true.'

'It is. You'll see.' He could tell she wanted to protest but didn't have the strength yet to do so, her eyelids too heavy to keep open. 'No more arguing. You need to rest.'

'Stay with me,' she managed to say as her eyes closed.

He repositioned himself so he was lying on the bed with her

cradled against his chest. Peace filled him, and for the first time in days, he felt like he could sleep.

But before he did, he glanced across the room.

Skye was crying, but happiness brimmed in her eyes. Jason's mouth quirked in a proud, relieved smile. And Shelley nodded at him, a faint smile on her lips, before she turned away to stare at a space beside Adam's bed, her face flashing to a pissed-off frown.

Sleep claimed him before he could worry about what that meant.

30

A week had passed since Eloise had almost died and she was still in the hospital room with Iain waiting on her hand and foot.

He hadn't left, not even when Marcus' body had been given up to the light like Gabbie's had with the help of Bron and Shelley and Skye and the McClune coven. She hadn't seen it, but Bron told them it had happened when she'd made a comment about the grief that still hung so thick in the air. Sending Gabbie into the light had helped the McVale Pack in a way it just didn't seem to be working for the McClunes. In fact, the suppurating wound of the loss of their Alpha and of Cordy's continued retreat into some dark place nobody could reach, leached out and touched her even in the hospital room deep in the earth.

'They won't recover from it,' Iain had said when Eloise asked him about it. 'Not until a new Alpha comes forth.'

'Isn't there someone to take his place?'

Iain shook his head, the sorrow in his eyes making her heart ache. 'No. Alphas are born and there have been none so far. The pack was hoping that Marcus and Cordy's child would be it.'

'Oh Goddess! She's pregnant?'

He closed his eyes briefly, and she knew. The loss of it made it difficult to swallow.

'She lost the baby?'

'The shock of loss, her grief, it was too much. Bron couldn't save it.'

'Oh, I'm so sorry.' She clenched his hand, her squeeze so weak, but he seemed to take comfort from it none the less. His fingers tightened around her hand, his thumb stroking the back of her hand, taking comfort and giving it in the way of the Were. She leaned against his chest, kissed his neck, knowing instinctively what he needed from her. After a long moment of holding and being held, she whispered, 'What are they going to do now?'

'Liam, the strongest lieutenant, has stepped forward in the interim, and Jason is helping as much as he can, but unless one of them Becomes, they're going to be without an Alpha until one is born.' He swallowed hard then fell silent as he stared into space, deep frown lines creasing his brow.

She touched his cheek to get his attention. He turned and smiled at her, warming her deep inside. 'What is it?' she asked softly. 'What's worrying you?'

He sighed. 'I have to go back to Melbourne. Jason needs to stay here with Adam—he's too unstable to move. Besides, the McClunes need whatever strength he and Skye have to give them to help them go forward as a pack and help their coven restructure without Cordy to lead them. He needs me in Melbourne to maintain the stability in our pack.'

'Of course.' Then she realised he was telling her he had to leave her. Panic seized her at the thought. 'I'll come with you.'

'I don't know if that's a good idea. You're barely strong enough to walk by yourself. Besides, you're safe here.'

'I would be safe with you. And besides, it's not like I have to walk back to Melbourne.' That made him smile. She was grateful to see his smile. Sadness wrapped around him, and she hated to see it. To feel it to the depths of her soul. 'Besides, I need to get out of these caves.'

She shuddered. 'I can still feel Cain here. I don't think I'll start to feel better until I'm away from that feeling.'

'Okay. If Bron says it's okay, we'll go tomorrow.'

Bron was fine with her leaving as long as she promised not to exert herself. 'You can stay at my place. But you aren't allowed outside for at least another week and then only out into the gardens until I have a chance to check up on you—which might not be for a couple of weeks depending on how long I'm needed here. Deal?'

'Deal.' Eloise would have shaken hands with the devil to get out of this sad, horrible place.

'At least you can start to study something about your powers while you're down there. I'll let Shelley know that you'll be wanting to look at the diaries in a week or so, but not before.' She held up a warning finger, wagging it at her. 'You must be fully recovered before you start using your powers again. Understood?'

'Yes, sergeant,' she said, doing a sloppy salute.

Bron laughed—the first laugh she'd heard from the usually bubbly woman since that horrible night. 'Good. Now rest up. The trip back to Melbourne tomorrow will probably be a drain, even though it's a short one.'

She was right. Eloise was so exhausted when they reached Bron's home in Templestowe that she fell asleep the moment Iain put her to bed and slept through the next day as well.

She got all the rest she would ever need over the next few weeks, with Iain ensuring that she barely lifted a finger when he was there. The times he had to be away from her to deal with pack issues— which increased with every day—he had his brother, Patrick, watch over her. It was a little maddening. She'd never been so cosseted in her life.

After a week of it, she began to feel edgy. Especially given Iain was barely there, and when he was, the sadness and worry that emanated from him was so great, she didn't feel like she could push him about it —about her need to spread her wings; her need to change and run free; her need to explore her new powers and learn more about them;

and most of all, her need to talk with him about their new mating, and how it had come into being.

She wanted to tell him that she loved him again. She wanted to hear from him that he loved her. But most of all, she wanted to know if he forgave her for forcing the mating in that moment, for taking the choice out of his hands, to know that she hadn't somehow damaged his Lone Wolf soul. She wanted to tell him that she needed him in her bed—and not in the next room where he wouldn't disturb her sleep during the night if he was called out on pack duties. She needed him to touch her like he'd touched her the nights they'd made love—not like she would turn into dust and blow away in the wind. She needed to touch him in return, share her desire, the passion and fire that built inside every time he came into the room— hell, every time she thought of him. But if she did that, then she'd have to face the fact that she might have to let him go, to wander, because he was Lone Wolf, and he couldn't be pinned down to any one place. Not even by his mate.

'*You're behaving like a coward,*' the voice she now knew was Bridgette whispered in her mind.

'No.' She shook her head. She wasn't a coward. She just didn't want to add to Iain's burdens. Not right now. Not when everything was so difficult.

'*Yes you are. Iain's sadness isn't what's stopping you from asking him. You're afraid to know the truth. Just like you're afraid to know if you can control your powers. You should have called Shelley and asked for her to bring some of the diaries over. You should address the fact that you feel power building inside you every day, tingling under your fingers. But you ignore it. Why?*'

'I did ask.' She'd brought it up briefly with Iain the day before. 'Shelley is using the diaries. Iain said she barely comes out of the study, she's so busy with her research of them. I don't want to disturb her.'

'*Excuses. You don't want to find out that the power you used to defeat Cain was just a fluke. You aren't truly sick anymore. You could ask for help, but you haven't.*'

'There's nobody to ask.' Bron was still at the mines with Adam, who was still too sick to move. Shelley was locked up with the diaries and Skye was, of course, with her mate, helping buoy the energies he was giving to Adam, his pack and the McClune Pack.

'They'd help if you asked. You just don't want to ask because you're afraid. Afraid that you don't belong. That you're not one of them. That they can't help you.'

'I do belong!' She knew she did. Had known for weeks. That wasn't her fear.

'Then don't let the mistakes of my past burden your present.'

She stared out the window, at the sun shining over the garden outside and realised something with a quiet clarity that wiped away all pretence as sure as a tsunami. 'Oh Goddess.' She'd been sitting around, allowing them to treat her like an invalid, allowing herself to sink into old patterns of behaviour. But she wasn't that person anymore. Didn't want to be that person anymore. Couldn't be that person anymore. She'd beaten Cain, beaten the Darkness. She hadn't ever let it in, even though it had always been there. It had touched Bridgette in the aether and had attached itself to a portion of her soul, and when that soul was reincarnated into Eloise, it had manifested as a deformity in her foot—but only because she had never let it in. If she'd let it in as Cain had, she would never have shown the deformity of its presence. It would simply have blackened her soul.

Her soul wasn't blackened. It was pure. And her foot was no longer deformed. It had healed when she got rid of the Darkness.

She was no longer an outsider. No longer less because of the presence of the Darkness. The canker of it was gone and she would never let it touch her like that again.

She was the Nexus. She had made her decision, chosen her side, and she was tied to that decision as certainly as she was tied to Iain and his pack. Her destiny was chosen. Now it was up to her to reach out and own it. Own herself. Own her claim to Iain and stand equal beside him.

There were things she could do. Things she had to do. And she was going to do them. Patrick leapt to his feet when she strode out of her room. 'What do you need?'

She waved him away. 'I'm going out into the garden.' He moved towards her. She saw the denial coming. 'I need to go out there. I need to change. I need to be with nature. Don't stop me.'

He wavered for a moment, uncertainty on his face, but then nodded. 'Okay. I'll need to call Iain though.'

'You do that.'

Then she was out the door and into the weak winter sun before he could say another word.

As the cool breeze wafted over her, the scents of the grass and earth and winter blossoms drifting around her, enticing, she changed into the wolf. Bounding off the patio and onto the gravel of the path beyond, she raced through the garden to its heart, its centre. This was where she belonged, with pack scents around her, in the arms of nature. She howled into the sky, calling her mate to her. Expectation filled her as power buzzed through her. He was coming. She could feel him. The pull of him, the constant presence through the bond that was now tied inextricably to her heart, to her soul. The knowledge filled her with a sense of place, a sense of purpose, a sense of who she was. It was unlike anything she'd ever felt before.

She didn't care that Cain and Morrigan—and the Darkness that held dominion over them—were still out there. They would be scrambling to find some way forward now that her powers were lost to them. They'd be afraid. Of her. Of what she could do now she had found herself. And they should be afraid. She had always been a threat to them, but she'd been too weak to see it, too gullible, too needy. Well, she was none of those things anymore.

Cain might have her blood, but he had nothing else. And he would never have any part of her again. The only person who had a right to any part of her had just entered the garden and was heading towards her.

And as he walked through the garden, she realised what the worry, the sadness, in him was truly about. He was worried that she hadn't truly chosen him; that she'd been forced by circumstances to bond with him.

She had to show him how wrong he was.

He appeared on the path and before he could say anything, she changed. She changed into Bluebelle first, then back to the wolf, and then, finally, into her human form. Standing naked before him, she met his gaze, chin held high.

'Eloise,' he breathed. 'It felt like you needed me. What's wrong?'

The burn of desire that flared in his eyes warmed her so that she didn't notice the coolness of the air. 'Nothing's wrong. But you're right. I do need you. I always need you.' She took a step closer to him. 'The question I've been too cowardly to ask you though, is do you need me? Am I enough?'

'You have always been enough. More than enough. You are everything.'

'As you are everything to me.'

He sucked in a breath. 'You accept me?'

'Always and forever.'

He was suddenly in front of her, cupping her face, fingers digging into her hair. 'Always and forever,' he said, repeating her words; the promise mates made to each other.

Then he kissed her.

She wanted to sink into the kiss, to lose herself in the feelings only he could bring to her and not think about everything else, but she had to tell him something more. She pulled away a fraction, enough to look into his beautiful eyes, to see the soul shining there that loved her throughout time; the soul that had always been, and would always be, hers. But more importantly, the part of that soul that was and would ever be, Iain.

'I love you, Iain. Me. Eloise. Not Bridgette. Not whoever came before. They will always have their share of my soul, but my heart is mine and I give it to you.'

His face broke into a smile brighter than the most glorious sunrise. 'As I give you mine. I love you, Eloise. And that love grows stronger every day. For you and the remarkable person you are and who you are to become. I will always be by your side. To find out your heritage. To discover your powers. To seek out the truth of what being the Nexus means.'

'And I will do everything I can to allow your wolf the freedom it needs to roam free.'

'I never need to roam free from you. Surely you know that?'

The smile bloomed on her face as she realised she did know that. The dreams had shown it to her. To both of them. Malcolm's words to Bridgette suddenly rang loudly in her head. Iain's need to roam free had changed. He was a Lone Wolf simply because he roamed to find his soulmate. She was found. He needed to roam no longer.

'Iain,' she whispered, reaching up to kiss him at the same time as he bent down to kiss her, her name on his lips. And as their names tangled together, their lips pressing and caressing, her sense of belonging and rightness increased, flooded through her, stronger than she'd ever imagined. It hummed like a glorious pure note, surging through her synapses, bursting through her skin and pores until she felt she *was* joy.

Iain flung back his head and howled at the night sky and without thinking, Eloise did the same.

Iain smiled down at her, his face glowing in the fairy lights and the light of the quarter moon. 'My mate,' he whispered. 'Always and forever.'

His words reverberated through her, touching a well of emotion hidden deep inside. 'Always and forever,' she whispered back. 'My mate. My love. My life.' She had no idea why she'd added those words, but they came from that same deep place inside and they felt right.

'My mate,' Iain repeated. 'My love. My life.'

Then their lips met again and Iain lifted her up, carrying her to the patch of grass still warm from the sun that was even now slipping from the horizon. Hands moving swiftly together, they removed his clothes, their lips never parting, and soon they were lying naked on the soft grass. She ran her fingers over the strong, silken planes of his chest, down his arms and over his shoulders to press into his back, pulling him down to her. She wanted to feel him inside her once more. It had been too long since they'd made love. She needed him now to complete the mating and make this a moment of true bliss.

'Love me,' she said against his lips.

'Always.' His lips left hers, but she didn't mind, because they ran down her neck, where he nipped and sucked and licked as his hands circled her nipples with teasing strokes, making her moan and arch up.

'Eloise,' he breathed against the pulse in her neck. 'Mine.' Then his teeth sank into her neck.

Lights sparked behind her eyes as he claimed her with his teeth and tongue and mouth. She clutched at his back, fingers raking over his skin. He groaned and she did it again.

'You're driving me insane, Little Bird,' he moaned. 'I'm not going to last.'

'I don't want you to. Take me. I need you inside me now.'

She wrapped her legs around him and as his teeth sank into her pulse point again, he slid inside in one firm push. The sparks behind her eyes went off and she pulsed around him. He uttered something she couldn't make out and went still.

'Don't stop,' she panted.

His lips met hers and he began to move. She clutched him tighter with her legs, her hands a fever over his back and into his hair. Rearing up, she bit him where the pulse pounded in his neck. He growled, the sound thrumming through her as the thick length of him slid in and out in that rhythm that was their secret dance. Everything tensed inside her to an unbearable point as Iain gave one last thrust.

Eloise screamed her pleasure into the night as the waves of sensation broke over her, Iain's cry a deep harmony to hers; the most wonderful sound she'd ever heard.

A few minutes later, he rolled over and stood up. But before she could complain about the sudden cold his absence brought to her, he pulled her up and into his arms, carrying her towards the house where he laid her down on her bed, snuggling her against his side.

Soft moonlight fell on them through the open curtain, silvering their skin.

'So, our mating is complete.'

'The most important part, yes. Patrick would have heard our mating cry—a pack member has to be present to hear it as well as feel it. But he wouldn't have seen anything. I promise.'

'I know,' she said, playing her hand over his chest. He would never expose her in any way she wasn't comfortable with. 'Is there anything else that needs to be done?'

'We'll have a binding ceremony with the pack to seal the deal for them, but for us, it's done.'

'It's there inside me. So strong. So beautiful.'

'Yes.'

She smiled. 'Why did you move us?' she asked as she pressed her cheek against his chest, the still fast pattering of his heart thrumming in her ear.

'The first part of a true mating must occur outside in nature, but I didn't want you to get cold.'

'I could never be cold with you next to me. Or inside me.'

He pressed a kiss to her forehead. 'I love you, my Little Bird.'

She moved to look up at him. 'I love you, my wolf.' She kissed him with all the wild joy inside her. 'I love you. I can't seem to stop saying it.'

Iain's lips curved against her brow. 'I feel the same way.' He touched his chest. 'You are my heart. I could never live without you there.'

'Iain.' She kissed him and knew that in him she had found someone who saw her for who she was and loved her for it, just as she saw everything he was and loved him. He knew that she could face up to anything the Darkness or Morrigan or Cain or the universe threw her way, just as she knew it. But she didn't have to do it alone. Nor did he. Alone they were strong. Together, they were more.

She would never let go of wanting the more. She loved and was loved. It was the most beautiful thing she'd ever experienced.

Always and forever. She reached out and embraced her destiny.

ABOVE THE HOUSE, the sky trembled and a light shot through night. The wolves as one lifted their faces to the moon and howled.

In the distance, the Darkness trembled and curled in on itself, squeezing tight to the hearts it had turned into blackest obsidian.

Morrigan and Cain clutched at each other, whimpering in pain, trembling.

'Mistress?'

Morrigan stroked Cain's hair. 'It will pass,' she gasped, holding tight to him as they collapsed to the ground.

'Yes,' the Darkness whispered. The fear, the loss, would pass. And then, when it had built its strength again, it would lash out. And this time, it would hit its mark and the world would truly tremble.

I HOPE you enjoyed Eloise and Iain's story as much as I enjoyed writing it and can't wait to sink into the next instalment with Shelley and Adam's story in *Wolf Bound*. Read on for the first few chapters.

Before you do though, I just wanted to let you know that I also have a FREE ebook copy of **Witch Bound**, a novella set 40 years before the events in the current day *Pack Bound Series*, to give to you.

More on that after the first few chapters of *Wolf Bound* ...

WOLF BOUND

PACK BOUND SERIES BOOK 4

LEISL LEIGHTON

PROLOGUE

Edinburgh, Scotland, 1502

Morghanna stared out at the crowd gathered to see the spectacle of a witch trial. Their greedy, avaricious faces taunted her. They were so eager to see her pronounced guilty.

These people she had helped through childbirth and sickness.

They wanted to see her burn.

She closed her eyes, sick of seeing the hate-filled faces around her, numb to the pain of her injuries. Even so, she couldn't escape their hatred and fear. It seeded the air with a foul stench. They clamoured and yelled, less than animals. She should hate them, but her hatred was held for one Were and the son he had never had the strength to control.

Her lip curled.

Iain MacCrae was to blame. If only he had done something about Lachlan when he began to show the seeds of his insanity; or if he'd allowed the Hunters to do their job as they should have done when Lachlan escaped, none of what had come to pass in the last ten years would have occurred.

She had lost so much because of his inaction, but never so much as in the last few weeks.

Alistair was dead trying to save her from Lachlan. And now Lachlan had done this! Turned her in to the Witch Finder after tricking her and Alistair to come on this supposed mission of mercy. He had known she would never be able to ignore a message from villagers who had once given her and her coven shelter.

She wasn't truly surprised by his actions. Nor was she surprised by Iain's continued lack of action where his son was concerned. But she was surprised by the others. When she had realised it was a trap, she'd called through the Packbond to ask for their help. She knew Iain would refuse to come, but his remaining lieutenants should have wanted to protect her, for she and Alistair were their last hope to keep their foundering pack together. But they refused. They blamed her for the fact they'd lost three quarters of their pack and nearly all of their coven to the exiled Dougal's new pack.

But she wasn't to blame. The Alpha they protected—an Alpha who, like the leech he was, drew on their strength and power to stay alive and keep his son from harm—was to blame.

If only she and Alistair had gone to join Dougal sooner, then this may not have happened. But like a fool, she'd stayed behind, Alistair along with her, the last of their coven to do so, their aim to convince those Were who stayed to leave the sinking ship that was Pack MacCrae and join them in Dougal's new pack.

She was only glad that Bridgette had come for the birthing of their son and had taken him to safety.

She was also thankful her sister, Morrigan, had not been there too. Although, why would she be? Her sister had begged her from the start not to listen to Bridgette Colliere. She'd begged her over and over not to share their powers with the Were. But Morghanna had believed as Bridgette did—she still did believe—that it was the only way they could survive.

And they'd been right. It had been the miracle they had prayed for. All the covens were safe now with their bonded packs.

It wasn't the fault of the Pact that things hadn't worked so smoothly for her coven. They couldn't have known they would be crushed under the weak leadership of an Alpha who wouldn't give over his position to Dougal and the others who were prepared to do what must be done:

Kill the insane Lachlan MacCrae.

But she'd taken care of that and her coven was now safe. However, was that enough? She'd been betrayed. Alistair was dead and soon she would be too. How could she make certain this would never happen to another one of her kind again? How could she make certain her son would be forever safe?

Her eyes burned with tears as she tried not to think of the son she was leaving behind. Tried to remember instead her mate's laughing face, his tender kisses, the way he'd held her face as if she were the most precious thing he'd ever beheld.

But all she could think of was that Lachlan's jealousy and Iain's weakness had killed Alistair.

Just as it was about to kill her too. Because of him, she would never see her child again. Never hold him to her breast. Never hear his first laugh, see his first stumbling attempt at walking, run to him when he was hurt, filling him with the certainty of her love. Iain and Lachlan had stolen all of that from Alistair and her.

For that, she could not forgive those who stood by and did nothing when they should have done what their Alpha was too weak to do. They were supposed to protect their coven as well as they protected themselves. Instead, their inaction had destroyed her and split her coven in a way she feared it would never recover from.

She *had* to do something to make certain this could never happen again.

Flames leapt to life around her as torches were put to the pyre at her feet.

And as it did, her need to pay back those responsible became a living flame inside her, building and building until everything she was focused with single-minded intensity on ending what remained of Pack MacCrae and ensuring this never happened to her kind again. She must protect her son and his progeny; only that mattered now.

The words of her curse leapt into her mind, and as they did, she spoke them out loud. Her words rang out above the angry cries of the mob and the crackling of the fire that licked at her with its hot, burning tongue.

Then the words were gone and she was empty, her power having been almost fully expended on making certain the Curse would carry through the ages.

It was then she truly felt the pain of the fire hungering for her flesh.

The flames weren't even touching her, but she swore her skin was blistering. She gritted her teeth, closed her eyes against the smoke. She wouldn't cry out. Wouldn't give those watching the satisfaction of her pain.

A prickling awareness shuddered through her and her eyes snapped open, going to the hill beyond the village.

A woman stood there, lit by the light of the moon above.

Morrigan.

No!

Oh, Goddess, no.

Her sister shouldn't be here. Not to witness this. Not to be touched by its evil.

She focused her magic so as to see Morrigan's features; she needed to read her to figure out what she had seen and heard. Despite the heat of the flames, cold slithered through her bones at her sister's expression—pure unbridled rage and hate. Oh Goddess, what had she done in speaking that curse aloud for her sister to hear?

Morrigan lifted her hands, drawing power.

Morghanna shook her head, whispered her denial, hoping the Goddess would carry her words to her sister's ears. '*No Morrigan. The Witch Finder will see you. Do not bring destruction upon yourself. Carry our line through the ages or all I have suffered will have been for nought.*'

Morrigan's hands stilled, the power falling away as devastation and grief pulled on her stunning features. Then her face screwed up and she shouted into the night, 'I told you this would happen. I warned you no good could come from aligning with those animals.'

'I know what you said. But I was right too. For many of our kind, the Pact has been a blessing.'

'How can you defend them?'

'Morrigan, listen. Not all of them are bad. Just this pack, and not even all of them.'

'Is that so? Then where are they now? These so-called good Were? They are supposed to protect you, so where are they?'

'I forced them away, to build a pack of their own where all of our coven can be safe.'

'And they let you?'

'They had no choice.'

'If you love some of them still, then why did you invoke that curse?'

'I had to. I had to ensure they protect Alistair's and my—' Her voice cut off as the flames licked closer and a cry of pain left her lips.

'Morghanna! I will kill them for doing this to you.'

Her sister's words helped her ride out the pain and say, *'No Morrigan. Do not go down that path. Believe me when I say, those responsible will pay. As will any others who seek to treat their covens as Iain McCrae and his ilk treated ours. The Curse will make certain this happens to no other witch or warlock again.'*

Morrigan shook her head, her rage and grief almost a physical thing. A dark shadow crept towards her down the hill.

No. It couldn't be. Panicked, she said, *'Please, Morrigan. Listen to me. You are inviting the Darkness to you. Can you not feel it all around you? It is what we have fought off with the Pact. Please, do not allow it entry into your heart. I beg of you not to—'*

The flames leapt higher, obscuring her vision, the smoke choking her, the flames catching her dress, touching her skin. She screamed, unable, despite her vow, to hold it in.

Through the pain, she cried out with her mind, desperate to make her sister hear. To make her stop from taking this most terrible of steps because of her hatred of the Were and her need to take revenge for something that only a few were responsible for. *'No Morrigan. Don't! Not for me. Never for me.'*

'Only for you,' she cried. 'They will pay for this. The Were will pay, but first every man, woman and child taking delight in this horror will feel each moment of terror and agony you endure.'

'No, Morrigan. It does not have to be like this.'

'You are wrong. They sealed their fate the moment they laid hands on you.'

'Then you give me no choice.' Morghanna looked up to the heavens and cried out, her voice carrying over the rabble, over the crackle of flames once more. 'Please, my Goddess. End this now. Take me as you always promised you would.'

There was no answer and as the flames took hold, Morghanna screamed again.

'Our Goddess has failed you,' Morrigan cried. 'I will not.' She raised her hands but Morghanna didn't see anything more. Light streamed from the heavens, surrounding her in a golden glow.

The pain fell away and she lifted her head to the heavens as the touch of her Goddess wrapped around her.

The light brightened, white and pure, as flames exploded around her. 'I knew my Goddess would never forsake me,' Morghanna cried out. Then in Morrigan's head, Morghanna said, *'It is not too late for you either my beloved sister to change your path. Fill yourself with the Goddess' light and love. Do not let the Darkness have you.'*

The light around Morghanna brightened, white and pure. Her bindings evaporated and she lifted her hands, crying out to the stars above, 'Save me.'

Flames exploded, whipping into a tornado that shot up into the sky. Screams sang out on the air as the mob fell away from the explosion of white-hot heat and flame. There was a brief flash of pain.

And then there was nothing.

She never saw the destruction her sister wrought in her name or the moment the Darkness wrapped itself around Morrigan's heart. It wasn't until much later when she was able to pull her consciousness together, that she looked down on the world and saw what had been started by her Curse.

She sobbed and railed and eventually cried out, 'Oh Goddess! How can I make amends for what I've done?'

'You can help me,' the Goddess Arianrhod said as she appeared beside her. 'Together, we can work to defeat the creature at the heart of this madness.'

'My Curse already took care of the MacCraes.'

'Not the MacCraes. The thing behind all the evil in this world. The thing I warned you we would have to face all those years ago when I helped save your mate the first time.'

'You did not save him this time.'

'No, I did not. But that was out of my hands.' A sigh. 'As you promised me your fidelity all those years ago, I now promise you I will do all I can to help lead you back to your soul mate in some future time.'

Hope thrilled through her. To be with Alistair again! 'You can do that?'

'I can try. But only after you do what must be done now.'

'And that is?'

'You will help me to destroy the Darkness.'

1

The smell was the first thing that hit Adam, a horrible burning of flesh and cotton. Then the punch as he was flung backwards. Time slowed, every bare millisecond separated as he flew through the air, giving him a chance to look down.

Fuck, there was a hole in his chest.

Time sped up as the pain tore through him. He hit the wall and there was a strange popping, wrenching sound that made him stagger. A thump behind him. He spun to see his body splayed on the ground, a stupid look of surprise on his face.

Marcus landed beside him. A black charred hole smoked in both their chests. Marcus' body was still in the super-empowered form that had allowed them to break down the door. Adam's was returning to normal. Well, as normal as it could be with a big black smoking hole in his chest.

Hang on. Why was he looking down at his body and not up at the ceiling?

The room span. There could be only one explanation.

He was dead.

Holy shit!

He was dead?

It had all happened so fast. One moment he'd been rushing into the room, feeling stronger than he'd ever felt before, the next—bam! Struck by warlock lightning. Dead.

It was the most curious sensation. Not at all like he'd thought it would feel. Quite freeing actually if you discounted the initial pain. Although there sure was a lot of wind in the afterlife—he couldn't feel it, but it was a loud whooshing in his ears. It made hearing anything else difficult.

Shelley had never mentioned it. Maybe she didn't hear it. Maybe you had to be dead to hear the noise of the afterlife.

He laughed, couldn't help it. It was so absurd.

Shelley's gaze snapped to him. His laughter died. She wasn't looking at his body lying on the floor with the smouldering hole in its chest. But at him. Ghost him. And the expression on her face made him want to howl.

Horror. Grief. Realisation.

He *was* dead. And there was no way they could ever be together. Not that there was ever really a chance that they would have been, but now that chance was completely gone. Whisked away between one breath and the next. It was like being punched in the chest with something worse than warlock lightning. He couldn't breathe. Couldn't breathe. He was dead! And every hope he'd ever had was gone.

Something brushed past him and he became aware of the pandemonium around him. What the fuck was he doing standing here worried about what he'd lost? There was a battle raging around him. Cain was about to throw a lightning bolt at Shelley.

No!

He threw himself in the way but he needn't have bothered. Power sizzled in the air as Shelley waved her hand and shouted out a word. Something buffeted him; the spirits around him wavered and crackled, like bad transmission on the TV. There was a faint amethyst outline hanging in the air around them all, like a bubble—holy crap, it was a shield! —protecting her, Cordy and the two bodies lying on the floor.

Cain loosed his lightning. It hit the shield, flared and skittered up to the ceiling, exploding there. 'Fuck, Shelley, that was amazing. I didn't know you could do that.'

She simply stared at him and then her gaze darted around him and he became aware of hundreds of spirits surrounding her too. He wasn't sure if they were being protective or staying in her protective cordon. He didn't have a chance to ask. Another bolt of lightning hit the shield. Sparks sprayed everywhere, delineating the edges of it; the strange amethyst tinge around the translucent edges fluttered. The bolt slid up and hit the ceiling. Rocks and plaster bounced off the shield and clattered onto the floor.

Shelley winced as if they'd hit her.

She was being hurt. Protective rage surged inside him. 'You bastard,' he shouted at Cain and leapt towards him—then fell right through him and onto the floor.

He rolled over, swearing, and rose, ready to try again. One of the spirits was whispering something in Shelley's ear. Another—he identified him as Harrison, Skye and River's grandfather, from photos he'd seen—shouted something, a general organising his troops. Half the spirits surged towards Cain.

Eloise's brother shrieked, his words lost in the strange wind that seemed to be a constant whistle in Adam's ears, then loosed another bolt and ran to the door.

'Don't let him get away!' Iain shouted, loud enough for Adam to hear. Shit. Iain was there. With Eloise cradled in his arms on the opposite side of the room. He'd forgotten about them. He turned to do as Iain bid, but Cain was already out the door, loosing another lightning bolt at Shelley as he went. More rocks and plaster rained down from the ceiling.

Cain was gone, but Adam didn't really care. He turned to check on Shelley.

Her look as it met his, it slayed him. Well, it would if he wasn't already dead. His lips quirked and he shrugged. 'I'm dead, aren't I?' he asked softly.

She didn't answer, but her eyes blinked faster.

'Am I supposed to go towards the light?' He glanced around, but he couldn't see any light except for what came from the lights in the ceiling.

'Don't go,' she said raggedly. His gaze snapped back to her as she whispered again, 'Don't go.'

He frowned. Strange that he could hear her so clearly when everything else was almost drowned out by the damned wind.

'Marcus. Marcus. Come back to me,' Cordy cried, her grief echoing through the wind. 'Don't you leave me alone. Not like this. Not like this.'

Her plea was useless. Marcus' spirit stood over Cordy, tortured grief written in every line of him. Adam swallowed hard the said, 'Shelley. Help her.'

Shelley jumped a little then started forward.

'Shelley.' Iain's voice, a sharp, desperate shout. 'Shelley. You can't help them. They're already gone. Eloise is still alive. We have to help her. Shelley!'

Cordy's wailing became even louder, the sobs so grief-filled they lashed him. He could see they were lashing Iain as well, the grief in his friend's eyes for him as well as the Alpha of Pack McClune and the mate he'd left behind. Yet, like a good lieutenant always would do, he put aside his grief and did what he could for the living. Adam understood. Just as he understood Iain would do anything to save his new mate.

Marcus was saying something to Shelley but Adam still couldn't make out his words through the howling wind—he could barely make out what the living were saying. Except Shelley. Her words were clear.

Shelley blinked and then very slowly turned to Cordy, her brow creased. She touched the grieving witch on the head and said, 'Sleep.' Cordy slumped over Marcus' body, the absence of sobbing a shocking silence. Shelley nodded slowly as Marcus said something else. 'I know. Are you sure?' She paused, then nodded. 'I'll tell her later.' Marcus looked pleadingly at her, then nodded and turned back to his mate.

'Who are you talking to?' Iain asked.

She swallowed hard. 'Marcus. He's standing right there. He couldn't bear Cordy's grief and asked me to make her sleep. She'll be no use to us anyway.' Her eyes slipped to where Adam stood and then away.

'We have to help Eloise,' Iain repeated.

'Yes.' Shelley blinked again and turned to look at him and the woman in his arms.

'Bron will be here soon.'

'We can't wait for Bron. We have to do something now.'

'You're holding her here.'

He grimaced. 'She's holding herself. She's using the bond and I'm holding her to it, but she's weakening. She's lost too much blood. The bond will tear if we don't do something. Please ... help. You're a nurse. Surely there's something you can do.'

She looked lost. Adam couldn't bare that look in her eyes. He had to do something. Had to bring her out of her grief and shock and bring her back to the here and now. He began to sing 'Suicide Blonde', doing his best Michael Hutchence impersonation. He knew she hated it. Knew it would make her angry. And anger would snap her out of her grief and make her move.

Her eyes flared wide and she snorted out on a laugh, 'Shut up you idiot!'

'Sure. As soon as you snap out of it and do what you're trained to do.' He pointed at Iain. At Eloise. 'She needs your help.'

She stared at him for a moment longer, her chin wobbling, then she moved, ripping the bloody sheet off the bed and racing to where Iain lay with Eloise clutched in his arms.

He smiled. *Good job Adam.* She was nurse Shelley again, action girl. One of the many sides of her he loved.

He watched her go to work, directing Iain to place Eloise on the bed, snapping out instructions. Despite Iain's injuries and obvious weakness, he complied, even to the point where he allowed Shelley to hook him up as a blood donor when they found no blood—Iain was a universal donor, thankfully.

As they worked, Adam became aware of a curious pull on him. Almost as if one of the pack pulled on the Packbond. Weird. He would have thought that bond was sliced clean the moment he died. Maybe it didn't fully go until the ceremony of light had been completed and his body taken in the flame of the power of his coven. He knew dead Were didn't stick around once the ceremony was done. Shelley had never seen any Were spirits—just human and witch and warlock. Perhaps he would be here, linked, until then. As Marcus was.

The pull became stronger, dragging him towards Iain and Eloise. He let it. He'd give everything he could to help Iain save his mate.

Jason, Skye, Bron and River charged into the room. Jason's gaze arrowed immediately to Adam's body, the gaping wound in his chest smouldering and black.

'Oh, my God!' Skye gasped.

'Adam!' Jason yelled. His brother's cry echoed through the wind; it was another tearing wound in his chest. Fuck! He'd never wanted to cause anyone that grief, let alone his big brother who had already been through too much. But what could he do? He was dead.

'Bron! Help.'

Alistair and June charged in behind them. They howled at the sight of their dead Alpha and went down on their knees next to Marcus and Cordy, keening at the ceiling.

Bron dropped down on her knees beside Adam's body, hands held over him, the anguish in her eyes only a fraction of what was in Jason's.

He held his breath, waiting for her to say the words that would make their grieving real.

Shelley's gaze flickered to him again. She took a deep breath and gripped Bron's shoulder. 'Don't. He's gone.'

Bron shook her head. 'No. He's still here. The bolt missed his heart. It's still beating. It's faint but still beating.'

'What?' Adam stared down at his body as Shelley slowly turned to look at him.

'That's impossible. I saw—'

He wasn't dead? Did that mean he was alive? He reached out to touch her, made contact.

She jumped, sucking in a breath.

'Holy shit. What was that?' He stared down at his hand. He'd felt her. Felt her! He looked up at her. She looked just as shocked as he felt. 'Shelley? Tell me you felt that.'

'Saw what?' Skye's voice intruded.

Shelley shook her head, at Skye or at him, he wasn't certain. 'I must have been mistaken,' she whispered and turned back to Bron. 'Can you heal him?'

'I'm trying. I'm trying.'

Skye and Jason began to question Shelley about what had happened. Adam waited for her to answer, for her to finish with them. Marcus began to speak to her again, gesturing at his pack-mates. She crossed to Alistair and June, spoke softly. They stopped keening and stood, fury and grief in their eyes. 'You have to stop them from doing something stupid, Shelley. You're the only one who can.' Shelley's gaze shot to him and then away, her lips working as if she was holding back some terrible emotion. He wanted to talk to her, wanted to ask her so many things, wanted to try to touch her again, but she got up and hurried back to help Iain with Eloise. Then she went back to Alistair and June.

More of the McClune pack arrived, and with words that Marcus spoke to her, Shelley managed to keep them focused, settling Cordy comfortably on a bed, covering and then carrying away Marcus' body. Some went in search of Cain.

'Catch the bastard and make him pay,' he whispered as they left.

There was a tug on him again and he stumbled a little towards Iain and Eloise. They needed his strength. He was happy to give it to them. He glanced over to where Bron worked on him, Jason's hand on her shoulder feeding his strength and Alpha power into her to use in healing his horrific wounds. He expected to be pulled back to his body any moment; Bron was the most powerful Healer they'd seen for centuries. She'd save him.

Minutes passed. Longer. But there was no tug back towards the shell that was once his. It was as if whatever had held him to his body had been completely severed.

But Bron would fix it. She had to fix it.

No point worrying right now. He was still needed even in this form.

He concentrated on Iain and Eloise, on the sensation that pulled at him. He needed to give them more.

'Don't do that.'

He turned. Shelley's eyes were wide, slightly panicked, as she stared at him. 'Don't do what?'

'Whatever you're doing. Stop it. You're fading.' Her voice was a mere whisper, but he heard it as clear as a bell.

'What do you mean?'

She looked around the room. Everyone was busy with what they were doing and took no notice of her. Not that Shelley talking to spirits was anything new—she tried to ignore them, but they weren't always ignorable. Except now. They weren't trying to talk to her now. They all hovered near his body or Iain and Eloise. Marcus and a few others stood over Cordy.

For the time being, Shelley had some peace from them all.

She turned back to him. 'I don't know.' She gestured with her hands, waving them up and down. 'You're less real looking. And flickering a little. I don't think it's good. What are you doing?'

'I felt Iain pulling on the Packbond so I channelled my strength into it to help him with Eloise.'

'Well stop it. I don't like the look of what it's doing to you.' She went to move past him.

He grabbed her arm. She hissed. He let go. 'Sorry. Did I hurt you?'

'No.' She stared at him, down at his hand, back up. 'It's just, you touched me. How did you touch me?'

'I don't know. All I know is I can. That I felt it. And so did you.'

She nodded. 'It's icy cold.'

'Oh. Sorry. I'll try and warm up a bit. I wonder if the fire pits of hell are close by?'

Her lips twitched. 'You're such an idiot.'

He couldn't help but smile at her epithet. 'Even in death.'

Her eyes clouded, gaze flickering to his body. 'You're not dead,' she whispered.

He leaned closer to grab her attention. 'Shelley. What's going on? If I'm not dead, then why can you see me? Why can I touch you? What am I?'

'I don't know.' Her gaze met his, a thousand troubled questions clouding the clear, almost violet, blue. 'I don't know.' Iain called her then. 'I have to go.'

'Don't tell them you can see me, Shelley. I don't want them more upset than they already are. I don't want them to give up hope of me. Not until we've figured out what's going on.'

She didn't look at him again, just pressed her lips together, nodded and walked away.

He turned back to the room, his thoughts whirring. There had to be some way he could find out what was going on. Why he was so separate from his body and yet wasn't dead. Was he a Shade like Cain had been? No. That couldn't be it. He'd touched Shelley and hadn't sucked her life energy from her as Cain had done when he touched others. There was something else going on here. Maybe one of the spirits could help him. According to Shelley, some of them were ancient and had knowledge of things that had been lost to the modern packs.

Perhaps there was one in the room with him now.

He caught a woman with long, tangled black hair, staring at him from across the room, her eyes a startling violet glow in the darkened corner in which she stood. She wore a gown that looked like it might be from the fifteenth or sixteenth century—although historical fashion wasn't his forte, so he could be completely off there.

But she was the only one showing him any interest. She floated over to him.

'You should touch her again. Do it as often as you can.'

'I can hear you.'

'Of course. We are the same. The others are not.'

'What are we?'

She waved her hand back towards Shelley. 'You must tie yourself to her more firmly through your bond.'

'Our bond?' He shook his head. 'There's nothing but the Packbond.'

She tipped her head, assessing. 'You truly believe that?'

'What else could there be?'

She opened her mouth as if to answer and then shook her head. 'You must come with me.'

'And why must I do that?'

'You want to know who you are, don't you? Why you're here? What your role is in all this?'

'What role? I'm here because I was stupid enough to get hit by warlock lightning.'

She tutted at him. 'You are important, Adam McVale. More important than anyone has ever given you credit for. But to learn all you need to learn, you must come with—' She jumped and looked behind her, then back at him, her face lined with worry. 'I must go. You need to come with me now. There is much you must learn.'

She reached for him. He edged away. The tug of the Packbond pulled insistently. He couldn't leave, no matter what the strange woman said. His pack needed him.

'They will always need you. But your role as Trickster is more important than you know and staying here won't teach you what you need to learn to save your pack.'

Her words skittered down his spine and he shivered, as if touched by magic or prescience. 'Who are you?'

She jumped again, looked behind her. She turned quickly back to him, eyes flared wide. 'You must come with me. Now.'

'I'm not going anywhere until you tell me who you are and what this is about.'

Frustration twisted her face. 'I can't. Not here.' She looked behind her again and when she turned back, her eyes were full of fear. 'You can stay, for now. Do what you must to help. But when I come back, I won't give you any choice. I only hope it won't be too late.'

'Too late for what?'

She glanced behind her, her fear palpable, and then, tossing her hood over her head, she turned and ran through the wall to his left, disappearing from view.

The roaring of wind around him crescendoed to ear-splitting proportions. He clutched his ears, trying to cut out the sound. It barely made any difference. By the Moon, it hurt. He bent over, trying to shield his head, his ears, from the ear-splitting noise. A dark shadow of movement emerged from the shadows in the corner, rushed across the room then disappeared through the wall where the spirit woman had run just moments before.

The deafening sound disappeared with the shadow.

'What the fuck?' All he could hear now was the whistling whoosh of wind that had been in his ears ever since he'd been kicked from his body.

He shuddered and looked around to see if anyone else had noticed the strange woman and the shadow that followed her.

A woman who looked strangely familiar—although he couldn't figure out why—was frowning at the wall. He strode over to her, waving to get her attention. 'Did you see that?'

She said something to him, but he couldn't hear her above the noise of wind all around him. He waved he couldn't understand. She shrugged then pointed over his shoulder.

He swung around. Shelley was staring at him. Their gazes met. She looked away and went back to tending Cordy.

For some reason, she didn't want to talk to him. Didn't even seem to want to see him.

But that was okay. She couldn't ignore him forever.

In the meantime, he had to figure out a way to hear one of the other spirits. That other spirit had seen her, he was sure of it. Someone here had to know who that woman was.

Perhaps he should have gone with her, but how could he, with the bond tugging at him like it was?

He sighed. The Packbond. At least he still had that. The violet-eyes woman had said he didn't know who he was or understand his true role of Trickster. What he did know was that he was still tied to his pack. Iain's need to keep Eloise alive pressed on him, pulling at him. He had to do whatever he could to help. It was what he'd always done. And despite what Shelley had said to him about not pushing his power through the Packbond, he had to help. It was the only thing he could do and he would keep on going until he could do it no more.

***

I HOPE you enjoyed that sneak peek of *Wolf Bound.* If you want to read more, you can find buy-links with the QR code here:

If you don't want to miss out on news about books in this series or the new prequel **Dawn of the Curse Series**, set 500 years before the Pack Bound Series takes place, as well as special giveaways, sales, book signings and information on my other books, then sign up to my newsletter.

As an added bonus, when you join, you will get a FREE ebook copy of *Witch Bound*, a novella set 40 years before *Pack Bound*. Just turn the page to find out more:

LOVE A FREE BOOK?

YOUR FREE BOOK IS WAITING

One Fate, one mate, a bond too strong to deny ...

Paul Collins, duty-bound Pack Warlock and seer, must marry a strong witch for the good of Pack McVale. But his hidden feelings for his best-friend's sister, maternal wolf Ivy McVale, make this a more diffi-cult pill to swallow every day. Especially when they begin to mate.

Then Paul has a vision: If they mate, Ivy will die. Desperate, Paul uses his powers to change destiny and make Ivy think she's always hated him. He can deal with any punishment the Fates make him pay for tampering with destiny, as long as Ivy lives.

After recovering from a bewildering month-long illness, Ivy notices her nemesis, Paul, is tormented by something. And strangely, she is the only one who can feel it. Unable to endure such unhappiness—even if he does call her Poison Ivy—she is determined to help him, no matter the cost. Because Pack McVale cannot survive without him, and curiously, neither can she ...

Simply sign up to my newsletter and I will email your free copy of Witch Bound to you. You will also receive the latest on upcoming books, sales, giveaways and relevant bookish news.

Get My Free Copy of Witch Bound Here:

But wait! There's more ...

If you're not into newsletters but think you might be into subscriptions that give you serialised content, exclusive chapters to new books, exclusive bonus content, signed print books and much more, then turn the page to find out about **Leisl's Legends** ...

JOIN LEISL'S LEGENDS

Subscribe to (or follow) me (via the QR code) at my Leisl's Legends page on REAM—a new subscription app like Patreon except it's designed especially for readers and authors for an amazing reading experience—and you will get early access to *The Huntress and the Vampire King*, my hot enemies to lovers, witch-and-vampire-licious urban fantasy romance that readers over there are already in love with. It's the prequel novel to the first book in the Blood-Rites Series - *The Blood of the Seer*.

Be the first to find out where it all began with Anita and Hei's love story.
BECOME A LEGEND NOW!
https://reamstories.com/leislleightonauthor

You will also find serialised chapters of the next book in my popular **Gods Cursed Series** there and can comment on the story as I write it! Not to mention you will also get extra bonuses like exclusive NSFW Bonus Epilogues, Bonus Prologues and cut scenes and chapters from all of my books.

Be part of creating the stories you love AND get exclusive access to a whole range of goodies including other WIPs, bonus content, voting rights, signed books and more.

Read on to find out more about The Huntress and the Vampire King PLUS read the opening chapters ...

The Huntress and the Vampire King

She hates the vampire who saved her; he holds the key to her fate ...

Hunter-witch Anita Middleton wants revenge against the violent vampire cults that murdered her father and has worked hard to become one of the best vampire hunters there is. But on a difficult hunt she is caught in an ambush and is mortally wounded ... only to be saved by a mysterious warrior. A warrior with brilliant blue eyes and long silver-blonde hair who fights with a grace and violence like nothing she's seen. It is only after she wakes in the heart of his palazzo that she realises her saviour is a vampire - and according to her brother and mentor, this vampire king is their ally.

Lord Hei rules over an empire of witches, humans and vampires who have been trying to keep the vicious vampire cults, the Wild and Dark Brethren, at bay for centuries. Then he saves Anita and knows with one look she is the prophecied Huntress who could be his downfall or his salvation - and she is also his fated mate. But she struggles to trust him as her hatred of vampires is deep-seated. And she *needs* to trust him because only he can offer the specialised training a Huntress needs so her power won't overwhelm her.

But with the Dark Brethren mysteriously amassing, he has little time to win her over. And Anita must go on a crash course to learn how to control her Huntress magic ... or go slowly and violently insane.

The Huntress and the Vampire King is the exciting action-packed prequel novel to *The Blood of the Seer*.

If you love your vampires hot with a bit of The Witcher thrown in and your heroines as kick-arse as Buffy and even more tortured, if you love fated mates, enemies to lovers, chosen ones and epically hot romance mixed with action and mystery, then *The Huntress and the Vampire King* is what you've been waiting for.

Sign up to Leisl's Legends and start reading exclusive early release chapters of it now!

BECOME A LEGEND NOW!
https://reamstories.com/leislleightonauthor

ALSO BY LEISL LEIGHTON

Love Cursed

Soul Cursed

Blood Cursed

Hearts Cursed

Fates Cursed

Witch Cursed

Dragon Cursed

(Coming 2026)

BLOOD-RITES SERIES

The Blood of the Seer

The Blood of the Sire

The Blood of the Son

(Coming 2027)

BLOOD-RITES PREQUEL AND BONUS MATERIAL

The Huntress and the Vampire King

The Middleton Manifesto

(Available now via Leisl's Legends subscription)

ANTHOLOGIES

A Perfectly Paranormal Valentine

A Perfectly Paranormal Halloween

A Perfectly Paranormal Easter

A Perfectly Paranormal Christmas

A Perfectly Paranormal Prophecy

(Coming in 2027)

As well as writing sexy, epic and romantic paranormal novels, I write mysterious and emotional romantic suspense novels too. Check out the following titles for amazing, suspenseful reads:

Storm Haven Series

Need You Tonight

The Devil Inside

CoalCliff Stud Series

Climbing Fear: Book 1

Blazing Fear: Book 2

Echo Springs Series

Dangerous Echoes: Book 1

Books 2-4 in this series, (written by Daniel deLorne, TJ Hamilton and Shannon Curtis) are also available now at all ebook retailers.

You can find all the buy links for Leisl's Books at her website:

ABOUT LEISL

Leisl Leighton is a tall red head with an overly large imagination. As a child, she identified strongly with Anne of Green Gables, and like Anne, is a voracious reader and born performer.

It came as no surprise when she went on to a career as a performer, script writer, script doctor, stage manager and musical director for cabaret and theatre restaurants.

After starting a family, Leisl stopped performing and began writing the stories plaguing her dreams. She now writes emotional stories mixed with mystery and a little bit of what goes bump in the night.

Her novels have won and placed in writing contests here and overseas. She is a passionate advocate for the romance genre, was President of Romance Writers of Australia from 2014-2017 and when she's not writing romantic stories of redemption, she is helping other authors reach their dreams with her Author Services. 
You can contact Leisl through her website via the QR Code above or here: https://www.leislleighton.com

And if you want to stay in touch and be the first to find out about new releases, appearances, special deals and exclusive content and give-

aways, sign up to her Newsletter and pick up your free copy of *Witch Bound* via the QR code.

Or sign up to *Leisl's Legends* via this QR code to get *Witch Cursed* plus serialised early access stories and bonus content including a bonus

NSFW ending for Love Cursed.

You can also follow her on social media:

facebook.com/LeislLeightonAuthor

instagram.com/leislleightonauthor

bookbub.com/authors/leisl-leighton

amazon.com/stores/Leisl-Leighton/author/BooDBYRGZY

ACKNOWLEDGMENTS

Getting this book ready for publication was more of an adventure than I'd bargained on. In the middle of the editing process, I had a bad car accident and fractured my sternum and a vertebrae in my back and spent four days in hospital with many months of recovery ahead of me. Then just after I was able to sit up for a few hours in front of my computer and get back to my editing, my son brought Covid home and promptly gave it to my husband and me. I was very sick with it and felt truly sorry for myself.

But so many people, both family and friends, helped out with food packages and running errands and keeping us all going and it filled me with a sense of such love and support that despite how sick I felt, and despite the Covid coughing and sneezing keeping my fracture from healing for a month—extending my healing time by another 4-6 weeks—I was able to kick myself in the butt and get up and do the work I needed to get this one finished and out in time and still have multiple rests during the day.

So huge thanks have to go to my mum and dad, Kerrie and Jim, who did so much for me during this difficult time, and to all the friends who cooked for me and sent messages of love and support. This wouldn't have happened without you.

Of course, my hubby, Mark, and my two beautiful boys, Jacob and Nathaniel, all stepped up too and when they were all feeling better, did so much to help me get back to work and took on extra duties (especially Jacob) in cooking and cleaning and washing so the house was kept in order given I wasn't able to do it.

Aside from great family and friends, a writer needs a Coven of writing peeps all their own. Thanks to my friends in my writing groups for encouraging me in this endeavour and giving me the strength to push on through all the highs and lows of doing this crazy writing thing—Laura, Chris, Marnie, Frana and Anita. I couldn't have gotten here without you. Especially Marnie and Anita who did all the hard yards so that we could still have our retreat together even though I was recuperating from my accident and was unable to help in the ways I usually do.

Big thanks to Laura and Chris as well for helping me to wrestle the old Pack Bound Series blurbs into something fresh and new and powerful—you are both amazing and talented and I'm so glad you're in my life.

Thoughts and thanks also to my bestie, Helen, and to the first writing friend I ever had, Liz. You are both gone but never forgotten and a part of you will always live on in my stories.

And a big shout out to all my friends in Romance Writers of Australia —you are inspiration and mentor rolled into a big ball of supportive writerly love. Thank you.

The final person I have to thank is my agent, Alex Adsett, for believing in me and my work and always backing every decision I make. Your confidence in me helps me believe I can actually do this writing thing. Eternal thanks.

www.ingramcontent.com/pod-product-compliance
Lightning Source LLC
Chambersburg PA
CBHW010536170726
48285CB00008B/2638